Wednesday Club

A NOVEL

KRISTINE JENSEN

PRAIRIEFLOWER PRESS

Cover design by Nicolle Rodriguez

Author photo by Joe Pierce

Cover image: iStock.com/YinYang

First edition: 2025

ISBN (Print Edition): 979-8-9992643-0-5

ISBN (eBook Edition): 979-8-9992643-1-2

For my grandmother, Adele, and my mother, Lou Ann—
From the wide prairie, you gave me roots to keep me grounded,
and from your love, I grew wings.
This story is for you.

Count That Day Lost
by George Eliot

If you sit down at set of sun
And count the acts that you have done,
And, counting, find
One self-denying deed, one word
That eased the heart of him who heard,
One glance most kind
That fell like sunshine where it went—
Then you may count that day well spent.

But if, through all the livelong day,
You've cheered no heart, by yea or nay—
If, through it all
You've nothing done that you can trace
That brought the sunshine to one face—
No act most small
That helped some soul and nothing cost—
Then count that day as worse than lost.

August 1963

Ivy

"MY LIFE IS OVER, goddammit!"

There was power in saying that forbidden swear word. A way to poke at her mother, even if it was only in her head. *You don't have all the power over me.* But the truth of the situation was, at that moment, her mother did.

Ivy leaned back and let the hot wind whip and tangle her hair, not caring if she ever got a comb through it again. Out the open window, the landscape blurred — row after row of corn in long rectangular fields, edged by sagging telephone wires. Ahead, the endless black ribbon of the highway melted into a watery blue. It was isolated here. Quiet. For a minute she closed her eyes and pretended she was hearing the dull roar of the city bus as it took her across town. But when she opened her eyes, there were none of her neighborhood's crowded streets and brick buildings. Just the dull roar of her mother's worn Chevy convertible. And more corn.

Ivy tested the word under her breath. "Goddammit." Then, a little louder. "Goddammit." She turned her head out the window and said the words in a normal voice. "Goddamn it, my life is over." Her mother, Vonda Marie, didn't respond; she just stared at the blacktop ahead and pressed the accelerator hard. *Caught up in her own world, as usual.* After a minute, Vonda Marie checked her reflection and smiled into the rearview mirror. The mirror reflected the things people always mentioned to Ivy when they described how beautiful her mother was: her freshly-Claireled platinum curls held back by a red triangle scarf, those startlingly deep blue eyes, and perfectly straight teeth. Ivy looked at herself in the side mirror and stretched her lips to force a smile, exposing her slightly overlapping eye tooth. Crooked. No one ever told Ivy she looked like her mother.

She pulled a small blue notebook and pencil from the canvas book bag at her feet, making sure the envelope was still securely taped to the back cover. She began to write, crooking her left arm across the book to hide her words and keep the pages from flying.

At least in her diary she could write everything she couldn't say out loud. Like what a stupid idea this was. How she couldn't wait to have a good laugh with Val when they came back to Omaha, her mother's tail between her legs. What terrible timing to be leaving Brad just when things...

Ivy's mother snapped her fingers in front of Ivy's face.

"Ivy! Did you hear me, sweetie? Can you find my cigarettes? They must have slipped off the seat."

Her mother pushed in the dashboard lighter. Bad enough the way the smoke blew straight back into Ivy's face, but how she hated being at her mother's beck and call. Ivy retrieved the pack of Pall Malls from the floorboard and slapped it into her mother's open hand. Her mother took her foot off the gas and leaned forward out of the convertible's wind, veering into the oncoming lane. Ivy grabbed the wheel and steered while her mother lit the cigarette. After three-and-a-half long hours in the car, Ivy knew the routine.

Her mother glanced at her and said, "I don't know why you're pouting so much. I've told you that as soon I get settled with a studio contract, I'll bring you right down to California. You're gonna love it there. Sandy beaches, big pink grapefruit that grow right in your front yard. Parties with all sorts of movie stars." She winked at Ivy. "Of course, you'll have to pretend to be my sister."

"Right, Mother." Ivy stared off into the distance. More rows of green, sometimes dotted with a red barn, white two-story house, and a tall metal-topped bin her mother had said were silos for holding corn and grains. She considered opening the car door and jumping out at the next stop sign, but how long would she have to walk before another car came along?

"Besides, it'll be good for you to be around your grandparents for a while. They haven't seen you since you were just a little girl. Your grandma is so excited."

"Well, that makes one of us." That should get her mother's attention.

Her mother squinted at Ivy through her heavily mascaraed and eye-shadowed eyes. "That's no way to talk."

"I wouldn't mind so much if they lived somewhere fun. But a farm — in the middle of Nowheresville, South Dakota!"

"It's not that bad." Vonda Marie forcefully exhaled a stream of smoke.

"Well, you never wanted to go back there. I've heard you say it a million times."

"That was different. I grew up there. Besides, you won't be there that long. Just until I get settled, see where this Pearl Soap contest takes me. Maybe a month or two at the most."

"That's forever in a place like this." Ivy stared out at the endless fields on either side of the blacktop road. The air smelled like dirt. "I don't see why you didn't let me stay with Val's family."

"We've been over this, Ivy. Val's father might be perfectly nice, but I don't trust that mother of hers. I can tell she doesn't like me at all." She glanced at herself in the mirror. "Besides, I'm never going back to Omaha. Too many bad memories of bad jobs and bad men."

Yeah, lots of both, Ivy thought.

"Now be a good sport and let me have my big break. You'll see. It'll be good for both of us." She turned on the radio and tuned the dial until she found a station with less static, then turned it up extra loud to hear Lesley Gore's *It's My Party*.

Ivy slunk down and leaned back against the hot vinyl seat, tipping her head to watch a lone hawk soar across the immense blue sky. She was right, her life was over. Goddammit.

Cora

IT WAS ONLY TEN o'clock, but already the sun was starting to beat down, hot as blazes, as Cora made her way from the farmhouse back door and across the wide gravel driveway to the garden, willow basket and shears in hand. Usually Cora loved this task, not really a task at all. But today, her stomach was tight with a mix of excitement and apprehension. There was still a list of things to do a mile long before the ladies arrived at two. And to add to that — Vonda Marie and Ivy were on their way. They could arrive almost any time now. Cora opened the latch on the metal gate and walked into the garden, the wind hot and dry against her cheek. Dirt from the nearby field swirled in the air for a second, then settled.

Let's see now. The gladiolus and tiger lilies, with a few delphiniums mixed in, would make a striking centerpiece for the dining room table. And some of those happy-faced white daisies for the kitchen counter. Nothing brightened a room quite like daisies.

Cora cut the tall flowers and laid them in the basket. She turned to the rose bushes. There were only a couple of tight Silver Sterling buds for Vonda Marie's room, but they would open more while she was here. Cora wasn't sure how long she was planning to stay, at least a few days she would think.

She snipped the buds and brought each to her nose.

Oh, and wouldn't a pretty little bouquet of snapdragons be perfect for Ivy's night table? So fragrant and sweet – just like her precious granddaughter. It was a shame it had been so long since she'd seen her. Ivy was already sixteen years old! You'd think they lived on the other side of the country instead of in the next state.

As Cora squatted to snip the snapdragons, her 55-year-old knees gave a familiar pop. Then she heard her husband's pickup, its rumbling engine unmistakable. *Oh Lordy — is he here already?* Cora gathered the flowers into her basket and headed to the house.

Delmar turned off the gravel road and sped into the yard just as Cora reached the front drive. He beeped the horn and cranked down the window. "Got it ready for me?" he hollered.

Cora hustled to the back door and yelled back, "Almost. Just lemme get the thermoses poured and the sandwiches put in."

Delmar shook his head and adjusted his Sokota seed cap, exposing whiter skin above his tanned forehead. "I told you the men would need their lunch right on time. Gotta get as much combining in as we can before the sun goes down."

Cora spun around and let the screen door slam behind her.

In the kitchen, she hurried to the sink and propped up the flowers in the corner. She would have to deal with them later. She set a cardboard box on the counter, took bologna sandwiches, deviled eggs, and carrot sticks from the refrigerator, and stacked them in the box. She filled one large thermos with lemonade and another with coffee and added them to the box. Glasses, napkins, cookies. This ought to hold the men until the noontime meal Norma was making.

Delmar leaned his face, leathery from so much sun, out the window and honked as Cora hurried out carrying the box. "Set it in the back," he said. "No sign of the girls?"

"Not yet. I sure hope they don't arrive in the middle of our meeting. I told Vonda Marie it would be best if she got here early, before all the commotion." Delmar pursed his thin lips into a smirk. "Since when did Marie listen to any dang thing we ever said? Most mule-headed girl that ever lived, that one. Let's hope Ivy turns out to be not a thing—"

Cora grimaced. "Now don't you be talking like that around your granddaughter. You're gonna need to be more careful of what you say."

Delmar noisily shifted his Ford pickup into gear and backed up. He gave Cora his index finger wave as he rolled out of the driveway and headed back to the fields.

Cora scurried back into the house and sat at the kitchen table, catching her breath for a minute. So much to think about right now. A daughter with some hair-brained notion of becoming a movie star. A teenage granddaughter coming to live with them. A husband who hasn't gotten along with his daughter since she was about thirteen. Cora always playing the peacemaker.

Cora removed her glasses, pulled a wadded Kleenex from her apron pocket, and dabbed her eyes. Last night's lack of sleep would catch up with her if she sat much longer. She got up from the table with a sigh and looked at her penciled list on the counter. She crossed off 'Cut flowers' and scanned the rest of the list. Bring luncheon trays from cellar. Set out dishes and silverware. Make coffee. Finish roll call topic. Arrange flowers.

Oh, right, the flowers. Cora moved to the sink, lifting the bright pink and yellow snapdragons to her nose, escaping into their sweet scent for a blessed moment. Then, reality seeped back in. Of all things, Wednesday Club today — in the middle of it all!

Ivy

As soon as they crossed a wide bridge over the Big Sioux River and Ivy spotted the highway sign, she could feel her stomach tighten. *Prairie View 5 miles.* She looked around but didn't see anything that resembled a city center or even a small town. Her mother fumbled for a stick of Beechnut from the package on the dashboard and crammed it into her mouth. She turned off the highway just past the sign, drove down a newly paved blacktop road, traveled about a mile, and then turned right onto a wide gravel road. Ivy looked around at the neat farmyards, family names plainly printed on the roadside mailboxes, and steep ditches lining the road. She had some vague sense of having been on this road before, but she wouldn't know how to get to her grandparent's farm from here.

Ivy's mom stared into the rearview mirror and scowled. "Get off my tail, idiot." Ivy turned around to see a red Ford pickup truck following them closely. The man behind the wheel stared straight ahead and didn't back off.

Her mom let her foot off the gas and the car slowed. She lifted her sunglasses and glared into the rearview mirror. "Oh hell! It's him." She pulled the gum from her mouth and flung it out the open window.

Ivy spun around; the pickup was even closer now. The driver was wearing a brown and yellow cap with lettering on the front, and he was almost near enough that she could make out the name on it.

"Of all the timing!"

"What do you mean?" Ivy asked. Why was her mother suddenly so irritated?

Her mother didn't answer but instead pursed her lips and switched on the blinker. They turned left into a long driveway edged with a perfectly trimmed hedge on the left and tall leafy bushes on the right. The pickup turned in behind them. Her mom tapped on the horn twice as she drove slowly past a square white house with black trim and shutters and gabled windows on the second floor. The expansive lawn was lush, and the house was edged with a colorful border of flowers along the front. Something about the flowers stirred a memory for Ivy.

They rolled to the rear of a circular driveway where five other cars were already parked, and Ivy's mom stopped behind the last car. "Looks like we didn't beat the club here either. Drat!" She slammed the car into Park.

"What club?" Ivy asked.

"Wednesday Club. Bunch of old ladies. At least they'll be a distraction."

Ivy grabbed her book bag off the floorboard, opened the car door, and got out, standing to look around. In the distance loomed a huge wooden barn with a tall, slanting roof. The siding looked freshly painted white and all the doors were shut. There were other buildings around the farmyard, both large and small, and a silver silo. She spied the red pickup parked in front of a metal hut-shaped building and watched as the driver strode toward them. He wore brown work pants, a short-sleeved plaid shirt, and dusty lace-up leather boots. Now she recognized him — her grandfather. She hadn't remembered the deep vertical lines etched between his eyebrows, noticeable above his black-framed glasses. He wasn't smiling.

Ivy's mother spoke first, "Hi, Daddy. You remember Ivy." Her voice sounded tight. And small.

Her grandfather barely glanced at his daughter before giving Ivy an appraising once over. His gravelly voice was flat as he said, "Welcome, Ivy. It's been a long time." He shifted his gaze to her mother, narrowing his eyes for a split second.

"Hi ..." Ivy meant to follow it with 'Grandpa,' but the word stuck in her throat. She followed with a weak "Thanks." She squirmed inside, suddenly shy.

"Where'd you get this car?" Delmar demanded.

"My friend Mel helped me find it. Low miles for a '57." Ivy's mom gave a forced-looking smile.

"Not much of a car for the snow." Delmar's thin lips registered his disapproval.

"Perfect for California, though." Her mother caught Ivy's eye and gave her a knowing glance. Ivy wished she wouldn't try to pull her into this — whatever *this* was.

Her mom opened the trunk and started to lift out Ivy's suitcase.

"Let me," her grandfather barked.

She pointed toward Ivy's large beige Samsonite. "Just that one."

"You're not staying the night?" He grabbed the handle of Ivy's suitcase and turned from the open trunk, hesitating.

"I told Connie I'd be in Hillsdale tonight. She's expecting me."

"What?" Ivy tapped her mother's arm, but her mother didn't respond — just twirled around and walked towards the house. Ivy grabbed her elbow, forcing her to stop for a second. "What?" she repeated.

"Buck up, bucko," her mother said in a low voice, shaking off Ivy as she marched toward the back steps. Ivy gritted her teeth. She should have known her mother would pull something like this.

Suddenly, the back door swung open, and her grandmother rushed out, dressed in a sleeveless cotton dress, nylons, and low heels. She grabbed her daughter into a long hug, then turned towards Ivy. "Oh my, you're all grown up into a beautiful young woman." She folded Ivy in her arms into a soft, welcoming embrace, and Ivy caught the scent of her perfume. It was Shalimar! Aunt Lillian had worn that same perfume. Even after all this time, it must be six years now, it still hurt that Aunt Lil was gone. When her grandmother let go and Ivy looked at her face, Ivy was shocked by how much the two sisters looked alike. Same small turned-up noses, same round, rosy-blushed cheeks, and the same kind eyes. Her grandmother was younger than Ivy had imagined.

"Come on in. The meeting is just getting started, but I'll fix you a sandwich while they go on. You must be starving," her grandmother said as they all entered the large kitchen, the smell of coffee and cinnamon filling the air.

"We don't need lunch," her mother said.

Her grandfather set the suitcase down. "Marie's not staying."

"What do you mean?" Her grandmother wrinkled her brow.

"Mama, I'm sorry. We got such a late start today, and my friend Connie is expecting me for the night."

Ivy's heart sank. She thought her mother would at least stay one night and help get her settled in.

"Can't you just stay a day or two?" her grandmother asked.

"I have to be in Los Angeles by Monday morning, and I'm not sure how long it will take me," she shrugged. "I just came in for a quick hi ..." Her voice trailed off.

A frown passed across her grandmother's face, but she quickly wrapped her arm around Ivy. "Well then, we'll take good care of Ivy until you get back."

"Which will probably be sooner than later," her grandfather said. *Let's hope he's right,* Ivy thought.

"What happens on Monday, honey?" her grandmother asked, ignoring her grandfather.

"That's the day I meet the Pearl Soap people. Find out what's next for Miss Vonda Marie." She lifted her chin and flashed a bright smile.

Her grandfather snorted. "The Pearl Soap people," he said, mocking his daughter.

Her mother clenched her jaw and spat out, "Well, it's not like they're farmers. They're important people who —."

"What's that supposed to mean ... not like they're farmers?" he snapped back. "Seems like farmers were good enough to keep sending you money all these years."

Cora slipped next to Delmar, grabbing his arm and squeezing. "I'm very excited for you, sweetheart. I know everything is going to work out just fine." She smiled at Vonda Marie, then turned towards Ivy. "We're so happy to get to spend this time with you."

"What are your plans for Ivy?" Delmar asked. "Or have you thought that far ahead?"

"I resent that attitude. My whole life has revolved around Ivy." Vonda Marie hissed.

Delmar's body tensed. He opened his mouth, then glanced at Cora and clamped it shut. He stormed out of the kitchen, slamming the door behind him.

Vonda Marie flung up her hands and shook her head. "As soon as I can get a place for the two of us, I'll come back for her. Or send money to get her to LA." She looked at Ivy. "You're in good hands with your grandmother. And before you know it, you'll be in California."

Ivy stayed silent, but her mind whirled, and she felt light-headed, almost numb. It was happening. Her mother was really dumping her here.

Cora hugged her daughter and held her by the shoulders. "Keep in touch now and let us know how everything is going."

Her mother walked over to Ivy and kissed her on the cheek, whispering into her ear, "Be my big girl now, Ivy." She pulled back and winked. Ivy knew she meant it in a teasing way — their little joke. But Ivy hated those words. She gritted her teeth as she remembered all the times she was asked to be a big girl. All those times she should have been allowed to be a little girl. With a mother who took care of her. That feeling came again – that cold spot in her chest, like a big dark hole in her heart.

She forced herself to squeeze out the words, "Bye, Mom. Good luck."

Her mother hurried out the door, not looking back.

"OK, sweetheart. Let's go meet the ladies." Cora grabbed Ivy's hand and tugged her towards the living room. "I just know they're going to love you."

Ivy swallowed hard, plastered on a weak smile, and followed her grandmother.

Etola

ETOLA WAS HAVING A hard time concentrating during the meeting. As soon as Cora, looking fit to be tied, had announced that they might be interrupted by the arrival of Vonda Marie and her granddaughter, Etola had felt all a'flutter. She was dying to see how Vonda Marie was holding up, since she was the prettiest girl these parts had seen for a long time.

Her mind wandered back to the start of the day. It began all in a funk with her and Bathilda having their usual kerfuffle about who would drive, why Etola should support Bathilda for president over Hattie Dunlop, and whether she had prepared sufficiently for the roll call topic. *What is there to say about the new national zip code system, for cryin' out loud?* Then she'd discovered that Eddie had gotten into their deviled ham and pickle sandwiches, and she'd started yelling at him. Course, it didn't do any good, he didn't know right from wrong, and he didn't mean any harm ever. Even though he was 45, just two years younger than Etola, you couldn't expect him to act like a grown-up man. So, they were already late after she'd whipped up a couple dozen more sandwiches — fancy ones with no crusts, so the members always ate quite a few. By then,

Bathilda was already behind the wheel, honking away, so Etola just let her drive without a big fuss. Good thing they only lived two sections down from Cora and Delmar's place.

And now they'd gotten through the saying of the club motto, the roll call, the treasurer's report, and the singing of "Make New Friends." Etola hated being stuck sitting next to Florence. That woman couldn't carry a tune in a bucket. And the way she slathered on that Avon Unforgettable could just about gag a maggot. They were partway through the election of officers when things had gotten interesting.

First, Etola had heard the toot toot of a horn and then muffled voices coming from the kitchen. She'd wanted to get up and say hello, but she knew Bathilda would skin her alive if she left during the election of officers. She'd tried inching her way to the edge of the couch and craning to peek into the kitchen, but she couldn't see anything.

But then she'd heard raised voices, something about Pearl Soap people, and then the back door slamming. She heard a pickup go rumbling down the driveway, and the kitchen door banged again in a few minutes. Ignoring the sharp look from Bathilda, Etola had stood up and looked out the window, worried this might be her only chance to see Vonda Marie. She caught a glimpse of a blue convertible speeding out the driveway, driven by a woman wearing black cat-eye sunglasses. It just had to be her, no one else around here gussied up like that.

Meanwhile, President Evelyn hadn't missed a beat. She'd kept pulling those folded papers out of the bowl and tallying them up like it was an ordinary August meeting. Etola thought it was ridiculous having formal ballots and all since there were only seven of them, but this club had always stood on formality.

After a couple of minutes, Cora came in, pulling the prettiest young woman by the hand and leading her into the living room. She was tall and slender, with dark brown hair and golden eyes.

Etola had never seen eyes quite that color, and the girl didn't look a thing like Vonda Marie. Then she remembered that baby's daddy.

"Ladies, this is our Ivy, Vonda Marie's daughter. She's going to be staying with us for a little while. Ivy, this is the Wednesday Club," Cora said.

Evelyn acted like nothing at all unusual was going on. "Welcome, Ivy. I hope you can join us for lunch so we can all get to know you."

Ivy squeaked out a hello and gave a wan smile, glanced around the room, and then made a quick exit. Etola thought that girl had stared at them like they were from another planet. And she did not look happy.

But Evelyn hadn't missed a beat. "Alright, ladies, let's continue with the meeting. It's time to recite the club creed by George Eliot."

Etola had a feeling this was going to be one humdinger of a year for Wednesday Club.

Wednesday Club Minutes

AUGUST 14, 1963

The Wednesday Club met at the home of Mrs. Cora Hanson. The meeting was called to order by President Mrs. Evelyn Fish, and the club motto was recited:

"Tis good to know

Tis better to do

Tis best to be."

Roll was called with all members telling what they thought about the new national zip code system.

Secretary Miss Hattie Dunlop read the minutes from the July meeting.

Mrs. Florence Lane gave the treasurer's report. Expenditures for July included $2.10 for a plant for Mrs. Dora Avery and $10.00 for the annual Bennett Home for Unwed Mothers donation. Receipts included $13.37 from our July cakewalk, leaving $45.48 in the Treasury. Hattie Dunlop made a motion to advance $12.00 to Tilly Halverson for supplies for next year's programs. Etola Baldridge seconded, and all members voted yes.

The flower committee reported that they delivered a plant to Mrs. Dora Avery in the hospital, and she was most appreciative. The song 'Make New Friends' was sung with Etola Baldridge assisting on piano.

The program for August was the election of officers. Election results were as follows: President Bathilda Baldridge, Vice President Florence Lane, Secretary Evelyn Fish, and Treasurer Hattie Dunlop. Flower chairman is Cora Hanson, music chairman is Etola Baldridge, and program chairman is Tilly Halversen.

Each member will take turns presenting on a current affairs topic for our programs this year. It can be about anything happening in our world that we should know more about.

Cora Hanson introduced a visitor, her granddaughter Ivy Hanson. The meeting was closed by reciting the club creed, 'Count that Day Lost' by George Eliot.

A lunch of deviled ham sandwiches, fancy lemon Jell-O with green olives and walnuts, oatmeal raisin bars, lemonade, and coffee was served.

Hattie Dunlop, Secretary

Ivy

IVY WAS IN THE back seat of her grandparents' Chevy Impala. Her grandfather called it "Cora's car," though he always seemed to be the one driving it. It was light green with vinyl interior, a color that was slightly unnerving to Ivy since both her Aunt Lil and her mother had always said that green cars were bad luck. Ivy had no idea where that superstition had come from.

It was hot. Not just warm hot, but steamy hot, the gray clouds so low in the sky it seemed like you could touch the bottom with a long pole and burst them. Ivy's grandmother dabbed at her upper lip with a fancy embroidered handkerchief as Ivy watched a drip of sweat crawl down the back of her grandfather's neck. Earlier, he had mentioned that once the rain came, it ought to bring some relief from the miserable mugginess.

They were all dressed up and on their way to church, which apparently had to be done every Sunday. Ivy's grandfather wore a suit and tie, which must have been unbearable. Her grandmother wore a short-sleeved belted dress, heels, and a white hat, and today she said she was leaving behind the white gloves because of the heat. She had insisted that Ivy wear a dress, too, and Ivy could feel the backs of her legs already sticking to the hot seat. Even though her grandfather had cranked up the air conditioning, a feature he said he was glad he had paid extra for, she didn't think any cool air was making it to the back.

"Maybe we'll hear something from your mother this week," her grandmother said, breaking the silence. They hadn't heard anything from her since she had left two weeks ago, except the night she called to say she had made it to Los Angeles. That call lasted only a minute because it was too expensive to talk very long, even on a Sunday night when rates were the lowest. "I wish she'd let us know how things are going."

"Typical." Her grandfather kept his voice low, but Ivy had no trouble hearing it. Ivy was getting the idea that he despised her mother, something they might have in common, but Ivy wasn't sure he was all that fond of her either.

Ivy's grandmother frowned at her husband and quickly turned back to look at Ivy. "Are you getting excited about your first day of school?"

"Mm, kind of." Ivy bit the inside of her cheek.

"I'm sure you'll feel better once you've met some kids your age. Remember Florence from Wednesday Club? She has a nephew your age or maybe a year older — Lance. I hear he's quite popular. An athlete."

Ivy forced a smile for her grandmother. She couldn't recall which lady was Florence. That day was a blur, and the ladies mostly seemed the same — old and boring. Except for the one named Tilly. Ivy couldn't imagine why a younger woman would want to join the group.

"I can drive you the first day and help you..."

Her grandfather interrupted, "Ivy can ride the bus just like every other farm kid. Don't need to coddle her right off the bat."

Her grandmother looked surprised. "But I just thought..."

"We don't need Ivy thinking she's better than anyone else, like Marie did. Maybe if she'd kept riding the bus, she wouldn't have ended up —"

"We'll talk about it later." The tone in her grandmother's voice, combined with the sharp look, shut him down. A heavy silence followed that made the air feel even thicker.

Finally, they pulled into the First United Methodist Church parking lot. Ivy noticed how her grandparents put on cheery smiles for everyone they greeted, as though nothing had happened a few minutes before.

They sat on the left-hand side of the fifth row of pews, the same place they had sat last week. While they were waiting for the service to start, Ivy looked down at her hands. She had forgotten to clean the black dirt from under her fingernails, evidence of the garden work she'd helped with. Her grandfather said there was harvesting to do: corn, cucumbers, beans, tomatoes, and vegetables she hadn't even known existed, like parsnips and rutabagas. It was tedious, but she liked it better than helping in the kitchen like she'd had to do for her mother. If they had wanted anything decent to eat, it was usually up to Ivy to plan and prepare. At least her grandmother did all the cooking while Ivy stayed in her bedroom reading. It seemed like that was most of what her grandma did — fix a meal, clean up from that one, and then start fixing the next.

Ivy slid her hands under her legs and looked at the round, stained glass window high above the altar. It was the shape of a colorful flower, and she might have liked it, except that she remembered it from when she and her mother last were in South Dakota. After Aunt Lil had died and the minister had said some kind words about her in the service and said to pray for the Hanson family. Then she remembered something odd from that day — a thin gold band on her mother's left hand. Ivy had never seen it before and never saw it again.

There were secrets her mother kept from Ivy. Maybe she would discover some answers in the short time that she was here.

September 1963

Ivy

IT WASN'T YET SEVEN-THIRTY when Ivy stood at the end of the driveway with her grandmother. The sun was warm on her face, but Ivy felt chilled and the oatmeal she had eaten for breakfast sat like a bowling ball in her stomach.

Ivy didn't want her grandmother waiting with her as if she were some six-year-old. But she had insisted and even called her old classmate, Bert Carsrud, to find out exactly what time he'd be pulling up.

Her grandmother chatted away about how exciting the first days of school had always been for her, how modern the new high school was, and on and on. Ivy just wanted to start walking down that long road and keep going. Anywhere but here, and her first day of her junior year in this godforsaken place. It was eerie how quiet it was without the buzz of traffic and street sounds of Omaha. Just bird sounds, so many bird sounds.

"Are you sure you don't want to run back and get a sweater? It might be chilly by the time you're on your way back."

"I'll be fine." Irritation crept into Ivy's voice.

"And are you sure about wearing slacks? I thought girls were supposed to wear skirts or dresses to school."

"Pants will be fine. We're wearing them in Omaha, Grandma." Ivy was wearing her newest black stirrup pants, a striped top, and white Keds. Her hair was held back with a wide headband. Stylish, but not too deliberate. City style.

Her grandmother looked towards the black-top section road. No sign of the bus yet. "Don't forget your lunch on the bus. Your mother was famous for that."

Ivy wanted to yell, "I am not my mother, and stop comparing me to her!" but held her tongue.

Finally, a small cloud of dust appeared up the road, growing larger until the yellow bus came into view and crunched to a stop in front of their driveway. Ivy looked up at the side of the bus and the strange faces staring out from the windows. When the door opened with a scraping metal sound, she trudged up the steps as her heart thumped in her chest.

Cora yelled after her. "Have a good day, honey. Bert, this is Ivy. You take good care of her now, won't you?"

"You betcha," Bert called back.

Ivy felt her cheeks burn as she made her way to the back of the bus to find an empty seat, and she heard Bert shout, "Hey kids, this is Ivy. She's new, so you all be nice to her, you hear?"

All the heads on the bus turned back to stare at her, but no one said a word. *What a bunch of cowpokes.* Ivy slunk down onto the cracked vinyl seat in the last row.

As the bus rumbled off, heads turned to whisper to each other, and a few faces turned back to look at her again. Ivy overheard 'Vonda Marie' several times above the muffled voices.

A young girl in the seat ahead of Ivy's, probably about eight or nine, turned entirely around and leaned over her seat. "Where'd you move from?" she asked, her hair a little matted, in need of a brushing. The chatter stopped.

26

"Omaha."

The girl stared at Ivy. *She probably has no idea where Omaha is. And is that sour milk smell coming from her or someone else on the bus?*

"Omaha." Ivy could hear the word repeating up the rows.

The girl looked Ivy up and down. "Got any cookies?"

Ivy glanced at her sack lunch, unsure what to say. She thought she heard giggling from the girls a couple rows up.

A boy in the seat across from Ivy smirked. "Don't mind her. Mary's a retard." Three rows up, another boy loudly announced, "Mary has a new friend." His audience responded with exaggerated laughter.

Ivy turned her head to look out the window and her reflection stared back. She barely recognized herself. Her eyes looked dead to her.

When the bus pulled into the driveway of the three-story brick building, Ivy gathered her things and stepped off the bus. As she watched the other students walking toward the school entrance, she saw the girls were all dressed up — plaid jumpers, bobby Sox, and patent leather shoes. Styles they were wearing in Omaha a few years back. Even the boys seemed to be making this first day of school a special occasion in their button-down shirts, slacks, and penny loafers.

Ivy found the small metal sign over the Guidance Counselor's door in the noisy hall of the high school wing. She opened it and walked in. Behind the desk, a cheery gray-haired woman greeted Ivy, ready to hand over a class schedule. "I'm Mrs. Bell. Welcome to Prairie View High School. You are now officially student number 80 in the graduating class of 1965."

Ivy took the paper without looking at it. "I won't be graduating here. I'm only here short term until we go back to Omaha."

Mrs. Bell gave a tight smile, followed by a once-over with small beady eyes set behind thick glasses. "Of course. Well then, please enjoy your time here, and I hope you make the most of it. I'm sure you'll find this to be an outstanding school with high academic standards and many extracurricular activities to get involved in. For the girls, we have band, chorus, pep club. And my program, FHA."

"What's FHA?" Ivy asked.

Mrs. Bell looked surprised by the question. "Future Homemakers of America. Your mother was in FHA until she ... quit." Mrs. Bell paused and cleared her throat. "We meet every Monday after school, and you'd be welcome to join us."

Ivy thought about being a homemaker on a farm — with its endless cooking, cleaning, and canning. "Um, probably not. Do you know where my locker is?"

"Yes, just halfway down the hall. On the right-hand side. You'll find the combination on your schedule." Mrs. Bell pursed her lips together tightly. "And by the way, we don't allow slacks at Prairie View High. We'll expect to see you in a skirt starting tomorrow."

Ivy decided not to give a smart-aleck response. As she turned to go, Mrs. Bell continued, "Please tell your mother hello from me. I certainly hope she's making something of ... doing well in her life."

Ivy looked back at Mrs. Bell. Wrinkled as a raisin. Hopelessly old-fashioned. Ivy didn't answer but as she left, she closed the door with a harder-than-necessary pull. The glass window rattled loudly, and students in the hallway turned to stare as Ivy searched for her locker. "What am I, a freak show?" Ivy said under her breath, but maybe loud enough for a few to hear.

When Ivy arrived at her locker, a tall blonde boy at the locker next to hers looked over and gave her a grin. "Guess you told her!"

Ivy glanced over at him. He was cute, but she was pretty sure he was making fun of her, so she ignored him and stared at her class schedule. First period, homeroom. Then, biology, history, English literature, lunch, PE, and algebra. She could do this, somehow. Just long enough to transfer the credits back to Omaha. Back to her friends Val — and Brad.

When she walked down the noisy hallway, she noticed a group of three girls whispering and pointing at her. She glared at them as she passed.

Ivy found the number ten classroom for homeroom, clenched her teeth, and swung open the door. Her mother was going to pay for this!

IVY CLIMBED THE NARROW rungs of the ladder leading to the barn's haymow. They were worn in the middle, and Ivy wondered how often her mother went up these same steps and if she had used the haymow as a getaway place too. It's not that Ivy was trying to hide, but she needed to escape her grandmother's hovering, always wanting to make sure Ivy was doing okay.

Ivy found the barn comforting, oddly familiar, and liked the smell up here, an earthy mix from the straw bales on one side and the hay bales on the other. The straw bales were less scratchy, so she chose a place with a natural straw bench on the far side of the loft, next to the large window her grandfather opened during the day to let the breeze through. As soon as she sat, a skinny calico cat ran up and rubbed against her legs, eager for attention. Ivy gave it a few pets, then pulled out the letter from her mother tucked in her waistband.

Dear Ivy,

I meant to get you written sooner, but life has been a whirlwind!

It turns out there are six of us finalists. They're getting all of us ready for the final vote by the Pearl Soap bigwigs. Mr. Hancock, one of the men at the Donovan and Doolittle advertising agency, says I've got the lead, hands down. He says I'm a Marilyn Monroe look-alike. He's real nice to me.

Hollywood is as glamorous as I thought it would be. First, they had us get settled in our little bungalows, they're mostly just a small room with a bathroom. If you want room to walk around, you have to fold the bed back up into the wall!

Then they had us go to a big fancy hair salon. They wanted to dye my hair chestnut brown, but I told them I'm a blonde through and through. They settled for giving me a new hairdo – straight across bangs and the bobbed ends all flipped up. Barely teased or sprayed at all. A 'girl next door' look.

Then we went to see a makeup artist named Billy Devine. He said I had perfect features and gave me black wingtip eyeliner and bright red lipstick. But then the agency people told him to tone it down, so it was back to pink lipstick and just the littlest bit of eyeliner.

We spent a whole week getting our pictures taken in different places: at the tennis court, walking along the beach, sitting in a living room with a fancy teacup, and standing in a dressing room getting ready for a night on the town. It was all so exciting!

They'll announce the winner in about a week, so keep your fingers crossed that I'm the next Miss Pearl Soap! There will be all kinds of magazine ads and TV commercials. It's the first step to becoming a full-fledged movie star.

Honey, there just isn't room to bring you here to California yet, but once the contest is decided, I'll be able to get a place big enough for the two of us. You're just going to love the weather. And the palm trees!

I'd better stop now and get some beauty rest (ha!). You mind your grandparents and don't give them any trouble.

Kisses and hugs,

Your Mom, aka Miss Pearl Soap

P.S. I suppose you've started school by now. I know how easy it is for you to make friends, so I imagine you're already Miss Popular.

Ivy folded the letter, then stood up and leaned over the open barn loft window. She began to tear the letter into small pieces, watching as they fluttered down into the cattle yard below, landing in mud dotted with piles of cow manure. Then she ripped the envelope into pieces and sent them flying, saving her mother's return address for last. She wouldn't be writing back any time soon.

Hattie

HATTIE PLOPPED DOWN ON the metal kitchen stool to catch her breath. She wiped her forehead and pushed back her short brown finger waves with the bottom of her apron. It was mighty hot today — one of those Indian summer days that almost made you look forward to winter. Almost.

After a day of canning her feet ached and her shoulders were sore. If this was how she felt now, at thirty-nine, what would she feel like in ten or twenty years? It was a lot of work getting thirty-six quarts of pickles put up. An hour of bending over to pick the cucumbers, then all the washing and slicing cukes and onions —standing at the sink the whole time. It might not have been so bad if she had somebody to help bring up the large canning vat and all the empty jars from the cellar. Maybe she should let Arlo help her like he was always offering. But that was probably why her mama had settled for marrying Ray, and Hattie didn't want help that badly.

There was something so satisfying about seeing all those jars lined up, labeled on the top with "Bread & Butter 9/63". There would be enough for the ladies in Wednesday Club, the church welcome committee pantry, and a few for Arlo, too. Hattie was famous for her tangy, sweet pickles, always being asked for the recipe.

Little Pup roused from her bed in the corner and scratched her spindly black legs at the door. She wanted out. Hattie reluctantly rose and opened the screen door, looking out into the yard and up into the sky. Buttermilk clouds, a long line of them, spilled out against a turquoise sky. And not a breeze – it was unusual for South Dakota not to have some kind of wind. That must be why it was so darn hot today.

Hattie walked to the hallway phone table. "Bainbridge 3468, please."

In a minute, she heard "Bathilda Baldridge speaking."

"Bathilda, it's Hattie. Do you have a few minutes?"

"I suppose those ewes won't starve if they have to wait a minute to be fed. What is it?" Bathilda's clipped sarcastic tone was predictable.

Hattie sat down. This could take a little while. "I had a call from Evelyn this morning with news that affects Wednesday Club."

"Is that so? Why didn't she call me? I'm the president."

Hattie rolled her eyes. "I'm not sure. Maybe she just forgot. At any rate, she and Charlie are picking up and moving west river. Now that Charlie's dad has passed, his mother is starting to fail, and someone needs to help Charlie's brother on the ranch."

"Probably not the most industrious if he's anything like Charlie."

Hattie continued. "Poor Evelyn didn't sound all that happy about it. You know how it is; west river is like a whole other state! She says it's a real big ranch, over five hundred head of Black Angus, so there's no choice in the matter but to go. They're starting to pack up now, planning an auction for next month already. We will certainly miss her."

"Certainly. She's the kind of no-nonsense woman who could always be counted on to volunteer for the extra committee. And she showed up for all the meetings on time." Bathilda made a funny noise in her throat. "Not like some."

"You bet, and I'm going to miss her potato salad. I'm sure Etola will miss having her on the music committee, too."

"An enthusiastic singer."

Hattie tapped her foot. "So, I've been thinking about how to fill the secretary role now that—"

Bathilda interrupted. "You know we'll never get Etola to budge from Music Chairman. What about Cora?"

"Cora said she was tired of being secretary after nine years."

"Tilly then. That's the only other option."

"You know as well as I do that Tilly has her hands full with those three little ones. I'm surprised she volunteered to do the program covers. No, I've been rolling this around in my head all day, and I think I have a good solution." She paused for a minute, gathering her resolve. "We should ask Ivy to be secretary."

"Ivy! You don't mean Cora's granddaughter?"

"Right, Ivy."

Bathilda half-shouted. "She's a child!"

"Sixteen and a half."

"But that's ridiculous. This club doesn't allow teenagers in, let alone have them as officers."

"There's no written rule that says we don't allow teenagers. Besides, I can only imagine how unsettled that young woman must feel. Cora is so worried about her fitting in at school."

Bathilda snorted again. "Well, she's probably come to town with her highfalutin ways like her mother Marie — I mean *Vonda* Marie. Thinking she's better than anyone else."

Hattie's heart went out to Ivy. Living under the shadow of a mother with such a big personality must be tough. She wondered what Ivy knew about her father. It was hard to grow up without a father, a real father. She ought to know. "Now that's not fair. Ivy seems very nice. I think a connection, even if it is with a group of mature ladies, might help. And we certainly need a secretary."

"But what about her school?" Bathilda said.

"If we move the meetings to three o'clock and Cora picks her up after school, she could make it. School is out for her at two-thirty on Wednesdays."

"I don't like it. You know how irresponsible teenagers are. We've been keeping proper club minutes for over twenty years now. We have a history to uphold."

Hattie stood up and rocked back and forth for a minute. Her hip ached. "I understand, and that's terribly important. But I think we should give her a chance. I'm sure Cora will show her how's it done. And if it doesn't work out after a few months, I'll take on both the treasurer and secretary roles."

Bathilda was silent for a few seconds. "This is highly unorthodox. Wednesday Club is for adult farm women who live within our five-mile radius — those with serious intentions. Not just a social club like that Extension Club. I don't want every teenage girl in the county trying to join."

Hattie swallowed a laugh. "Don't worry, I doubt that will happen. Can we just try it?"

There was a long pause on the other end of the line. "Well, I suppose we could give her a try for a month. Since we don't have anyone else."

"I'll give Cora a call and see what she thinks."

"One month. That's all I'm willing to gamble on."

"I understand. And, of course, we'll take a vote on it at our next meeting. See how everyone feels." It was good to remind Bathilda from time to time that she was not their queen. "Goodbye now."

Hattie was about to dial Cora when she heard Pup barking at a car coming up the driveway. *Oh dear, it's Arlo. Hopefully, he's only here to pick up eggs and won't be planning to stay for coffee. That man is such a nuisance.*

Like all men seemed to be.

Cora

CORA WAS PICKING APPLES when she heard the school bus rumbling down the road. Waiting for that sound was familiar, yet it had been at least fifteen years since Vonda Marie had gotten off that bus. That was before she'd refused to ride it anymore, and one or another of her friends had dropped her off after school. Delmar never would let her drive. He always said she wasn't responsible enough.

Of course, Delmar had a different idea of what it meant to be responsible. His own father had died in a terrible farm accident when Delmar was just thirteen. Everything changed after that — Delmar suddenly became the man of the house, constantly helping his mother and the three younger kids. Sometimes, Cora wondered if Delmar even remembered what it was like to have fun. Before it was all work, *every possible minute,* all the time.

Cora watched Ivy trudge down the bus steps and up the driveway, head down and shoulders low. Not at all the way her mother would have bounced down those steps, ready to share the latest gossip. Later, Vonda Marie had clammed up and that's when she knew something was wrong.

Cora picked up the bushel basket half full of red apples and walked to the driveway to meet Ivy. "Hello, sweet pea. How was your day?"

Ivy shrugged. "Okay." They walked up the driveway without saying anything more, through the back screen door, and into the kitchen together.

Cora set the basket on the counter. "Would you like a snack, sweetheart?"

"No thanks."

"Well then, do you want to help make a pie?"

Ivy put down her schoolbooks, looked at the apples, and frowned. "I guess ..."

"Wash your hands, and we'll get started. I'll show you how to make a pretty lattice top. First, we'll get these nice apples peeled."

Cora watched Ivy head to the sink and turn on the water, her mouth downturned and her eyes sad looking. Cora wondered if Ivy was as unhappy as she looked. "So, how's school going? Are you making any friends yet?"

Ivy shook her head. "Not really. I don't think they're interested in being friends with anybody new." Her voice raised. "And I'm not all that interested in them either."

Cora recognized hurt behind that defiance. "Well, I'm sure it will take a little time to feel at home here." *Maybe now's the right time to bring it up.* "I had a call from Hattie today. You know, from my Wednesday Club. It seems that Evelyn, our secretary, is moving away. So, they want to ask you something."

Ivy shut off the water. "Me? What's that?"

Cora willed herself to sound nonchalant, un-invested, as she handed Ivy a paring knife. "Hattie and Bathilda think you'd be a perfect secretary for the club. That is, if you're interested."

Ivy was silent for a few seconds. Cora held her breath.

"No thanks. I don't think so." Ivy turned away and began to peel an apple.

Cora knew she'd have to tread lightly; she was learning that Ivy was no pushover. "Well, you might think it over. It could be a nice way to get involved with a group of wonderful women."

"But aren't they all old ladies?"

Cora smiled at her granddaughter's frankness. "Well, most of us are older. But Tilly is only twenty-five or so. Not too far from your age."

Ivy furrowed her brow. "I'm sixteen, Grandma."

Cora laughed. "Oh, right. When you're in your mid-fifties, twenty-five seems young. Besides, it's not about the age. These women are the heart of this community. Always there for you through thick and thin. They were the only ones who stuck by me when ..." She trailed off, then added, "Every woman needs a Wednesday Club in her life."

Ivy kept her head down, peeling apples. After a time, she asked, "What does the secretary do?"

Cora kept her voice neutral. "All you have to do is take notes at the meetings and write up the minutes. You know, record the main things that happen, decisions made. Then you read the minutes at the next meeting, and the club votes to approve them. We have several books of minutes from past years, so you could see how they've been done before."

Ivy was silent.

"And I could help you," Cora continued. "Maybe just try it for a month and see what you think?"

"Maybe just for one month. I won't be here that much longer, anyway."

Cora felt relief flood her body. "Why, that's wonderful! Let's start on the crust now. A pie is only as good as its crust." Cora opened the icebox. "And it all starts with cold lard."

Cora looked at her granddaughter. That sweet girl was doing this for her. Ivy didn't look happy about it, but that was okay.

Maybe some day Ivy would come to love the Wednesday Club ladies as much as she did. If she were here long enough.

Tilly

THE SUN PEEKED ABOVE the horizon, sending a weak yellow light through the narrow window. Tilly sat hunched over the kitchen table, wrapped in a pink chenille bathrobe and wearing scuffed brown moccasins. The overhead light spilled a haloed glow above the table in the otherwise dark trailer house.

How Tilly loved this time of the day — everything was so blessedly quiet. Just the tick-tick of the hands of the wall clock. Time seemed to move more slowly when it was quiet. For Tilly, it was worth getting less sleep to have these precious minutes of silence.

Two rows of yellow construction paper lay on the table, each of the seven pieces trimmed to eleven inches tall by four inches wide. On one half, Tilly had painted an image of a ring-neck pheasant, the state bird of South Dakota. She had used an elaborate, layered effect to illustrate the red, gold, and black tail feathers and the white ring at the base of the bird's neck. Now Tilly used a sharp black pencil to painstakingly print "Wednesday Club 1963–64", her lips pursed in concentration. Then, she wrote the club motto on the back of each program cover:

'Tis good to do

'Tis better to know

'Tis best to be

She sat back in the chair, rolled her head to relax the kinks in her neck, and ran her fingers through her golden blonde curls. She couldn't remember the last time she had washed and set her hair. Poor James, she used to have time to spend on her looks.

She heard a creak of bedsprings, then heavy steps clomping down the hallway. Tilly smiled as James entered the room, yawning. She loved the boyishness in her husband's face when he first woke up, that same sweetness imprinted on all three of his sons' faces.

James came up behind her, leaned down, and wrapped his arms around her shoulders, looking at the table. "They're looking good, honey. You should be real proud of 'em."

Tilly smiled. "Almost done. Just the lettering on three more, and I'll be finished. I sure hope the group likes them."

"They'd be fools not to. What time's your meeting?"

From the back bedroom, a baby whimpered. "Three." The whimper ramped up to a full-fledged wail, and then another tiny voice called out, "Mommy!"

Tilly sighed, getting up from the table. "Your mother has agreed to watch the boys and Hattie is picking me up."

"Mommy, baby Milo is crying!" Four-year-old Robby entered the cramped kitchen and made his announcement as if this was something new and not an ongoing occurrence.

Tilly bent down and gave Robby a loud smacking kiss on top of his head. "Thank you for letting me know, big boy. You're mama's good helper." Robby beamed, impossibly long eyelashes surrounding his chocolate brown eyes. Tilly hurried to the bedroom, where she could still hear the conversation through the thin walls.

"Are you going to work at the big eggevator, Daddy?"

Cereal rattled into a bowl. "Yes, sir, I'm off to the elevator. Lots of truckloads of oats coming in today."

Tilly walked back into the kitchen, holding a crying baby with one arm and clutching the hand of 2-year-old TJ with the other. James grabbed the milk bottle from the refrigerator and looked at the few drops left in the bottom. He let out an expletive under his breath.

"Oh darn! I was hoping it would last until you got your ... I'm sorry." Tilly rocked Milo back and forth. "I could make some toast."

James grabbed a bun from the metal breadbox. "It's OK. I know you're trying to make things stretch. Payday on Friday. I've got enough to pick up some milk after work." He kissed Tilly and the baby as he headed for the door. "Good luck today. Have fun with the ladies."

Tilly didn't even hear the door close over Milo's wails. "Shh. There now, sweetheart. Mommy will get your bottle ready. TJ, you sit down, and I'll make you and Robby some toast with cinnamon and sugar."

Robby pulled on Tilly's robe. "Can I help with the formala?"

"Sure, sweetheart, you can help me mix it. Get the can from the cupboard."

Tilly rocked the baby back and forth, then suddenly remembered and whirled around to the table. TJ had a fistful of the construction paper covers he waved overhead, pretending to make the pheasants fly. His little fingers had wadded and bent the corners of several of them. "TJ! Stop!" Tilly shouted. He dropped the covers and as they floated to the floor he began to cry. Robby rushed over to comfort TJ, stepping on the covers as he went. "Stop, don't move!" Tilly yelled. Milo continued to shriek in Tilly's arms, right next to her ear.

"Oh my gosh! I'm so sorry I yelled. Just give Mommy a minute to get these picked up." Tilly clutched the howling baby, grabbed the program covers with one hand and put them on top of the refrigerator. At that moment, there was a loud rapping on the aluminum door and the door flew open.

"Everything all right in here? I heard a lot of crying." Mildred, Tilly's mother-in-law, stomped in and plunked down on the couch, her hair still in pink plastic curlers. She held out her thin arms. "Come to Grandma, TJ, and stop your crying now." TJ rubbed his eyes and sidled over to his grandmother.

Tilly kept rocking the baby. "Everything's fine, Milo is colicky again, and that set everyone off. I hope they nap for you this afternoon."

Mildred raised her thin eyebrows, and her angular features became sharper. "This afternoon?"

"Remember, you're going to watch the boys while I go to Wednesday Club? Only for a couple of hours."

Mildred pursed her lips. "Why no, dear. I never said I could watch them today. I'm going to Ortonville with Nelda. We've been planning this trip to the fabric store for weeks now."

Tilly felt her shoulders tighten. "But we talked about this on Friday. It's our regular meeting ... I'm bringing the program covers I made ..."

"Well, you'll just have to take them next month. Or bring the boys ... oh, maybe not." Tilly hated that sarcastic edge Mildred sometimes had. "Those Wednesday Clubbers probably wouldn't want their fancy meeting disturbed. Think they're so dad-burned special."

Tilly turned toward the cupboards, her eyes pricking with heat. She opened a door and pretended to search for something on the shelf.

Mildred plopped TJ on the floor and stood. "Well, I'd best be going. Nelda will be here soon. Wanted to make sure you were treating these precious boys right. Bye, boys."

Tilly didn't turn around. "Goodbye, Mildred."

The metal screen door quivered, then slammed shut, and Tilly sat at the table, her whole body hot and tight. She looked around at the boys as the old familiar voices filled her head. *I hate living in this dumpy trailer, so close to that spiteful woman. This is not how I thought my life would turn out. I do love James; he's a good man, trying his hardest to support us. It's just that every day is so hard.*

Tilly's thoughts were interrupted by the phone ringing, and she took a moment to compose herself. "Hello? Oh, hi Hattie!" She listened for a minute. "I'm so sorry, it turns out that James' mother can't keep the kids after all. So maybe I could just send the program covers with you." Tilly bit her bottom lip. She would not cry!

Hattie's voice was calm. "Never mind all that. I'll give Arlo a call. You know he loves kids, and he's got nothing better to do. You sit tight, and I'll call you right back after I've talked to him."

Tilly squeaked out a goodbye and hung up. She sat down with the fussing baby still in one arm. Robby came over and loudly kissed the baby's cheek. "Are you crying, Mommy? Your birdies will be okay. We can make them fly again."

Tilly hugged Robby. "Mommy's fine. Come over here, sweet little TJ. Everything is fine. Mommy loves you all so much. I'm gonna make your breakfast now and then we'll go outside to play. Won't that be fun?"

Tilly roughly wiped at an annoying tear with the back of her hand, then pushed her uncombed hair off her face. She'd make it through, somehow. Wouldn't she?

Ivy

IVY SLAMMED THE DOOR on her way into the house a little louder than she had intended. This day had gone from bad to worse, if that was even possible, given how bad things already were.

Her grandmother came scurrying into the kitchen. "You alright, Ivy?" A worried look crossed her face.

"Fine." Ivy glanced over to the counter where the day's mail was always left. "No mail for me?"

Her grandmother shook her head. "Not today, honey. Were you expecting something?"

"Not really." Her mother was MIA. And Ivy had only had two letters from Val since she'd been here, even though they had promised to write each other twice a week. Probably that stupid Marilyn was trying to suck Val into her crowd now, asking her to the movies or whatever. And what about her so-called boyfriend Brad? She hadn't heard from him at all.

Her grandmother's gentle voice interrupted her thoughts. "Were you helping your grandpa out there?"

"He probably wouldn't call it that."

"What do you mean?"

Ivy meant to hold back her frustration, but it bubbled out. "He asked me to bring a bucket of oats from the granary for the cows. I couldn't get the dang trap door pulled down fast enough and the oats overflowed the bucket and spilled all over the ground. I shoveled them up, but you'd have thought I killed a cow or something."

Ivy's grandmother let out her tinkling laugh. This was not the response Ivy had expected and she couldn't help but feel defensive. "Well, you should have seen the way he shook his head and scowled at me!"

"Oh, believe me, I know that look. Sorry I laughed, Ivy. It's just that that's happened to me a few times too. The oats come shooting out so fast you just can't get that door shut in time. It'll be fine, no harm done."

Ivy let out a deep sigh. Nothing seemed to work for her around here. She didn't fit on the farm or at school. Everyone at Prairie View High either seemed to hate her or acted like she didn't exist. It didn't really matter, Ivy hated them too, they were all a bunch of backward hicks. What difference did it make if no one ever talked to her at lunch? She could just sit with her book and ignore them.

"What are your plans for the rest of the afternoon, Ivy? Should we finish working on the Wednesday Club minutes?"

Good grief, Ivy thought. That's about the last thing in the world she wanted to do. *I can't believe I let her talk me into being the secretary of that stupid club. What a waste of time meeting with those old ladies. They did the most ridiculous things, like have a motto and a creed they said out loud.*

Ivy gave a forced smile. "Um, maybe not right now, Grandma. I really should work on my Algebra homework."

She turned and slowly climbed the stairs to her bedroom. There was a phrase she found herself repeating every five steps as she climbed up and down the stairs each day: I miss O-ma-ha. I miss

O-ma-ha. Two times, both up and down the stairs. Two times that felt like two hundred.

Wednesday Club Minutes

SEPTEMBER 11, 1963

The Wednesday Club met at the home of Miss Bathilda Baldridge and Miss Etola Baldridge. The meeting was called to order by President Bathilda Baldridge. She announced that Mrs. Evelyn Fish had resigned from the club and her role as secretary. Bathilda said there had been a suggestion for Miss Ivy Hanson to be acting secretary. All members agreed. Bathilda said this could be a temporary situation.

The club motto was recited, and roll was called with six members telling their favorite recipe for Spam. Ideas included fried Spam burgers, Spam with tater tots hot dish, scrambled eggs with Spam, and Spam and olive salad.

The minutes from the August meeting were read by Ivy Hanson, as written by Miss Hattie Dunlop. Mrs. Cora Hanson moved, and Mrs. Tilly Halversen seconded to approve the minutes. All members voted to approve.

Hattie Dunlop gave the treasurer's report. Expenses for August were $3.50 for a going-away hanky for Evelyn Fish. The balance in the Treasury is $38.80. A motion was made by Cora and seconded by Etola to donate $3.00 to the Milk Fund at Prairie View Elementary.

Etola Baldridge led the Club in singing *The More We Get Together*.

Hattie Dunlop gave the program based on a speech titled "I Have a Dream." Martin Luther King, Jr. delivered this speech on the steps of the Lincoln Memorial in Washington, D.C., on August 28. Hattie said over 250,000 people were at the Civil Rights March. She said that Martin Luther King, Jr. called for an end to racism and civil and economic rights for all, and she read a part of the speech. Afterward the club had a discussion. Tilly asked what the word racism meant, and Hattie said it was when people got judged by the color of their skin. Etola noted that she never saw anyone except white people in Prairie View, but if she did, she would go out of her way to be nice to them. Hattie reminded her that a few Sioux Indians were living in Prairie View, and she saw them in town occasionally. Florence said that when they lived in Texas, a few Mexican families were there, but they didn't talk to them because they might try to rob them. Hattie said there can be racism towards Indians and Mexicans too, and that just because they weren't white didn't mean they weren't good people.

The meeting ended with reciting the club creed. A lunch of orange Jell-O with mandarin oranges, lunch meat sandwiches, rolls, and chocolate cake was served.

Ivy Hanson, Acting Secretary

Etola

WASN'T IT ALWAYS THE way? Whenever Etola thought a day was going to be ordinary, often it turned out to be a whack-on-the-side-of-the-head sort of day. It had started without a hitch, a typical Indian summer day — hot, dry, and breezy.

After she and Bathilda had washed up the breakfast dishes and figured out how to keep Eddie occupied and out of trouble, Bathilda had asked if she could go to town and get a few groceries at the Red Owl. They only needed a few things: coffee, canned mandarin oranges, and marshmallows. Etola also wanted some of that new powdered Tang. Bathilda asked if she'd need a list, and Etola said no, she could remember four things since she *was* only forty-seven and not anywhere near having old-timer's brain. Bathilda had warned her not to forget the marshmallows since they were a key ingredient in the Jell-O salad she was making for the church funeral luncheon.

Etola had changed out of her barn shoes and thought about putting on a different dress, but she figured it would be a quick trip, and she'd be working in the garden as soon as she got home, so why change twice? Besides, the Red Owl should be quiet on a

Tuesday, what with most women shopping on Thursdays when the coupons came out. Plus, Thursday was Green Stamps Day.

She should have known it would be an off-kilter day when she walked out to the machine shed and there was a big old dead rat next to the car door. That dad-blasted gray tabby was always leaving presents for them instead of eating those ugly rodents.

Etola grabbed an old exhaust pipe from the corner and pushed the stiff carcass out of the way. She'd have to tell Eddie to bury it later since he was way off in the barn, laying down some fresh straw for the sheep.

Next thing you know, she was stuck behind Bud Chester's tractor pulling a manure spreader, and he was going about five miles an hour down the highway. Nothing to be done but crawl along since there was no passing on the curve, and some of those cars coming toward her were whipping past at about fifty miles an hour. At first, she had the window rolled down, but then the stench was so strong she had to roll it back up. That started the inside of her car heating up faster than the shake of a lamb's tail.

By the time she finally got to town, there was a line of cars six deep behind her. Her blood pressure was rising, she had a lot to do today, and Bathilda was always complaining about how Etola dawdled around in town.

As soon as she pulled into the parking lot of the Red Owl, she spotted Mildred Halversen's car. She probably should turn around right then. That woman was the meanest old biddy in all of South Dakota. Poor Tilly, Etola didn't know how she could stand it, living right in her backyard the way she did. Maybe she could avoid Mildred since she only had a couple of things to pick up, and she could get out of there fast.

Etola gathered the Folgers, the oranges, and the Tang and headed toward the register. Then she heard Bathilda's voice in her head saying, "Don't forget the marshmallows!" She headed back to the baking supplies aisle. Sure enough, there was Mildred stopped midway down the aisle with her back to Etola, having a big old gab session with Nelda Monroe. They had their two carts completely blocking the aisle like no other shoppers were in the store besides them. And those confounded marshmallows were on the shelf right beside them. Etola came behind them and said with a polite but firm voice, "Morning, ladies. Excuse me, please." You'd think she'd asked them for a handout the way they begrudgingly moved their carts. She grabbed the marshmallows and hurried back up the aisle and around the corner toward the checkout stand.

Then, don't you suppose, with all her juggling of those groceries and no basket to put them in, Etola dropped the Folgers. And it didn't only fall on the floor, it rolled all the way back to the end of the baking aisle. She scurried after it just in time to hear Mildred's loud voice braying up the aisle, "Looks like she came straight from the barn." Then Nelda: "Harvey and I call them the spinster sisters. They'll be living on that farm with their halfwit brother til they're all six feet under. Couple of bitter old maids."

Etola snatched the can off the floor, paid for the groceries, and skedaddled out to her car. It wasn't until she was behind the wheel that it sunk in what Nelda had said. Her whole body sagged. Straight from the barn. Spinster sister. Bitter old maid. Those hurtful words hit her hard and she broke down, right there in the parking lot. Etola thought she might never stop bawling, quiet at first and then those hiccup-y kinds of sobs where she couldn't catch her breath. Her nose was dripping like a garden spout, and she'd be darned if she had no hanky in her purse. Had to wipe it on her sleeve like a heathen.

She finally got her wits about her and took off for home. She sure as heck didn't want Mildred seeing her there, blubbering away. At first, she'd felt sorry for herself on the drive back to the farm. Is that what everybody in Prairie View called her and Bathilda, the spinster sisters? Did they all say poor Eddie was a dimwit? Didn't she have a right to a little bitterness, having lost her beau, John, only a month before her wedding?

But the further she drove, the more her feelings changed. *How dare those old biddies talk that way about me! Old maid? Living on the farm until I'm six feet under? Why, I'll show them. Just wait and see.*

October 1963

Bathilda

BATHILDA STOMPED ALONG THE hard-packed dirt lane of the shelterbelt and up to the pasture fence facing the road. She wanted to make sure the hand-painted sign was still hanging there: *For Sale – Quarter Horse, 15 ½ hands, 17 years old. A good horse for occasional work or pleasure riding.*

They hadn't had a single question about that darn horse, which made Bathilda suspicious that Eddie had taken down the sign. Etola said they should add a telephone number and a price on the sign, but that just seemed silly. Everyone knew who lived on this farm, and they just needed to come and talk to her about the horse. Besides, she didn't want to list a price for Bearcat. Better to have a chance to haggle.

Bathilda had made up her mind — there was just no reason for keeping that horse when neither Eddie nor Etola paid it the least bit of attention. It was a waste of hay and oats and good grazing land for the sheep. What with hail destroying half of the bean crop last spring, they'd be lucky if they didn't need a short-term loan to get them through the winter.

Sure, Eddie was fond of that old, dappled horse, but feeding and petting were not enough. Bearcat needed to be ridden and fooled with more. And he was getting up there in years — if they waited too much longer, nobody would want him. Bathilda whistled for her dog Shep to catch up, then closed and latched the gate to the pasture and headed toward the house. Looked like the barbed wire was sagging down in the southeast corner; she'd need to have Eddie get on that soon.

She paused for a moment to gaze at the V-shaped formation of Canadian geese in the sky, announcing their trip south. Better get that horse sold before winter.

"C'mon, Shep, time to get you your supper." At the mention of the word, the heavy-coated herding dog ran to the barn. Bathilda unlatched the small feed room door and scooped a cup of dry food into a bowl. She gave Shep a few rubs on his soft head as he gobbled down his food and then turned and walked toward the house.

The first thing Bathilda noticed when she stepped into the utility room was the smell. Ammonia. It wasn't like Etola to take up some cleaning on her own; goodness knows that girl would just as soon keep her nose in a magazine as make sure this house was presentable. Had Eddie gotten into something he shouldn't have?

Bathilda removed her rubber boots and put on her house shoes before entering the kitchen, the smell getting stronger. She didn't know how this farm would function without her. Eddie had an excuse, but that Etola! Bathilda had to remind her of every little thing that needed doing. Maybe it would have been better if her younger sister had married and moved away. Etola was nothing at all like their German mother, who was the hardest worker Bathilda had known.

Her mother's words echoed through Bathilda's head, a constantly recurring memory. *"Now, you take care of your little sister until we get back."* Those words were always followed by the image of them driving off, young Eddie waving from the back seat, and the dust from the driveway eventually obscuring her last view of their 1934 Chevy pickup. And her parents. How many times had she replayed that scene in her mind?

Bathilda's thoughts were interrupted by the whirring of a small motor coming from the living room, and she followed the sound. Etola was slumped on the sofa as a flexible tube pumped air into the inflated cap encasing her head, making her look like some kind of Martian. It was that ridiculous Sunbeam hair dryer. Etola was sound asleep, her head tilted sideways and her mouth half open, a thin line of dribble coming from the corner. On her lap was a magazine open to a close-up photo of some movie star and beside her on the couch were two more magazines: *Movie Mirror* and *Silver Screen*.

Bathilda walked toward Etola to see if she'd wake up, but Etola was dead to the world. Even when Bathilda called out her name, she still didn't respond, so Bathilda switched off the hair dryer and watched the pink rubber cap slowly deflate. Etola woke with a start.

"I thought you'd of started supper by now. Do you think that hotdish is going to make itself?" Bathilda asked.

Etola's eyes widened. "What time is it?"

"Darn near five o'clock."

"Murgatroyd!" Etola disconnected the wired tube from the hair dryer and dashed up the stairs to the bathroom, the tube still connected to the cap and dragging behind. It was the fastest Bathilda had seen her move in a long time.

From the kitchen, Bathilda heard some muffled sounds and a few "oh no!" s, each one getting a little louder and sounding more distressed. *Now what?* Bathilda shook her head. She didn't know what had come over Etola lately, why she'd suddenly become so concerned about her looks. Almost every day, she'd been making a trip to the drug store, coming home with some kind of cream or potion. And then buying that crazy hair dryer. Not to mention the way she'd been slathering on the makeup. One day, Bathilda asked her if she was fixin' to become a clown and run away with the circus. Eddie thought that was funny, but Etola just glared at her.

Bathilda set to work on the hamburger hotdish, starting by peeling the carrots. It was going to have to be an easy-to-fix meal tonight. In a few minutes, Bathilda heard Etola's heavy footsteps on the stairs and then the half-stifled gasps of her sister standing in the doorway. Bathilda turned around.

Etola was a sight to behold. Her previously greyish brown hair was now bright orange, sticking straight out from her head and looking for all the world like a clown wig. Bathilda quickly bit her lip to stop herself from mentioning the circus again. The look on Etola's face kept her from saying anything at all.

Finally, Etola spoke, "I must have fallen asleep. I was only supposed to let it process for 10 minutes."

"How long was it?"

"Almost an hour. Now I've ruined my hair!"

Bathilda took a couple of steps towards Etola, looked more closely at her hair, and then that snorting sound escaped her throat. She couldn't help it. "What color were you going for?"

"Auburn!" Etola sobbed. "Like Maureen O'Hara." She slumped down in the kitchen chair and put her head in her hands.

"Well, isn't that just like you? How many times have I said you need to use the kitchen timer because you're always going off into dreamland, not paying attention. Serves you ..."

At the sound of Etola's sobs and the sight of her quaking shoulders, Bathilda closed her mouth. She hadn't seen Etola like this since she'd gotten the news of John's death over 25 years ago. She walked over to Etola and touched her hair. It felt like straw. Bathilda slid her hand down to Etola's shoulder and gave it a quick pat.

"There, there. No use crying over spilt milk. It will grow back, and you'll look just like you did before."

Etola looked up long enough to spit out, "That's just it — I don't want to look like I did before. Like some barren old maid. Can't you see, I'll never get away from here then."

Bathilda stepped back, caught off guard by the hateful tone in her sister's voice. Since when was it so bad around here? She whirled around to the counter, chopping the carrots with a lot more vigor. After all she did to keep this place going, and now her sister couldn't wait to get away.

After Etola left the room weeping and Bathilda had finished making the hotdish, she considered whether she should have tried to sound a little more sympathetic. It wasn't like Etola to sound off like that. Surely, Etola was just upset about her hair and would eventually come around to her good humor. Still, Bathilda couldn't help thinking that something about Etola had changed.

Florence

FROM THE BASEMENT, FLORENCE listened to the phone ring once, twice, three times, four times. Finally, she heard her husband heave himself from his faded brown easy chair and amble towards the phone stand in the hallway. Florence could picture the dent left in Lloyd's leather chair, a scoop that fit his backside like a perfectly worn baseball glove.

Florence heard more heavy footsteps on the wooden floor above her, then "Florence!" She called up to him. "What?"

After a few seconds, Lloyd shouted, "Florence!"

Florence yelled louder this time. "Down here, Lloyd."

Lloyd opened the door to the cellar and called down, "What are you doing down there?"

"Getting the punch bowl and cups."

"Telephone. It's Coast to Coast Hardware."

Florence trotted up the stairs as fast as she could manage. Which was pretty good for a 42-year-old, she thought. She bumped into Lloyd as she rushed for the phone.

"Hello? Yes, that's right. Oh – that's wonderful news. I'll be right in to pick it up."

Florence ran for her purse as she called out to Lloyd. "The wallpaper's in. Just in the nick of time. I'm on my way to town to get it."

"Wallpaper? I thought your meeting is tomorrow."

"It is. I'll have just enough time to get it hung tonight." Florence stopped for a quick check of her appearance in the front hall mirror. Despite today's humidity, her carefully teased and heavily sprayed hair was still in place. She added a fresh coat of lipstick, then blotted it with a Kleenex pulled from her pocket.

Lloyd stared at her. "You can't do the whole dining room in one night. That's damn foolhardy!"

Florence didn't have time to linger. "But I have to, Lloyd. Tomorrow's Wednesday Club." With that explanation, she was out the door.

Later, around midnight, Florence thought that maybe Lloyd had been right; perhaps this was a bit foolhardy. She'd only gotten two rolls up so far, and already she'd had to redo things four times. It had been a while since Florence had hung wallpaper, and she'd forgotten the delicate balance between getting the glue on, getting the roll positioned just right so the patterns lined up, and getting it even from top to bottom. Perhaps she should have chosen a more forgiving pattern, too. The large fleur-de-lis looked terribly wrong if it wasn't matched up exactly.

It was probably a bit ambitious to think she could finish the whole dining room in time. But it seemed important to set a good example for the club. Especially now, with a young impressionable girl in the club who could learn from her. Where she was from, in Dallas County, women were well-versed in the art of hostessing. After all, creating a beautiful and inviting setting put your guests at ease and said a lot about how you were managing your household. Everything needed to be considered: the welcome by the hostess, the table setting, the serving dishes, the linens, and the bathroom. So much to consider and prepare for.

Florence would do her usual dress rehearsal in a few hours, pretending she was a guest and gathering impressions from the front door onwards. Were there any eyesores? Unsightly clutter? Dirt? Smears? Everything should be spotless and perfect. Including her own appearance, of course.

Florence had been to Wednesday Club at everyone's house except Tilly's, and, frankly, some of these women could use an example of how-to hostess well. Who better than Florence to show them? She was the only member with big city out-of-state experience, and Texas was well advanced over South Dakota when it came to sophistication and refinement.

Florence wished they were still living in Texas and closer to their son Todd, who was in basic training in Georgia. If only Lloyd hadn't made it so they had no choice but to come back to where he'd grown up, back to where Robert could take them in, give Lloyd a way to make a living. She hoped his brother didn't tire of Lloyd's health problems. There were days when Lloyd couldn't manage the long hours of heat and dust. He was trying. And it did seem like those dark days were behind him.

He had promised Florence.

With her mind given over to remembering, Florence lost herself in the repetition of measuring and cutting, the spreading of the glue, and the positioning of the paper. Two walls down, two to go. If only this rickety step stool weren't so wobbly — she'd been after Lloyd to fix it for so long, even before they moved into this old farmhouse eight months ago. Why couldn't he ever just do what she asked instead of her having to remind him three or four times? She'd better go ahead and fix it herself — it would be just her luck to topple over and glue herself to the wall.

Florence grabbed a flashlight and headed out the kitchen door to Lloyd's shop. Maybe that was what all this fuss about women being less dependent on their husbands was all about. Maybe it was just about being tired of waiting for men to get things done.

No reason why Florence couldn't find the large Philips head and tighten up the ladder herself. Sometimes, when she laid awake in bed, she imagined herself like this: taking charge, managing the place on her own. Being able to do things the way she wanted; the way she knew they should be done. It felt good thinking about being alone, no Lloyd to worry about.

Florence kept the big overhead light in the shop off — better not to take a chance on Lloyd waking up and giving her what for when he saw the walls half done. She shone the flashlight toward the shelves above the workbench and the drawers below it. *What a mess. Are all men this way — not an organized bone in their bodies? How can you put the WD40 in with the drill bits and the wrenches? Wouldn't it be logical to put all the cans of oil together? Where are those dang screwdrivers?*

Florence pulled open a drawer: paintbrushes, sanding paper, glue. Another drawer: rope, gas funnel, and leather gloves. What was in this large drawer? Under this rag?

Florence pulled up the greasy cloth and then stood, her breath catching in her chest. She bent back down and pulled out a couple of bottles. Then, more bottles. A whole big drawer filled with empty liquor bottles. Florence stood motionless; her heart washed over with a wave of dark liquid heaviness.

Then she clenched her teeth, replaced the bottles, covered them with the rag, closed the drawer, walked to the shop door, and quietly left. She'd just have to manage the wobbly stepladder.

Still, she wrestled with the deep sadness threatening to overtake her. He'd promised.

Ivy

WHEN IVY ARRIVED AT her locker, the boy next to her had his locker door swung wide open, blocking hers. She recognized him as a football player. Not that she followed sports, but he always seemed to have a small crowd around him on Mondays, talking about Friday night's game. He was one of the popular students. Her grandmother had said he was Florence's nephew. She waited for him to notice her and move out of the way, but he was preoccupied, crouched down, and digging for something in the bottom of his locker. Finally, she had to say, "I need to get into my locker."

He looked up, then stood up and moved his locker door to make room for her. "Oh, sorry." He looked at her more closely, his blue eyes boring into hers. "I'm Lance. Lance Lane."

She pretended she didn't know. It seemed to Ivy that he was pretty proud of that name. She really couldn't stand guys like this, so full of themselves. She stared at her locker combination dial as she said, "That's your real name? Lance Lane?"

"Uh, yeah, I know. It's like my mom thought I would be a movie star or something," Lance quipped. His blonde hair was parted on the side and swept over, grazing the top of his eyebrow.

Ivy couldn't stop herself. "Or a ventriloquist's dummy, maybe."

Lance looked a little surprised, then gave her a wide grin. "Guess it's true what they're saying, then. You are a sassy thing."

"Yep, sassy, and smart. Too smart to waste time talking with you."

Ivy grabbed her book bag and marched toward the exit. Guys like that needed to be taken down a notch. She knew the type. He was nothing at all like her Brad. If only her Brad would write to her.

Wednesday Club Minutes

OCTOBER 9, 1963

The Wednesday Club met at the home of Florence Lane. The meeting was called to order by President Bathilda Baldridge. The club motto was recited.

Roll was called, with five members naming their favorite television shows. These included *The Ed Sullivan Show, The Andy Griffith Show, The Dick Van Dyke Show, The Danny Thomas Show* and *Bonanza*. Bathilda told the club that Etola had a small accident and was unable to attend but would be back next month.

Ivy Hanson read the minutes from the September meeting. Bathilda said the minutes should be corrected to put a Miss or Mrs. in front of the names the first time they are mentioned. A motion was made by Florence Lane and seconded by Tilly Halversen to approve the minutes as amended for the records. All members voted to approve. President Bathilda said that since Ivy had done an adequate job with the minutes, she recommended that Ivy continue as the club secretary. All agreed.

Hattie Dunlop gave the treasurer's report. There was a $3.00 Milk Fund donation for September, and the balance in the treasury is $35.80.

Bathilda, covering for Etola, led the group in singing "Brighten the Corner Where You Are."

The program for October's meeting was a talk from guest Mrs. Vivian Wills. Vivian showed slides from her recent trip to London with her husband Oscar and daughter Ruth. They visited Buckingham Palace and saw the changing of the Royal Guard and the London Bridge. She told us that the highlight of her trip was a tour of the city in a double-decker bus. She passed around a British pound that she said was worth about $3.39 in American dollars. Mrs. Wills said everyone would enjoy visiting London, especially if they bring an umbrella.

The meeting closed with the members reading the creed "Count That Day Lost," Florence served a lunch of lime Jell-O with sour cream topping, brioche rolls, honey ham, and angel food cake. Sanka, tea, and a fruit juice punch were also served.

Ivy Hanson, Secretary

Ivy

Ivy HOOKED ONE OF her grandmother's aprons over her neck and tied it around her waist as she waited for her grandmother to return with the apples. Another day of canning applesauce. Another Saturday on the farm.

In Omaha, she would have been on her way to a movie with Val and then lunch at the Woolworth's counter. Maybe Brad would have met them after he got off work. Val wrote that Brad was working a lot; that must be the reason he wasn't writing. It had only been two months since she left Omaha, but it felt like an eternity.

Her grandmother came into the kitchen, flushed and smiling, and set the bushel basket on the counter. "Okay, let's get them washed and sliced."

This was the second time they'd canned applesauce in two weeks, and Ivy didn't even like the taste of it. She started to rinse the first apple under the running faucet when the phone rang.

"Can you get that, honey?" her grandmother asked.

Ivy walked to where the phone was mounted on the wall and answered. "Hello, Hanson house ... oh, hi, Mom." It was about time her mother called.

"Hi, darling. I can only talk a minute. I'm in this nice gentleman's office. I just wanted you to know the results of the contest. It turns out they're calling all of us the winners."

"Oh yeah?" Ivy twirled the phone cord around her finger.

"They're doing a series of ads with all six of us. They're going to use the photo of me on the beach."

Ivy rolled her eyes. "That's nice."

Ivy continued listening as her mother described the beach photo in detail, not saying anything as she gazed out the window at the garden and the open pasture beyond. She wondered how long it would take her mother to realize she'd been silent. Finally, her mother asked, "How are things going for you?"

Ivy glanced at her grandmother. "Pretty good, it's fine. Not much, really, just going to school and helping out. And reading." Then she pulled on the telephone cord and tiptoed around the corner into the dining room, lowering her voice to a whisper. "I'm so bored! When are you getting me out of here?"

She listened for a couple more minutes to her mother's excuses and then hissed, "I want my life back!" Her mother ignored her and said to give her grandparents her good news. "Fine, I'll tell them. Bye."

Ivy hung up the phone and came back into the kitchen. "They picked all six to be Miss Pearl Soaps. There's no real winner at all."

"Oh. I see." Cora peered at Ivy. "How is your mom doing? Does she sound good?"

"Yeah, she sounds excited. Seems like she's enjoying all the photo sessions."

"What did she say about you coming to California?"

"She said it's not a good time right now. Maybe after Thanksgiving when she gets moved into a bigger place."

Ivy kept her jaw set and her focus out the window as her grandmother gave her a pat on the shoulder.

"Well, that's good for us. More time to spend with you until then."

"Grandma?"

"Yes, dear?"

"I'll be back. I need to use the bathroom."

"Okay, sweet pea. See you in a minute."

Ivy ran up the stairs and into her bedroom, throwing herself face down on her bed. She let out a long, slow scream into her pillow. Thanksgiving was six excruciatingly long weeks away.

IT WAS COOL AND cloudy, a row of dark, ominous-looking clouds sitting low in the sky when Ivy set off from the house and walked past the barn and the granary and on past the machine shed. Her grandmother had mentioned it might rain, so Ivy had slipped her blue notebook and pencil into her canvas bag. She didn't much care about getting herself wet, but she wanted to protect her diary.

Ivy kept walking down the packed dirt road that led to the fields behind the farmyard, each field surrounded by rows of crab apple, pine, and poplar trees — shelterbelts her grandfather called them. She walked until she was past the sorghum field and the mowed alfalfa field and out to what they called the south pasture. She'd seen a place where she wanted to land — a large, flat gray rock on the pasture's edge, set back almost into the trees. Even if her grandfather drove past on his tractor, he probably wouldn't see her. She liked the idea of being gone today, her whereabouts unknown.

It was a good rock, cooler than Ivy expected, and big enough to lie back on and let her legs hang down. She settled in for a minute, relaxing her back and touching the sandy granite texture with all ten fingers. She wondered whether there had ever been another person who had laid on this rock before, maybe someone hundreds of years ago.

After a few minutes, Ivy opened the front buckle on her bag and took out her notebook. She opened the back cover where she'd taped the envelope and removed the dog-eared black and white photo she'd kept there, a photo she had stolen from the bottom of her mother's jewelry box. She looked for the hundredth time at the picture of the man — a cowboy holding a golden horse with a white mane. The man was tall and muscular, with a relaxed posture. He looked comfortable with the horse. The front of his white straw cowboy hat was slightly tilted down, and the sun cast a long shadow that obscured his face, only the bottom of his square jaw showing. His wide mouth was slightly upturned in a shy smile. Behind him was the edge of a white barn with a steep roof and a tall sliding door partially open. To the right of the barn was a white three-rail fence. Ivy was sure of it now, that was the barn on her grandparent's farm.

She slipped the photo back into the envelope and turned to the first blank page, two-thirds of the way into the diary, and reached for a pencil.

Dear Diary,

I finally heard from Val. It's been three weeks since her last letter, I guess she didn't really want to tell me the news.

Ivy looked up and saw a stocky black cow chewing grass and looking at her. Behind that cow were a dozen more.

Central High had their homecoming last week. This year there were six seniors and two juniors voted into the Homecoming Court.

The first curious cow walked closer to Ivy, and a handful more watched, and then they began to follow the lead cow. Ivy kept writing.

It turns out that Brad and Marilyn were the two juniors on the court.

The cows were cautiously walking towards Ivy and the rock, moving in a group towards her.

And then, on the night of the Homecoming Dance, they won. They were crowned Queen Marilyn and King Brad. Val says it was ridiculous how Marilyn acted for two weeks before the voting — all nicey-nice to all the unpopular kids, even bringing homemade cookies and passing them out at lunchtime.

Ivy watched the cows amble towards her in a tight semi-circle and heard their snuffling noses and tails swatting against each other's backsides.

I guess that's how Marilyn bought her votes. As for Brad, well, he's the kind of guy that's always nice. He doesn't have to fake it to have people like him.

Val says not to worry, it's not like Brad and Marilyn are dating or anything. They kind of had to hold hands after they were crowned. And when they walked off the stage together.

By now, the cows were six feet from the rock, crowded together to get a closer look at Ivy. She looked at their big brown eyes with long lashes and moist leathery noses. She could hear their loud breathing.

Val says a few people asked about me at the dance. I've only had one short letter from Brad since I've been here. That was six weeks ago. He signed it: Love, Brad.

Ivy jumped up on the rock and yelled at the top of her lungs, "Go away! I hate you, you stupid cows!"

The startled cows scrambled to retreat, almost trampling each other as they ran away. Ivy slapped the notebook shut and shoved it into her bag. She wondered how long it would take to die, slowly starving herself to death, on top of this rock, at the edge of this pasture, on this farm, in the state of South Dakota.

THE NEXT AFTERNOON, Ivy asked Bert to drop her off at the corner so she could walk the rest of the way to her grandparents' farm. The afternoon was warm, almost like summer, and there was barely a breeze. Ivy was tired of riding in the back of the bus and tired of little Mary talking to her. She felt sort of sorry for her — Ivy wondered if she was getting enough to eat; she was always asking for handouts. At least a walk from the corner would give Ivy a break from the constant chatter. And she'd seen a sign on the fence of the Baldridge's pasture that she was curious about.

Ivy walked on the part of the gravel road packed smooth by the wear of tires. There were no cars in sight, only the road stretching straight ahead and fields and pastures on either side until the next road. Her grandmother had told her that the roads divided the fields into sections. It all looked like one big boring grid; flat rectangles broken up by occasional rows of trees.

Ivy kept walking until she saw the small hand-painted sign hanging on the barbed wire fence. She could read the "For Sale" part, but the rest of the letters were small, and she was curious what they said. Ivy hesitated a moment before she ventured into the deep ditch and over to the fence. She hadn't heard of snakes in these ditches, but she worried about them hiding in the tall grass. If not snakes, who knew what was in there?

Ivy waded into the grass and up to the sign where she read: *Quarter Horse, 15 ½ hands, 17 years old. A good horse for occasional work or pleasure riding.* Ivy pondered the strangeness of the description. *What's a quarter horse? Fifteen and a half hands? It's like a foreign language around here sometimes.* As if on cue, a gray spotted horse trotted across the field and straight towards her. Ivy backed up a bit, wondering if the horse would charge at her, but the horse came to a stop right beside the sign and leaned its head over the fence, staring straight at Ivy. She took a few steps closer to the horse, sticking out her hand, palm up, like her grandfather had shown her.

The horse clomped two more steps closer to Ivy and then leaned in, its big nostrils taking in the smell of her. It had huge brown eyes, fringed with long lashes on the top and bottom — beautiful. The horse moved close enough to gently nudge Ivy's hand with its nose. Ivy touched its nose with one finger – so soft – then ran her fingers down the side of the horse's face. The horse stood quietly. Ivy leaned slightly over the fence, patting the horse's neck and feeling its long mane. She'd never been close to a horse before and hadn't realize how big they were. She rubbed the horse's head and touched its velvety nose again.

Suddenly, the horse let out a loud snuffling sound, and Ivy jumped back. The horse backed up too and then stepped away, stretching its neck to nibble at the low grass, ambling in the other direction and swatting at flies with its tail. Ivy watched for a while, then decided she'd better get home before her grandmother started to worry.

As Ivy walked into the driveway of the farmyard, her grandpa's pickup truck barreled towards the driveway. As he turned the corner, Delmar leaned out the window, waving at Ivy and motioning for her to follow him. Was that a smile on his face? She followed the truck to the back of the circular drive near the barn. Delmar hopped out of the cab. "Got us two birds. Take these on up to your grandmother, should be time to get 'em cleaned for supper."

Delmar picked up two pheasants from the back of the pickup. Their necks were bound together with twine, and their legs and feet hung limp and motionless.

Ivy looked at the birds and backed away. "No thanks."

"For god sakes, girl! They're pheasants. Delicious."

Ivy didn't move.

Delmar scoffed. "They're not gonna hurt you. Take 'em on up to the house." He held out the birds to Ivy, raising his voice this time. "Just grab them around the necks."

Ivy hesitated, then approached her grandfather and gingerly took the birds by the twine around their necks, holding them far away from her body.

"C'mon now, we don't have time for prissy attitudes. You're as bad as your mother."

Her grandfather's words felt like a slap. Ivy walked toward the house, not looking at the birds. She felt light-headed and her stomach clenched. When she got to the kitchen door, she laid them down on the back step and looked at their lifeless bodies.

The legs were scaly, like a chicken, their long claws limp and curled up. Their feathered bodies were gold, copper-red, and chestnut brown with iridescent sheens of green and purple, the long tail feathers brown streaked on black. Ivy had never seen such beautiful feathers. She put her finger out and stroked the back of a still-warm body.

The twine binding together the shimmering turquoise heads wrapped around the white neck rings, as if they were marked for that. Their yellow and black eyes were surrounded by red patches and were open, empty, as if they had frozen the moment the bullet hit, and they fell from the sky, wings useless against the earth's gravity.

In her sixteen years, Ivy had never seen anything or anyone dead. Her Aunt Lil had already been taken away by the time Ivy had gotten home from school that day. Her mother had said she died peacefully, but Ivy couldn't envision a peaceful heart attack.

Ivy wanted to look away but couldn't stop staring at the eyes. *Did birds go to heaven? Did anyone?* That dark hole in her chest felt bigger today. And even colder.

Cora

When Cora walked into the kitchen, she spotted Ivy through the dusty screen door, two dead pheasants beside her on the stoop.

Cora opened the squeaky door, shutting it gently so it didn't slam. She picked up the birds and moved them to the base of the steps, then sat beside Ivy. Cora waited, not saying anything. She remembered when Vonda Marie had found the newborn lamb in the field, stillborn and stiff, and how she had cried, inconsolable, for quite a time. These two were both tender-hearted. But where Vonda Marie would dramatically sob, Ivy was quiet, with no tears. She put her arm around Ivy.

Finally, Ivy spoke. "I won't help you get them ready for supper."

Cora didn't respond.

"And I'm not going to eat them." Her tone was defiant.

"I understand, honey. It's tough sometimes. But that's why God created these creatures — to feed us."

Ivy didn't say anything.

"I know it's different in the city. You're used to getting meat from the butcher, all packaged up and ready to cook."

Ivy shook her head, her long hair partially covering her face. "It's not the pheasants. I mean, it's sad and all. They're pretty birds. It's just everything — about being away from my friends, about how Grandpa hates me."

Ivy's words cut deep. "Oh, sweetie, Grandpa doesn't hate you. Whatever makes you think that?" She'd need to talk to Delmar about this.

"He's always saying I'm like Mom and complaining about her."

Cora sighed. "Your mom and your grandpa had some rough times. He's had a hard time moving past them."

"What happened? Why is he still so mad at her?"

Cora weighed how to answer the question she knew would come up one day. "Things didn't turn out as your grandfather had hoped. He wasn't happy with your mother's decisions."

"Like what decisions?"

"Well, I guess he wanted her to settle down around here. Marry some nice farm boy."

Ivy looked up at her grandmother. "Mom never talks about my dad. Just says she made a mistake, and he wasn't in the picture. She won't tell me anything about him. It sounds like he's not alive anymore." She looked away when she asked. "Is that true?"

This must be so difficult for Ivy. Cora had promised Vonda Marie she wouldn't say anything, but still. Perhaps a partial truth would suffice. "I really don't know. He left town a long time ago."

Ivy raised her voice. "But what happened?"

Cora put her hand across Ivy's shoulder, pulled her long hair back into a ponytail, and gave Ivy a peck on her cheek. "Sweet girl, that is up to your mother to tell you. But you should know that you are very loved, no matter what. No use wishing for the past to be different." Cora wondered if she'd said that last part to Ivy or to herself.

She stood. "Now, I'm going to get ready for supper. You can eat or not eat the pheasant. Whatever you want. They are delicious, though."

Cora picked up the birds, then walked towards the side yard, where she'd make a slice down the middle of their breasts and pull the skin off. She was used to it by now.

So much pain was still being caused by a teenager's actions. If only things had been different. But then they wouldn't have sweet Ivy. One of these days, maybe she'd just have to tell Ivy the truth.

November 1963

Etola

FOR CRYIN' OUT LOUD! If somebody had told Etola what that dye would do to her hair, she would have run screaming from Rexall Drug. Maybe she should have ponied up a little more dough and bought the Clairol instead of the cheap brand. If only she hadn't fallen asleep. When she took that dryer cap off, it was like looking at a pile of straw so dry they wouldn't feed it to Bearcat. Her hair broke off and fell out for days — it was like the wrath of God himself had singed her. Like she was being cursed for her vanity.

Etola had spent the first three weeks not leaving the farm. She had to skip Ruth Foster's Tupperware party — even missed Wednesday Club in October, the first time in the last six years. Not since she'd had that terrible flu in January of '57. Finally, Bathilda said she was tired of having to do all the errands in town, and why didn't Etola just get herself a wig?

Course, she'd had to cover her head with a big sun hat and drive all the way to Ortonville to look at wigs at the Glamour Beauty Salon. She'd prayed the whole time she wouldn't run into anybody from Prairie View.

Turned out shopping for a wig was just the ticket. Wearing a wig, Etola could be anybody! She'd looked at short, straight blonde cuts like The Pixie, long platinum hair done up in a bouffant they call a beehive, shoulder-length red hair called The Bombshell, and brunette hair in a flipped-up bob. She almost went with the bob because it looked exactly like the First Lady's hair, but then she decided, what the heck, she might as well go all the way into Beautyland, and she went with The Bombshell, down to her shoulders and very thick — they called it voluminous. That should come in handy what with winter coming on. Plus, the length seemed to hide her double chin. It was just the auburn shade she was going for. Why, if her own hair was longer and the dye had worked, she might have looked just like this naturally.

Bathilda had had a fit when she saw her in the wig for the first time, but Etola didn't care. She had to take charge of her life while there was still time.

The wig was only part of her complete makeover. Etola bought herself one of those sweating suits that would melt off the pounds. It looked like a giant tinfoil jumpsuit, but the advertisements guaranteed she would lose thirty pounds in just one month. She didn't dare let Bathilda see it, so she locked herself in her room and laid on the bed in it. So far, she'd only sweated a little and hadn't lost any weight, but the instructions said to give it some time.

Etola had also been practicing with all the new makeup she'd bought: peony pink blush, moonlight blue eye shadow, midnight black eyeliner, and pearly white (with a hint of coral) lipstick. Plus, powder to keep it all from coming off if she got the hot flashes. And the icing on the cake: false eyelashes, extra-long like Brigitte Bardot's. She'd kept a whole scrapbook of pictures cut out from movie magazines, so she had a guide for applying all this makeup.

Now, she went through her high school yearbook to narrow down the options for her victims, or rather potentials. It turned out to be quite the sorry lot. Of the twenty men in her graduating class, three were dead, five had moved away, nine were married, two were widowers, and one was still a bachelor. So that narrowed it down to three. Etola decided to home in on the widowers first because at her age, there was probably a reason a guy was still a bachelor in his late forties. Best to leave that option for last.

Next Friday might just be the first day of the rest of her life. It took only one phone call, and Willard had said he'd be happy to meet her for dinner to talk about growing cucumbers. Etola figured he couldn't resist giving his gardening advice since he was always winning blue ribbons at the county fair for his cukes.

Etola and Willard. It had a nice ring to it. Now she just needed to figure out what to wear!

Ivy

WHEN IVY ASKED BERT to let her off the bus to walk, he'd looked surprised. It was a cold day, only 32 degrees, and the wind was blowing hard enough that Ivy felt like there was dust spitting at her. It was a sharp change from yesterday's 50 degrees, as if the door to winter had suddenly been thrown open. But Ivy insisted she wanted to walk the rest of the way home. She'd noticed that sign was still up on the fence.

There wasn't any snow on the ground yet, but the long brown grass crunched as Ivy tromped down into the ditch and over to the edge of the pasture. She didn't see the horse this time, but she remembered how it showed up before and figured it could happen again. The pasture looked empty as Ivy let out a whistle. She didn't know if horses responded to whistles, but sure enough, the gray horse came from behind the trees, trotting towards her.

Ivy reached out to pet the horse when it stopped in front of her and leaned its head over the fence. "What's your name, pony?" The horse backed up slightly but continued to stand beside the fence. Ivy dropped her book bag on the ground and carefully climbed through the fence, bending low to keep from snagging her coat on the top row of the barbed wire. She tiptoed toward the horse, talking to it in low tones and running her hand across its back. The horse didn't move; only turned its head to watch her. Ivy scratched its neck, feeling the coarseness of its long grey mane. The horse bowed its neck and nuzzled closer to Ivy, who kept her movements slow and gentle. Again, the size of the horse, its height and weight, sunk in — she could get hurt by an animal this big. But for some reason, she wasn't afraid, transfixed by the horse's gentle brown eyes.

"Do you want him?" Ivy jumped at the shout from the man walking toward her in the pasture. She hadn't seen him coming — but it was too late to climb through the fence and head down the road. She waited as the man walked toward her, then felt her body tense when she got a closer look at him. He had a long, angry scar from his hairline to his eyebrow, and his head looked slightly misshapen, a little caved in on one temple. His eyes darted back and forth, never looking directly at her.

"I'm sorry I came into your pasture. I just wanted to see the horse. Is he yours?"

The man motioned towards the trees. "He belongs to me and Bathilda and Etola. All of us. He's for sale."

"Oh, you must be their brother Eddie. I'm Ivy. My grandparents are Cora and Delmar Hanson, up the road a little way."

Eddie didn't respond. He removed a leather contraption from his shoulder and brought it toward the horse's head. The horse didn't move as Eddie opened his mouth for the piece of metal and then positioned narrow straps over his ears and down his face. Then Eddie pulled the reins over and left them on the horse's shoulders.

Ivy watched the process. "What's the horse's name?"

"Bearcat. You ready?"

"For what?"

"To ride him."

Ivy stepped backwards. "I don't really know how. I mean, I've ... only ridden a couple of times before." Ivy didn't know why she had lied. Now she'd dug a hole for herself.

Eddie stepped around to the front of the horse, nearer Ivy, and leaned over, making a stirrup from his two hands. "He's broke. Won't hurt you. Climb up."

Ivy hesitated. "But isn't there supposed to be a saddle?"

"It's ok, just walk him, bareback." Eddie continued to make his hand stirrup, and Ivy stepped in with her left foot and swung her right leg over, like she'd seen on TV. The horse stood completely still.

"Use the reins to tell him which way to go." Eddie slapped the horse's rump, and Bearcat started to walk.

Ivy clutched the reins, then leaned forward to put her arms around the horse's neck, feeling equal measures terror and thrill.

"Sit up. Hold on to his sides with your legs." Eddie said, walking alongside them.

Ivy sat up, squeezing her legs, and feeling the muscles of the horse's sides against her legs. Bearcat walked forward. Ivy remembered about the reins and pulled hard on the right rein. Bearcat turned to the right sharply, his head jerking up.

"No, not like that." Eddie showed Ivy how to use the reins as a guide on Bearcat's neck. If she wanted to turn left, she should lean the right rein on Bearcat's neck. To turn right, use the left rein. Ivy practiced, surprised by how Bearcat responded to such light pressure.

They walked for some time, Ivy getting used to the rhythm of Bearcat's gait and feeling his muscles and warmth. She'd had no idea this was how it felt to ride a horse. She thought about what it must be like for Bearcat, having her on his back.

"If you want to stop him, pull back gently with both reins," Eddie said.

Ivy pulled, and Bearcat came to a quick stop.

Eddie made a clucking sound, "Do this to have him go again. Or go faster." Ivy tried it, and Bearcat went from a walk to a trot, bouncing Ivy and almost dislodging her from his back. Ivy yanked on the reins.

Eddie made an awkward laughing sound, "Not a smooth trotter. His canter's better."

Ivy wasn't sure what a canter was, but she was pretty sure she didn't want to do it without a saddle to hang onto. "I'd better get off now. I need to get home."

Eddie shrugged and grabbed the reins while Ivy slid off. "He's forty dollars."

"Oh, I don't think I can buy him. I only wanted to pet him."

"You can get him tomorrow. Talk to Bathilda." Eddie still hadn't made eye contact, but Ivy felt more comfortable with him. He seemed like a gentle man, almost an overgrown boy. She wondered what might have happened, something seemed not right with him.

"Thank you for the ride. I can't buy him." Ivy repeated her statement, but Eddie was removing the bridle and no longer paying attention to her. He sauntered off toward the trees at the end of the pasture.

Ivy gave Bearcat's long head a few more scratches and then touched his nose. In between the bristly whiskers, his nose was as soft as a rose petal. "Goodbye, Bearcat. You have a funny name."

Finally, she climbed through the fence and picked up her bag. She was almost halfway home when she realized she was smiling. She was light on her feet and almost felt like skipping.

And she had an idea.

Hattie

THE WIND — SOUTH Dakota wind — was blowing so hard Hattie had to brace herself against it, leaning forward as she inched along with slow, deliberate steps, her boots crunching in the whirling snow. The snow was eight or ten inches now and higher where the wind had pushed it against buildings and fences. The clouds were iron gray and low, another sunless day. A large wire basket dug into the crook of Hattie's arm.

She lifted the latch on the door and entered the low building, steeling herself against the smell: that heavy combination of warm feathers, dried corn, dusty straw, and acrid ammonia. Only a chicken coop smelled like this.

The chickens rustled their feathers, most of them crouched down in their three rows of small round cribs. They poked their necks forward as they cackled to one another, announcing the interruption of their quiet. Taking off her right glove, Hattie moved toward the first chicken. She reached under the soft, feathery breast, pulling out a large brown egg, as the chicken pecked at her half-heartedly.

"Now, now. You stop that, little miss. C'mon now." Hattie continued her soothing as she made her way up the row, ignoring the chickens that, not yet resigned to the inevitability of losing their eggs, pecked harder.

When she was done, Hattie left the coop, latching the door and testing it to make sure it was secure against the wind. *Can't let those raccoons get in.* She trudged through the blanketed barnyard, her metal basket filled with white, brown, and pastel-green eggs. She entered the large three-story Victorian farmhouse from the back door and set the eggs on top of the white metal cupboard in the utility room. Hattie unfastened her rubber galoshes and removed her thick knitted scarf and wool barn coat.

"Pup. I'm back." Pup ran in, wagging her black wiry tail. "Chickens are laying good again."

She put on a full-length apron and then began to wash the eggs, rolling each one gently back and forth in her palms under the running water. This was her least favorite part, feeling the chalky shell of each perfect egg, still warm from their mothers' breasts. It was a shame, plucking them away like that.

She was lost in thought, washing the eggs, when suddenly Pup barked from the living room. Hattie wiped her hands on her apron and hurried to the front window. It was Arlo, coming up the drive, scooping a pile of snow with the front loader as he went. "Right on time." Pup cocked her head, listening. Hattie returned to the kitchen and measured coffee from a small Folgers can into the percolator.

A while later, there was a knock at the kitchen door. Arlo stood there, red-nosed. Hattie thought there wasn't anything wrong with Arlo's looks; he was average height and weight, with a pleasant enough face and an easy smile. Not particularly handsome, but not unattractive. And in his late forties, Arlo seemed neither young nor old.

"Come in, come in. It's a nasty one out there," Hattie said.

"Yep, must not be more than five or ten degrees."

Pup ran up to Arlo, bouncing up and down and clawing at his legs. Arlo pulled a small Milk-Bone from his pocket and gave it to Pup, who ran to the living room with her prize.

"You spoil that dog, Arlo. Sit down, have some coffee. Really appreciate you coming out on a day like this."

"My pleasure. Know you got your club ladies comin' tomorrow. Don't want anybody gettin' stuck tryin' to get to the meeting."

Arlo took off his gloves, hat, and boots near the door. He placed his heavy canvas coat on the back of a kitchen chair and sat down.

"Hopefully, this wind will stop, or it'll undo all your hard work." Hattie brought over a cup of coffee on a saucer and a plate piled with sugar cookies. She caught a whiff of Arlo's Old Spice cologne and turned away.

"How're you doin' with firewood? Got enough to keep you warm for a while?"

Hattie brought herself a cup of coffee and sat down across from him. "I'm not bothering much with that old wood stove. Just using the fuel oil, and it does the job. A lot less fuss and mess."

"It sure was a good thing Ray did – puttin' in that furnace when he did."

About the only good thing that man ever did. The words formed in her head, but Hattie didn't speak them. No use speaking ill of the dead.

"And your car? Does it seem to be runnin' okay? Need me to take a look? See if the oil needs replacing?"

"It's fine. I take it in to the Texaco station, and Wendell takes care of it for me."

"Seems a shame, you tryin' to take care of everything all by yourself. How long are you gonna try to hang on to this big old place?" Hattie didn't say anything, and Arlo kept going. "You know how hard it was for your mom before she married Ray. It near about killed her, trying to do everything by herself. And you were only a young girl then."

Hattie pushed up from the table, taking her coffee with her. She gritted her teeth before she answered. "I'm doing fine. Just need a little help with things like plowing my driveway. The rest of the land is taken care of by the renters." She grabbed a worn bill from a ceramic jar and laid it on the table next to Arlo. "Thanks again for coming out in this weather."

Arlo glanced briefly at the five-dollar bill, then back at Hattie. "Your money's no good with me, Hattie. You know I'm more than happy to help you any time. Any time at all." He pushed the money across the table.

"Well then, you'll at least take some eggs." Hattie picked up an egg carton and remained standing, signaling that the visit was over.

Arlo stood. "Say, I don't suppose you'd like to come along on Friday night? The Lutheran Church is startin' up their bingo again."

"Nice of you to invite me, but I'm afraid I have other plans." Hattie put a half-smile on her face.

Arlo's shoulders drooped. "Well, maybe another week?"

"Maybe. Not much of a bingo person, myself."

Arlo finished bundling up to go out. "Hope you have a good club meeting tomorrow. Say hello to the ladies for me. Heard Cora's granddaughter has joined the group." Placing his cap across his chest, he nodded his goodbye.

"Will do. Thanks again, Arlo. Have a good day now."

Hattie closed the door behind him and picked up his coffee cup and the cookie plate. She went to the living room window to watch his departure and then sat in her chair, rocking back and forth. Her chest heated up and she breathed faster. She just hated it when his name came up. Ray. She'd like to go the rest of her life without hearing that man's name again. Because with the name came the smell. That rancid odor of old sweat. That rotten smell of bad teeth from behind his heavy, labored breath.

Once, when she had complained to her mama about Ray's smell, her mama had just laughed and said all old men smelled like that. Hattie tried to see if that was true and snuck up to the attic to remove her father's suit from the old trunk. But it was too late. Only the smell of mothballs remained.

It was uncanny how the mention of Ray's name brought back his smell. She will never forget waking up to that smell. Even twenty-six years later, the memory was still as strong as ever.

Hattie stopped rocking and called for Pup. She picked her up around her barrel belly and placed her in her lap, then bent down and buried her nose in Pup's fur, inhaling deeply the sweet smell of dog.

Etola

AT FOUR O'CLOCK, ETOLA was dressed and ready to go. It was plenty early, but Etola wanted to give herself extra time for her makeup. Those long eyelashes were tricky — it took her several times on her left eye to position them just right. The glue looked a bit thick, but Willard probably wouldn't notice. He'd worn Coke bottle glasses for as long as Etola could remember. Of course, it had been a couple years since she'd seen him. Not since Annabelle's funeral.

Etola had decided on her navy dress with the large white polka dots and big, flared skirt. It was still a little tight but with her new girdle, and since she hadn't eaten hardly anything in the last three days, she could now cinch the belt in one more notch. Etola wished she hadn't gone with the girdle from the discount rack, she could barely stretch the garters long enough to reach the tops of her nylons.

She stepped into her black patent leather heels with sparkly bows on top. She wasn't used to wearing high heels, but the magazine articles had all talked about how heels extended the look of the legs and made them shapelier. They were a bit tight, but Etola knew you had to suffer for beauty — every woman would tell you that.

After one last twirl in front of the bathroom mirror, Etola decided she was as ready as she'd ever be. She might as well sit downstairs awhile before she needed to leave. She teetered down the stairs, clinging to the handrail — wouldn't want anything to happen before the big date. Of course, Willard didn't know it was a date; he probably thought they were going to be talking about vegetables. But soon enough, he'd be mesmerized.

Eddie was sitting in the living room when Etola came in; his soft body slouched against the back of the couch. Looked like he hadn't been reminded to comb his hair today, and it was sticking straight up on the side of his head, the side that was slightly caved in. Eddie gave her a long stare up and down. "Etola, you look different."

"Why, thank you. I have supper plans."

"Where ya goin'?"

"To the diner. Going to meet an old high school friend."

"What will you eat?" Eddie asked.

"Why, I'm not sure. I do like their Swiss steak and scalloped potatoes. But I'll probably just have a bowl of soup. I'm trying to eat light these days."

Satisfied with Etola's answers, Eddie returned to watching *Make Room for Daddy*. Etola watched too, and for a minute, as she admired the star Jean Hagen, she wondered if she should have chosen the shorter red wig. This long Bombshell sure was hot.

When it was time to go, Etola put on her brown wool dress coat and minced out to the car, her heels unsteady on the gravel driveway. Good thing there wasn't any ice on the ground, and the snow had all melted. She hoped she could leave before Bathilda spotted her since Bathilda was sure to have something smart-alecky to say. She hadn't told Bathilda about her plans, had just left her a note on the kitchen counter.

Dad blast it, here came Bathilda from around the corner of the barn, pail in hand, just in time to see Etola.

"Heavens to Betsy! Where you goin' all gussied up like that?" Bathilda yelled across the driveway. She stomped toward Etola.

"Not that I owe you an explanation, but I'm going to meet a friend."

Bathilda smirked and made her trademark sound. "You both runnin' off to join the circus?"

"That joke is getting old. If you must know, I'm going to supper at the diner."

Bathilda raised one thin eyebrow. "This must be why you've been spending so much time in the bathroom lately — I was beginning to wonder if you were having intestinal problems."

"Not funny."

Bathilda shrugged. "Will you be home in time to watch *The Jackie Gleason Show* with Eddie?"

"I'm not sure, but most likely."

Etola slammed the car door. She saw Bathilda trying to get her attention, but Etola figured she had some other stupid question, so she just drove off. Her sister could be so annoying, and if she made that stupid snork one more time, Etola just might punch her. Bathilda had been making that nervous sound — halfway between a snicker and a snort — for so long that Etola and Eddie had always referred to it as Bathilda's snork.

When she got out at the diner, she noticed that part of her polka dot dress had been caught in the car door and dragged along the ground; the bottom of it was all soiled now. *Booger snot!* But there was nothing to be done about it now.

Willard was already waiting for her in a corner booth. Etola hadn't known Willard had gained so much weight in the last few years, but who was she to judge?

"Why hello, Willard!" Etola struggled out of her coat and threw it over the back of the red vinyl booth. Willard remained seated as Etola slid into the booth, settling into the dip left by so many others.

"Howdy do, Etola. You sure are all shined up."

"Thank you. I try," she said, looking at Willard's plaid flannel shirt with frayed cuffs and worn black suspenders.

There was a long silence until Willard said, "Nice sunny day."

"Why, yes, it was."

Mabel sashayed over with the plastic-coated menus and a pitcher of water. "Hello, Etola. You sure are looking all fancy. What brings you out tonight?"

Why does everyone in this town have to be so dang nosy? Etola forced a smile. "Just a dinner with my old classmate. Catching up."

Mabel grinned. "You two know what you want?"

"I'll have the liver and onions, Mabel," Willard quickly replied.

"I'll have the soup ... oh, never mind, I'll have the Swiss steak with scalloped potatoes."

After Mabel left there was an awkward silence as Willard stared at Etola, his eyes extra-large and bug-like through his thick glasses. "I didn't remember you had red hair," he said finally.

"Just a new look." Etola would be damned if she was going to let Willard know it was a wig on the first date. She was suddenly aware of a horrible stench, and she hoped she hadn't stepped in something in the driveway, like Shep's poop. She hadn't noticed anything on the drive over.

"So, how are you, Willard?"

"Doin' pretty good. The price of hogs is way up, and the crops were good this year. Plenty of rain and no hail."

Willard continued to go into detail about the price per bushel of his soybeans, corn, and sorghum. Etola was slightly distracted. Hogs! That's what she smelled. Nothing else stunk like hog manure. She put her arm on the table and leaned her nose against her fingers, wishing she had sprayed a bit more perfume on her wrists.

Mabel returned with a basket of dinner rolls and pats of butter. "How you two doin' here? Everything goin' okay?"

"Just fine, thank you!" Etola snapped.

There was another awkward silence when Mabel was gone.

"How're you getting along now that Annabelle has left?" Left? That made it sound like she took off on a trip or something. She should have said 'passed on'.

"Well, it's mighty hard to keep up with everything. You like to cook?"

"Oh my, yes. I'm the main cook at our house. Course, nothing fancy. I'm a regular meat and potatoes kind of gal. Baking's what I love."

Willard put two pats of butter on the bottom of the dinner roll, then folded the top over and took a big bite. With his mouth full, he said, "Well, that works fine for me. You a good housekeeper, too?"

Things were moving awfully fast — she wasn't sure about this. Etola crossed her legs under the table and felt the top garter on her right leg stretch and then snap with a *thwap*. In a second, the bottom garter went too. *Thwap.*

She might as well be honest. "Can't say as I really enjoy cleaning house." Was that her nylon starting to creep down her leg? Etola's forehead felt hot.

Willard took the rest of the roll into his mouth in one big bite and raised an eyebrow.

"Kind of a never-ending task. I mean the dust just keeps coming back," Etola tried to make a joke of it. "But I guess it has to be done," she added weakly. Willard just gawked at her. This was not going the way she'd hoped.

She crossed the other leg, hoping to stop the slow descent of her nylon down her leg. Thwap. Thwap. *My god, now the other one's blown!* Etola was nauseated now, and the smell coming from under the table wasn't helping. Etola felt a melting-from-the-inside hot flash coming on and sweat started to run down her temple.

"Nothin' much has gotten done around the house since Annabelle's passed. Usually wait until I've run out of dishes, and then I'm forced to wash 'em," Willard chuckled at his own cleverness.

Mabel sauntered over to the table with the two plates. She stared at Etola's dripping face but didn't say anything as she slid the plates down and walked away.

Willard immediately dug into his fried liver. Etola intentionally dropped her napkin and leaned down to look at her ankles under the table. Horse patootie! All four garters had snapped open, and her nylons had slipped to her knees. While under the table, she looked at Willard's brown leather lace-up boots. They were caked with manure. Hog manure. The smell made her want to gag. She sat back up and stared at her plate of Swiss steak, swimming in greasy brown gravy and mushrooms.

"So, you wanted to know about my cucumbers? There's a reason for all those blue ribbons. I grow extra big ones." Willard winked, then gave a big leering grin with bits of liver stuck in his teeth.

That was it — she'd had enough. Enough thinking she might overcome Willard's poor manners and slovenly appearance, and even his manure-caked boots. But she was not about to accept his downright rude behavior, no matter how disappointing it was to eliminate him from her meager husband options.

"Oh, shut your pie hole, Willard!" she shouted at him.

Willard's eyes widened, and his mouth clamped shut. He looked around to see if anyone else had heard Etola's outburst.

Etola stood, grabbed her coat, and stomped towards the exit, her nylons pooling around her ankles. She rushed out the door, the bell tinkling loudly as she left.

That damn Willard! Well, he wasn't the only fish in the sea. There were at least two others.

Wednesday Club Minutes

NOVEMBER 13, 1963

The Wednesday Club met at the home of Miss Hattie Dunlop. The meeting was called to order by President Bathilda Baldridge. The club motto was recited.

Roll was called, and the topic was each member's idea for their Thanksgiving table settings. All six members gave ideas, including an arrangement of cattails sprayed with hair spray to keep them from bursting open, a turkey centerpiece made from a big pinecone and felt, and pilgrims made from empty toilet paper rolls. Everyone had plans to be with family or friends for Thanksgiving.

Secretary Miss Ivy Hanson read the minutes from the October meeting. Miss Bathilda Baldridge asked to see the written minutes and pointed out that our guest speaker last month spelled her name with two n's and an e at the end: Vivienne. Miss Etola Baldridge made a motion to approve the minutes with that correction. Miss Hattie Dunlop seconded, and everyone voted in favor.

Hattie gave the treasurer's report. There was a balance of $51.98, and Hattie suggested that we give $8.00 to the First Lutheran Church for their turkey giveaway to needy families. All voted in favor.

The members discussed the raffle basket fundraiser. Hattie handed out 50-cent raffle tickets that everyone should try to sell in the next month. Bathilda, Etola, and Mrs. Florence Lane will buy the items for the raffle basket with $20 from the treasury to be reimbursed. The winning ticket will be drawn at our December Wednesday Club meeting. Last year, the Club raised almost $50.

Etola played the organ, and the club sang "My South Dakota."

The program was "A Day in the Life of the JFK White House," given by Etola. She reported that inside the White House First Lady Jacqueline Kennedy is hostess for many dinners that bring famous writers and artists together. Mrs. Kennedy has been seen in recent magazines showing her impeccable style with the renovations of the White House and her wonderful fashion sense. Daughter Caroline is attending first grade and riding her pony Macaroni around the White House grounds, and young John-John is going to a preschool inside the White House. The president is kept busy with several issues, including the Civil Rights movement, the establishment of the Peace Corps, speaking out against communism and the Berlin Wall, and the President's Commission on the Status of Women. President Kennedy and the First Lady will be traveling to Texas next week on a campaign tour.

After the program, members discussed that our president is working on so many important things and doing a good job. Hattie remarked that if she were still teaching, she might have gotten a raise from the school district because of the Equal Pay Act that was signed in June. Florence says she wishes she could be back in her home state of Texas to have a chance to see the President Kennedy and First Lady. Everyone agreed that they were setting an example of class and positive American ideals to the rest of the world, even if he is a Democrat.

The meeting ended with the club creed. Hattie served a lunch of chicken and green bean hotdish, cheese balls, and pumpkin pie dessert squares.

Ivy Hanson, Secretary

Ivy

IT WAS HOT AND stuffy in Mr. Hoagland's U.S. History class. The chalkboard said in large letters: November 22. Another completely boring fifty minutes at Prairie View High. Ivy wished Mr. Hoagland would stick to being the wrestling coach and stay away from teaching altogether. He just slouched at the front of the room with the history book open and read out loud from it, droning away in a monotone voice. Occasionally, he scribbled something on the chalkboard or asked a question from the back of the chapter.

Ivy heard that all the wrestlers liked Mr. Hoagland, and they'd had a winning team for a few years now. Apparently, Mr. Hoagland had been a wrestling star himself. Ivy daydreamed, looking at his short, blocky body, paunchy belly, and receding hairline. It was hard to imagine him as a high school student. She'd never seen him smile or heard him crack a joke. He was probably just as boring back then, like all the drips at this school.

Today they were talking about the end of World War I and the soldiers returning home. Mr. Hoagland was midway through another droning chapter read-through when the box on the side of the wall squawked. There were hardly any announcements during the day — only first thing in the morning at the start of homeroom — so all the students froze and looked at the loudspeaker.

"Attention students and teachers." It was Principal Webster. "I regret to inform you of some unfortunate news." There was a pause. Everyone in the classroom was silent, waiting.

"At twelve-thirty pm Central Time, President John F. Kennedy was shot while traveling in a motorcade in downtown Dallas, Texas." There was a collective gasp in the room.

"He was taken to Parkland Hospital where he was pronounced dead at one o'clock Central Time."

Mr. Hoagland sat down at his desk and his face crumpled.

"In honor of President Kennedy, we will dismiss school early today. Please proceed quietly to the exits. For those of you who ride the school buses, they will be arriving shortly to take you home."

Everyone sat frozen in disbelief and some girls started crying. Ivy wished she could cry, but she just felt numb. After a little while, the students gathered their things and headed out the door, no one saying a word.

Before she exited, Ivy looked back at the front of the room where Mr. Hoagland now slumped forward. He was quietly weeping at his desk, his head in his hands and his shoulders shaking. Ivy considered moving toward him to say something, but she couldn't imagine anything she could say. Today, it seemed there were no words that could make a difference.

Tilly

THE SNOW CRUNCHED UNDER Tilly's feet as she balanced a sleeping Milo and the large sack from Coast to Coast in one arm and held the hand of TJ in the other. They climbed the worn steps to the door of the trailer house. It was another cold and windy day, but at least the sun was shining. For that, Tilly was thankful.

"C'mon, TJ. Let's get inside. Mommy has to get ready for Robby's party." Why was TJ moving so slow today when Tilly had so much to do before James got home and stopped by his mother's to pick up Robby? Mildred had begrudgingly agreed to watch Robby while Tilly ran to town. It would have been so much easier if Mildred had offered to take TJ and the baby, but she didn't. Sometimes, Tilly felt Mildred wanted to punish her for having three kids so close together — more than a few times, Mildred had remarked that "people make their beds, and now they have to lie in them."

Tilly ushered the kids inside and closed the door. There it was, that smell. She'd hated that smell since she first stepped into this trailer house. It smelled sour and musty, like things were rotting underneath the thin floor. Like one day a foot could just go through the bottom of this flimsy box. Oh well, it was a place to live for now, until they could save up enough money and move to a real house in town. What Tilly wouldn't give to escape her mother-in-law! She was dreading the get-together at Mildred's tomorrow for Thanksgiving.

"Okay, TJ. You sit here, and I'll bring you a cracker." She tucked Milo in his crib and handed a cracker to TJ. Then she went to work. She only had a short time to get Robby's present wrapped and supper started before James and Robby got home.

There was barely enough wrapping paper to cover the sides of the large metal toy tractor. It was a bit of a splurge, but Robby loved it so; he made a beeline for this green and yellow tractor every time they were in the hardware store. He knew better than to beg, but Tilly could tell from his eyes how much he wanted it. James wouldn't be upset about the purchase, he always said he trusted Tilly to manage their budget. She'd just have to cut back on something else — like the new paintbrushes she was hoping to buy for herself.

Tilly hid the present in the bedroom and started preparing supper. They'd have hamburgers with Robby's favorite — tater tots. And chocolate 'pupcakes', as Robby called them. Tilly had just lifted the iron skillet onto the burner when James came in with Robby. "There's that birthday boy! And his handsome daddy. We'll be ready to eat soon; go wash your hands, Robby."

James kissed Tilly and then sat beside TJ at the table to keep him occupied while Tilly finished supper.

Mealtime was chaotic, as usual, with Milo waking up right as they sit down to eat and TJ being fussy about his food and needing to be cajoled to eat anything. Robby chattered on, excited to be celebrating his special day. His grandmother had given him a 30-piece puzzle of a black stallion, and he was looking forward to putting it together. James seemed quiet, but some days were tough at the elevator, and Tilly tried to be understanding.

After Robby blew out the candles on the cupcakes, and the two little ones had made a huge mess with the chocolate frosting, it was time for the present. When Tilly saw the enormous grin on Robby's face as he unwrapped the tractor, she knew she had done the right thing in spending a little more than usual. James gave her a questioning look, but Tilly nodded to say, 'It'll be okay.'

Finally, the birthday celebration was over, and James and Tilly got the boys washed up and into bed. It had been a long day, but Tilly knew they could grab a little extra sleep with tomorrow being a holiday. Too bad James didn't have Friday off, too.

By the time Tilly climbed into bed, James was already there, on his back, staring up at the ceiling. "You all right, hon? Tough day at work?"

"Well, yeah, about the toughest, I would say," James said, not looking at her.

"Oh no, what happened?"

James let out a big sigh and rolled over towards Tilly, grabbing her hand, his mouth downcast and brows tight with worry. "Leroy let me go. Says there's not enough work this winter to keep me on."

Tilly froze.

James continued. "He says I can come back again in the late spring. Felt real bad about it."

Tilly could feel her heart beating fast inside her chest. It was hard to breathe.

"Leroy says maybe I can get work at the school. I guess Ed is going to retire in February."

"February?" Christmas was less than a month away and February was a long way off.

"I know, Tilly. It's pretty bad news."

Tilly squeezed his hand and struggled to keep her voice steady and her words convincing. "We'll figure it out. Something'll come along."

Tilly laid awake for a long time after that, long after she heard James' gentle snoring, hoping to still her racing heart.

Now what would become of them?

December 1963

Ivy

IVY HAD NEVER SEEN so much food prepared for one meal. Her grandmother said it was traditional to have all these things on Thanksgiving. Ivy had been helping her since early morning to prepare roast turkey with Pepperidge Farm stuffing, cranberry sauce, green Jell-O with olives and walnuts, homemade dinner rolls, sweet potatoes covered with melted marshmallows, mashed potatoes and gravy, corn, and green beans with onion crispies on top. Yesterday, they had baked two kinds of pies. The cooking smells had permeated the house for hours, and Ivy could even smell turkey when she went out to the barn to feed the cats. Apparently, the cats could too, and they rubbed against her ankles and pooled around the feeding dish.

There had been plans for more than just the three of them for dinner, but one by one the invited guests had called with polite declines. Hattie wasn't feeling well, her grandmother's high school friend Kathryn had decided it was too far to travel from Minnesota with the weather turning bad, and widower Willard Holzmann had an ailing sow he needed to keep an eye on. Her mother wouldn't be here, but she had sent a card with a turkey all covered with glitter. Her grandmother said it was a very Hollywood kind of card and proudly displayed it on the fireplace mantel. There was no letter, just a big 'Happy Thanksgiving' and a sprawling signature, a heart used to dot the i in Vonda Marie. Ivy hadn't seen this signature before; her mother must be practicing for her future fan club.

Her grandmother had insisted that Ivy set the table with the fancy fall tablecloth and good China. It was, after all, a holiday, and that's what the good China was for. She even had Ivy add a crystal cordial glass at the head of the table for her grandfather's shot of Irish whiskey. Ivy hadn't seen alcohol served in the house before this, so it must be a special day. Maybe this would be the right time to bring up the subject that had been on her mind for days.

At one o'clock, almost on the dot, Ivy and her grandfather sat down to the Thanksgiving meal, Cora rushing from the kitchen to the dining room with one dish after another, flushed and happy. She was wearing a special apron, the pocket made to look like a spread-out turkey tail. "Don't forget to save room for pie," she cautioned, but it was doubtful they would want pie for a long while after this huge meal.

"You've outdone yourself, Cora," said Ivy's grandfather.

Her grandmother beamed. He dished small scoops of everything except the stuffing, which he heaped into a big pile on his plate. It must be his favorite. He seemed in a good mood today, helped along by the tiny sips of whiskey. They talked about the weather and whether they'd get more snow in the next day or two.

"The *Farmer's Almanac* is predicting more snow than usual."

"What does that mean?" asked Ivy. Asking about the weather was a sure way to engage her grandfather in conversation. She'd never known people to be so obsessed with the weather.

"Oh, probably around thirty-six inches or so. A good amount, can use that moisture for spring planting."

Ivy savored the taste of the sweet potatoes. "Think we'll get any blizzards? I heard the school plans for four snow days a year."

"Hard to say, but most likely." Cora chimed in. "It wouldn't be a South Dakota winter without at least one blizzard."

Ivy nodded, hoping like mad she wouldn't be around to experience it. As if this life weren't dull enough, she couldn't imagine being stuck inside for days on end.

Ivy's grandfather became animated, his eyes shining brightly when he talked about the crops he was planning for the spring. It had been a good year for prices, and he was going to stay the course on soybeans, maybe plant another 150 or so acres of it. He let slip in, "I'm thinking of buying that Baldridge pasture to the east."

Her grandmother's mouth tightened but she didn't say anything. He kept eating.

"I've heard once they get that horse sold, they're looking to sell that quarter section."

This was the opening Ivy had been waiting for. "Maybe you could buy the horse with the pasture."

"No good reason to have a horse. No one to ride it."

"I'd ride it," Ivy said, a little more forceful than she had intended.

Delmar stopped chewing for a minute, his eyes fixed on Ivy. "What do you know about horses?"

"I've been stopping to see Bearcat a couple of times after school. He's a beautiful horse. And Eddie let me ride him one day. Bareback..." Ivy trailed off.

Her grandmother jumped in. "That is a wonderful horse, Bathilda's always talking about how gentle and well-trained he is. And we still have Vonda Marie's saddle in the barn."

Her grandfather set down his fork, his face flushed, and raised his voice. "Stop. Both of you. There will be no horse around here. If it hadn't been for that goddamn horse of Hank's..."

"Who's Hank?" Ivy asked. And why did her grandfather get mad so fast?

"Conversation is over." He went back to eating, his head down, and the vein on his temple pulsing.

Ivy saw her grandmother steal a long, sidelong glance at her grandfather.

"More corn, sweetheart?" her grandmother asked.

"No thanks."

Ivy didn't want any more corn — she didn't want any more food. Her appetite for Thanksgiving dinner had vanished. She didn't know why her grandfather was determined to ruin anything remotely positive in her life. He was just a mean, hateful person. And now, what would she do to survive around here?

Bathilda

IT WAS ALREADY EARLY December when the basket committee of Etola, Florence, and Bathilda finally met. It was terribly late with the holiday basket being raffled off in a little over a week but getting this group together had been quite a challenge. First, Florence had been taking care of a sick husband, and then Etola kept clamoring for a later meeting date. Bathilda figured it was because Etola wanted that Miracle Length hair product to finally kick in. She was always hiding her head under that flowery silk scarf, even from Bathilda, so things must still be bad in the hair department.

They had a lot to accomplish in the next few days: decide which items were going into the basket, split up the shopping, then meet to put all the things together and wrap them up all fancy-like. At least last year's winner has donated the large willow basket back to the club, so they didn't have to worry about finding a new basket.

The women were seated at the metal kitchen table when the phone rang. Bathilda looked at Etola, and Etola looked back at Bathilda as the phone kept ringing. Finally, Florence said, "Is one of you going to get that?"

Bathilda shot Etola an irritated look and scooted back the chair, drawing out the scraping metal sound made by the chair leg. She glared at Etola as she answered the phone, "Baldridge's. Bathilda here." She put an extra emphasis on "Bathilda."

After a moment: "Oh, hello, Hattie!" She listened for a few minutes, inserting an occasional "Oh my!" and "Oh dear!" into the conversation.

Etola and Florence exchanged glances.

Bathilda finally wrapped up the conversation. "Well, we'll certainly discuss it. I'm not sure what the rules are. Thank you for letting us know." Bathilda hung up and sunk into her chair. "That poor girl can't catch a break. Seems Tilly's husband has lost his job at the elevator."

Both Etola and Florence exclaimed, "Oh no!" at the same time.

"So, Hattie is wondering if there's a way we might include some items that Tilly's family could use. Just in case Tilly wins the basket."

"But how would that work?" asked Florence. "Is that even legal for a club member to win?"

Bathilda shouted. "Legal? This ain't some official national sweepstakes."

Etola frowned. "I don't recall seeing any written rules about who can win."

"Has it ever happened before?" asked Florence.

Etola said, "We've never had a Wednesday Club member win the basket. But then, we don't usually buy our own raffle tickets."

"Oh, there is that. Even if we did manage to draw her ticket, how would we get Tilly to buy one?"

"She's in no shape to be buying a ticket. And if one of us buys it for her, it will surely look too rigged," Bathilda reasoned.

"Maybe James would buy it?" Etola asked.

"No, I don't think so. Besides, that might be too obvious." Bathilda absently scratched her hair. Etola motioned to let her know that she had a left a piece sticking straight up.

Florence offered, "Maybe Mildred would buy a ticket for her?"

Bathilda snorked, then loudly proclaimed, "Hell will freeze over the day that old biddy has anything to do with the Wednesday Club. That won't work."

"I've got it!" Etola said. "Hattie said Leroy felt bad about letting James go. Surely, he could be talked into a ticket or two. Especially if we let him know that Tilly's chances are good."

"That's perfect!" Florence said. "But how will we make sure Tilly's ticket is drawn? Who gets to draw the ticket?"

Bathilda raised her hand. "The Wednesday Club President. And that gives me an idea. Etola, you go talk to Leroy and get at least one ticket out of him. And make sure you don't put that ticket in the can just yet."

Etola adjusted her headscarf and then nodded in agreement.

"Now, let's think about what goes into the basket," said Bathilda.

Florence said, "I'll drive over to the department store in Madison tomorrow for some toys and clothes for those boys. How old are they again? Isn't it four and two, and what's that baby's age?"

Etola answered, "Ten months. Bathilda, you go to the Red Owl and load up on some groceries. Maybe a big canned ham. I'll talk to Leroy."

"But how are you going to make sure you draw Tilly's ticket without it being obvious?" Florence asked.

Bathilda was confident now. "Leave that to me. The fewer people that know, the better. You all must act as surprised as can be."

And with that, the raffle basket committee swung into action.

Ivy

December 8

Dear Diary,
Sometimes, I wonder what's the point of trying. Everything in my life is old, dead, or gone. After four months here I can honestly say it's even worse than I imagined. President Kennedy is dead, my mother has abandoned me, my grandfather is a mean old man, and my old friends have moved on.

It's official. Marilyn and Brad are now a couple, according to Val. I don't know why it took her so long to tell me.

At least Val still writes. But she doesn't seem to get how bad things are here. She keeps telling me to try to make the best of it until I get back to Omaha. She doesn't realize that hardly anyone here will even speak to me – not that I care.

The only person I even talk to is that guy Eddie who's helped me learn how to be around a horse. It's going to be sad when they finally sell Bearcat. Too bad Grandpa is so stubborn about us not getting him.

Better go now, I have to figure out something for the gift exchange for Wednesday Club. I need a gift for Bathilda – of all people! – and it must be homemade or under $2.00.

I haven't even told Val about the Wednesday Club. She'd die laughing about me being the secretary.

Miserable in Prairie View,

Ivy

Etola

THE DECEMBER MEETING WAS the most fun Etola had had in a long time. Of course, considering the dark cloud that had hung over her since her date with that slop heel Willard, most anything could've perked her up.

Still, just about everything had gone well. She was so pleased when the order worked out for her to be the December Wednesday Club hostess. She and Eddie did all the decorating and getting ready. They were in a flurry right down to the last minute, but they got it all done, and the house looked festive and smelled like cinnamon and pine.

Even the weather cooperated. They'd had the lightest little dusting of snow the night before; everything was white and sparkly with the sun shining on it. All the bushes were wearing little crystal shawls, like a postcard of how Christmastime was supposed to look. And there wasn't the slightest wind; it was a balmy forty degrees.

Etola had made the cutest table decorations. She had seen how to make Christmas trees and angels in a magazine by folding the pages of old *Reader's Digest* magazines. She and Eddie did all the folding while they watched *Lassie* and *Gunsmoke,* and then Eddie spray-painted them green and gold. Etola lined them up down the middle of the table. Of course, Bathilda had said she thought they were a little 'simple,' and where would Etola store them since the attic was already full? But Etola said it didn't matter if they threw them away in January; they were just old magazines anyway.

Etola wore 'The Bombshell,' so the gathering started off with lots of compliments on her long hair. Cora said she looked ten years younger, and Hattie said the color went so nicely with her skin tone. She noticed that Florence kept stealing looks at her — but, good grief, she wasn't the only one in this group who could show a little sophistication and style.

A highlight of the December meetings was always the Secret Santa gift exchange. They used to try to keep the Santas secret, but with such a small group, it was obvious who gave what.

Here's how the gift-giving turned out: Cora gave Florence a fancy hostess apron she had sewn with ruffles all around the bottom and the pockets. It was perfect for Florence, and it got them all talking about reviving their apron parade, which they hadn't done for a few years. Cora said it would be a good way for Ivy to learn to sew. Ivy didn't look too excited.

Tilly gave Ivy the sweetest little fairy house. It was all made of things Tilly found in the trees near her home. The walls and roof were tree bark; there was a little bed made of twigs and covered with a moss quilt and a very tiny teddy bear, a little stone fireplace in the corner, a small table with tiny acorn cups, and even a little sofa with tiny square pillows. Ivy couldn't have looked more pleased. That Tilly is so creative, they all oohed and ahed over it.

Ivy gave Bathilda a small ceramic sheepdog that looked just like Shep.

Bathilda had made a giant garden scarecrow for Cora with some of Eddie's old clothes and a burlap head. Bathilda remembered how Cora had complained about the birds stealing all her raspberries, so maybe this would help. That scarecrow was downright creepy (and looked a bit like Bathilda, truth be told), but Cora seemed to like it and said it would do an excellent job of scaring the birds.

Since there was an odd number again this year, Hattie had stepped out, saying she didn't need one more thing to find a place for in her house, as she was trying to pare down.

Etola gave Tilly a set of three paintbrushes. She had asked the high school art teacher for recommendations on which ones to buy. Etola had spent a little over the $2.00 limit, but nobody else needed to know that. Tilly was so happy to open the brushes Etola thought she would cry. Little did she know what was to come.

Last, but not least, Florence gave Etola a box with dozens of different makeup samples: lipstick, rouge, eye shadow, and nail polish. Etola didn't tell Florence she had already spent a fortune on makeup from Rexall's Drug. A little card at the bottom of the box said, 'Good for one deluxe makeup session.' Florence said she used to sell Avon in Texas, so she had learned from some real pros all about the feminine art of makeup application and had a lot of samples left over. She told Etola she had a box of tiny lipstick samples in over 50 shades they could try. Etola guessed Florence had heard how she was transforming herself. Nothing goes unnoticed around here!

The real highlight of the meeting was the drawing for the raffle basket. As president, Bathilda took over that part of the meeting. First, she made it all dramatic by having the basket covered with a sheet in the middle of the living room and said she would unveil it after the winner was drawn.

Then Bathilda announced they'd sold a record number of raffle tickets, so the raffle committee had spent a little more on basket items this year. That got everybody excited. She said one person even bought ten tickets and wrote someone else's name on them and made a real point of letting us know that was certainly allowed.

Then Bathilda said that she thought it made sense for somebody other than a Wednesday Club member to draw the winning ticket, so there would be no question of fairness, and since the only non-Club member around was Eddie, he should draw. Everyone agreed. She called for Eddie, and there he was, right in the hallway. This was a little suspicious since Eddie normally hightailed it out the door before the ladies arrive. But nobody else seemed to notice this or that Eddie was wearing a bow tie and white gloves with his flannel shirt. People usually gave Eddie a lot of leeway, Eddie being Eddie.

All the tickets were in a large Maxwell House can with a slot cut in the top. Bathilda took the lid off and asked Eddie to pick a winner. Eddie pulled a little black wand out of his back pocket, waved it over the coffee can, put his hand in, moved it around a little, and then pulled it out quick-like. He handed the ticket to Bathilda and beat it out of the room. Bathilda read the ticket and said extra loud, "And the 1963 Wednesday Club raffle basket winner is — Tilly Halversen!" Then she flung the sheet off the basket with a dramatic flourish; poor Cora got hit in the face with a corner of it.

There was so much stuff in that basket! It was piled high with ham and cheese and canned food, kids' toys and books, new dish cloths and towels, and even some personal things for the lady of the house, like smelly soap and hand lotion. Tilly was floored; she kept saying "For the love of Pete" over and over. Then she asked if it was allowed for a Wednesday Club member to win the basket. But Bathilda insisted they could all prove the ticket was drawn by an impartial outside person, so of course, it was fine. Within a few minutes, Tilly's excitement and tears had us all using our hankies.

Etola sure was glad they had given Eddie that box of magic tricks for his birthday all those years ago. You just never knew when you'd need a magician in the house.

Wednesday Club Minutes

December 11, 1963

The Wednesday Club met at the home of Miss Etola Baldridge. The meeting was called to order by the President, Miss Bathilda Baldridge. The club motto was recited.

Roll was called, and the topic was "Christmas in other lands". Members reported on St. Lucia's Day in Sweden, where a young girl would be dressed in a white dress and a crown of candles. In England, everyone gets a Christmas cracker that they pop open, and it's filled with sweets and little toys. In Italy, the Christmas cake is called a Panettone. In Denmark, feeding animals like birds and other wildlife on Christmas Eve is traditional. In France, they eat 13 different desserts. In Germany, Advent calendars are popular, and they are credited with bringing the first trees into their homes. Club members remarked that they often include some of these international traditions in their own homes at Christmastime.

The minutes from the November meeting were read by Secretary Miss Ivy Hanson. Bathilda noted that it was stated that Etola played the piano, but in fact, she had played the organ. The minutes were approved as corrected. Mrs. Cora Hanson led the club in a prayer for poor Mrs. Kennedy, Caroline, and John-John.

Hattie gave the treasurer's report. The current balance was down to $2.80 since the raffle basket committee spent $25 instead of $20, and we donated $8.00 to the turkey giveaway. She stated that she did not have the latest numbers from the sale of Christmas raffle basket tickets, but we had excellent sales this year, and she would give a full report in February.

The club discussed the January meeting that will be the community get-together held in the Methodist Church basement. Everyone was encouraged to bring family, friends, and plenty of food for the potluck. The club will provide punch and coffee. Hattie will lead the icebreakers. For young people, there will be a cookie decorating table and games. Adults will be encouraged to visit with one another. Tilly volunteered to make the nametags and be at the nametag station.

Etola played the piano, and the club sang 'Joy to the World.'

The program was a gift exchange; all members received a gift from their Secret Santa.

The winning ticket for the raffle basket was chosen by an outside, impartial person, Eddie Baldridge, and the winner was Tilly. President Bathilda declared the drawing to be fair, even though the winner was a Club member.

The meeting ended with the club creed. Etola served a lunch of chili, cornbread, cinnamon applesauce Jell-O, and cinnamon thumb cookies.

Ivy Hanson, Secretary

Cora

CORA WAS IN THE kitchen preparing lunch when Delmar got home. She heard his familiar stomping on the stoop outside the door, removing chunks of snow stuck to his boots.

Delmar, his nose red from the cold, clomped into the kitchen dressed in winter layers and threw his heavy parka over the back of a chair. He glanced at the stove and gave his usual noontime greeting, "Lunch ready, Cora?"

"Just about. Wash up, and it'll be ready." She was making his favorite — grilled cheese sandwich and tomato soup, and she'd been careful to grill the sandwich just the way he liked it, golden brown but not too brown, a little mustard and mayonnaise on the cheese.

"How is it out there?" she asked as she brought the lunch to him at the table.

"Not too bad, no wind."

"Looks like we've had a couple inches so far."

Delmar didn't reply; just nodded as he dipped his sandwich into the steaming soup.

She waited until he was halfway through eating before she mentioned it. "Bathilda called this morning. She says they still haven't found a buyer for that horse."

"Not surprised. Tough time of the year to sell a horse."

"She said they'd be willing to loan that horse to Ivy for a few months to see how she does with it."

"I thought Vonda Marie was going to be sending for Ivy soon," Delmar said, his mouth full of food. His mother never did teach him good table manners, but now was certainly not the time to mention it.

She set her jaw. "Well, we shall see about that. Eddie's been showing Ivy how to get a bridle and saddle on."

Delmar shook his head. "Dammit, Cora. She has no business being over there with that horse. I told Ivy this conversation was over."

Cora put down her spoon and leaned in, speaking slowly and firmly as she planted her feet in a wide stance. "Well, maybe this conversation is not over with *me*. I think we should give it a try with the horse..."

Delmar peered at Cora over the top of his glasses. She'd only used this tone with him a few times, but enough for him to know she was serious. He tried a lighter tone. "C'mon now, we've been over this. Ivy will lose interest in two weeks, and then I'll be the one taking care of the damn thing."

"How do you know that?"

"Because she's just like her mother."

Cora was not having it. "If you were paying attention, you'd see that she's not like her in many ways. Besides, when are you going to get past all that?"

"You don't get past somebody ruining two lives. Maybe more."

"Really? You might be the only person who sees it that way." She wouldn't let it go this time. She'd done that too many times in the past, desperate to keep the peace.

Delmar kept his spoon in the soup, glancing at the kitchen clock. His voice had a sharp edge to it. "I'm the only person who sees it that way? Damn girl gets pregnant at sixteen, and I'm the only one who sees it that way? Takes up with the best hired man I ever had, says he's giving her riding lessons, and they're off messing around at all hours of the day and night?"

They'd been down this road so many times, so much pain and anger still there. Usually, Cora would stop here, leave it alone. But this time she won't.

"I still say he really cared for her," she said.

"Yeah, well, I'm not sure the feeling was mutual." Delmar picked up his spoon and glared at his soup.

"I just thought, over time, she would come to appreciate what a good man he was. Other couples have married that young and made a go of it."

Delmar had had enough. He leaned back from the table and raised his voice this time. "Cora, for god's sake! You know what Hank is!"

Cora recoiled briefly, then grabbed her plate and bowl and marched to the sink. There was a strained silence for a few minutes as Delmar finished his soup — only the quiet slurping from the table as Cora weighed her options. Finally, she said, "Are you still planning to buy that Baldridge pastureland?"

"Yep, figured we'd go into the bank and sign the loan next week."

"And you'll need my signature?"

Delmar didn't answer, but he got the message loud and clear.

Hattie

HATTIE WORKED AT THE kitchen table, listening to polka on the radio and carefully pasting S&H Green Stamps. She had almost a complete book, 1,200 points, saved up for a crystal candy dish. She didn't need another candy dish, but she might as well do something with those stamps from the Texaco. Besides, there was something so satisfying about pasting in all those stamps and seeing a book fill up.

Pup barked at the car coming up the driveway. She always heard cars before Hattie did. Hattie rose with effort, her knees were hurting again, and peered out the kitchen window. It was Arlo. She watched him climb out of his pickup and hurry towards the kitchen door. Was that a present in his hand? Hattie hoped it wasn't, because she didn't have a reciprocal gift and didn't want anything from him. It was embarrassing.

Sure enough, when Hattie opened the door, Arlo was there, hatless and gloveless, his softly wrinkled face blushing as he held up a small, wrapped package in his thick fingers.

"This is for you, Hattie." He shifted his weight back and forth as Hattie grimaced, hoping the present would just disappear. Finally, she took the gift and invited Arlo to come in. She tucked the package at the back of the counter and motioned Arlo to have a seat. Pup scratched and clawed against Arlo's calf, whining, and was rewarded with a Milk-bone.

Clenching her jaw, Hattie served Christmas-decorated sugar cookies and coffee, and they made small talk about the weather and the news of the raffle basket that Tilly had won. Arlo asked if the Wednesday Club would have their annual January get-together at the church again this year, and Hattie confessed the date and time. After all, he was bound to hear about it from someone in town. Everyone liked Arlo; she'd often heard people remark that it was strange Arlo had never married. By the time he was done taking care of his sick mother all the women in town had moved on to someone else. Except for Hattie.

After about fifteen minutes, Hattie rose to clear the table. Arlo got the hint.

"You can open your present now. You don't have to wait until Christmas, you know."

Hattie tucked her hands into her apron pockets, then took them out and retrieved the present. She shoved it against Arlo's chest until he was forced to grab it. "Why, you know I don't need one more thing in this house! I'm about bursting at the seams as it is. Now you just return this and get your money back."

Arlo's eyes widened and he reared back in his chair. Then he gave a slow, disbelieving headshake. He stumbled to put on his coat and let himself out, turning back to say, "Merry Christmas, Hattie. I hope you have a nice one."

Hattie stood at the counter, barely looking up at him as she put the dishes in the sink. "You too, Arlo. Merry Christmas."

Arlo was halfway to his truck when it struck Hattie how rude she had been. She scurried to the door and called out, "Thank you, though. Very thoughtful of you."

Arlo gave her a half-wave and got into his truck. Then Hattie saw him look out the window and give her a long, pained look.

She slowly closed the door and leaned her body against it, her heart sinking and a flush warming her cheeks. What in the world had gotten into her?

Ivy

WHEN IVY WALKED TOWARD her usual seat, she could hear snatches of excited conversation all the way to the back of the bus. It was the last day of school before the Christmas break and the students were talking about their plans for the break, the toys they hoped to get, and how happy they were to have no homework for a while. Ivy wished she were feeling happy too.

Ivy pulled out her diary and began to write.

Dear Diary,

I guess it's true, Christmas really is for kids. And I'm not a kid anymore.

I remember how excited I used to get; it was the one time Mom would put a lot of effort into something for me. When I was little, she always took me to see Santa at the Brandeis Department Store, and then we'd go to Toy Town and I'd get to pick something I wanted. I'd have to pretend to be surprised when it showed up under the tree on Christmas morning.

On Sunday, I got my hopes up that I'd be out of here soon. When Mom called, she told me that the Pearl Soap Company had decided to end their advertising campaign. I guess they're not going to be making her into a big star after all. I crossed my fingers, waiting for the good news, but she's not moving back to Omaha any time soon. She says one of the advertising guys 'believes in her' and can get her work with other companies. He has a pool house behind his mansion where Mom can live until she gets established. Most of the rest of the conversation was about Mr. Hancock this and Mr. Hancock that. She said she's been so busy she hasn't had time to get anything in the mail for me but will send something soon. I won't be holding my breath.

I tried pleading with her to let me go back to Omaha, but she wouldn't hear of it. Guess I'm stuck here for a while longer.

In the meantime, I just need to pretend to enjoy this stupid holiday.

Merry damn Christmas.

Suddenly, Ivy remembered the little package she had for Mary. She slipped it out of her book bag and put it down on the seat across from her, where Mary always sat. One of the sixth-grade boys watched her put it there, but she gave him her best evil eye and he turned away.

When Mary got on the bus she spied the gift with her name on the tag. She looked over at Ivy, but Ivy shrugged as if she didn't know where it had come from. When Mary ripped it open, she got a huge smile on her face. It was only a troll doll with ratty purple hair that Ivy had found in the five-and-dime, but you'd have thought Mary had won the jackpot from the look on her face.

Ivy turned and stared out the window so Mary wouldn't know she'd been watching her. She hoped Mary still believed in Santa Claus.

Florence

FLORENCE WAS IN THE kitchen mixing up the buttermilk chocolate cake that her sister-in-law Delores had specifically requested for tonight's Christmas Eve supper. It tickled Florence that Delores would ask for this cake since she considered it one of her signature recipes and it was Lloyd's favorite. So light and yet rich at the same time; the buttermilk keeping it extra moist. Florence preferred baking to cooking; the preciseness of measuring ingredients was so satisfying compared to the guesswork of a bit of salt, a little grease, and a little flour, the way most cooking was done. Of course, Florence must be careful about eating what she baked; the last few years, keeping her weight down had been much more difficult. She only allowed herself a tiny portion – just a taste.

Florence was looking forward to a pleasant evening at Lloyd's brother's house. They didn't spend much time with Robert and Delores and their teenage son Lance, but Florence always felt welcome there and appreciated that Delores worked hard to keep a clean house. Since leaving Texas, they were the only family close by, and goodness knows where they'd be if Robert hadn't offered his brother a job and a place to live. Florence tried not to think about that.

The timer went off, and Florence opened the oven door. She touched the cake in one of the pans on the bottom rack. It sprung back, just as it should, after baking for 35 minutes in a 365-degree oven. The recipe called for 350, but this oven was so old she had to compensate for the variance. She tested the top cake and was satisfied with the result, so she took out both pans and set them on the cooling racks.

She might as well get the frosting started while the cakes cooled. Frosting was always tricky; it had to be cooked just right to keep it smooth and satiny.

Florence carefully measured a cup of sugar into a small saucepan. Then two squares of unsweetened chocolate. She had remembered to soften the butter, so she spooned out ¼ cup, carefully measured, and put it in the pan. Finally, she poured ¼ cup milk into the glass measuring cup, getting down to eye level to make sure the amount was precise. She turned the gas burner to slightly past medium heat and began to stir the ingredients with a wooden spoon.

She continued stirring, thinking she'd bring the cake on her cranberry-cut glass plate, perfect for Christmas. She was glad she'd splurged on that Tupperware cake carrier with the red traveling handle; it would go perfectly with the red plate.

Florence watched the ingredients blend and begin to thicken. She must be careful to get the frosting to a rolling boil, but not beyond. If it boiled too long, it got that unpleasant grainy texture. She breathed in the smell of the cooling cakes, that comforting chocolate aroma that permeated the kitchen and the rest of the house, covering any traces of worn carpets, old wood, and settled upholstery that Florence smelled in this old farmhouse when she woke up.

Then Florence thought she heard a muffled cry. She stopped stirring but she didn't hear anything. It was probably Lloyd hollering about something he couldn't find and wanting her to rush right out to point out something that was right in front of him. Why was it that men could never see what was in plain sight? She couldn't leave now, or the frosting wouldn't be right, so he'd just have to wait.

When the frosting was ready, Florence moved the saucepan to a cool burner and checked the clock. She'd let the frosting cool for two more minutes. She could check on Lloyd, but then she'd miss that perfect window of time for beating the frosting to get it satiny smooth.

She heard her name called again, this time a little louder. Damn that Lloyd! He always had the worst timing. Well, he'd just have to wait. She beat the frosting, carefully applied the frosting to the bottom layer, then placed the other layer on top and began to cover both layers with frosting. She used the bottom of a spoon to create lovely circular swirls, all perfectly spaced across the sides and top. Florence smiled, admiring her handiwork. *Just perfect.*

Then she remembered Lloyd, put a winter coat over her housedress and apron, and headed out to the shop. She had an idea that something might be wrong when she saw the shop door had been left open; Lloyd was usually careful to keep it shut when he was running the little electric heater. Through the door, Florence could see Lloyd sprawled on the cement floor. *Dear Lord – he's had a heart attack! It's all my fault for not coming sooner!* Florence ran on shaking legs to Lloyd and bent down, putting her face close to his nose to see if he was still breathing. It was then that the overwhelming stench of alcohol hit her.

She barked his name, "Lloyd!"

Lloyd's eyelids half opened, and he gazed blankly at Florence.

"Get up!" she ordered as she put her arm under his shoulders and tried to pull him up. Lloyd lifted his head and mumbled something she couldn't understand. He tried to sit but fell back in a heap. It was no use; Florence couldn't lift him. But she couldn't leave him here passed out on the concrete floor; it was way too cold, and what if he had hit his head when he fell?

Florence cursed Lloyd as she stomped back to the house. It was Christmas Eve for god's sake! Could he have not even waited until they were home from their supper to start drinking? If only Todd was here. *Shouldn't a son be spending his Christmas leave at home with his parents?*

Florence marched toward the house, clenching her fists. When Delores answered Florence's phone call, she said that Robert was out checking on the cattle. Florence explained that Lloyd had complained about not feeling well earlier in the day; maybe he was hit with some bug and got too weak while working in the shop. Delores said she'd send Lance over right away.

When Lance arrived, and they hurried to the shop, Florence told a detailed story of how Lloyd must have come down with the flu. It was a struggle for the two of them to get a stumbling Lloyd into the house and onto the couch. Lance didn't say much, but Florence was sure he knew his uncle was flat-out drunk. The smell of liquor was all over Lloyd. Lance promised to send their regrets that they could not make it for supper.

It was only a minute later, after Lance had left, that Florence remembered the cake. She trotted to the front door to catch Lance, but his pickup was down the driveway and turning onto the gravel road by the time she leaned out the door to call for him.

She returned to the living room and covered Lloyd with the crocheted afghan Delores gave them last year for Christmas. For a fleeting moment, she fantasized what might happen if she covered Lloyd's face with the afghan, placed a heavy sofa cushion on top of it, and then sat on the cushion. Only for a minute or two. She quickly pushed the thought from her mind and went to the kitchen.

There, she poured a tall glass of milk and set it on the gingham-checked placemat. She grabbed a serrated knife, cut a large piece of cake, and placed it on a fancy China Christmas plate. She began to eat. It was sinful how delicious this cake tasted, the chocolate rich and gooey and the sweet, sweet frosting melting around her tongue.

When she finished that piece, she cut another. This one didn't taste quite as good, but it was comforting to simply keep chewing, the rich depth of the chocolate soothing her soul.

By the time she came to her senses, the cake was half gone, and Florence felt sick. Over-sugared. She should cover up the cake and save the rest for Lloyd's Christmas dinner. Instead, she rose and dumped the rest of it in the trash. She'd be damned if Lloyd was getting any cake.

Cora

CORA WAS ALREADY IN the kitchen, kneading the white dough for the cinnamon rolls, when the sun began to rise. She took a minute to look out the east-facing kitchen window. The glorious sunrise covered the fresh snow with a dusting of pink and gold for as far as she could see, like a sprinkling of colored sugar all over the farmyard and down the drive. For the first time in a long time, Cora felt all was right in her world.

She even had time to sit with a cup of coffee and browse the latest *Life Magazine* while the bread rose in a glass bowl covered with a dish towel, nestled in a larger bowl of warm water to coax things along.

After twenty minutes, Cora floured her countertop and wooden rolling pin and flattened the supple dough, snapping air bubbles as she rolled. Then she spread it with soft butter and shook a generous amount of sugar and cinnamon over it. She rolled the dough tightly, using a clean white string to cut one-inch slices. Delmar came in as she was placing the pieces in a greased round pan.

"Merry Christmas, honey." He sounded especially chipper.

"Merry Christmas to you, sweetheart. Beautiful morning, isn't it? Coffee's ready on the stove."

Delmar poured himself coffee and sat at the table, absently looking through the magazine Cora had left behind. He started to hum softly but stopped when he noticed Cora watching him. She loved it when he was happy, when he had taken an idea and made it his own.

"How long you gonna let her sleep?" he asked.

"I thought for a bit longer; it is a holiday."

Delmar tapped his foot up and down. It was clear he was ready to go. "I'll go check on things. Be back in a while."

Thirty minutes later, Cora removed the baked rolls from the oven, pleased with how they had turned out. Nothing said Christmas morning like the sweet fragrance of cinnamon rolls.

As if drawn by the smell, Delmar returned to the kitchen. "She's not up yet?"

"Not yet. I'll see if I can rouse her."

Cora slowly climbed the stairs and knocked gently on Ivy's door. "Morning, sweet pea." After no answer, she knocked again. "Merry Christmas, Ivy."

Satisfied with a muffled "Morning, Grandma," she returned to the kitchen. She knew Delmar was feeling anxious. "I'll send her out as soon as she's up and dressed," she promised.

Delmar nodded and ducked out the door.

As soon as Ivy came downstairs, Cora grabbed a bowl filled with milk and food scraps. "Here, sweetheart. Grandpa says those cats are already hollering for their breakfast. Let's you and I head out to the barn to feed them."

Ivy looked slightly surprised that Cora already had her wool coat, gloves, and hat waiting for her on the kitchen chair, but she slipped into them, and they headed out the door.

Cora chattered all the way to the barn, commenting on the beautiful fresh snow and the mild temperature. Such a lovely Christmas morning.

Ivy lifted the metal latch of the barn door and stepped over the well-worn threshold onto the hard-packed dirt floor. Cora entered behind her, carefully balancing the bowl, and shutting the door to keep the heat in. Five skinny cats of various colors came running, meowing, and circling their legs as they walked towards the empty stall where they always fed the cats.

Then they hear a soft snuffling and a clap of a hoof. Cora saw Ivy's eyes widen, a look of recognition, then doubt crossing her face. Cora nodded and said "Yes."

Cora stayed back as Ivy walked to the stall at the back of the barn. Let this be Delmar's moment. She heard Ivy's hesitant question and then Delmar's answer, "He's on loan from the Baldridge's. Just while you're here. As long as you take care of him, he can stay. As soon as he becomes my problem, he's gone."

Cora came around the corner toward the horse's stall in time to see Ivy throw her arms around her grandfather. Delmar accepted the hug with stiff arms and a big smile. Suddenly, Cora experienced that tingly feeling she'd heard people call déjà vu. She'd seen this exact scene before, about eighteen years before. Maybe this time, it would end well.

January 1964

141

Ivy

Dear Val,
I don't really like the TV show that much, but this Mr. Ed postcard is meant to be a clue. There's a new man in my life. And he's very handsome, much more handsome than Brad. And a lot more hairy – ha-ha! Write back, and I'll tell you more about him.
Happy New Year!
Ivy

Ivy would have preferred to stay home and hang out with Bearcat in the barn, but her grandmother insisted she go to the community-wide Wednesday Club social. Apparently, the club had been hosting this family event for as long as they all could remember. Because the men can't be out working in the fields in January, it's a good time to get all the neighbors together. Ivy thought it all sounded hopelessly old-fashioned.

Her grandmother had been baking all week to stockpile sugar cookies for the kids to decorate and Ivy had helped her roll out the dough and cut snowflakes, snowmen, and mittens. They had dozens of plain cookies ready to go, to be frosted in white, red, and green, along with colored sprinkles, and little silver balls called dragees.

Even Ivy's grandfather seemed to be looking forward to the event. He had mentioned at breakfast that he was anxious to hear what everyone was putting in this spring. It had been a good year for most crops, and prices were holding steady. Plus, there had been no major lousy weather events like hailstorms or too much rain at the wrong time — overall a good year for South Dakota farmers.

Promptly at one-fifteen, Ivy and her grandparents loaded up the back of the pickup with the boxes of cookie supplies, covered them with a tarp, and headed to the Methodist Church. With the low-hanging clouds and wind from the north, it might snow later in the afternoon, so the pickup was better if the roads got bad. At least it had warmed up to a tolerable 25 degrees after last week's below-zero temperatures.

Several cars were already in the parking lot when they arrived, and they parked near Tilly and her family, who were getting the kids out of their Rambler station wagon. James waved at the Hansons as he held onto Robby's hand. Tilly held the baby, and James' mother Mildred grabbed the back of TJ's coat to keep him from running ahead.

Tilly spoke to her mother-in-law. "Mildred, I don't think you've met Ivy. Ivy, this is James' mother, Mrs. Mildred Halversen."

Mildred gave a half-smile to Ivy, "Yes, I knew your mother." She pursed her lips together.

Ivy wasn't sure what Mildred meant with that statement but replied, "Nice to meet you, Mrs. Halversen." Ivy's grandmother had said that Mildred could be 'a little prickly sometimes', but Cora was careful to never speak too negatively about anyone. She was constantly reminding Ivy that if you can't say something nice about someone, it's better not to say anything.

When they descended the narrow linoleum steps to the church basement, they were greeted by Hattie, who had already set up the name tag table. "Tilly, your name tags are a big hit. Everyone says they're so beautiful." Tilly beamed. Hattie said she wanted Tilly to hear the compliments firsthand, so she traded places at the table.

Ivy admired the name tags, each a unique and intricate snowflake, its edges frosted with silver glitter. Tilly said she'd worked on them for days.

Ivy wrote her name on a tag and then pinned it to her sweater with a small safety pin. She walked further into the large meeting hall and looked around to see if there was anyone her age there. She saw two girls from her gym class, Tammy and Susan, and gave them a half-wave, but they both turned to talk to each other, ignoring Ivy. There was Lance talking with his aunt Florence. He glanced over at Ivy, and Ivy quickly looked away.

Ivy heard Milo start to fuss. Tilly looked a little overwhelmed; it seemed that everyone was right on time and were all arriving at the same time to get their name tags. Ivy walked back to the table. "Should I take the baby for a few minutes?"

Tilly gave a grateful smile and handed him over. "That would be great. He'll probably quiet down if you walk around a little."

Ivy held the baby against her shoulder as she circled the room. Milo stopped crying. There must be almost fifty people here already, and the steady buzz of greetings and conversations was getting louder.

Exactly at 1:40, Bathilda marched to the front and banged a metal spoon on a large Mason jar to get everyone's attention. The crowd noise subsided. Bathilda welcomed the group on behalf of the Wednesday Club and announced that Miss Hattie Dunlop would kick things off with an icebreaker. After that, the adults could visit, children could decorate cookies, and teenagers were invited to join in games at the back of the room.

For the icebreaker, Hattie explained they would go through the alphabet from A to Z. If your first name started with an A, you should stand up and shout out your first and last name. Parents should speak for their children if they were too young.

Ivy watched as folks introduced themselves — she'd heard her grandparents mention some of these names in conversation. When the alphabet got to I, Ivy waved from the back of the room and said, "Ivy Hanson." It felt like everyone was suddenly staring at her and she heard murmurs and then remembered she was holding Milo. Did they think this was her baby? With a start, she realized that her mother had been about this same age when Ivy was born. Ivy knew her mother had left Prairie View before she was born, and a lot of these people probably knew this too. Ivy felt a tingling crawl up the back of her neck and the baby suddenly felt very heavy in her arms.

By the time they got to M, Tilly had arrived and made a point of standing near Ivy as she held up the baby and said, "My son, Milo Halversen."

After the icebreaker, Ivy went to sit with her grandmother, but Cora pushed her to join the young people. This was exactly what Ivy had been dreading. How long would it be until they could get this stupid event over with and go home?

Ivy reluctantly joined a dozen teens who were seated in a circle on the floor. Lance was directly across from her. Hattie said they were going to play 'the telephone game.' This seemed like a childish game for kids their age and Ivy only half-listened as Hattie explained that this was a good exercise in communication skills and a lesson in how messages could get misinterpreted as they were repeated. They'd start the game with one person coming up with a phrase and whispering it to the person next to them; then that person would whisper to their neighbor, and so on, down the line. At the end of the circle, they'd see how far off from the original the message ended up. What made the game more fun, according to Hattie, was to come up with a phrase that could be easily misinterpreted, especially phrases with alliteration like: Two tiny toads ate fat flying flies. Or: the funny bunny hid the colored candy in the coffee can.

They played for several rounds, giggling at how the messages went off track after being repeated. When it was Ivy's turn to begin the phrase, she whispered, "Six small snails crawled across the gray garden gate." The group continued passing along the message until the last person around the circle, Susan, exclaimed to the group, "Sixty slimy snails left their sickening juice on the poison ivy." She shouted the word 'ivy'.

The teens erupted in raucous laughter. All eyes were focused on Ivy, and she felt a burning heat spread across her cheeks. Hattie quickly jumped in, "Why don't you tell us what you started with, Ivy."

Through clenched teeth, Ivy spit out, "Six small snails crawled across the gray garden gate." The group laughed again, led by Susan and Tammy, who gleefully repeated the phrase 'poison ivy.' Ivy glared at them and when the game concluded, she jumped up and headed for the bathroom. What a stupid game for stupid people; she should never have let her grandmother convince her to join them.

When she came out of the bathroom, Lance was loitering nearby, and he sidled up to her. "Hey, sorry about that. They can be a little mean sometimes."

"Yeah, obviously. I could care less, really."

"My aunt Florence talks about you. You're in the Wednesday Club." He flashed a big smile.

Ivy hadn't noticed before how deep blue his eyes were. "Yeah, well, they needed a secretary, and I said I'd do it for a little while. Until I move to California, where my mom lives. Or back to Omaha ... who knows ..."

"When will that be?"

"I dunno, maybe in a month or two."

"Other than the telephone game, how do you like it here?"

Ivy wondered why this guy was talking to her. Maybe Florence had insisted. "Not very much. But my grandpa is letting me have a horse, so that's one good thing."

Lance put both hands in the back pockets of his tight Wrangler jeans. "Do you know Becky Dahl? She lives about a mile from you. She's got a horse, too."

"I think she might be in my algebra class. I didn't know she had a horse."

"Yeah, you should meet her. Maybe you two could ride together sometime."

Ivy noticed Susan and Tammy standing nearby, staring at them, and whispering to each other. Lance saw them too. "Well, I'd better check in on my folks. See you at your locker next week."

"Yeah, maybe."

Ivy headed towards the table where her grandmother was sitting. As she walked past, Florence caught her eye and smiled. She must have told Lance to talk to her. Still, when Ivy sat down, she couldn't help but remember Lance's smile. No wonder he was one of the popular kids. He sure knew how to turn on the charm.

She glanced over at Lance, and he was looking at her. She quickly turned towards her grandmother. Guys like that thought all the girls were dying to talk to them. She couldn't care less about him. But maybe she would introduce herself to Becky Dahl sometime.

Etola

ETOLA LOOKED AROUND THE room at the people gathered for the January social. Things were starting to wind down. It had been a humdinger of an event, with a lot more folks than last year as the word spread that it was open to *everyone*, not just the Wednesday Club. There was just one person in particular Etola had her hopes up about seeing: Hans Burdett. Hans' wife Eloise had died last spring, and he was the last remaining eligible bachelor in town now that Willard had proven himself to be a complete dud. Well, there was Arlo, too, but everybody knew he was smitten with Hattie.

She scanned the room, searching among the clusters of men who sat along the edges, most wearing a cap advertising their favorite brand of seed corn. The socials never started out segregated, but after the icebreaker ended, the men just seemed to naturally migrate together, leaving the women on the other side of the room.

Just as Etola had determined that Hans was not among the men, she spied him entering the room, looking a little confused. Tilly was no longer at the name tag table and was helping with the cookie decorating. *Now's my chance.* Etola hustled over to the table at a half-run.

"Why hello, Hans! Welcome, it's so nice to see you here." She didn't mean to sound so breathless.

Hans' eyes widened. "Hello, Etola. Cold one out there, ain't it?"

"At least the sun is out. Let me get you one of these beautiful name tags. Do you know Tilly Halversen, Mildred's daughter-in-law? She made all the snowflakes by hand; she's so artistically inclined."

Etola chose one of the snowflakes and wrote Hans' name on it as she stole a glance at him. Still such a handsome man. Not an extra pound on his tall frame, and his thick curly hair was sandy brown, with hardly any gray. And he was wearing clean shoes, not manure-covered boots.

Hans searched the room, then spoke with a soft voice. "I guess I don't know her. I don't get out much, not since Eloise passed. She was the social one in the family."

"Why, that's a shame. It does a person good to get out once in a while."

"I suppose," Hans said.

Etola glided to the front of the table with the name tag and a safety pin, moving right up to Han's shoulder and grabbing his blue and grey plaid flannel shirt. Hans stepped back from her.

"Now, don't you worry. I'm not going to stick you." Etola leaned in close.

Etola heard Hans take in a deep breath, no doubt breathing in her Jean Nate After Bath Splash. He wiggled his nose, and Etola wondered if he was going to sneeze. Perhaps Bathilda was right that she had put on a little too much.

"Maybe you and I should get out together sometime. Have a nice meal at the diner." Etola tried to sound casual as she fastened the pin.

Hans turned his head to look at the group of men and kept his eyes on them as he said, "I'm not a big fan of the diner's food. It never seems to compare to the home-cooked meals my Eloise used to make."

Etola backed up a step but still stayed close. "Yes, I heard that Eloise was a wonderful cook. I'll bet you really miss her meals."

"Sure do."

"I'm sure there's no comparison, but I make a pretty good meatloaf if I do say so myself. Why don't I make an extra one and bring it over?"

Hans shuffled two steps back. "Oh, you don't need to trouble yourself like that."

Right at that moment, Arlo walked up to the table.

"Why, it would be no trouble at all. Just as easy to make more than one at the same time. I'll come by with it at about 5:30 next Saturday. You know the Wednesday Club ladies are always looking to be of service."

"There's no need. My son's wife Debbie brings me meals for my freezer."

Etola noticed Arlo standing nearby and forced a half-hearted smile.

"A person can always use an extra meatloaf, Hans."

Suddenly, Arlo piped up, "If you're handing out meatloaves, I'll take one. I'll be home on Saturday."

Etola wasn't expecting Arlo's comment, but there was nothing she could do but be polite. "Why sure, Arlo. I'll make you one, too," she said weakly.

Arlo winked at Hans, and they walked off towards the other men, leaving Etola to stare after them. For Pete's sake, now she'd have to make another meatloaf. Pretty soon, she'd be making them for the whole dang-blasted town!

Wednesday Club Minutes

JANUARY 11, 1964

There was no official meeting of the Wednesday Club this month. Instead, the club members, their families, and many town visitors came to the January social in the basement of the Methodist Church.

At the social, members and their families decorated cookies, played games, and visited with each other. Tilly made beautiful, one-of-a-kind snowflake nametags. A variety of desserts, coffee, and Kool-Aid was served.

A good time was had by all.

Ivy Hanson, Secretary

Florence

WHEN THE PHONE RANG, Florence was sipping her coffee and listening to the morning news on the radio. She thought it would be her brother-in-law Robert, asking why Lloyd was late again. Florence ran through a list of excuses in her head as she answered the phone.

"Lane residence. Florence speaking." She was relieved and surprised by the voice on the other end of the line. "Etola!" She listened for a minute. "This morning? I guess that works. Maybe at nine-thirty? Alright, see you then."

As soon as Florence hung up, she sprang into action. So much to do in the next ninety minutes! The first thing, of course, was to get Lloyd out of bed and off to work. If he didn't work for his brother, he likely wouldn't have a job by now. He seemed to be sick all the time. She had begged Lloyd to see a doctor and find out if there was anything seriously wrong, but he refused, saying he was too old to do this much physical work. Florence knew the work in January was light, tuning up machinery and feeding the cattle in the feedlot, but she bit her tongue.

Florence trotted up the steep stairs to their bedroom. Lloyd barely moved when she shook him and told him it was already eight o'clock. Finally, he grunted something about getting up shortly and to leave him alone. How was she supposed to have Etola over for her makeup lesson in the bathroom if Lloyd was in the bedroom with the adjoining door? God only knew when he'd finally get up. She should have told Etola that today wouldn't work, but Etola had sounded desperate.

She'd just have to improvise, set up a makeup station at the kitchen table, and keep Etola downstairs. Florence raced back downstairs to inspect the kitchen. Everything had to come off the table. Now where was that light pink tablecloth? That would be the best background for displaying the 'beauty enhancers', as she called them.

Florence scurried up and down the stairs multiple times, bringing down all the makeup samples left from her days as an Avon representative. She had loved that job, helping women achieve their best look— and she was good at it, too. It was hard to leave that all behind when they had to move.

After all the tubes and sticks and containers and brushes were laid out in multiple curving rows, in order of use, plus two wet washcloths, it occurred to Florence that she had forgotten the most essential item: a mirror. She had a beautiful mother-of-pearl hand mirror, but it wasn't big enough for a proper makeup lesson. She'd need to bring down the large tri-fold vanity mirror. If only Lloyd was awake to help her.

She hadn't realized how heavy it was until she tried to lift the large mirror off the vanity. She braced herself against the bathroom wall as she lifted it and folded the sides over the front. It was going to be challenging getting it downstairs.

With the mirror in front of her, Florence couldn't even see the stairs, so she leaned against the wall and gingerly descended the steep steps one by one, sitting down halfway to rest her burning arms and legs. *My stars, this mirror must weigh forty pounds!* She finally made it to the kitchen and heaved the mirror onto the table. Her back complained loudly, and she sat down for a minute, bending over to stretch her screaming muscles. She would have iced it if she had more time, but she needed to get the percolator going so there would be fresh coffee. Good thing Florence always kept a couple dozen home-baked cookies in the freezer.

Wait! What about her own makeup? A makeup professional could hardly expect to inspire confidence unless she was perfectly made up herself. Florence hastily applied makeup at the table, accenting her high cheekbones with rouge and penciling her arched eyebrows. She was just finishing her lipstick when she heard the knock at the door. She took a final look in the mirror and practiced a big smile.

Etola arrived all a-flutter, and said she was excited to cash in on Florence's Christmas gift. It took a little coaxing to get her to remove her wig, but Florence finally convinced her that they didn't want to do anything that might mess it up, and, anyway, a woman's hair was her crowning glory and meant to be dealt with last. Florence promised they would consider the vibrant hair color when choosing shades of rouge, eye shadow, and lipstick.

As instructed by the Avon handbook, Florence began by applying a creamy moisturizer to Etola's bare skin, commenting that the wrinkles and fine lines were Etola's reward for having lived a good, full life. It was always interesting to notice how women's faces seemed to settle into and reflect the most dominant expressions of their inner lives. Contentment, worry, longing, tiredness. In Florence's case, when she looked at her own face in the mirror, more and more days, she wondered if she just looked sad.

She continued with the next steps in the makeup process: a special cream to reduce puffiness, concealer to cover the dark shadows under Etola's eyes, and then foundation to smooth out the dark spots and redness. Now, there was a seamless canvas upon which to add color.

Florence showed Etola how to apply subtle rouge to her round cheeks, nothing too noticeable. Soft green eye shadow would bring out her hazel eyes and contrast beautifully with the red hair. Then, a cotton square to blend, blend, blend the rouge and eye shadow. Florence advised against eyeliner for women over forty; it only accentuated the crow's feet and added a 'cheap' quality to the overall look. Next, brown eyebrow pencil to create the perfect frame around the eyes. Florence showed her how to use the pencil in short, thin butterfly strokes to mimic the look of hairs; everything meant to enhance, not stand out, and work with everything else. Etola looked delighted with what Florence had done so far. In her forty-seven years, she said no one had ever shown her how to apply makeup, and she loved what she saw. She told Florence she thought she looked at least ten years younger, and Florence agreed. At least ten.

Florence had just lifted the box of tiny lipstick samples to choose the perfect shade when they heard heavy footsteps clomping down the stairs. Lloyd entered the room, shirtless, hair askew, and his skin grey and creased from sleep. It was clear he wasn't expecting anyone besides Florence to be in his kitchen.

Lloyd stared at Etola's head, covered with short spikes of orange-tipped gray hairs, just as Etola remembered her wig was lying on the table. She reached for a nearby washcloth and threw it over her head as Lloyd burst out laughing.

"Lloyd!" Florence reprimanded him. How dare he humiliate Etola like that?

Lloyd mumbled, "Sorry, Etola. Wasn't expecting anybody here this early." The reality that it was after ten o'clock was lost on no one. He turned and made his way back up the stairs as Florence delicately removed the washcloth from Etola's head.

"Now, now, don't mind him. He wasn't feeling well this morning, so he was late getting up. I didn't have a chance to tell him you were coming. You look so pretty, Etola; let's finish up with the perfect lipstick color. You can take everything with you that we've been using this morning. My treat."

But the spell was broken. Etola's face never returned to the same delighted expression she had earlier, and both women knew that Etola looked forty-seven. At least.

Florence did her best to prop up Etola's enthusiasm as she chattered away, and Etola said she was grateful for the lesson as she left with a bagful of makeup goodies. Florence gave her extras of everything.

After she was gone, Florence slumped at the table and looked at herself in the mirror. Why did Lloyd seem to ruin everything in her life that was happy? Yes, that *was* the settled expression etched on her face. Sadness.

Ivy

WHEN IVY WALKED UP to her locker Lance Lane was at his locker too. She deliberately took a long time hanging up her coat and pretending to look for a paper at the bottom of her locker. But he didn't seem to get the hint.

"Hi Ivy. You still upset about the Wednesday Club social?" he asked. He sounded genuinely concerned.

"Of course not," she said.

"Nice poster," he said, motioning into her locker. "I like The Beatles too."

"Yeah, they're my favorite."

"Say, are you gonna go to next week's wrestling match?" *Cripes, was he a wrestler and a football player?*

"No, I don't really like wrestling."

"Oh." That seemed to shut him up. "Well, I'd better get to class."

Just then, Lance spotted a girl walking past. "Becky! Come here a minute, I want you to meet someone."

When the girl came over, Lance introduced her as Becky Dahl. "This is Ivy, I told you about her."

Becky gave Ivy a big grin. "Oh, great to meet you. Lance said you've got a horse too. Maybe we could ride together some time. Our farm is just kitty-corner from your grandparent's farm."

"I'd like that," Ivy said. Just then the hallway bell rang for the first class. "See you around."

As the three of them walked off to class, Ivy had a mix of feelings. She might actually have someone to hang out with. Becky seemed nice. The bad thing was, Ivy didn't have much practice riding and Becky was probably really good at it.

Oh well, it wasn't like they could ride any time soon. It was the dead of winter, freezing outside, and the most Ivy could do was hang out with Bearcat in the barn. It was probably a stupid time of the year to get a horse. Still, her life was better with him in it.

Etola

MEATLOAF SATURDAY WOULD GO down as the day Etola officially gave up looking for a husband. That day, she worked her fool head off for nothing. First off, she had to bake four meatloaves instead of only three on account of that darn Arlo.

In Etola's recipe, there were the usual ingredients: ground beef, onions, green peppers, celery, mustard, ketchup, eggs, half and half, saltine crackers, garlic, salt, and pepper. It was her secret ingredient that really took it up a notch: horseradish.

Most people didn't realize that the secret to a good meatloaf was a lot of green pepper and a lot of onion. That meant a lot of chopping. The green peppers weren't so bad but chopping up those four doggone onions just about put her under. She'd tried all those numbskull things you were supposed to do to keep yourself from crying: light a candle beside the onion, hold a piece of bread or a teaspoon in your mouth, or even pinch your nose with a clothespin. None of those things worked for her, she still ended up with a running nose and eyes that felt like she had poured acid in them.

The best way to get the ingredients mixed together was with her hands. You couldn't use a spoon because it was impossible to stir. You just had to dig in and knead with your fingers. Etola had hunted for the most giant bowl she could find to mix up all those meatloaves and she thought she might need to use a clean milk pail until she finally remembered the extra-large stockpot. It was so tall she had to stand on a step stool to lean way into the pot on the kitchen counter.

That was just the time when Bathilda stomped into the kitchen. With her butt sticking up and up to her elbows in ground beef, Bathilda snorked at her and asked if she was running a soup kitchen now. Etola didn't even try to explain. Bathilda and Eddie would have two meatloaves ready for their supper, so it was no skin off her nose what Etola did with her own time.

She finally had the meatloaves mixed up, and while they were baking, she trudged upstairs to get gussied up. She used a variety of the makeup samples from Florence and remembered to blend, blend, blend. Maybe she didn't look ten years younger, but this would have to do.

As soon as the meatloaves were out of the oven, she slathered ketchup all over the top of the two for Hans and Arlo. That was another secret to her magnificent meatloaf.

It was blowing and snowing full tilt, and Etola wondered if it was a damn fool thing to be risking her neck to drive those meatloaves around the countryside. But she'd come this far.

Etola decided to stop at Hans' house first so the meatloaf would be nice and warm for him — silly Arlo would have to wait. She stood on the front porch, knocking and knocking for the longest time. She swore she could see someone peek out from behind the living room curtain, but there was still no answer. She started to bang on the door. Then she looked up at the long icicles hanging from the eaves; just her luck one of them would fall off and hit her in the head with all her pounding! The meatloaf was getting cold, and so was Etola since she'd come out hatless, not wanting to mess up her wig or risk it coming off when she removed the hat. As it was, she had to hold onto it with one hand, with the wind blowing as hard as it was.

Finally, Hans opened the front door and peeked out through the screen door. Etola asked, "Were you sleeping? You took so long."

He grunted, "I didn't recognize you as a carrot top."

Baloney! He'd just seen her a few days before.

"It's not carrot colored. It's auburn. Now can I come in?"

She wondered if he was going to just take the darn meatloaf from her and close the door. Hans slowly opened the door. She carried the meatloaf in and set it on the stove, expecting to see the typical bachelor mess in the kitchen, but everything was neat as a pin. No dirty dishes, no piles of magazines and newspapers, and no muddy boots in the corner.

In fact, every surface was bare as a baby's butt, except the sideboard, where a dozen or so pictures of Eloise were all lined up in frames: Eloise in grade school, Eloise in high school, Eloise as a bride, Eloise with her baby son, and Eloise and Hans in their church picture. And on and on. The whole thing was a shrine to Eloise.

Then Etola noticed the kitchen table was set — for two.

"Were you expecting your son?"

Hans blushed. "I always sets a place for Eloise so I can tell her about my day." He looked so sweet and sad that Etola's hopeful plan to win over Hans crumbled in an instant. Even though his Eloise had been gone for over five years, clearly, this man had no room in his life for another woman. With a painful lump in her throat, Etola said goodbye and limped back to her car.

By the time she got down the road toward Arlo's house, it was blowing ground snow to beat the band, and she couldn't see more than a couple of feet in front of the hood as she crept along. Right before Arlo's driveway, she took the turn a little too soon, and the car sailed through the air straight down the steep ditch, landing only inches from a big old cottonwood tree. *Son of a biscuit eater!*

Etola was so shaken up that she left her purse and the meatloaf in the car, clawed her way out of the slippery ditch, and shuffled along the driveway to Arlo's house. Good thing it was pink, so it stood out from the white snow. She banged loudly on the door, and it was thrown open by Arlo, a blast of warm air coming from behind him. He raised his eyebrows and leaned in towards her.

"Etola! Whatever has happened to you?" He placed a comforting arm around Etola's shoulder and gently guided her to a kitchen chair, keeping his warm palm on her for a minute as she settled at the small round wooden table. Then she started to blubber.

"Are you okay, dear?" Arlo searched her face with his soft grey eyes, his voice comforting and low. Through her tears, Etola managed to choke out that she was fine, but her car was in the ditch — along with her purse and his meatloaf! Arlo brought her a cup of steaming coffee and, seeing as how it was a full-fledged snowstorm, convinced her to call Bathilda and let her know she was safe. As soon as he went out the door to check on her car and retrieve her belongings, Etola let out a shoulder-shaking wail. She didn't know if she was crying because of her car mishap or because it had suddenly dawned on her that she would probably die an old spinster sister after all. She had been so hopeful about Hans.

When Arlo returned with her purse dangling off his arm and bearing the meatloaf regally in front of him like a butler carrying a silver platter, Etola couldn't help but giggle. He set the meatloaf in the middle of the table with a flourish. "It's a beauty! I'll rustle up some vegetables, and we'll just wait out this storm. Your car will be just fine until after we eat."

Arlo was as nice as could be. They sat and ate the meatloaf with peas and fried potatoes, and Arlo had three helpings of meatloaf. They chatted about anything and everything, and before she knew it, Etola had told him about the horrible, ridiculous date with Willard. Arlo threw back his head and let out a deep-throated laugh that sounded like rumbling music. And because she never was any good at keeping a secret, she spilled the beans about the accident with her hair, too. Arlo's snickering was contagious, and soon they were both leaning onto the table and roaring with laughter, Etola's ending in embarrassing hiccups. That set them off again.

When they finally wound down, Arlo leaned close and said, "But you know, I think that auburn wig is mighty attractive. And the truth is, I liked your gray hair just fine, too."

The hours flew by at the drop of a hat — that Arlo sure was an interesting man! He smelled good too; was that Old Spice he was wearing? She always liked that aftershave on a man.

Maybe it didn't matter if she ever got hitched again. Maybe there were just nice men like Arlo to be friends with and share a cup of coffee with from time to time. And maybe that was enough.

Cora

JANUARY IN SOUTH DAKOTA can be a long, hard month. It wasn't unusual for the temperatures to be well below zero degrees and sometimes, with wind chill factored in, twenty degrees below. And the way the wind tore across the frozen fields without any buffers made it miserable to be outside for more than a few minutes at a time.

Cora and most farm wives had adapted by keeping themselves busy with indoor activities like sewing, needlework, and baking. But Cora knew the winter weekends were hard on Ivy. She was used to going to the movies or shopping with friends, and none of that could be done here. Even getting out to the barn to see Bearcat had been difficult lately. Every time Cora went upstairs, Ivy was lying on her bed, reading a book from the school library.

Today Cora would teach Ivy to sew, to get ready for the Wednesday Club apron parade next month. She knew Ivy wasn't really interested, but she was being a good sport.

By the time Ivy finished her breakfast, Cora had the sewing machine, iron, and ironing board all set up in front of the south-facing dining room window. They needed as much light as possible for sewing.

"Tell me again what the apron parade is all about?" Ivy asked.

"I know it sounds kind of silly, but it's simply a way for us to have fun. Everyone goes through their fabric scraps and trim and uses them to create an apron. Then, we model them with a spin around the living room. It's all for laughs, but it's fun to see what everyone comes up with."

Cora might have seen Ivy roll her eyes when she said, "Is it going to take a long time?"

"Oh no, aprons are one of the easiest things to learn. Probably won't take us more than a couple of hours to sew yours, and I'll do mine afterwards. And the fun part comes first: picking out the colors and design."

Cora and Ivy looked through the piles of fabric on the dining room table and the saved odds and ends of rickrack, lace, buttons, and hem binding tape. Cora showed Ivy a few examples of aprons from previous years to get some ideas, and Ivy quickly chose a bright green fabric covered with polka dots in yellow, blue, and orange. Cora wasn't sure if she was always this decisive or just wanted to hurry things along.

Cora told Ivy this fabric had been used to make a spring dress for her mother when Vonda Marie was about four.

"Let's use this yellow stuff around the edges," Ivy said.

"That's called rick rack. And do you want to put a pocket on it?"

"Sure, we could put some rickrack on the top of the pocket, too."

With that, they began the apron. Cora showed her how to cut the three pieces of fabric for the apron body, top, ties, and pocket. They held up the apron body to size it against her; since she was so slender, they didn't need to gather the top, making it easier for her first sewing lesson.

While they were holding up the fabric, Ivy decided. "Let's make the bottom of it curvy like that one." She pointed to one of Cora's examples.

"Wonderful idea. That's called a scalloped hem."

Ivy cut the bottom of the hem, trimming carefully until she was satisfied that the scallops were even. Scallops could be challenging, but Ivy had a good eye for detail and seemed comfortable with the heavy sewing scissors.

"Let's pick a thread color and get the bobbin filled." Threading the machine confused her, but Cora explained it was confusing for everybody the first few times.

She showed Ivy how to start the process by carefully folding the apron tie in half and pressing it flat. "Now we're going to make the seams, leaving a space to attach the body. We'll put in a couple of pins to know where to stop sewing."

Cora taught Ivy how to use the foot pedal and how to guide the fabric through the moving needle. Ivy seemed a little nervous at first but caught on quickly. They turned the ties so the seams were on the inside and pressed them flat. Next, they turned the seams on the pocket, pressed them, and sewed the rickrack on the top. They pinned the pocket to the apron and sewed it on.

Ivy's face brightened and eyes shone as the sewing lesson continued. Cora loved that, unlike her mother, Ivy had the patience for it and gained more confidence with each step.

They were beginning to work on the hem, the trickiest part with that scalloped edge, when Delmar came in the house, ready for his mid-morning coffee break. He stomped his feet in the utility room to remove the snow with his predictable pattern: stomp, stomp, stomp-stomp, stomp-stomp. Always the same pattern, always the same number of stomps.

On his way to the kitchen, he stopped by the dining room. "What're you two up to?" His ruddy complexion was flushed deep red from the cold.

Ivy said, "We're sewing aprons for the Wednesday Club apron parade."

Delmar smirked. "Is that still happening?"

Cora shot him a warning look. "At the next meeting."

He looked at Ivy's apron and tried to make a joke. "Are you gonna parade as the Easter Bunny?"

Ivy recoiled, then frowned, looking at the apron. She jutted out her chin. "No, I'm not."

What a killjoy Delmar could be! "Don't be mean! This is a wonderful fabric for an apron; don't you remember that sweet little dress Vonda Marie had? It makes me happy that Ivy has chosen this."

Delmar lifted, then let his shoulders drop. "Well, it looks like Easter eggs to me. I don't know what you women are trying to do with a parade, anyway." He made a half-chuckling sound and wandered out in search of the coffee and cookies Cora had ready on the kitchen counter.

"Now, don't you mind him. He's just cranky that the weather is so cold, and he has to be out doing chores in it." Ivy nodded and went back to her sewing. They finished the apron and starched and ironed it, but the little joy light Cora had seen in Ivy's eyes was turned off, and Ivy said she was going to her room to finish some homework.

Cora waited until she heard Ivy close her bedroom door before she put down the apron and pushed back her chair from the sewing machine.

Poor Ivy. That darn Delmar was picking on her just like he did with his daughter. Maybe Cora had let it ride back then, but she wouldn't let him get away with it this time. She stood up and girded herself for a confrontation. This just had to stop!

Ivy

THE NEXT MORNING, IVY was in her bedroom, sitting under the warm woolen quilt and writing in her diary, even though it was almost eleven. She was grateful her grandmother was leaving her be. She needed to go feed Bearcat soon, but she was having a hard time getting going today. She had an ache that started in her stomach and went up into her chest. She could tell her grandma, but she figured she'd get all worried and would want her to go to a doctor right away. She was pretty sure the ache was caused by boredom. Or maybe loneliness. It had been a while since they'd heard from Ivy's mom, and even Val hadn't written since Christmas.

Ivy heard her grandfather's heavy stomping. When he turned down the hallway towards her bedroom, Ivy shoved the diary under the covers. He was probably going to ask why she hadn't fed the horse yet.

He knocked on her door. "Ivy? You up yet?"

"Almost, Grandpa."

"Can I tell you something?"

Ivy pulled the covers around her. "Um.... okay."

Her grandfather opened the door and stood outside in the hallway, not looking at Ivy.

"Looks like it's gonna warm up today, maybe in the teens. Heard you've been wanting to ride that horse, so I plowed a path around the edge of the feedlot. That outta be enough of an area to ride around on. At least until the next big snow."

"That sounds great."

Her grandfather almost shut the door and then opened it again, pivoting his wiry body. "I can give you a few pointers if you want. I was a pretty good horseman in my day."

"I'll get dressed and come out in a few minutes."

"Okay then." He turned to leave.

"Grandpa?"

"Yep?"

"Thank you!"

He gave a slight nod and shut the door.

Ivy jumped out of bed. Her stomach felt better now that she was getting dressed. Maybe it was just something she ate last night.

"HERE IT IS. WHAT do you think of it?" Ivy pointed to the path around the feedlot her grandfather had cleared with the snowplow. She was eager and a little nervous to have Becky Dahl come home with her. Becky's dad wanted to look at Grandpa's new hayer, so it was a good day for her to get picked up by him later. Even though she and Becky lived so close, Becky almost never rode the bus because her older brother drove them to school.

"It looks like a perfect place to ride in the winter. That was nice of your grandpa," Becky said as she looked around.

It had taken Ivy's grandfather a full morning to plow the rectangle, so Ivy agreed it was nice of him. Surprisingly so. She let out a loud long whistle and Bearcat came running up from the nearby pasture.

"He's beautiful," Becky said. "I remember him from the Baldridge's pasture. I'm so happy your grandparents bought him for you."

"I don't exactly own him. It's more like he's on loan to me." Ivy grabbed his halter, and they walked Bearcat into the barn and tied him in his stall. Ivy grabbed a brush for herself and a curry comb for Becky. Becky stood back for a minute, watching. Ivy stood beside Bearcat, not behind him, and ran her hand down his rump to let him know she was going to brush the back of his legs. She hoped Becky noticed that she knew to do this. Her grandfather had taught her these rules to keep from being kicked by a horse.

Becky began to comb out Bearcat's mane. "He is a handsome horse. Still has a lot of good years ahead, too. Are you planning to show him?"

"I don't know much about that," Ivy said.

"The 4-H show happens every spring – they have a bunch of different events you can compete in. Even a confirmation class where you just groom your horse and lead them beside you. You could start with something easy like that."

Ivy thought for a moment about what it might be like to be in a horse show, to be seen as a girl who showed horses, probably even wearing a cowboy hat and boots. It was hard to imagine herself in that way. "Sounds like fun. But I probably won't be in Prairie View by then." She didn't elaborate and Becky gave her a questioning look but didn't ask more.

"Do you want me to show you how to braid his mane?" she asked.

"Is it like braiding human hair?"

"Pretty much; it's just that their hair is much coarser." Becky showed Ivy how to divide Bearcat's mane into small pieces. They didn't have ribbons, so they used short pieces of twine to tie the ends. Becky chatted about her classes and the latest goings-on at Prairie View High. She seemed to know everyone, but then again it was a small school.

"Do you know about the Valentine's Day Dance?" she asked.

"I've seen the posters." Ivy said.

"My boyfriend Matt and I are going. Have you thought about it? You know Matt and Lance are good buddies, they're both on the wrestling team."

"Oh, that's nice." Ivy wondered why Becky was mentioning Lance.

"Lance said maybe the four of us should go together."

"What?" The conversation had leaped ahead to a place Ivy wasn't prepared to go. "I don't think so. Lance isn't really my type."

'You should think about it. Lance is not stuck up at all, he's a nice guy."

They were interrupted as Ivy's grandfather and Mr. Dahl came into the barn.

"Ready to go, Beck?" Mr. Dahl asked. "Your mother's probably wanting your help to get dinner ready."

Becky handed the extra twine to Ivy and turned to Ivy's grandfather. "Say, could Ivy come with us to the wrestling match Friday night? They're competing against Palmer. And there's always a hot dog roast afterwards."

Ivy's grandfather asked, "Who's driving? And what time would she be home?"

Mr. Dahl said, "I'll drive them. Get her home by 10:30."

"That'll be fine then."

As they were leaving, Ivy thought about the fact that nobody had asked her if she wanted to go. She supposed it was okay, though she had never wanted to go to a wrestling match. At least it might be better than the usual Friday night watching *Bob Hope Presents*.

And then it occurred to her: she might no longer be friendless in Prairie View. That felt good.

IVY SAT ON THE edge of her bed and quickly tore open the letter.

Dear Ivy,

I hope the winter weather isn't too bad. I hate to tell you, but here in sunny California the flowers are blooming, and the weather is still warm. Honestly, I don't know why the whole world hasn't moved here. I hope to move you here soon, I just need a little longer to make a name for myself.

It's not that I haven't been trying. I've been SOOOOO busy going from one audition to another. I don't know what I'd do without Richard's help. His advertising agency has accounts with all the top companies here, so he is getting me auditions with the best directors in town. He says it's only a matter of time until my 'look' matches the 'look' they are 'looking' for. Haha! It's all about the looks!

Richard's pool house is tiny and there's only a couch for me to sleep on, but I don't pay any rent so I'm lucky to have it. He says I can stay here until his wife comes back to town in June; she's staying with her sister in France until then. (Can you imagine the glamorous lives these people live?) Of course, I have no intention of staying that long. Soon I'll have a larger place and I'll bring you to California!

I hope you're being good for your grandparents. Your grandmother tells me you're learning to sew and that you have a horse to ride. You must be having the time of your life!

Your soon-to-be movie star Mom

Ivy let the letter fall to the floor. She'd been here almost six months now. Six long months. She really couldn't stand her mother.

Tilly

IT WAS LIGHTLY SNOWING when Tilly pulled into an empty parking space in front of Coast to Coast. One more errand and she could head for home before it snowed any harder. They'd already had a foot this month, but it had been plowed and piled up, and the streets and highway had been easy to drive for several days now. Tilly liked how the new white layer covered the dirty edges along the roadways. It felt like a fresh start.

Tilly hurried out of the car and walked toward Downtown Shoe Repair. It should only take a minute to pick up Robby's shoes — shoes that will now be TJ's.

The bell on the inside door handle announced her arrival, and Tilly breathed in the cobbler's world: a heady mix of leather and shoe polish.

In a few seconds, Lester Hill appeared from the back room. "Afternoon, Tilly."

"Hello, Lester."

Lester stopped at the front counter and peered at Tilly. "How are you today?"

"Doing pretty good. It sure is nice to see this fresh white snow."

Lester hesitated and then pivoted to the long wooden shelves facing the counter, cubbyholes filled with shoes and boots of various shapes and sizes. He retrieved a pair of small black leather lace-ups and set them on the counter. "Did the best I could, Tilly. The leather's almost worn through on the insides here. But the soles will last for a while now."

Tilly avoided looking at the worn leather. "They look great. And all shined up."

"Yep, Margaret is the shoe shiner around here. That's all her doing. She said to say hi when you came in, was wondering if James has found a job yet?"

Tilly's put on her public face. The optimistic one. "Not yet. But he's picked up a few odd jobs. Things folks need help with for a day or two. And there's still a chance he can get a job at the school next month."

"Oh, right, I heard that Ed is due to retire soon. Hope that works out for him. Margaret said to be sure to let you know if you folks need anything, to just ask. Anything at all."

"Thank you, that's so nice of her." Tilly smiled and reached into her purse for her wallet. "How much do I owe you?"

"Oh, there's no charge today. Only took a minute to fix those up."

Tilly felt a hot stinging behind her eyes. She snatched up the little shoes, keeping her head slightly down but smiling extra big. "Thank you so much. My best to Margaret now."

She left the store and hurried to the car, sitting at the wheel behind the white windshield. The fresh snow provided an opaque curtain to the street, hiding the tears that streamed down her face.

Why was it that she cried the most when people were kind to her?

Tilly sat motionless for a few minutes until the freezing seat penetrated her rear end, reminding her to start the car. She turned on the wipers and noticed that the windows of the hardware store were painted for Valentine's Day: hearts in all sizes and a Cupid shooting an arrow. The drawings looked simple, kind of amateurish really, not nearly as detailed as the Valentine doodles she'd been drawing for TJ.

Tilly gazed at the window and the hearts, and suddenly felt hopeful. She wiped away her tears with her coat sleeve. A plan began to take shape.

Ivy

Ivy PACED BACK AND forth as she waited for Becky and her dad to pick her up. She thought Becky had said they were coming at 6:45, but it was almost 7:00 before she saw the headlights cutting through the dark. She wasn't that excited to go to a wrestling match, but it was nice to be included. It was the first time Ivy had attended an evening high school event.

She yelled as she put on her coat and grabbed her hat and gloves. "See you later."

"Have fun, Ivy," her grandmother called out.

"Don't get in trouble," her grandfather said.

Ivy squeezed into the front seat of the warm pickup cab with Becky and Mr. Dahl. A low ground fog made it difficult to see down the road, and Ivy was glad that Becky's dad was driving. He seemed confident as he maneuvered the gravel roads, then onto the blacktop and into town.

Becky chatted nonstop about the wrestling match and why Palmer High was such a big rival. Everyone knew this would be the hardest match of the season, and her boyfriend Matt said Coach

Hoagland has been practicing them almost to death to prepare for this one.

Mr. Dahl dropped them at the front of the high school and said he'd be waiting for them promptly at ten-fifteen. "Don't want Delmar to worry!"

Ivy heard the cheering and shouting as soon as they walked in the front door, and the crowd noise was almost deafening when they reached the gymnasium. She was struck by the smell of popcorn, hot bodies, and sweat, and for a second she wasn't sure why she'd agreed to come. She and Val had avoided sports; the newspaper staff and debaters were their crowd, not athletes and cheerleaders.

Becky navigated them around the edge of the gym, where two wrestlers grappled with one another, and located a spot for them about a third of the way up the bleachers, directly behind Susan and Tammy. Ivy saw the big elbow Susan gave to Tammy's side, but Becky seemed oblivious as she tapped Susan on the shoulder. "How's it going?"

Susan turned around. "Oh, hi. You just missed Matt. He got a pin. And the JV team won, so they're going to sectionals."

Maybe this was a good time to join the conversation. "What's a pin?" she asked.

Susan and Tammy half-smiled at each other and neither answered.

Becky got Ivy's attention and shrugged at their rudeness. "It's when one of the wrestlers holds their opponent's shoulders down for two seconds. The match is automatically over then, and it scores six points for the team. That's so great for Matt!" She joined the crowd in cheering for the next Prairie View wrestler.

Ivy tried to follow along with the action on the red mats, but it all made no sense. All she saw were two guys in stretchy one-piece suits and headgear over their ears, rolling around with their legs wrapped around one another. Every couple of minutes, the referee, who kept himself crouched down inches from the action, blew the whistle, and the wrestlers assumed a new position and went at it again.

Finally, it was Lance's turn, and the crowd grew quieter. Ivy thought he looked so goofy with his headgear on and a mouthpiece that made his lips stick out. But she couldn't help but notice his strong legs and muscular chest and arms.

She tried to follow along, but it was only because of the crowd's hushed reaction that she sensed that Lance wasn't doing well. He didn't get pinned and kept slipping away, but Ivy could tell he was mainly on the defensive.

At the end of the match, the referee declared the Palmer wrestler to be the winner, and he held up his hand in victory. Ivy was sorry Lance lost, but the whole thing seemed silly. A couple of guys rolling around on mats together.

In the end, Prairie View Varsity lost by only two points. The crowd was subdued as they filed out of the gym, the parents and kids heading for the parking lot, and the high schoolers heading for the cafeteria. It was stupid they called it a hot dog roast since the hot dogs were just steamed in the cafeteria kitchen.

They found a table in the middle of the cafeteria, and Becky gave her the lowdown on who was dating who and how long they'd been together. The cheerleader Wanda Vanliere and Lance used to be a couple, but Lance recently broke up with her when he caught Wanda in the back seat of Tom Nordvet's car. Wanda insisted they were just talking, but it was a big deal when she and Lance broke up. Apparently, Wanda wanted to get back with Lance.

Ivy missed hearing the latest gossip from Omaha. Probably Brad and Marilyn were in the back seat by now, kissing. And maybe more. Maybe right now.

Lines formed for the hot dogs and chips, and there was a little mingling between the students from Prairie View and the Palmer students. Some of them seemed to know each other from other events, and there was a general spirit of friendliness.

A few minutes after Ivy and Becky sat down with their food, Matt joined them. Becky and Ivy congratulated him on his win, and they talked about the match and what it meant for the chances of going to regionals next month. Then Matt asked Ivy, "So, did Lance ask you yet?"

"Ask me what?" *What was he talking about?*

Matt's eyes whipped over to Becky. "About the dance."

Ivy wasn't sure what to say, and Becky jumped in. "Where is Lance, anyway? Licking his wounds?"

Matt chuckled. "Something like that, I guess. A few of the guys are sharing a little peppermint schnapps in the parking lot. A post-match warm-up."

Becky rolled her eyes. "Hey, speak of the devil." She pointed to the door where Lance now stood scanning the room.

As soon as Lance noticed Matt and started to walk toward them, he was approached by a curvy red-headed girl in a cheerleader's outfit. Becky whispered, "That's Wanda." The redhead grabbed Lance's arm, and they moved to a corner of the room, where they put their heads close together to talk. Ivy looked away. So much for him. She could care less anyway.

Becky pointed to the large clock on the wall. It was 10:10. "We'd better go, my dad said to be on time."

They said goodbye to Matt and headed out the front door towards the parking lot. As they were standing on the sidewalk by the curb, they heard someone yell, "Ivy!" It was Lance.

"Hey, can I talk to you for a second?"

Becky motioned for Ivy to go. "I'll get my dad to wait."

Ivy walked towards him, butterflies in her stomach. "Hi, Lance." He was back in his blue jeans and wearing a leather and black wool letterman's jacket. His blond hair was tousled on top, and it felt like his bright blue eyes were boring deep into her. "Did you see my match?"

"Yeah, sorry you lost."

Lance looked away for a second. "It's okay. I got too weak from trying to cut weight. That'll teach me."

Ivy could smell alcohol on his breath.

"So, Matt says Becky says you might go to the dance with us?"

What a stupid way to ask. She wasn't going to let him off that easy. "Are you asking me to the dance, Lance?"

They both laughed at the unintentional rhyme.

"Right, the four of us. We can go together."

Ivy had rehearsed this moment ever since Matt had mentioned it, but this invitation wasn't anything like she had imagined. "I guess so. When is it again?"

"Saturday the fifteenth."

"Okay. Well, see you then."

Lance smiled. "I'll probably see you before then." His voice was confident.

Ivy pointed towards the pickup Becky had climbed into. "I gotta go. Becky's dad is here." Lance put his hands on her shoulders and pulled her close, staring into her eyes. Her heart raced as he leaned in to kiss her. The lights of the parking lot swirled around her, and she melted for a second. Then she pushed back from his embrace, ran to the pickup, and climbed in.

Becky looked at Ivy and asks, "So?"

Ivy felt her lips burning. She nodded, and Becky gave her a big grin. She sat back against the seat, lost in thought as they traversed the foggy roads home.

She was way more excited than she thought she would be about a stupid Valentine's dance. And Lance's kiss.

February 1964

Ivy

Ivy GLANCED AT THE February 1st postmark from Pomona, California, and tore open the letter her grandmother had left on her bed. For a second, she wondered if she'd even be around for the Central High Valentine's dance.

Dear Ivy,

I am so excited to tell you my news! I got my first commercial! We just finished a day of shooting, and I am on CLOUD NINE!!!

I had a call at 6:00 this morning from the Tipton Marshall Agency. The girl said an actress had called in sick, and they needed a quick fill-in for a commercial and could I be at the soundstage at 8:00? Ivy, you never saw me get ready faster in your life!

They had a makeup girl for me and a wardrobe person, and I felt like a real actress the way I was being fussed over. I never thought to ask what kind of a commercial it was until I was standing under the lights with these big white cue cards in front of me.

Turns out it was a commercial for Feel Right, a brand-new medicine to stop diarrhea. It's a little embarrassing, but as the director said, we're practically providing a community service,

183

letting those poor people with stomach problems know about this great product.

We did it over and over so many times it wasn't long before I had it memorized. It went like this:

When you're suffering from intestinal distress or a simple case of flatulence, reach for FEEL RIGHT. Only 1 dose and you'll have your happy bowel back again. Available in 8- or 16-ounce bottles at your local pharmacy. You deserve to FEEL RIGHT.

I almost cracked up when I had to keep saying the word flatulence. And you try saying intestinal distress over and over! I guess if I can do a good job on a commercial like that (the director said I was excellent!), almost everything else will be easier.

I made $25.00 for just one day's work. And that's only the beginning! Actresses can make a lot of money in this town.

Anyway, I wanted to share the good news. I'm so excited I'm not sure I'll be able to sleep tonight. Maybe I'll have to take a night swim. Sometimes Richard joins me in the pool. He's just a friend AND married, after all.

Luv, Your Mom

Ivy leaned back against the headboard, staring at the water stain on the ceiling of her room. Her mother's words 'friend' and 'married' brought back a memory she'd tried to bury.

It had happened two years ago when Ivy came home from school an hour earlier than usual. Her English teacher had gone home sick that afternoon, and there wasn't time to get a substitute, so the principal had let the class leave early. Her mother wasn't usually off work when Ivy got home, so she was surprised when the front door was unlocked. And even more surprised to find Val's father putting on his sports jacket in her living room. He seemed extremely flustered, and then her mother had come out of the bedroom in her robe. They had quickly made up an excuse about how Mr. Bowers had stopped by to see if Val was there, but the whole explanation was ridiculous, and Ivy could tell they were lying. She and her mother never spoke of it again, but Ivy thought it explained why she wasn't allowed to stay in Omaha with Val.

There was good reason to not trust much of anything her mother said. Things were always this way — Ivy got her hopes up only to be knocked back to the reality of who her mother was. You'd think she'd learn after all this time.

At least Ivy had a dance to look forward to.

Cora

IT WAS ALMOST TEN, and Cora was still at the sewing machine. The last few days, Cora had been sewing nonstop.

Not that she minded. She couldn't be happier that Ivy had finally made a friend and seemed to be finding a way to fit in with kids her age. She was so opposite from Vonda Marie; she just seemed to sit on the sidelines, never really letting herself join in.

Cora was tired but she still had a long way to go on Ivy's dress, and there were only a few days before the dance. In hindsight, they probably should have picked a different fabric; this one was so slippery. But Ivy had fallen in love with this royal blue satin, which would be beautiful with her sandy brown hair and hazel gold eyes. So striking, those eyes.

Cora studied the instructions from the Butterick pattern one more time. Zipper next? Cora dreaded putting in zippers; they were always the most challenging part, so she'd baste it by hand first. She grabbed her tomato pincushion and looked for the right-sized needle.

As she took a stitch one by one, Cora's mind wandered. If only Vonda Marie could be here to see Ivy get ready for the dance. If only Vonda Marie could have experienced a few more of these dances herself instead of cutting her teenage years short. How different things might have been if only Hank hadn't been in the picture.

Cora felt a deep pang of sadness, a regret that had permanently etched her heart. On purpose, she pricked the end of her finger with the sharp needle to stop the thoughts. There was no point going down that path again. No use thinking about what she couldn't change.

She hoped Lance was a nice young man. She was glad he was Florence's nephew and seemed to come from good stock. Hard-working. Their farmyard was tidy, and the buildings were kept painted. Delmar always said you could tell a lot about a farmer by that. And by the number of weeds in his fields.

When Cora finished stitching in the zipper, she ended things for the night. She'd get back to it as soon as Delmar's had finished his breakfast and Ivy was off to school. Oh, and she had to remember to ask Ivy about the Wednesday Club program. With all the excitement about the dance, she wondered if Ivy had remembered that she volunteered to present the program this month.

As she turned out the light, Cora's head buzzed. But it felt good. It was true what they said: busy hands kept the worries away.

Wednesday Club Minutes

FEBRUARY 12, 1964

The Wednesday Club met at the home of Mrs. Cora Hanson. The meeting was called to order by the President, Miss Bathilda Baldridge. The club motto was recited.

Roll was called. The roll call topic was the apron parade. Members took turns modeling the aprons they had designed from fabric scraps and other leftover decorations. Members tried to agree upon a description of the aprons in one word.

Cora – light blue fabric with a panel of various fabrics in a quilt pattern along the bottom. Finished on top with a zigzag of blue rickrack. Soft.

Hattie – navy and white gingham fabric with a cross-stitched flower panel on the bottom. Large pocket and another small pocket for Kleenex. Practical.

Tilly – fabric with red pansies on a white background. Appliqué of hand-cut red rooster sewn over fabric. Finished with red rickrack around the pocket and on the scalloped hem. Artistic.

Bathilda – small, floral print fabric. Square-shaped, geometric apron with flaring wings. Finished with black hem tape. Unusual.

Ivy – green fabric with colored polka dots. Yellow rickrack on pockets and scalloped hem. Youthful.

Florence – purple and white plaid fabric with small yellow flowers. Zig zag hemline trimmed with ruffled white lace and bordered by yellow rickrack. Fancy.

Etola – top panel in chartreuse plaid and bottom panel in bright chartreuse. Bordered in brown rickrack and finished in looping rickrack along the hem. Colorful.

There were no formal minutes from the January meeting, but Ivy read a short description of the social, and everyone agreed it was a successful day.

Hattie gave the treasurer's report and noted that final sales from the December raffle baskets were $65.00, an all-time high, so the balance in the treasury was now $30.98. The club approved a donation of $5.00 to the Cancer Fund.

Etola led the group in singing 'The More We Get Together.'

Ivy gave the program on the Beatles. She told the club the history of the four English rock musicians taking the country by storm. They became very popular last year in the United Kingdom with their songs 'Please Please Me' and 'She Loves You' and are now touring the world. Their latest song 'I Want to Hold Your Hand' is the #1 song in the US. Ivy reported that the Beatles had appeared on *The Ed Sullivan Show* last Sunday night, and if you missed them, you have a chance to see them again this Sunday night, broadcast live from Miami Beach.

Tilly said she heard there was something called 'Beatlemania' where fans would scream hysterically when they saw the Beatles and some of the girls were even fainting. Cora expressed concern for the girls' safety. Bathilda questioned what kind of influence this group had on young people and what was meant by the title 'Please Please Me'? Florence said she didn't like their unkempt long hair, but Etola said she thought all four band members were cute. Everyone agreed it might be worth tuning in to Ed Sullivan to see what all the fuss was about.

The meeting ended with the club creed. A lunch of hamburger soup, carrot hotdish, and sorghum drop cookies was served by Cora.

Ivy Hanson, Secretary

Ivy

Ivy was getting ready ridiculously early, but she wanted to leave plenty of time for her hair. She'd been practicing the chignon, ratting and smoothing her hair to give it a lot of height. She was determined to show the other girls what a sophisticated teenager looked like — from her hair to her slingbacks with kitten heels.

She'd wait until the last minute to put on her dress, so it didn't get all wrinkled. If only Val was here to see it. She was kind of surprised her grandmother had agreed to it. At first, she had hesitated, asking if it wasn't a little sophisticated for a high school dance. But Ivy had explained that in Omaha, girls were always wearing dresses like this, and in the end, her grandmother had agreed.

Her grandmother had done a beautiful job sewing it. The smooth satin fabric was perfect for the sleeveless boat neckline, tight bodice, and slim A-line skirt with a short slit up the back so she could walk, and dance, in it. They finished it with a narrow belt and bow at the empire waistline. None of that 'full skirt and ruffles' for Ivy; the last thing she wanted was some old-fashioned prairie girl look.

She was halfway finished pinning up her hair when the phone rang, and a minute later, her grandmother knocked gently on the bathroom door.

"Ivy honey, it's Becky."

"Okay, be right there." Ivy hurried downstairs to the phone in the hallway.

"Hi, Becky! How's it going?"

"Um, well, I don't know how to tell you this. I'm so sorry." Becky sounded strange. Like she had something in her throat.

"What's the matter? Are you sick?"

"Oh no, nothing like that. It's just, well, I guess the double date is off."

"What do you mean?" Ivy's heart skipped a beat.

Becky hesitated before she said, "Lance should be the one to tell you this. He's such a chicken. Apparently, Wanda's mother put some pressure on Lance's mother. So, he kind of had no choice."

Ivy felt the hallway walls begin to move, undulating back and forth. She leaned against one, thinking maybe this wasn't happening. Becky's words sounded muffled: "I bet you were getting ready and everything ..."

Suddenly, she was back in her mother's bedroom, sitting in front of her low dresser, watching her put on her makeup. "Do you want some lipstick, too, Ivy?" her mother asked. She watched in the mirror as her mother carefully feathered the bright pink on her lips. She looked so different, glamorous like her mother, and ready to go out. Then she remembered her mother's words, "You be my big girl now, Ivy. I might be home late, so get yourself ready for bed and go to sleep. Don't answer the door for anyone. When you wake up, I'll be home." As Ivy heard her mother's high heels clicking down the apartment hallway, her chest ached, that cold spot so large it threatened to swallow her.

There was a long silence before Becky said, "I'm sorry, Ivy. I tried to talk to Lance."

"It's not your fault. I should have known better. Lance Lane is a bastard!" Ivy's words were loud enough that her grandmother heard her. She rushed into the hallway, alarmed.

Becky replied, "Yeah, he is. I will hate being with him and Wanda tonight."

Now, the living room floor rolled in waves, and Ivy wondered if she was going to be sick. "Try to have a good time. Thanks for letting me know."

Ivy hung up the phone. Her grandmother held out her arms to her, but Ivy turned away and ran up the stairs to her bedroom. She slammed the door loud enough to let her grandmother know she needed to be left alone.

Hattie

HATTIE FINISHED WASHING THE cookie sheets and cooling racks. She'd made two dozen cookies for Tilly's boys, and they were boxed up and ready to go. She'd better give Tilly a quick call to make sure TJ was feeling better, and they'd be attending church together the next day.

Hattie went to the living room and pulled the afghan from the back of the couch to cover her legs as she sat on the phone bench. The hallway felt chilly compared to the warm kitchen. Within a flash, Pup was on her lap, always waiting for an opportunity; Hattie could hardly land for a moment before Pup jumped up. She lifted the receiver to make her call and heard voices. Darn party line — always someone blabbing when you just want to make a quick call! Before Hattie could hang up, she heard: 'It's just, well, I guess the double date is off.'

Then: "What do you mean?" Was that Ivy's voice?

Hattie didn't mean to listen to the rest of the conversation, but she couldn't help herself. It was all so shocking. When she heard the word 'bastard,' she decided it was time to gently set the receiver down. She sat for a second, taking it all in. That poor Ivy. Damn men, anyway.

"Okay, little Pup. Time to get off. I've got to go." She set Pup on the floor and went to her bedroom. This dress would be fine. Just a quick comb of her hair and a little lipstick. As she headed out the door to warm up the car, she realizes she wasn't even sure what time it was. Never mind, they'd make it work.

When she showed up at Cora's door, Cora looked surprised but graciously welcomed her in.

"Where's Ivy?" Hattie asked.

"She's upstairs in her bedroom. She's had a bit of a blow; I'm not sure she'll want to talk right now."

Hattie removed her boots in the entryway but didn't bother removing her coat. "Trust me on this, Cora."

She hustled up the stairs and knocked softly on Ivy's door. When there was no answer, Hattie knocked again. "Ivy, it's Hattie. I need to talk to you."

After a few seconds, Ivy opened the door. Her long hair was half pinned up on the back of her head and her eyes were red. "Hattie?"

Hattie launched in. "Listen to me, Ivy Hanson. I know what it's like to let a man make you feel you aren't worth anything, like they can treat you like a piece of dirt. Well, that's nonsense! There's no better time to hold your head high and show the world that nobody gets to tarnish your shine."

Ivy stared at Hattie with wide eyes. "How did you know?"

"Party line. I went to make a call and can't help what I heard."

Hattie continued, aware that Ivy had never seen her this worked up. "*My Fair Lady* with Audrey Hepburn is playing at The Bijou tonight, and I need a movie companion. Even if I am an old lady to you, it's still going to be a lot more fun than staying home thinking about some foolish boy who doesn't have the sense to know a good thing when it's in front of him."

Ivy looked almost ready to smile.

"Can you be ready to go in ten minutes?"

Ivy broke into a grin. "I've been wanting to see that movie."

"Great, I'll be downstairs. And don't forget to finish pinning up your hair. Whatever you were starting will be perfect for this movie."

Bathilda

BATHILDA MINCE-WALKED ON THE ice-covered snow and was halfway to the barn when she heard Etola let out a blood-curdling scream from the upstairs bathroom.

What the devil has happened to her now? It seemed like Etola was always getting in some pickle that required Bathilda to be the rescuing older sister, a role she was used to but still resented.

Bathilda could tell this was not an 'I'm in a life-threatening situation' kind of scream, so she walked back towards the house at a pace not likely to cause an unnecessary fall. When she was about ten yards from the house, Etola emerged from the kitchen door, wearing a pink chenille bathrobe and house shoes.

"My wig is gone!" Etola yelled.

"Your ring is gone?"

"MY WIG IS GONE!" Etola gestured repeatedly towards her head, bristling with a thick covering of stick-straight hair.

Bathilda shrugged. "You can see I'm not wearing it, can't you?"

"Well, did you put it somewhere?"

"Of course not," answered Bathilda with an added snork. "You probably lost it in bed."

Etola threw up her arms in frustration and went back into the house. Bathilda headed back to the barn with her measured steps. She needed to check on those ewes; they were just a few weeks away from birthing, and she wanted to make sure they had easy access to water and feed. She was almost to the barn when something triggered a vague memory from earlier this morning. It had been so cold last night she let Shep sleep in the entryway. When she heard Eddie let him out early this morning, she had looked out her bedroom window to watch him head towards the barn. She had chuckled about how Shep always managed to find a frozen cow patty to carry around, a strange habit he had started when he was just a puppy and one of the many quirks she loved about him. She'd heard it said that you get one great dog in your life, and, for her, it was Shep. At ten, he was moving much slower than he used to, but he was still the best sheepdog she'd ever known.

On a hunch, Bathilda headed to the corner stall where Shep had an old saddle blanket and his food and water bowls. He was sleeping there now, curled up with his nose tucked under his big fluffy tail. As soon as he heard Bathilda, he got up, wagging his tail, and stepped stiffly towards her.

Bathilda gave him some rubs and then bent down to peer at the blanket. There was something brownish-red peeking out from the edge of it. She lifted the blanket and held up the hairy clod. Sure enough, it was Etola's wig: half-chewed, caked with straw and manure, and almost unrecognizable.

"Shep, did you do this?" Shep bowed his head and looked away, then looked back at her. Bathilda could swear he was wearing a slight dog grin.

She looked more closely at the stolen object. "There will be hell to pay, Mr. Shep."

She stuffed the hairy mess into her coat pocket and continued to the side of the barn. Things looked okay with the steel livestock waterer; the water remained unfrozen. She dragged a bale of hay into the corner of the feedlot and used a pitchfork to divide it. That should be enough until she could get Eddie out to do more.

By the time she returned to the house, Etola had gone upstairs, and Bathilda could hear doors being flung open and drawers being slammed shut. "Etola, I found it!" Bathilda yelled up the stairs.

Etola came clamoring down the steps but jerked to a stop when she saw what Bathilda was holding. She repeated the same blood-curdling scream Bathilda had heard earlier. Only this time, it was in close range. Bathilda covered her ears.

Etola started to yell. "Mother of pearl fartknocker! What the hell happened?"

"You must have left it where Shep could get it."

Etola grabbed the pitiful wig. "Shep? I had it on the kitchen table drying after I washed it last night. How could Shep have gotten it?"

"Got down to fifteen below last night. I let Shep sleep in the entryway. At his age, the poor dog would have frozen to death in the barn."

Bathilda hoped Etola would have a little sympathy for Shep's elderly condition, but Etola was having none of it. She collapsed with drama onto a kitchen chair, examining the ruined remains of her wig, a glare set in her eyes.

"Poor dog didn't know any better; it looks just like one of those cow ... um ... squirrels he likes to chase."

Etola was silent, shaking with rage.

"Look, I'm sorry. But your hair is growing out nicely now." They both knew this was a lie; Etola's hair more closely resembles a chopped-off whiskbroom that had been dipped in orange paint.

"I could even give you a permanent if you'd like. You could have some nice tight curls like Hattie."

Etola's look sent daggers, but her words cut even deeper. "I wouldn't let you touch my hair if you were the last person on earth. What would you know about anything related to beauty? When I see you from a distance, you look like an old man. An ugly, skinny old man."

She dropped her head and Bathilda could tell that Etola regretted her words. But there's no unsaying what's been said in anger.

Bathilda couldn't speak; a painful tightness filled her throat. She walked on trembling legs out the door and headed to the barn. Faithful Shep followed closely behind her.

She continued her trek in the biting cold. She'd welcome the warm barn, fragrant with animals' breath. And the comforting feel of the pregnant ewes' bellies, thick with wool and growing with new life. It was true. She did like animals more than people. They never let her down.

Florence

FLORENCE HAS BEEN DREADING the knock on the door. Usually, she was happy to see her nephew, such a tall, handsome, strapping fellow. She couldn't have been more excited to hear about the Valentine's Dance plans. Of course, her mind had leapt way ahead to the fancy wedding she would be asked to help plan, then the clever baby shower she would host for the expectant mother. Perhaps even a chance for 'Auntie Florence' to babysit. What a cruel ending to her fantasies.

She wished she could slam the door in his face, but that's not how polite people act. Instead, when Lance arrived to take Lloyd to the stock auction, Florence greeted him with a simple "Hello" and invited him in.

Lance replied in his usual cheerful, outgoing manner. "Hi, Aunt Florence. Beautiful day for mid-February. Might get to forty degrees."

"Why, that's nice to hear. I'll let Lloyd know you're here." Could he detect the distinct coolness in her tone?

She left him standing in the entryway as she stomped upstairs. When she returned, Lance had seated himself at the kitchen table. "Your uncle will be down in a minute."

"Sure thing. Say, do you have any of your famous sugar cookies?"

"Why no, no, I don't. I think we ate them all on Valentine's Day." Florence hoped Lance would take the hint and confess his heartless actions, but he didn't respond. Florence decided to push it a little further. "How was the dance?"

"It was fun," Lance shrugged.

"Wasn't that the prettiest blue dress your date was wearing?"

Lance glanced at the floor for a second, scrunching his eyebrows. "Yup, very pretty."

There was an awkward silence. That brat, he wasn't going to admit it. She'd just have to force the issue. "I heard you uninvited Ivy at the last minute."

Lance's eyes widened, and then he looked toward the stairs. "Oh yeah, well, that was all a big misunderstanding."

Florence knew she should bite her tongue before she went too far. But she didn't. "A misunderstanding. I'm not sure that's what Cora would call it when she worked all week to get Ivy's dress sewn in time. Not sure that's what Ivy would call it either – all dressed up and ready to go when she got the news."

Lance stared down at his feet, blushing. He stammered out, "But, I..."

"True gentlemen don't get themselves in those kinds of *misunderstandings*." Florence emphasized the last word perhaps more strongly than she intended. She'd said enough now and walked to the kitchen counter. She opened the lid of the cookie jar and took out two sugar cookies, putting them on a small plate and setting them in front of Lance.

"I guess I misunderstood. I do have cookies left, after all." Florence hoped the sweet sugar cookies would feel like dry sand in Lance's mouth.

Lance stared at the heart-shaped cookies, covered in thick white frosting and sprinkled with red sugar crystals. Florence turned and left the room.

Ivy

IVY HAD BEEN DREADING this moment. Of all the times to have a locker right next to Lance's! There he was, loitering in front of his open locker door. Ivy did a U-turn in the hallway to go the long way around and circle back to her locker in a couple of minutes. If only she hadn't left her written assignment in the back of her English book — in her locker. For a minute, she considered turning it in late just to avoid him, but she worried she'd get called on to read today. And Mrs. Nichol kept praising Ivy for her writing style, encouraging her. Maybe she could even consider becoming a real writer, after college.

By the time she got back to her locker, Lance was still there, obviously waiting around for her. Ivy lifted her chin and marched past him, avoiding eye contact and turning her back to him as she twirled the combination lock. Her stomach felt tight.

"Hi, Ivy." His voice was low and tentative. Ivy didn't answer.

Lance tapped on her shoulder. "Hey, can we talk? I wanted to explain ..."

Ivy opened her locker door and slammed it into the locker on the right. She kept her head turned away from Lance, her jaw clenched.

"I brought you something." He held up a small paper bag and pulled out a heart-shaped sugar cookie. "My aunt Florence made it." When Ivy didn't look, he came around to the other side, holding the cookie closer.

Ivy swatted at the cookie, sending it flying into the hallway and down onto the gray-tiled floor. It lay there for a second until a group of four students walked past. One of the boys accidentally kicked it down the hall into the middle of the hallway traffic, and before long, it was smashed underfoot, a small trail of cookie bits and white frosting left behind.

"Hey..." Lance protested, but Ivy cut him off. "I don't want your stupid cookie or anything to do with you!" she shouted. When the activity in the hallway came to a silent halt, she yelled even louder. "I can't stand you or any of the pathetic losers in this school."

The students in the hallway were looking at her. "You're all a bunch of dolts ... and country hicks!" Then Ivy saw Becky a few yards down the hall, her eyes wide and mouth open. "Except for Becky."

Ivy slammed her locker door shut and stomped off towards her English class; her eyes focused on the floor. She was breathing so hard she felt like there was fire coming out of her mouth. Then she felt a small ping of regret and then a bigger one. She didn't mind what she'd said about the other students, but she hoped she hadn't hurt Becky's feelings. Becky was her only friend in this terrible town.

February 25

Dear Val,
It's been a while since I've written, and I haven't heard from you since Christmas. I know you must be busy. I wanted you to know I'm still alive. Barely.
Life on a farm in South Dakota in the winter is even worse than you can imagine.
I hate to ask but I was wondering if you might talk to your parents again about the possibility of me moving back to Omaha and staying with your family. I'm not sure how much more of this place I can take, and my mother can't be counted on to get me out of here. You are my best hope. Seriously, Val, my life kind of depends on getting out of here soon.
Say hi to everybody I know, even though they have all probably forgotten about me by now.
Lotsa luv,
Ivy

March 1964

Ivy

"THEY'RE PREDICTING A BIG snowstorm," Bert told Ivy as they both stared out the windshield at the blowing snow forming little ridges like waves across the road. It was only four o'clock, but the sky was already blanketed with thick, gunmetal gray clouds.

Ivy had slid to the front of the bus as they got closer to her grandparents' farm.

"According to the *Farmer's Almanac*, we're in for a late spring on account of an extra-long, hard winter this year. One of the longest in a decade," Bert continued.

Ivy nodded, the information settling into the swelling gloom she already felt. It was only the beginning of March. And only Monday.

After she climbed off the bus, Ivy tromped through the snow down the driveway, the sharp sting of blowing snow slapping against her cheeks like sharp little ice crystals so she lifted her wool scarf and tucked her head lower, exposing only her eyes. She entered the back porch, removed her scarf, gloves, hat, and snow boots, and then hung up her coat before she entered the warm kitchen. The coconut smell coming from the back of the stove was yummy.

"Hi, Grandma."

Ivy's grandmother was stirring something with a wooden spoon in a large metal bowl and didn't turn around to greet Ivy. That was odd. "Your grandfather would like to talk with you. In the living room."

"What about?"

Cora turned, barely making eye contact. "Go on in there." She pivoted back to her stirring.

Ivy's grandfather put down the newspaper when she entered. "Have a seat, Ivy."

Ivy sat, racking her brain to recall what she might have done to make her grandfather mad.

Delmar's jaw was clenched as he leaned forward, removing his black glasses, and rubbing the bridge of his nose. "What the devil is going on with you, Ivy?"

"What do you mean?"

He put his glasses back on before he asked, "Just how ungrateful are you?"

"I don't know what you're talking about." Suddenly, Ivy's skin prickled with uneasiness, and she felt like running.

Delmar sat tight-lipped for a moment. "The guidance counselor, Mrs. Bell, called me into her office today. Seems she had a call from Mrs. Bowers."

"Mrs. Bowers?" For a moment, the name didn't register.

Delmar's voice rose. "Mrs. Bowers. Valerie's mother. 'My life depends on getting out of here soon.' That Mrs. Bowers."

Heat swept across Ivy's face as she remembered the words in her letter. Did she really say it that way?

"Do we not do enough for you around here? Your grandmother is working so hard to try to make you happy. Me going out on a limb to get you that horse."

"But I didn't mean it like that. I was only asking if I could stay with Val ... finish out high school with my old friends."

Cora had quietly entered the room and was standing in the doorway, her arms folded across her stomach. Her voice sounded tight and low when she said, "And you didn't think you should maybe talk to us about something like that first?"

Delmar continued, "Do you know how humiliating it was to have Mrs. Bell ask if everything is all right at home? As if we were beating you or something!"

Ivy looked at her grandmother. "I'm sorry, I never meant it that way. I just really miss my old life."

Cora sat down next to Ivy. Her eyes were red and watery. "I'm sure you do."

"That's no reason to make us out like torturers. Do you think we asked to have you here?" Delmar's words instantly cut into Ivy, and she imagined this was how it felt to be stabbed without warning from behind.

Her grandmother reached out to put her hand on Ivy's leg. "Now, Delmar, you know we're happy to have Ivy here. I'm sure she was merely being dramatic. Let's all forget about this. I've got a nice tater tot hotdish for dinner, and coconut pudding for dessert. Ivy, you wash up now and then help me set the table."

Dinner was quiet, with only a few attempts to make small talk, mainly about the storm that raged outside, blowing the snow harder and rattling the windowpanes. Ivy forced herself to eat, but even the coconut pudding she usually loved tasted overly sweet, almost sickening.

After the dishes, she excused herself and headed to her room to finish her homework. Later, she lay awake, listening to the wind as it screamed across the farmyard. It sounded just like the airplanes taking off from the Omaha Airport she and her mother used to watch, dreaming of all the places they could travel to.

At midnight, Ivy was still awake, confused about her intense feelings: deep regret for hurting her grandmother and anger about her grandfather's biting words. Finally, she got out of bed and dressed to go outside. Maybe being near Bearcat, in the comforting barn, she could find peace.

As soon as she slipped out the back door, she realized she had underestimated the storm's fury, but she was determined to reach the barn. It wasn't that far, maybe only 150 yards. After a few minutes, Ivy stopped, realizing she could barely see her hand when she held it in front of her. She was pretty sure she was headed in the right direction, but the whiteout was disorienting. Normally, the top of the yard light, halfway between the house and the barn, would be visible, but all she could see now was a faint glow where the top of the pole must be.

She didn't dare turn back to look at the house or she could get really turned around. Why hadn't she grabbed a flashlight — or her cap and gloves?

Ivy kept plowing through the snow, wondering how far she'd come. She tried, unsuccessfully, to push away the stories she'd heard of people getting lost in blizzards and freezing to death only a few feet from their house. One foot in front of the other, she trudged along, hand outstretched so she didn't run into something. Ivy couldn't remember being this scared, her heart hammering louder than the howling wind.

After what seemed like an eternity, her icy fingers hit a solid object. It was the front of the barn. She leaned against the building, sliding along until she felt a seam where the door edge must be. Then she reached for the metal latch, opened the door, and stepped in.

Inside, with the door closed behind her, the barn was warm and quiet. Ivy paused for a minute, inhaling deeply. She never thought she would love this smell so much: dusty hay, pigeon feathers, and warm animals. She called out, "Bearcat?"

From the opposite corner, Bearcat softly whinnied. Ivy was at the other end of the barn from where she thought she was entering. It was pitch black, but she knew the bones of the barn and blindly edged to Bearcat's stall. Bearcat stood up as Ivy came near.

When she reached him, Ivy wrapped her arms and freezing fingers around his neck and buried her head in his long mane. She was safe. Her tears escaped into sobs, and Ivy let herself go into her fear and relief. After a few minutes, she was spent, her weeping slowing down as she struggled to catch her breath. It was then she noticed a flashlight's narrow beam as the door creaked open and she heard her grandmother's voice.

"Ivy, you in here?"

"Over here, Grandma. With Bearcat."

Her grandmother used the flashlight to navigate to the corner stall, and Ivy reached out for her. "I'm sorry." She burst into tears again. "I'm so sorry."

Her grandmother wrapped her arms around Ivy. "There, there. Shh ... everything will be okay, sweet pea. I promise you."

Tilly

TILLY WAS ALMOST FINISHED. She chose a smaller brush, one Etola had given her, to paint the smiling features on the faces. She checked her watch — still fifteen minutes before the store opened, so she might as well add a few more clovers using the Tempera Kelly Green.

Tilly stood back to admire her work. It had turned out great, especially as she'd had to paint everything backward since she was working inside the windows. Maybe not an artistic masterpiece, but she'd had a lot of fun creating the dancing leprechauns, four-leafed clovers, and silver horseshoes. She had even painted a pot of gold with colored streamers shaped like a rainbow coming out of it. She considered putting her signature in the window's bottom corner but decided against it. As her late mother always said, nobody likes a braggart.

With all these symbols of good luck around her, Tilly thought about her own recent bit of good luck. It was almost as if someone else, someone braver than she, had inhabited her body when she had come into the store last week with her sketch pad under her arm. She had waited until Mr. Cranston had finished with a customer and then asked if he could spare a minute.

Tilly said she'd like to paint the store window, and she had an idea all sketched out for him: a Saint Patrick's Day Sale window. Mr. Cranston loved the idea, and when he peered more closely at the drawing, he said everything looked perfect except the little sign the leprechaun was holding that said, "Kiss Me, I'm Irish." Oh, and maybe the beer stein overflowing with sudsy bubbles would have to go. He didn't think Prairie View was quite ready for beer in the front window of a hardware store.

Mr. Cranston had said Tilly could come in at six o'clock and have three hours to paint without interruption before the store opened at nine. He would pay her $10.00 if she supplied the materials. And if it worked out, she could replace the St. Patrick's Day window with an Easter window.

Then Tilly had to tell James she'd gotten the job and see if he would babysit. She hadn't told him in advance about the idea, hadn't wanted to jinx it. But when she told him, James was excited for her and even offered to watch the kids so she could get the paints she needed.

There was just one niggling bit of dread lurking in the back of her mind. As Tilly cleaned up her brushes and paints, the reality of the future began to creep back in. Wednesday Club. It was her turn to host the group next week. It isn't that she minded doing the cooking and cleaning in advance of the meeting; it's just that their trailer house was too small for company. Not to mention old and shabby. That worn-out brown plaid couch, a hand-me-down with a broken spring and a threadbare cushion, had been ready for the dump when they got it two years ago.

She could ask her mother-in-law about hosting the club at her house, but she was sure she already knew the answer. And she couldn't bear the sharp-tongued lecture she would get both before and after the meeting as penance for Mildred's generosity.

And then, in the way that lovely coincidences happen, Hattie entered the store. It must have been barely nine o'clock, but Hattie was all dressed up for a day of errands. Tilly noticed her beige wool coat, brown gloves, and brown felted pillbox hat. A light coat of orange-red lipstick. Brown shoes with practical low heels.

"Tilly! Is that your painting?" Hattie pointed to the window.

"Yes! I'm so excited Mr. Cranston let me do it. It's been so much fun."

Hattie squeezed Tilly's arm. "It's darling. I'm so happy you're getting to share your talents. How wonderful."

"Thanks, Hattie. I'd better get this cleaned up. I guess I'll be seeing you next week?"

Hattie hesitated for a second. "Oh, right! Wednesday Club. I need to get going on my program. The US Surgeon General's report on the dangers of smoking. Quite important. I'll see you then, dear."

As Hattie walked off into the store, Tilly knew what she could do. Hattie had always said if there was anything Tilly ever needed, she should let her know. But it was the asking that felt so impossible. Tilly had never been one to ask for anything. Even when her momma died when Tilly was only fourteen (her daddy long gone before that), Tilly didn't reach out for help in raising her younger brother. It felt like imposing, and her momma had always said it's better to just rely on yourself. She'd told Tilly that fourteen was plenty old to be acting like a grown-up anyway. When Tilly married James at twenty, she felt like she'd already been an adult for a long time.

But maybe part of getting older was about asking for help when you needed it. Look how well things had turned out when she talked to Mr. Cranston. Tilly appraised the window one more time. Then she walked down the aisle in search of Hattie. It was going to be hard to ask her. But not asking was harder.

Wednesday Club Minutes

MARCH 11, 1964

The Wednesday Club met at the home of Miss Hattie Dunlop. President Miss Bathilda Baldridge called the meeting to order, and the club motto was recited. Miss Etola Baldridge asked if any of the members thought it might be time to get a new club motto, but Bathilda said her question was out of order according to *Roberts Rules of Order* and should be addressed later. Etola would need to ask for it to be officially added to the agenda.

Roll was called, and the topic was Irish jokes or sayings. One of the jokes was: what do you call a big Irish spider? The answer: A Paddy long legs. Cora said her mother was half-Irish and shared her favorite Irish saying that hung on her kitchen wall: 'May your heart be light and happy, may your smile be big and wide, and may your pockets always have a coin or two inside.' Florence said she was always careful with Irish jokes as some of them might be seen as offensive, and she really appreciated all the things the Irish had brought to this country, especially potatoes.

Ivy read the minutes from the February meeting, and they were approved.

Hattie gave the treasurer's report, and the balance was $62.80. Etola said Margaret Hill was in the hospital after gallbladder surgery and she had visited and brought a small African violet from the Wednesday Club. The club voted to reimburse Etola $2.15.

Music chairman Etola Baldridge played the organ and led the group in singing "My Wild Irish Rose."

Hattie gave the program on the recent report by Surgeon General Luther Terry, M.D. He and his committee members have linked cigarette smoking with dangerous health effects such as chronic bronchitis and heart disease. Hattie said the report showed that people who smoke cigarettes are 10 to 20 times more likely to get lung cancer. Hattie hoped everyone would take the information seriously and give up smoking, a habit she had always found disgusting. Florence said her husband Lloyd smokes, and she didn't think even God himself could get him to quit. Cora said she was glad Delmar quit smoking; he only does his dips of chewing tobacco when working in the fields.

The meeting ended with the club creed. Hattie served corned beef and cabbage, and Tilly brought hand-decorated St. Patrick's cookies in the shape of four-leaf clovers.

Ivy Hanson, Secretary

Etola

ETOLA WAS RETURNING FROM the Cut-n-Curl when she saw the truck pulling into her driveway, just ahead of her. Maybe it wasn't an unlucky day after all. Bathilda had told Etola she was a damn fool to schedule a hair appointment on Friday the thirteenth. But six months after her hair accident, Etola was more than ready for a new hairdo. Maxine had cut off all the old color but had maybe gone a little overboard with her permanent. Of course, everybody knew that time would relax the curls — and about everything else with your body.

Anyway, that sure as heck looked like Arlo's pickup. What could he be here for? As soon as she got out of the car, Arlo stepped out of the pickup, a small paper bag in his hand.

"Hello. What have you got there?"

Arlo grinned and held up the bag. "A mess of garlic from last summer's harvest. Enough to keep at least a dozen vampires away."

"Or a beau bent on kissing, I imagine." She couldn't believe those slipped out of her mouth. She was sure she'd turned as red as a beet. "Well, I didn't mean you, I mean, you know ... what they say about garlic and kissing and all ..."

Arlo grinned some more. "I grew a lot more garlic than I can ever use, and I figured you might be able to use some."

"That was mighty nice of you, Arlo. Want to come in for a cup of coffee?"

"Sure, I guess I have time for coffee before I get back to my chores."

Etola made coffee and served up a plate of ginger cookies and applesauce bars. She and Arlo sat in the kitchen, talking for the longest time, as natural as could be. They talked about everything from the latest news from the White House to the Coast-to-Coast window Tilly had painted. It was like they'd been friends all their lives; nothing awkward or odd about it. That is until Bathilda showed up. Then it was like a cold draft had suddenly blown into the kitchen.

"Why, if it isn't Arlo Wilcox."

"Hello, Bathilda. I hope you're doing well. I just stopped by for a minute to drop off some garlic. Had a bumper crop last summer, and I don't want it going bad on me."

Bathilda looked at the two of them sitting there, and Etola thought she noticed a little smirk when her eyes landed on Etola's tight curls.

Arlo stood up. "I'd best be on my way and let you two get on with your day. Never enough time when you own a farm, is there? Even in the winter."

Etola thanked him for the garlic and said he should drop by any time.

She was hoping Bathilda would keep her big mouth shut, but as Arlo was putting on his coat, Bathilda just had to get her digs in. "What do you hear from Hattie these days, Arlo?"

Dad blast her! She knew perfectly well how Hattie was; they'd just seen her two days earlier.

Arlo gave a slight shrug. "I'm not sure. I haven't seen her for a few weeks. Didn't you see her at Wednesday Club?"

Well, that shut her up. "Oh, that's right. I guess I did."

"Thanks for the hospitality, Etola. Surely do appreciate it."

Arlo gave Etola a big smile that about melted her heart. She wanted to hold onto that smile for as long as she could, so she grabbed a mop and went upstairs to scrub the bathroom, where she could be alone. No sense letting sourpuss Bathilda take any bit of that warmth away.

Hattie

HATTIE LOVED THE WAY the four wide steps up to the door of the Geiss Feed Store were worn down, curved in the center where all those feet had trodden over the last fifty years. She always remembered her daddy — her real daddy — holding her hand and helping her climb these steps when she was little. Geiss Feed had been an institution in Prairie View for as long as most folks could remember, and now the store was run by old man Geiss's son Denny and grandson Luke.

When Hattie reached the top step at the wide covered porch, she paused to peruse the large bulletin board. Almost better than the weekly paper, this was the place to learn about local church and high school events, see who had barn kittens to give away, or whether there was a farm auction happening nearby. Looked like the Trygstads had some Plymouth Rock chicks for sale; she thought she might get a couple.

When Hattie stepped through the heavy sliding doors, halfway open on this warm early spring day, she breathed in the comforting smell of the place: livestock feed and leather mixed with sweet hay bales and bags of dried molasses. They made her think of shopping here with her daddy, how she would look to see if there were any bunnies in the large metal cage, and how her daddy would let her poke a finger in to touch their soft fur. Later, her momma would try to get Hattie to go to the feed store with Ray, but she always refused, not wanting to taint her old happy memories.

Today, Hattie didn't look around for bunnies but simply went to the counter where Denny was bent over some paperwork.

"Howdy, Miss Hattie!" Denny had a wide smile for everyone who entered; he seemed to have been born for this job.

"Hello, Denny. How are you doing?"

"Just dandy. What can I do for you today? More chicken feed?" Denny asked, the small talk out of the way.

"Yes, please. I'll take four of those fifty-pound bags. And another bag of oyster shells; they seem to be working well."

"Yep, sure is the best way to get those eggshells nice and hard. Not like the old days when they used to chop up glass..."

As soon as Denny said it, Hattie knew he regretted it. Of course, Denny knew the story of how Hattie's mother had lost sight in her left eye when a tiny shard of glass had pierced it. For as long as Hattie could remember, her mother's blue glass eye had been a part of her, always staring straight ahead. It didn't bother Hattie; she was used to it, except when strangers stared at her mother. Once, as a teenager, she overheard someone call her 'Martha with the glass eye.' At times, when her anger faded, Hattie almost felt sorry for her mother.

Hattie didn't want Denny to feel embarrassed to have brought it up. She smiled, "Nope, not like the old days."

"That'll be seven dollars and ten cents."

Hattie took her checkbook out of her handbag.

"I'd be glad to have Luke deliver those for you."

"Oh no, I expect Arlo will stop by one of these days. If Luke could get them into the trunk, that'll be plenty good enough."

Denny looked at her for a second longer than Hattie expected. "It's no trouble at all for Luke to stop by and put 'em right into the hen house."

"That's kind of you, but just the trunk is fine." Hattie ripped the check from the checkbook, looking forward to what came next.

"Okay, Scout. Your turn." Denny's old black lab lifted himself from where he'd been resting at Denny's feet and came around to the counter. Hattie handed the check to Scout, who gingerly took it in his mouth and padded over to Denny. This had been the routine for the last ten years or so, and the whole town would mourn when this gentle dog was gone.

"Bye now, Denny. Give my best to Beulah."

"Will do." Denny hollered to the back of the store. "Luke! Load four bags of chicken feed and one oyster shell into Hattie's trunk!"

As Hattie was leaving, Eddie came in the door. "Afternoon, Eddie." Eddie nodded at Hattie, then looked at the ground as he walked toward the back of the store. Hattie navigated the steps down to the parking lot where Bathilda was waiting in their pickup. Hattie tapped on the driver's side door and Bathilda, lost in thought, startled, and then rolled down the window.

"Nice to see you, Hattie. Picking up some chicken feed?"

"That's it. Figured I'd wait for some better weather to venture out."

Bathilda nods, "Sun is a welcome sight after so many of those gray days."

"Certainly is! How's Etola doing?"

"Oh, she's fine. Keeping busy these days, what with all those visits from Arlo."

Hattie held her face motionless, not wanting to give anything up to Bathilda, then managed a smile she hoped was convincing.

"That's nice. Arlo does enjoy visiting with folks, especially in the winter."

Bathilda smiled back at Hattie. "He sure seems to."

Hattie heard that funny, nervous sound Bathilda made in the back of her throat. It was so annoying. She smiled wider at Bathilda. "Well, you take care now and give my best to Etola."

Hattie walked to her car, started the engine, and pulled out of the parking lot, her smile still firmly in place. Only when she was a few miles down the road, her fingers clamped tightly around the steering wheel, did she realize what she'd done — driven off without waiting for Luke to load the chicken feed. That encounter with Bathilda had been surprisingly upsetting.

Ivy

Dear Diary,

As of yesterday, I'm officially seventeen years old. Only one more year until I'm eighteen and can live where and how I want. It feels close and far away at the same time.

I thought my birthday was going to be a big bust. Before I got on the bus, Grandma said she would pick me up after school, and we could shop for new clothes. Boy, was I surprised when Becky got in the car, too, with an overnight bag! Grandma had surprised me and planned for Becky to spend the night!!

Becky helped me pick out a new blouse, twinset, and pair of Keds for when the weather finally warms up. Shopping in Prairie View is nothing like the big department stores Val and I used to go to. But better than nothing.

Becky and I had the best time together. We hung out with Bearcat, braided his mane, and fussed over him. Grandma made a Chef Boyardee pizza for dinner, and then we went to my room and played on the Ouija board Becky had brought along. Every time we asked *who my next boyfriend would be, the little pointer kept spelling out 'Lance.' That got us laughing so hard Grandpa had to knock on the door and ask if everything was ok. We stayed awake until two a.m. It was a total blast!*

It turned out to be a pretty good birthday, thanks to Grandma. I really should be nicer to her; it's not her fault Mom dumped me here. Maybe I should just surrender and make the best of things until I can get out of here. Unless Mom does make something of herself.

I can't believe I'm rooting for the success of a diarrhea commercial,

Ivy

Cora

CORA WAS IN THE living room folding the load of white clothes she'd taken out of the dryer. She preferred to hang laundry outside on the long clothesline Delmar built for her — nothing like that fresh outdoors scent — but in late March, it was still too cold for that.

She separated Ivy's clothes into a pile for Ivy to put away herself, laying her tiny bra beneath her shirts. Ivy was so slender, still growing. Lithe and muscular and tall. Seventeen now. Cora hadn't seen much of Vonda Marie at that age, and Vonda Marie's body was completely different by then. Her name was different, too. She'd been just Marie then before she added the fancy part after she went to Omaha.

Cora was lost in remembering when she heard the crunch of gravel along the side of the house. She walked to the kitchen to peer out at the circular driveway. It was the sheriff's car. Holding her breath, Cora took a quick inventory of her loved ones. Delmar was helping Eddie with some new fencing. Ivy was in school. Vonda Marie? Cora had no idea where her daughter was other than somewhere in Southern California. It had been several weeks since they'd heard from her.

With her heart pounding, Cora opened the back door for Sheriff Palmer. As classmates, they'd known each other for over forty years, so Tom Palmer was a friend too.

"Now, Cora," Tom said as he stepped into the house, "nothing to worry about. I'm only here for a minute; wanted to check with you on something."

"Come in, Tom. You know you're always welcome. It's just—"

"I know. The car always makes things seem official, whether they are or not."

Cora motioned for Tom to sit and poured him a cup of coffee from the pot that was always ready for a drop-in guest.

"Delmar around?" Tom didn't remove his jacket.

"No, he's over at the Baldridge place helping Eddie put in some new fence lines. Bathilda is worried their lower pasture is too close to the riverbed. With all the snow we've had this winter and all."

"We sure have had more than our fair share. Let's hope maybe we're done now." Tom sipped his coffee.

Cora sat down but didn't say anything, eager to get past the weather talk.

"I'll get right to the point. You been in contact with Hank recently?"

Cora leaned forward. "Why no. It's been over seventeen years since we've seen him. You remember..."

Tom nodded and set down his coffee cup. "Hate to ask you this; I know it might be a sore subject. Do you think Vonda Marie has been in touch with him?"

"I have no idea. She's never mentioned anything about it."

"And Ivy?"

Cora bit her lip. "Ivy doesn't know anything about him. Why? Has something happened to him?"

"I got a call from Sheriff Rasmussen over at Elmdale, in Lincoln County. Apparently, they're holding him in jail ... until the arraignment."

"For what?"

Tom tilted his head back and then said quietly, "Manslaughter."

What? "That's got to be a mistake! Hank was one of the gentlest persons I've ever met."

"That's what the sheriff thinks, too. He's looking for anybody willing to be a character witness. Right now, Hank's boss from the slaughterhouse is standing up for him."

"Slaughterhouse?"

"Yeah, Redfield's, that big place in Elmdale. His boss says he's worked there for fifteen years without so much as a day calling in sick."

Cora shuddered when she thought of Hank working in a slaughterhouse for fifteen years. It must have been tough, as tenderhearted as he was. But steady, good-paying jobs around these parts were hard to find.

"Manslaughter." Cora let the word sink in. "What happened?"

"Hank was walking down the street when he heard a ruckus behind a tavern. When he went back there, he saw a man threatening a woman with a knife. Hank intervened, and somehow the guy was stabbed in the neck and died. Hank swears he was only protecting the woman and never meant to hurt him, but the man's family is pressing charges."

The gravity of the situation made her heart sink. "What does the woman say?"

"She says the man was trying to kill her, and Hank was only trying to help. Says it was an accident."

"Then what's the problem?"

"She was intoxicated. And the dead guy is the son of one of the wealthiest ranchers in the county — Monte Sears. Sears is saying, without any evidence, that Hank had threatened his son in the past. It seems to be his word against Hank's."

"Oh, dear Lord. Poor Hank. Is there anything we can do?"

"Like I said, Sheriff Rasmussen is looking for character witnesses. I always liked Hank, so I thought I'd let you know."

Tom stood and pushed his chair back under the table.

"I appreciate you letting me know, Tom. I'll talk to Delmar."

Cora closed the door behind Tom and sat back down with her head in her hands. She remembered the day she opened the door to the barn and saw Hank crouched down, crying over the body of a stillborn baby calf, the umbilical cord wrapped tightly around its neck.

Cora was still at the table, lost in thought, when Delmar came home. She willed her voice to be steady. He was not going to talk her out of this.

"Delmar, I'll need the car tomorrow. I'm going to Elmdale."

April 1964

Ivy

WHEN IVY GOT HOME from school, the house was empty. That was unusual. Normally her grandmother would be there, to ask about her day and offer fresh baked cookies or a bowl of applesauce. Instead, there was a note on the kitchen table saying she'd be home by 4:00 but no explanation of where she was. Things had seemed strange lately, her grandparents both acting more secretive about something, but Ivy couldn't put her finger on exactly what was going on.

At five o'clock her grandfather came in and started pacing back and forth in the living room. When Ivy asked him where her grandmother was, he spit out, "None of your business, young lady!"

Geez, Ivy thought. *What the heck is his problem?* She went upstairs to work on her homework and stay out of his hair. He seemed to be in a worse mood than usual.

A few minutes later she heard the phone ring and thought she heard her grandfather say the name Hank a couple of times. She might have been imagining it though. She crept down the stairs to have a closer listen, but her grandfather heard her footsteps and said into the phone, "Talk to Ivy." He shoved the phone in her direction.

It was Ivy's mother, and she sounded all fakey happy.

"Are you doing any commercials?" Ivy asked.

"I'm sure I will be very soon, darling. I've been going to a lot of auditions and I'm just waiting to hear." Ivy could tell she was only acting hopeful.

"Ivy dear, I have to rush off now, but I'll be sending you a letter soon."

Ivy thought that seemed odd since they were on the phone, and her mom could just say whatever she needed to right now.

"That'll be great," Ivy said. The truth was she couldn't care less about a letter from her mother. They were always just filled with more promises that she wouldn't keep. Ivy hung up the phone and went back upstairs.

When she heard her grandmother's car, she looked out the window at the driveway below. Her grandfather had gone out to meet her and when she watched them talking, Ivy thought her grandmother looked worn out. And kind of sad.

What was going on around here? Something was different.

Wednesday Club Minutes

APRIL 8, 1964

The Wednesday Club met at the home of Mrs. Florence Lane. The meeting was called to order by President Bathilda Baldridge. The club motto was recited.

The roll call topic was your favorite modern invention for the home. Each member chose a different invention.

Cora – touch-tone telephone

Tilly – felt tip pens

Ivy – portable record player

Hattie – electric vacuum cleaner

Florence – side-by-side refrigerator (she had one in Texas)

Bathilda – toaster oven

Etola – portable hair dryer

Ivy Hanson read the minutes from the March meeting. Bathilda noted that the minutes again said that Etola had played the piano when it should have said organ. Bathilda said there was a significant difference and asked that Ivy be more careful in her minutes. Etola made a motion to approve the minutes with the correction. The motion passed. Ivy also read a thank you note from Margaret Hill. She said she is doing fine now and welcomed any visitors to her home.

Hattie Dunlop gave the treasurer's report; the balance was $60.65. There were no expenses. Cora reported that Grandma Harrington had passed away in her sleep on Monday night and asked that the club send flowers for the funeral. The club agreed.

Music chairman Etola Baldridge led the group in singing "My South Dakota." Some of the members didn't know the words, and Etola agreed to bring the words next time for any song that wasn't well known.

Bathilda led the program: a recent newsworthy event. She reported on the Great Alaskan earthquake that had happened on Good Friday, March 27, in south-central Alaska, including the city of Anchorage. Bathilda described how the ground had cracked, buildings had collapsed, and giant tsunami waves had rushed onto land. So far, this has been the most powerful earthquake ever recorded – a 9.2 magnitude. Bathilda said the shaking had lasted four minutes and 30 seconds. Etola suggested that we close our eyes for four minutes and 30 seconds and imagine the shaking, but Bathilda said that was not a part of her program.

In all, 131 people died: nine died from the earthquake itself and 122 deaths were because of the tsunami waves. A 27-foot wave destroyed the village of Chenega, and the tsunami affected the entire west coast.

Tilly asked if there was anything the club could do to help the poor people of Alaska, and Bathilda said we could donate to the Red Cross. Florence said she was glad we didn't live in an area affected by earthquakes. The club then discussed ways South Dakota had experienced their own disasters, including tornadoes, hailstorms, and floods. Cora remarked that with all the snow this winter we must be cautious about spring flooding.

The meeting ended with the club creed. Florence served a delicious lunch of dried beef hotdish, raspberry ring salad, and lemon meringue pie.

Ivy Hanson, Secretary

Florence

As soon as Florence was aware of the morning light filtering in the bedroom window, she closed her eyes and burrowed her head under the quilt. *Dear Lord, let this be a bad dream I can awaken from, not my real life.* Florence was not religious, having long ago given up on having her prayers answered. Still, sometimes, when she felt hopeless, she gave it another try.

Everything had gone so smoothly. The house looked spic and span, the weather had cooperated, and even her lemon pie had turned out perfectly, the meringue browned evenly and the curled edges weeping ever so slightly. Florence had worn her new outfit: an old dress she had transformed by adding a new striped belt and matching pocket trim.

And then Lloyd had ruined everything — stumbling in the front door right in the middle of the creed, swaying in the living room doorway, and slurring his words as he called out to the ladies. Even now, his mocking words burned into Florence's head: "Well, if it isn't the wacky Wednesday Club! The high society of Prairie View." The creed reciting had stopped on a dime, as the club members froze. Was it shock or pity on their faces?

Florence had hastily escorted a wobbly Lloyd up to the bedroom, where he passed out on their bed almost immediately. Her mind raced for excuses, and she finally settled on a weak explanation as she served the lunch later. "Seems like Lloyd and his brother took to celebrating his birthday a little too much today. I'm terribly sorry for his rude manners."

The ladies had been gracious enough, but Florence could hardly wait until they were all gone, and she could be alone to wash the dishes, the water scalding. A fitting sensation for the burning shame she felt.

More awake now, Florence glanced over at Lloyd's sleeping face, his mouth half-open and snoring; then she rose and began her morning routines: getting dressed, teasing and spraying her hair, putting on lipstick, getting the coffee on and the breakfast ingredients laid out on the counter. She was lifting the heavy iron skillet from the cupboard when she heard the knock at the door. Peering out the living room window, she saw Delmar standing on the front porch and hurried to open the door.

"Delmar, come on in."

"Morning. Is Lloyd around?"

"Well, he's still asleep," Florence said. Had Delmar been told about yesterday's disaster?

"I'd like to speak with him if you don't mind waking him up." From the severe expression on his face, Florence knew Delmar had heard.

"Yes, of course, I'll go get him. Would you like to sit down and have some coffee?"

"No thanks, I'll wait in my truck for him."

Florence wanted to ask Delmar what was happening but thought better of it.

She climbed the stairs. Lloyd was already up, having heard the knocking and the voices downstairs. He looked like death warmed over, his eyes red and puffy, and his skin a pale gray.

"What's he want?" Lloyd asked.

"He wants to talk with you. He's waiting in his pickup." No farmer in the county was more respected than Delmar, so Lloyd was not likely to refuse the summons. And word had it that Delmar had a brother who used to drink too much.

Downstairs, she tiptoed to the living room, perching on the edge of a chair to get a clear view of Delmar's truck. She watched Lloyd shuffle out to the pickup and stand beside it, talking with Delmar through the open driver's window. Lloyd's head was low, mostly looking down at the ground. After about ten minutes, he returned to the house, Delmar's pickup still in the driveway. Lloyd limped up the steps without saying a word, and Florence heard water running, and the closet door opened and closed.

Finally, Lloyd descended and stood in the living room, his hat in his hand with his shoulders slumped. "I'll be back in a couple of hours. Delmar is taking me to a meeting. Friends of Bill W."

Florence's stomach clenched. Bill W. was the founder of Alcoholics Anonymous.

Lloyd stared at the floor, ran his hand through his hair and put his hat on. He glanced at Florence and said in a quiet voice, "Honey, I'm sorry."

She wondered if he was going to break down. She hoped not.

She sat motionless for a long time after Lloyd and Delmar drove off, her eyes closed, and her hands folded tightly in her lap.

Dear Lord, let this not be a dream.

Ivy

IVY FELT CRANKY AS she waited for the school bus to take her home. It felt strange that she was now calling her grandparents' farm "home". Sometimes it felt like her old life in Omaha had never happened. She still got a letter from Val every few weeks, but Ivy could tell by the tone of the letters that Val had started to give up on Ivy ever moving back. And even though Val reported that Brad and Marilyn were no longer an item, Ivy never heard from Brad anymore.

Ivy dreaded her bus rides home from school. Last week when she walked down the aisle to take a seat, she had heard someone whisper "half breed" as she walked by. When she asked Becky about it, Becky had said it was a word kids used when they were razzing each other, and it didn't have anything to do with Ivy. She said it meant that someone is half-Indian. Ivy guessed it was a way to put people down since South Dakotans didn't seem to think too highly of Indians. Maybe that's why kids on the bus made fun of little Mary. With her dark skin and hair and last name of Bear Eagle, Ivy was pretty sure Mary was Indian.

Now, as Ivy trudged up the steps and made her way to a seat in the back, she wasn't looking forward to seeing Mary either. It wasn't that she minded helping Mary with her homework; it's just that she didn't want to do it every day. She regretted starting in the first place, but Mary did seem to be improving with her reading and writing. At least Mary got off the bus before her, so Ivy had a few minutes to herself every day.

The weather wasn't helping Ivy's mood. Yesterday was warm and beautiful, and Ivy hoped for another day of riding Bearcat up and down the field roads, getting used to the feel of the saddle and his responsiveness to her signals. And on Saturday, she was going to ride him over to Becky's place to watch her do barrel racing with her horse Storm. There were plenty of piles of dirty brown snow still on the ground, but it was melting fast. After yesterday's blinding sunshine, today's heavy gray sky was quite a contrast. And the rain was coming down hard.

"Weird weather!" Ivy remarked to Bert as she moved to the front of the bus.

"Yep. Not good for places along the river. Imagine it's rising mighty fast."

"See you tomorrow." Ivy climbed down the bus steps and onto the road. She quickly pulled her hood up. It was pouring rain, the clamor drowning out the sound of the bus driving off.

Ivy noticed the big sliding barn door was open. Curious, she stepped into the dark barn. Eddie was there, putting the saddle blanket on Bearcat's back. What the heck? Why was he riding her horse? Ivy felt her irritation rise but then remembered that Bearcat didn't belong to her; her grandfather was clear that the Baldridges could take him back whenever they wanted.

Eddie hadn't notice Ivy, so she came to the front of the stall where she wouldn't startle him. "Hi, Eddie. What's going on?"

Eddie glanced at her for a minute, then lifted the saddle and settled it on Bearcat. "Get the bridle." Eddie's somber tone meant this was serious. She had a lot of questions but decided they could wait. She set down her book bag and hurried to the tack room. When she returned, Eddie fastened the back cinch and took the bridle.

"River is coming up fast. Sheep are in trouble." He stuck his fingers in the back of Bearcat's mouth, encouraging the horse to open his teeth for the bit. Bearcat complied, and Eddie lifted the top of the bridle over his ears, fastening it below Bearcat's chin. He led Bearcat out of the barn and climbed on the saddle. "Hop on the back. You can help."

Ivy thought about telling her grandmother first but decided they'd better hurry. Eddie took his foot out of the stirrup so she could step in and swing up behind him. He gave Bearcat a gentle kick to get him running, and Ivy grabbed tight around Eddie's waist to keep from falling off. They took off down the driveway and onto the road as the rain pelted down. At the Baldridge driveway, they turned in and raced through the farmyard to an open gate leading to a large pasture.

The river water had flooded a corner of the low-lying pasture and Bathilda was there, sloshing through the shin-high water towards a flock of sheep. There must be fifty or so. As they waded closer, Bathilda motioned for Eddie to go around the other way behind the flock. Bathilda's dog Shep was near her at the edge of the flock, but he seemed reluctant to go into the water, instead barking loudly and pacing.

"You get off now," Eddie told Ivy. "Go help Bathilda."

Ivy wasn't sure how to help, but she slid off Bearcat's back and stood, looking at the situation. The sheep were running back and forth, uncertain which way to go. It was then that Ivy spotted baby lambs among the group, some of them barely keeping their heads above the water. The water was quickly rising.

Eddie circled to the left of the sheep, attempting to get behind them and herd them to higher ground. The sheep were bleating, and Shep barked more loudly. Bathilda headed the other way, wading in water almost up to her knees now. The rain was coming down hard, but Bathilda seemed oblivious to it. Some of the sheep were frozen in place, looking for a leader to follow. The mothers bleated loudly to their babies, and the lambs answered with a mournful high-pitched sound, like nothing Ivy had heard before. She didn't know which way to go, then decided to head to the left, away from Bathilda and Shep, when some of the flock headed that way.

One of the larger sheep took the lead and headed directly towards Ivy. She looked up to see Eddie gesturing wildly, but she didn't know what he was trying to tell her. Now, the whole group headed towards Ivy, and she ran to the right, but her fast movement seemed to panic the group, and they turned around, heading back towards the higher water. She had made things worse! Ivy's chest felt tight, and her throat scratched with thirst despite the water all around her. Her light tennis shoes were heavy with water and her feet were numb with the cold. The rain continued to pour and Shep kept barking as the frantic sheep held their heads up and continued bleating. Ivy could feel her nerves on edge and her whole body felt brittle.

The sheep were treading through the water more slowly now, and Ivy couldn't understand why they didn't know how to rescue themselves. Eddie and Bathilda were circling in closer behind them and Ivy traversed around to the edge of the herd. Bathilda grabbed a lamb, lifted it out of the water, and ran to a high spot in the pasture. Eddie dismounted and yelled "Stay" to Bearcat, grabbed another baby, and headed to the same location. Bearcat stood in place, not moving. They were picking up the exhausted babies one by one and Ivy waded into the flock and picked up a lamb. The little animal was almost limp with exhaustion, and Ivy was surprised by how heavy it was, its wool soaked up like a sponge.

Some of the adult sheep followed their babies to higher ground, and the rescuers continued until finally only a few more lambs were left in the water. Shep guarded the flock to ensure those out of the water stayed put, but his barking added to the cacophony as the terrified bleating continued.

Bathilda and Eddie grabbed the last two lambs and carried them to safety. Ivy took one last look around and noticed a light spot in the water about ten feet away. Was that another baby over there? She waded over and pulled a tiny lamb out of the water. It was completely limp, motionless. Ivy stood for a second, unsure what to do until Bathilda motioned for her to bring it. When she got close, Bathilda grabbed the lamb and held its back end high, so its head hung down. Water trickled out of its mouth when she slapped it on the back several times. She laid the still body on the ground, gently pushed on its chest and then opened its mouth to blow air down its throat. She repeated the motions as Ivy stood watching, hoping and praying that Bathilda could save this wet little bundle of wool. After a couple of minutes, the baby began to breathe; its movements were weak, but it was alive. Bathilda held the lamb close to her body, rubbing it gently up and down to warm it. A nervous mother approached.

"Your little guy might make it," Bathilda told the ewe. "We're going to take it to the barn and warm it up."

Then, Ivy saw how Bathilda looked: drenched from head to toe, her face and hair smeared with mud. She was smiling, pure joy lighting up her face. Ivy had never seen Bathilda look so happy.

"Ivy, you saved this little guy." Bathilda beamed.

"You're the one who saved it," Ivy said.

"But I didn't see him, you did. You did a good thing."

Eddie came closer, leading Bearcat. He, too, was sopping wet, breathing heavily, his cheeks flushed and the scar on his temple an angry red. Bearcat looked calm, unfazed by the whole situation.

"C'mon, Eddie, let's get these babies in the barn to warm up. We only have a little time." Bathilda turned to Shep. "You never did like to swim, did you, Shep?" She pointed to the barn. "Get 'em in the barn." Then she showed her hand to the dog, palm up. "Slow."

Following her command, Shep slowly herded the flock towards the barn, nipping at their heels to get the exhausted sheep moving. The sheep slogged along in a group, finally headed in the right direction.

"You go on and take your horse home," Bathilda directed Ivy. "Get yourself dry."

Eddie handed the reins to her and smiled. "Bearcat did good."

As they walked out of the pasture towards the barn, Ivy was surprised by how warm she suddenly felt, even though she was soaked to the bone. She couldn't wait to tell her grandfather she had saved a baby sheep. That should make him so proud.

Etola

ETOLA HAD HIGH HOPES for the day, but everything seemed to go downhill from the minute she woke up. The first thing she noticed was the sickening smell of melting manure in the barnyard, always pungent this time of year. Then she realized it was going to rain — on the one day she and Arlo had planned a nice picnic. They needed to wait until Arlo finished his chores and Etola had said a mid-afternoon picnic was fine with her since it should be the warmest part of the day.

The plan was to take a drive over to Highplains — they had a big county park with an old carousel, a romantic gazebo, and a large tulip garden. Etola figured the tulips wouldn't be blooming yet, but just the sight of those green shoots coming up should cheer them up after this miserably long winter. Not that she'd told Arlo, but she'd heard that the gazebo was a popular place for men to propose. It might be a little early for that, but they had been seeing each other steadily now for about two months.

Etola was in charge of the picnic, and she went all out. Fried chicken, potato salad, homemade pickles, buttermilk biscuits, and black bottom pie. She had the wicker basket all packed and ready to go when Arlo showed up at two o'clock. When Etola let him in, he didn't look very excited.

"Howdy, Etola," Arlo said, giving her a peck on the cheek. "You sure you still want to try to do this? It's looking awful dark to the north. Can't see that it's going to stop any time soon."

"You never know, Arlo. I've seen the weather turn around more times than not. And even if it doesn't, we'll enjoy an outing. I can use some new scenery after all this time of being stuck inside."

Arlo looked a little dubious, but he reluctantly agreed. "OK then. I can tell you've got your heart set on going."

It was only sprinkling when they left the house, but as they drove closer to Highplains, it rained harder. "Starting to rain cats and dogs now," Etola said.

Arlo gripped the steering wheel a little tighter and slowed down. Finally, Etola spotted the sign for Oakwood County Park, and they turned in. Theirs was the only car in the parking lot, and they sat there for a bit, listening to the rain pounding on the metal roof.

At the edge of the park, Etola spotted the sweet little gazebo. It was octagonal, with white wooden slats and a low railing surrounding it. Above the railing were tall, narrow pillars and a steep, pointed roof, like something out of a fairy tale. Four little steps led the way to the center. It looked just perfect for a romantic picnic for two.

"Should we just eat in the car?" Arlo asked. "I'm mighty hungry after that drive."

"Let's make a run for that gazebo. I need some fresh air." Without waiting for a reply, Etola opened the car door, grabbed the picnic basket, and took off for the gazebo. Arlo trotted behind her. Etola had hoped for a table or a bench in the gazebo, but there was nothing but a bare wooden floor. It was a small space, not as big as it looked from a distance.

On top of that, the roof had sprung a leak. A steady stream of water was pouring down in the middle of the floor. No dry space was large enough for a picnic, even if they sat on the floor.

"Not what it's cracked up to be," Etola said.

Arlo looked around. "There's a band shell over there. They have concerts in the summer. Looks like it should be dry. Here, let me carry the basket."

They scurried across the wet and muddy lawn, climbed up the steps to the small stage, and headed toward the back, where it was covered and dry.

"You sure you want to do this?" Arlo asked.

Etola was determined to salvage the day. "Why sure, Arlo. Someday, we'll look back on this and have a good belly laugh."

Etola spread out the red-checkered tablecloth and they eased down onto the cold cement, both sopping wet. Arlo repeatedly said how delicious everything was, but it wasn't even close to the picnic Etola had imagined. She didn't mention it, but she could swear the whole place smelled like a colony of feral cats had taken up residence there.

On the drive back home, Arlo turned up the heat as high as it would go. They both were wet and shivering and Arlo was quiet all the way home. When they pulled into the driveway and stopped, Etola put her hand on Arlo's shoulder and leaned closer. "Well, that was fun, Arlo. Even if Mother Nature didn't cooperate."

"Thanks for the picnic food. You outdid yourself." Arlo said. His voice sounded tight, and he tapped the steering wheel with his index finger.

There was an awkward silence. Surely Arlo would lean over and give her a kiss? Arlo did lean slightly towards her but then seemed to change his mind and backed away, looking straight ahead. Was it her breath?

Suddenly, there was a loud rapping on Etola's window, and she jumped in alarm. She rolled down the window, and there was Bathilda's mud-streaked face, leaning in and looking intense.

"I need your help in the barn. Lambs nearly all drowned." Then Bathilda stomped off, hunched over and looking like some kind of mud monster.

"I'll stay and help," Arlo said.

"Probably better if you just go. Thanks again for the drive."

Etola grabbed the basket and opened the door. Nope, not at all the day she had hoped for. And why was Arlo acting like there was something stuck in his craw that he couldn't seem to spit out. Etola didn't imagine it was anything good.

Ivy

THE HOUSE WAS QUIET when Ivy got home from school. Her grandmother had left her a note saying she was picking up her grandfather at the implement dealer. Then they'd stop at the grocery store on the way home, so it would probably be four-thirty before they were home. She told Ivy to help herself to peanut butter cookies. Beside the note was a letter from her mother. Ivy bit her lip and ripped it open.

Dear Ivy,

I wanted to let you know that every so often, I see my Feel Right commercial on television late at night. I know this is just the beginning! When I watch the commercials for Alka Seltzer I know I could do a lot better than that actress.

In the meantime, I've taken a part-time job at a dry cleaner – just until I get a few more acting jobs and can stockpile some money. It's taking so much longer than I thought to get my big break.

Your grandmother said it's time for me to tell you. I thought about telling you a few times before this, but then I didn't know why it mattered. After all these years, I've tried to forget about it.

You do have a father. Haha, well I guess that's not a surprise since everybody has a father. Anyway, he's still alive, and his name is Hank. Hank was a good person with a big heart and wanted to marry me. But I was too young and it wouldn't have worked out.

After that I went to live with Aunt Lillian in Omaha, where you were born. So everything turned out all right in the end.

I don't think Hank knows anything about you, and he probably has a big family of his own by now, so it's better to leave well enough alone. I know I pretended he wasn't alive, but some things just cause too many bad feelings.

Luv ya bunches,
Your Mom

Ivy reread the letter, more slowly this time, hoping there was essential information she'd missed the first time. But that was it, that was all there was. Her mind boiled with a stew of emotions: at first, she was shocked that her mother had lied to her all these years. Then mostly angry. Jaw-clenching, teeth-grinding, "I hate her" kind of angry.

She stuffed the letter in her back pocket and slipped into the dining room. She knew the family photos were stored at the bottom of the buffet, so she sat on the floor and opened the heavy drawer. Ivy searched through all the albums and all the loose photos gathered in small boxes, especially looking for a man with a white straw cowboy hat or a man with a horse. Or a man with her mother. But she never saw anyone who looked like he could be her father. No one at all.

She sat on the floor for a long time until she heard a car in the driveway. Then she quickly shut the drawer and scurried to her bedroom so her grandparents wouldn't see her tears.

Hattie

THE SUN WAS SHINING brightly, and Hattie felt like the whole countryside was smiling at that moment. After the seemingly endless winter, both two-leggeds and four-leggeds seemed giddy with relief that spring was on its way. Today was a lovely fifty-five degrees, and Hattie noticed a little patch of purple pasque flowers peeking out from the side of the yard near the clothesline when she returned from feeding the chickens. Pup was sniffing under the big cottonwood tree, the seeds just beginning to fall, when Hattie arrived at the kitchen door.

"C'mon Pup. Do you want to go in now?"

Pup ignored Hattie, scampering to the other side of the tree where he couldn't be seen.

"Alright then, you stay out for a while. I can't blame you for wanting to soak up this sunshine."

Hattie opened the screen door and left the storm door open; the house could use a good airing out. She washed her hands, then lifted the flour sack dishtowel from a bowl of rising bread dough. She gave the dough a solid punch, heard the burp of air escaping, and covered the bowl again. She was reaching for her recipe box when she heard a car on the gravel driveway. Alarmed about Pup, who was prone to chasing cars, Hattie trotted out.

"Pup! Come here!" Her heart leapt for a second when Pup ran across the yard and straight toward the car's tires, racing on his short little legs to bark at the intruder and defend his territory. But luckily, it was Arlo who had spotted Pup and stopped his car midway up the drive.

Arlo opened the car door and Pup ran to jump on his favorite visitor. "Now, Pup, you could get yourself killed running after cars. What's the matter with you?" Arlo chided the dog as he got out of the car and walked toward the house, stopping once to give Pup his usual Milk-Bone.

Hattie was happy to see Arlo. It had been weeks since he'd come to visit, and though Hattie had told herself that Arlo was a nuisance, she missed his regular visits.

"Hello. I don't have the coffee pot on, but it will take only a minute. C'mon in."

"No need to bother with coffee; I'm only here for a few minutes. It's so nice out. How about we just sit on the porch swing?"

Hattie agreed though it felt odd to be sitting so close to Arlo on the two-seater swing. They'd never sat here together, and she felt uncomfortable about the whole thing, especially because his Old Spice seemed particularly strong today. She was relieved when Pup begged to be up on the bench with them, and she squeezed the little dog between them. They looked out across the front yard, the lawn lush green and dotted with elm trees. Across the road, in the distance, a tractor was slowly plowing the dark black soil.

"How have you been? I haven't seen you for a while."

"Yep, I know. That's what I'm here to talk about."

Hattie stared at Arlo. "Uh, oh. I did something to offend you."

Arlo laid his hand on her forearm. She felt herself tense up, and Arlo must have felt it too, because he removed his hand.

"No, it's nothing like that. It's just that ... I'm not sure how to tell you this. You know I think the world of you, and I've been trying to show you that for the last two years."

Hattie looked over at the row of poplars along the driveway, their leaves gently swaying. Her stomach churned and her ears felt suddenly hot.

Arlo continued. "Seems like I've been making you more uncomfortable than anything else."

"Now, that's not true. You don't make me feel uncomfortable," Hattie denied, feeling uneasy even as she said it.

"Well, that's the impression I was getting. So anyways ..." Arlo looked off into the distance. Hattie was silent.

"I wanted to make sure you agreed that we had broken up."

"Broken up? There was nothing to break up!" Hattie's voice rose more than she intended it to.

Arlo's eyes widened and he shifted in the chair. "I wanted you to know that I've been seeing Etola lately. Wanted to make sure that I told you myself and see that you're okay with it."

Hattie lifted her mouth into a smile. "Arlo, of course, I'm okay with it. You and I are just friends, always have been. And I'm happy for you and Etola."

Arlo's shoulders relaxed, and a soft smile crossed his face. "Etola's a real nice lady, and, well, it seems like she's enjoying spending time with me." Hattie saw a slight shimmer in his eyes and for a moment he looked more handsome than she had remembered.

"Of course she's enjoying it. You're good company." Hattie managed a small pat on his shoulder as she stood. "I'd best be getting in the house. My bread dough is probably rising sky high by now. Thanks for coming by."

"You betcha. And you know, if you ever need anything, anything at all, I'm only a phone call away."

Hattie nodded and picked up Pup. "You take care of yourself. And give my best to Etola."

She stood in the doorway holding Pup and watching Arlo walk to his car, his shoulders slumped. Out of the sunshine in the shady part of the porch, she felt a shiver run through her tired body. She hugged Pup closer to her. "Poor Pup. You're going to miss him, aren't you?"

For a minute, Hattie felt like she might cry. But she steeled herself and set Pup on the floor. "C'mon. Let's get that dough into the oven."

Hattie looked forward to the taste of the soft white bread, warm from the oven and covered with extra butter and stubble berry jam. It reminded her of how her mother would provide comfort when Hattie was having a particularly bad day. After a particularly bad dream. Dreams that always included her stepfather, Ray.

Tilly

TILLY TOOK A MENTAL inventory of the supper menu: beef goulash, French-style canned green beans, and peach pie. She wanted everything ready for James to sit down to one of his favorite meals as soon as he got home from work. For the last three days he'd been helping to pour concrete for Bob Hauge. It was only temporary, and it was back breaking work, but it was something. Tilly appreciated that James was the kind of man willing to do almost anything to help feed his family. Not like some men she'd heard of. She knew James constantly worried about making ends meet so maybe her news would help him relax.

The kids seemed to be picking up on Tilly's excitement too. TJ kept pulling his big brother Robby by the arm over to baby Milo and telling Robby to kiss Milo. Robby obliged, and then the baby would shriek in laughter, and Robby would run off to hide again. The game continued as TJ found Robby and pulled him back. It wasn't often the three boys played together, and Tilly was delighted, even if the baby's piercing shrieks were a little hard to handle. She hoped Mildred didn't hear them and come stomping over to find out if Tilly was torturing her children. Even in the tiny trailer, Robby found multiple hiding places, and the game continued for a long time. All three boys were worn out when James came through the door.

James looked tired, too. And dirty. His brown Dickie work pants were covered with a layer of white concrete dust, and his face was streaked with grime. Undeterred, Tilly kissed him as he removed his steel-toed work boots by the front door. Robby and TJ came running up to hug him, and James smiled at the homecoming.

"Hi, honey. You go wash up. Supper's ready. Goulash tonight!"

Tilly got the older boys seated at the table and Milo into the highchair. When James sat down, she asked him to say grace and watched to see that the boys all folded their hands and bowed their heads.

"God is great, and God is good; let us thank Him for our food. Amen." James said.

The boys and Tilly dutifully repeated, "Amen".

Tilly passed the goulash, and James put a pile on his plate and then looked around at the other empty plates. "Don't worry, there's plenty. I made a double batch; I knew you'd be hungry."

James heaped more onto his plate and took a big mouthful. Tilly passed the bowl of green beans. "How'd work go today?"

Between mouthfuls, James said, "Good. Big job. Old man Brandt's gonna have the longest paved driveway in the county. Guess hog farming has been pretty good the last few years."

"How long until you're done?"

"Probably only two more days." A shadow of concern crossed James' face.

Tilly decided this was the moment. "I had a call from Mr. Cranston. He was happy with the St. Patrick's and Easter windows I did for him."

"That's nice, sweetie. You did a good job." James continued eating.

"He liked them so much he called to offer me a job. Part-time. He wants me to keep painting the windows and work on all the smaller signs in the store. You know, the ones that announce sale items or new products. And do the artwork for the newspaper advertisements!"

James stopped eating to gaze at her. She'd fixed her hair in the way she knew he loved, pulled up, and twisted at the back. She thought it accented her eyes.

"That's great. But what about the kids?"

Tilly had known this would be his first question. "Well, he said I could do most of the work after hours in the evenings and on the weekends. It sounds like it would be about twelve to fifteen hours a week. $1.50 an hour."

James leaned back in his chair, chewing his food. "Tilly, you know I never wanted to have you have to work. I'm doing the best I can with lining up odd jobs ... wouldn't be surprised if work at the elevator starts up in a few weeks."

Her words rushed out. "But I want to do this! I've always dreamed about being able to do something artistic. I won't let it interfere with the kids. I could even go in after the kids are in bed and do all the work late. Mr. Cranston says he'll give me a key and I can set my own hours."

"Now, sweetheart, I don't want you in that store alone in the middle of the night. We'll work it out. I'll watch the kids after supper, or if I'm not working that day, you can go in earlier."

"Right! I could have supper all ready for you to feed the kids." Tilly felt a wave of relief now that James was on board.

"Maybe my mother will be willing to help out once in a while."

"Maybe." *When hell freezes over.*

James added, "But let's see how it goes. I'm not sure I'm okay with this as a permanent thing, maybe just until I can get back to steady work."

Tilly smiled at James. "That's fine. We'll see how it goes. I'll give Mr. Cranston a call tomorrow. I think he wants me to start this weekend."

Before James could change his mind, Tilly got up and hugged him from behind on her way to the kitchen counter. "Did you see what I baked? Peach pie!"

She held up the pie and looked at the scene across the room. A handsome husband and three darling boys, all enjoying the meal she had prepared for them. And a new job. Tilly couldn't imagine her life being any better. Well, maybe a different house, something a little bigger. And not in Mildred's backyard.

But it felt like they were on their way.

May 1964

Etola

IT WAS ONLY SIX o'clock when Etola was awakened by Eddie knocking on her bedroom door and telling her to come to the barn. One of the ewes needed help. Usually, this was Bathilda's job, but Bathilda had been under the weather the last few days, hit by a gallbladder attack that had laid her low. Bathilda was in a lot of pain, so Etola didn't mind helping — even if this wasn't how she had planned to spend the morning. She had in mind getting herself gussied up to run a few errands in town in the hopes she'd run into Arlo. It had been over two weeks since she'd seen him, and their last date had been a bit of a bust. A picnic gone sideways.

Half asleep, Etola hurried to the utility room and threw on the first barn clothes she could find. Then she remembered how Bathilda was always preaching about the importance of cleanliness in lambing, so she tromped back to the kitchen and washed her hands with hot, soapy water.

When she entered the dim and dusty barn, she heard a weak, bleating sound coming from one of the stalls. Etola walked over to where Eddie stood and kneeled on a burlap bag on the straw to have a look. Suffolks are known for being good lambers, but this ewe was in trouble. Etola could see the tip of one leg and the black nose of the lamb emerging from the birth canal, but the tired ewe was panting hard, and Etola didn't think she could push the lamb out any further.

"How long has she been in labor?"

"Dunno, but too long." Eddie stroked the thick oatmeal-colored wool on the ewe's back to try to calm her.

Etola leaned in for a closer look at the black-faced ewe lying on her side, panicked with her eyes rolling back. "Is she a maiden?"

"Yes."

If only Bathilda were here, she'd be so much better in this situation. Etola scanned the checklist in her head: first, make sure the lamb was in the correct position. In this case, Etola needed to make sure both forelegs were coming first, and that the lamb's head was lying over its knees. She could only see one leg, so the other must be bent at the knee. She'd have to reposition the lamb. She'd rather have Eddie do that part, but she knew that her hands were much smaller and there was less chance of injuring the uterus if she did it. Together, they lifted the ewe from under her chest and back legs to get her to stand up.   "Got the lubricant?" Etola asked.

Eddie handed her the bottle, and Etola pushed back her shirt sleeve and covered her hand and forearm with the slippery gel. She squeezed lubricant into the birth canal and gently inserted one hand to slide the lamb back toward the uterus. She could feel the lamb's head. *That's good, it's in the right place, so just the foreleg needed to be moved.* She inched her hand along and found the second leg. This was the part she hated; made her stomach do flip-flops. But it had to be done, so she gritted her teeth and closed her eyes, cupped the hoof in her palm and carefully corrected the leg so the toes were pointed forward. Bit by bit, Etola removed her hand. Now, both legs were barely emerging from the ewe's birth canal.

Etola looked at the ewe's slender face. "C'mon, little mama. Can you do it now?"

The ewe was still panting, her dark eyes glassy and unfocused. Eddie and Etola sat down to wait. After another ten minutes, the lamb had emerged about one-third of the way out of the birth canal, but the ewe was completely exhausted.

Eddie hauled over two straw bales, stacking one on top of the other. Together they lifted the weak ewe and positioned her over the bales, her back legs dangling. Eddie stepped away and came back with three small birthing cords. He had often assisted Bathilda in this process, so he was steady in his movements. He placed a cord with a running noose on each leg above the fetlock and the third cord behind both ears and between the jaws. Then he kneeled.

"I'll pull, you steady her,"

Etola felt a little sick to her stomach. "Be gentle."

Eddie nodded, a frown on his face. "I know."

As Etola held the ewe's back legs, Eddie applied traction to tug the lamb downward, pulling one foreleg slightly ahead of the other to narrow the width of the lamb's chest. He tugged slowly and steadily; his face contorted in concentration. The lamb emerged inch by heart-pounding inch. Etola held her breath, her chest tight. That poor mama and baby. It wasn't until the lamb was entirely out that Etola could feel herself exhale.

Once the lamb was freed, Eddie cleared the mucus from its mouth and airways and held it up by its hind legs. It was a miniature version of its mother, black-faced and black-legged, with a creamy beige body. Eddie swung the lamb back and forth ever so slightly to remove more fluids from its airways. The lamb let out a weak bleat, but the ewe didn't look at him. Etola and Eddie lifted the ewe off the bales carefully and laid her down in the straw.

"Here you go, mama," Eddie said. He placed the lamb by the mother's head. She still didn't look at her baby. The first minutes between the ewe and her lamb are critical, so Etola picked it up and moved it closer to the ewe's nose. Finally, the ewe sniffed the lamb, and it bleated again, a little stronger. The ewe nuzzled the baby and then lifted her head to lick it. In a few minutes, the ewe dragged up her tired body to stand, and the lamb struggled to its feet and began to nurse.

Etola and Eddie watched for a while, smiling at each other. Etola felt the sharp prick of tears welling up. There was nothing quite like the miracle of birth and the bonding between a mother and a newborn. Sometimes she wondered what it would be like to give birth herself. It was something she would never know.

After some time, when they were satisfied that both mama and baby would be all right, Eddie and Etola stood.

"I'll wait for the afterbirth and make sure there's not another one on the way. Can you make us some coffee?" Eddie asked. Etola nodded. Coffee sounded good, and she looked forward to getting herself cleaned up.

As she walked out of the barn, a pickup was turning off the road and coming up the driveway. *What the heck? Who is here this early?* At the same instant that Etola recognized Arlo's pickup, she realized what she must look like. She was wearing one of Eddie's old plaid shirts, a pair of brown work overalls (about four sizes too big) that she had thrown on over her flannel pajamas, muddy boots, and a red handkerchief tied over her uncombed hair. To make matters worse, she was covered with birth fluid and muck. Heaven only knows what her face must look like.

Arlo had spotted Etola and waved, so there was no turning back now. She walked toward the pickup, wiping her hands on the overalls, and Arlo stepped out, holding a pink tin cone with a thin metal handle, brimming with colorful goodies.

"Here you go. I meant to hang it from your door and slip away before you caught me," Arlo admitted, blushing. Etola hesitated to take the basket. She had almost forgotten about the lovely May first tradition she'd celebrated as a girl — delivering a May basket to someone you liked and sneaking away before they spied you.

"Why, Arlo, you're about as sweet as a pecan pie. I forgot that today's the first of May. It's been a long time since I've thought about May baskets."

"Well, take a look." Arlo shifted from one foot to the other, his arm outstretched.

Etola looked more closely. Arlo had arranged a jumble of candies with a few bright orange and red tulips. Poking out from the middle was a small envelope.

"Go ahead, open it."

While Arlo held the basket, Etola pulled the card out and opened the envelope. She felt a little wobbly. On the front was a May Day greeting, and when she opened it, she read these hand-printed words: Will you be my sweetheart? Forever?

Etola was stunned, rendered motionless by the powerful emotions of the morning. First, the breathtaking birth, and now this.

"You don't have to answer me now. But since you caught me delivering the basket, you owe me a kiss."

Etola hesitated. "Lordy, Arlo, just look at me! I must look like something the cat dragged in."

Then, Arlo spoke the words that Etola would remember the rest of her life. A moment in time that changed how she thought about herself forever.

"Etola, you have never looked more beautiful."

Ivy

IVY COULD FEEL THE blood rushing through her veins as she rode Bearcat down the dirt lane home from Becky's farm, beside the shelterbelt of tall poplars and blooming crab apples that smelled fresh and sweet. She was careful to walk Bearcat after their afternoon adventure. She had never heard of barrel racing before Becky mentioned it earlier in the week and couldn't believe how much she loved it.

It only took one time watching Becky and Storm to catch onto the pattern: around to the left, circling counterclockwise around the barrel, then race to the barrel on the right, rotating around it clockwise, and then head towards the barrel in the back. One more clockwise circle and then race back to the finish line. Becky said you could start to the right or left as long as you went in a cloverleaf pattern. In the beginning, Ivy had mostly had Bearcat trot, but after a few times, she trusted her ability to stay in the saddle, leaning in as he turned and urging him to run. Becky said Bearcat was a natural.

They didn't have a way to time how fast they're going, but Becky said the winner at last year's 4-H horse show had a time of seventeen and a half seconds. She had placed third at nineteen seconds, winning a pretty red ribbon she hung from her bedroom mirror. The year before, she had won first place and had a silver belt buckle to show for it.

It had been a fun afternoon. What a difference it made to finally have warm weather and bright sunshine. Everything was green and ready to bloom, and spring was shaping up to be her favorite season in South Dakota. If she had to be stuck here a little longer, at least the weather was nice.

Ivy's grandfather had seemed pleased that Ivy was learning to barrel race, but he warned Ivy to take it easy with Bearcat and let him cool down slowly — after all, he was a seventeen-year-old horse. Ivy made sure they walked all the way back to the barn, even though he pulled on the bit and wanted to hurry back, anticipating the oats he always got after a ride.

Closer to the barn, they rode past the pasture that adjoined the cattle feedlot. Bearcat veered toward the gate, where the lush, brilliant green grass stood six inches tall.

"I bet you'd love to get in there, wouldn't you?"

She rode Bearcat to the barn, then got off and slid the heavy, wide wooden door that opened to the three stalls. She led him into the first stall, removed his bridle, and guided the halter onto his head, tying the rope to the round hole in the worn manger. Then she unbuckled the cinches and carried the old leather saddle into the tack room, where she heaved it over the wooden post. She laid the saddle blanket upside down over the top, like her grandfather had shown her, so any sweat could dry. Then she grabbed a brush and a small pail of oats.

Ivy liked the sound of Bearcat's munching, the way he nibbled at the oats to grab a mouthful and then chewed slowly with his powerful molars. She liked the way the stiff brush bristles felt on Bearcat's hide as she worked her way down his neck and across his back, Bearcat occasionally giving little shivers as the brush moved across his body. She even liked the horsey, sweaty smell that lingered in her hands and clothes after riding. It was a rich animal smell that seemed wholesome and athletic. Different from the city Ivy.

She made her way to Bearcat's head, brushing around his large brown eyes with care. She stroked his velvety nose, and he nibbled her fingers in affection. She kissed his head.

"You're such a good horse. I think you deserve a reward."

She untied the rope and led Bearcat out of the barn. Instead of putting him in the feedlot pen, she continued past it to the gate of the bright green grass pasture.

"How about some nice fresh grass instead of that dry old hay?" She opened the gate and removed the halter. Bearcat trotted into the pasture a few feet and then bent his head to nibble the grass.

"Happy springtime, Bearcat!" Ivy felt happy as she hung the halter on the post and locked the gate. Maybe Grandpa had a stopwatch she could borrow for their next barrel racing practice. At least this should give them something to talk about.

Cora

CORA WAS POOPED. IT had been a long day of gardening, laundry, and cooking. But a good day — as measured by how much she'd accomplished. She might as well get ready for bed early. It was only nine o'clock, but the dishes were done and the kitchen tidy; Ivy was in her room doing homework, and Delmar was staying up to watch the nightly news.

Cora was reaching for her Ponds cold cream when she heard Delmar bellow up the stairs, "Ivy, get down here! Now!" It was a tone of voice Cora didn't hear from him often. *Was that panic in his voice? What in the world?*

Ivy opened her door, and Cora hustled to the landing.

Delmar was red-faced. "When did you put that horse in that grass pasture?"

"After I came back from Becky's," Ivy said, her voice defensive as she went down the stairs.

"When was that?"

"About noon." Cora hurried downstairs to be a part of the conversation.

269

"Son of a bitch. Stupid, stupid, girl! You're gonna kill that horse!"

Ivy's eyes went wide as saucers. She held up her hands and looked at Cora.

Cora went to Ivy's side and put her arm around her. "Delmar, you stop that! You're scaring her."

"Well, she should be scared. That horse is gonna be either crippled or dead!"

"Founder?" Cora asked, her voice almost a whisper.

"Likely. He's got his front feet stretched out like a sawhorse. Hooves hot as coals. I'm heading to Doc Toefte's to rouse him. You get Ivy out there walking that horse to the creek to cool down his feet and then back again. Just keep him moving."

Delmar stormed off. Cora turned to a white-faced Ivy, who asked, "What's happened?"

"Sweetheart, putting a horse out to green grass first thing in the spring is not good. Too much sugar in the grass can cause a horse to founder."

Ivy's brow furrowed and she asked in a trembling voice, "What does that mean?"

"It makes the hooves swell up, and then the foot bones can shift forward and cause lameness."

"Or worse?"

"In rare cases. But we don't need to think about that right now."

Ivy blinked back tears. "But I didn't know!"

Cora gave her a quick hug. "Of course you didn't. Now, you go ahead and walk Bearcat down to the creek, and I'll be out shortly. We might need to keep this up for a while."

Ivy hurried to the back door, head down, to get her boots, and Cora climbed the stairs to her bedroom to change into her barn clothes. In the hallway, she stopped in front of the crucifix on the wall and bowed her head. She hadn't done that for a long time.

Dear God, if you never answer another prayer for me, let it be this one.

Later, when she reached the creek, Ivy stood there with Bearcat, silhouetted against a sky barely lit by a crescent moon. The air was still and cold, probably only thirty degrees or so. Even from a distance, Cora could see Ivy was shivering.

"Ivy, you run back to the house to get warmer clothes on. And rubber boots. I'll walk the horse to the barn to wait for the vet."

"But I don't want to leave him!"

Cora was firm. "Go on now; we don't want you catching pneumonia."

Cora arrived at the barn with Bearcat at the same time Delmar and Doc Toefte showed up. Ivy soon joined them, her eyes red and swollen, and hovered in the background as Doc Toefte examined the horse, listening to his heart and lifting his feet to feel the temperature of his hooves. The vet took a small hammer from his leather bag and gave the front hoof a tap — Bearcat lifted his hoof quickly and gave a slight whinny. Cora moved close to Ivy to hold her hand, but Ivy pulled away. The poor thing, she must be so scared.

Finally, Doc spoke. "Could be laminitis, but too soon to tell. Good thing the horse isn't overweight, that'll help. Best thing to do is keep doing what you're doing: walk him down to the creek, get those hooves in the cold water for a half hour at a time, then out of the water. Keep that going for the next twelve hours or so. Don't feed him anything during that time, then start up slowly. No green grass — or grain. Just hay. It'll take a while to know if he's gonna be lame."

He turned to Ivy, "Don't make yourself sick standing in that cold water all night, young lady. Get some help. And don't take it too hard."

Ivy nodded, then glanced at her grandfather. Delmar's jaw was set, and he avoided her eyes. Ivy led Bearcat back to the creek, her

271

shoulders hunched over and her head down. While Doc Toefte gathered his things, Cora whispered to Delmar, "She couldn't have known." Delmar didn't respond.

Cora hustled to the house and picked up the phone. "Davis 4214, please." In a minute, she spoke again. "I'm sorry to call you so late, Hattie. Ivy's horse was in the green grass too long and might have foundered. We'll need to keep him in and out of the creek overnight. Can you start the phone tree to see who can help?"

Confident she could rely on Hattie for anything, Cora pulled out the coffee pot she used for large gatherings. They were going to need a lot of coffee. She took a loaf of bread from the freezer and grabbed a long roll of beef salami from the pantry.

In a little while, Hattie called back to tell Cora she'd organized the Wednesday Club into rotating sixty-minute shifts. The Baldridge's, including Eddie, were taking the first three hours starting at eleven, followed by Hattie, Florence, Cora, and Tilly. Then, back to Ivy. Arlo would show up at seven.

After Eddie arrived, Cora encouraged Ivy to rest, but when Ivy came down for breakfast, she looked exhausted from worry and said she'd been too worried to sleep. Cora made a hearty meal of eggs and bacon that no one seemed to have the appetite for. Delmar sat silent and scowling. Cora made small talk, but neither Ivy nor Delmar looked at one another. To Cora, it seemed like something between them had broken.

Ivy

IT WAS A WARM spring morning and Ivy loved feeling the sun on her shoulders as she and Bearcat walked back from the creek. She'd been taking him there almost every day to stand in the cold water to help prevent founder as the vet had advised. She also wasn't feeding him any grain or letting him into the pasture. So far Bearcat showed no signs of limping. Ivy gave her grandfather a report on his condition every evening at dinner and though he didn't seem as mad at her, he still didn't say much, just nodded and pursed his lips together. Her grandma said it would take time to build up his trust again, but it seemed like he'd been holding a grudge way too long.

Ivy let herself relax into the gentle swaying rhythm of her feet in the stirrups and her arms loosely holding the reins. She felt so comfortable in the saddle, soothed by the creaking sound the leather made as they walked along. She reflected on her life — only three more weeks until her junior year would be finished, and she was finally hanging out with a couple of other girls at lunchtime. And she liked Becky a lot. She appreciated that they could complain together about the clod Lance Lane. He and

Wanda had never really lasted as a couple after the Valentine's Day dance, and though Lance tried to be all sweet to her, always saying hi and telling her she looked nice, Ivy pretended she didn't hear him. She could tell that bothered him, but she didn't care.

Ivy was just entering the farmyard when her grandmother came rushing out of the house. "Here, I'll go tie up Bearcat. You run in the house now, there's a phone call for you."

The overly cheery voice on the line said, "Ivy! I was hoping you'd be there!"

Ivy wished she had stayed at the creek longer and had missed this call. She'd had a sinking feeling it would be her mother, given what day it was.

"Hi, Mom," Ivy wondered if her voice sounded as flat as she felt towards her mother. She hadn't spoken with her or written back since she'd gotten her mother's letter almost a month ago.

"And?"

"And what?" Ivy asks, her mind racing ahead for an excuse to get off the phone.

"Don't you know what day this is?" Her mother had that fake, coy tone of voice. Like she was acting.

"Uh ... nope," Ivy lied.

"It's Mother's Day," Vonda Marie said brightly.

"Great. Happy Mother's Day."

"You could sound a little more enthusiastic, young lady."

Ivy held the phone away from her face, stuck out her tongue at it, and then brought it back to her ear again. "I don't feel very enthusiastic after that last letter from you." There was a long pause on the other end of the line. Surely, her mother hadn't forgotten. Ivy heard a deep exhale of breath. "There's so much you just don't know, Ivy. Things that weren't appropriate to tell a child."

Ivy felt the blood rush to her face, and she was suddenly hot all over. "Yeah, well, I'm not a child now. So why don't you tell me more about him? Like, if he's not dead, is he around here? Have

I been seeing my father and not even known it? What the heck, mom!" Ivy was yelling now.

"Listen to me, Ivy, I don't know where your father is, nor do I want to. He wasn't a part of your life, and I don't know why he even matters to you now. He wasn't the one raising you all these years. I was!"

There were so many things Ivy could say: about how it was Aunt Lillian who had raised her. About how she was the adult in the house after Aunt Lil was gone. About how she felt like her mother was burdened by having a child, and not happy about it. But she didn't say any of that. What good would it do now?

"Why did you lie to me?" Ivy was surprised by how her voice sounded so small, like a little girl's.

"It was just a little white lie; I was only trying to protect you. I never thought you'd be so upset about it."

Ivy let the silence speak for her. A long silence.

Finally, her mother said, "I really need to go. I'm at a phone booth and someone else needs to use the phone now. Tell your grandmother Happy Mother's Day from me."

Ivy didn't say goodbye, she just slowly put the receiver down to hang up the phone. She leaned against the wall, her chest heaving. Then she closed her eyes and covered her heart with both hands. To warm herself.

Wednesday Club Minutes

MAY 13, 1964

The Wednesday Club met at the home of Miss Bathilda Baldridge and Miss Etola Baldridge. The meeting was called to order by President Bathilda. The club motto was recited.

The roll call topic was the ideal characteristics of a mother. Each member told what they felt was the most important characteristic.

Tilly Halversen – patience

Cora Hanson – attention

Bathilda Baldridge – teaching children how to do things correctly

Hattie Dunlop – protection

Florence Lane – generosity

Etola Baldridge – grace and charm

Ivy Hanson – honesty

Ivy read the minutes from the April meeting and Bathilda made a correction to the treasurer's report. The balance was $60.56, not $60.65. A motion was made to approve the minutes as corrected. All members voted yes. Ivy read a card from the Harrington family thanking the members for the funeral flowers. Club members commented that the funeral had been well attended, as Grandma Harrington was well-loved in the community. Ivy thanked the Wednesday Club members for helping with Bearcat when they were concerned about founder. She reported that he was doing well, and she had learned a valuable lesson.

Hattie Dunlop read the treasurer's report. The balance is $58.13 after deducting the cost of the funeral flowers. Members voted to donate $8.00 to the Salvation Army.

The club was led in singing by the music chair Etola. She played the piano, and members sang "South Dakota We Love You Best."

This month's program, a newsworthy topic, was presented by Etola. She reported on the wedding of movie stars Elizabeth Taylor and Richard Burton. Etola said that Elizabeth and Richard met on the set of *Cleopatra* in 1961 and fell in love. *Cleopatra* was the biggest box office hit of last year. After a short engagement, they were married only nine days after Elizabeth's divorce from Eddie Fisher came through. Their small wedding was held March 15 at the Ritz Carlton in Montreal, with just nine people in attendance.

Etola reported that Elizabeth wore an empire style, short chiffon dress in daffodil yellow, and her hair was styled in a long ponytail entwined with lilies of the valley and white hyacinths. She wore the wedding present from her husband, a brooch that was an 18-carat emerald surrounded by diamonds. This was Elizabeth Taylor's fifth wedding and Richard Burton's second.

A short discussion followed, with members saying that the wedding was quite scandalous; even the Vatican condemned their behavior. Florence remarked that getting married on the Ides of March did not bode well for the success of the marriage. Bathilda said that she did not consider a Hollywood marriage to be the kind of program topic the Wednesday Club should be discussing, as there were many other newsworthy issues happening in the world.

Etola said this was a topic of importance to her, as she would be planning her own wedding to Arlo in June!

After congratulations and more discussion, the Wednesday Club decided to forgo next month's program topic of The War on Poverty in favor of a wedding shower for Etola. The meeting will be held at Hattie Dunlop's home.

The meeting ended with the club creed. Bathilda and Etola served a lunch of deviled eggs, asparagus with lemon sauce, and rhubarb custard pie.

Ivy Hanson, Secretary

Bathilda

WHEN BATHILDA RETURNED TO the house for breakfast at seven-fifteen, Etola was just getting up. By this time, Bathilda had fed Shep, done a complete walk-around in the pasture to check on the ewes and lambs, fed the chickens, and pulled some weeds in the vegetable garden. She had hoped she could get in and out of the kitchen without having to deal with Etola at all, but there she was, looking all sunshiny and cheerful.

"Good morning!"

"Is it?" Bathilda didn't feel like playing the happy game. She went to the icebox and pulled out the eggs, then decided she'd have the leftover piece of rhubarb pie for breakfast instead. She put the egg carton back and slammed the icebox door.

Etola raised her eyebrows. "Are you mad at me?"

Bathilda wished she could walk out of the kitchen and never have to speak with Etola again for as long as she lived. "No, why would I be mad at you?"

"Well, you haven't said a word to me since Wednesday Club. Not even a congratulations or anything."

Bathilda wanted to be happy for her sister, but she couldn't stop the words that spilled out. "Did you think that was the best way for me to learn about you and Arlo getting engaged? At Wednesday Club?"

Etola was quiet for a moment. "You're right, I'm sorry. I should have talked with you before I told the rest of the club. It just slipped out – I was all caught up in the Taylor-Burton wedding story."

"A ridiculous topic for Wednesday Club! We're supposed to better ourselves, not wallow in movie star nonsense." Bathilda sat down with her pie and ate in large bites, barely swallowing before shoveling in the next forkful. "Well, what's done is done. I suppose I should have guessed you and Arlo were getting serious. What are the plans for the big shindig?"

"Just a simple ceremony out at the little Lutheran church at Lake Dorena. Arlo knows Reverend Gerhardt, and we can get married on June twenty-seventh." Etola's words were matter of fact, but Bathilda could hear the excitement bubbling out of her.

"Then what?"

"Florence said she would host a little reception in her backyard. Probably only a few people, nothing too big. I've been making a list—"

"No, I mean, then what? You movin' into Arlo's house, or what?"

"Well, of course. You didn't think I'd get hitched and then stay here, did you?"

Bathilda finished eating her pie and then went to the sink to put her plate in. She'd wash up later. Right now, she just wanted out of the kitchen. On the way out the door, she mumbled to herself, loud enough for Etola to hear. "That figures she'd leave me to take care of everything. Me and Eddie."

Etola didn't say anything, but Bathilda could feel Etola's hurt hanging heavy in the air as she stomped out the door.

On the way to the barn, Bathilda kicked at a rock in her path. All morning, she'd been thinking about this conversation and how it would go, and this was not how she'd wanted it to go. She wanted to be more gracious. After all, Etola had waited all these years for another husband after losing her first fiancé John in such a tragic way; didn't she deserve another chance at happiness? But some other part of Bathilda had leaked out. The part that was tired of always taking care of everything. The part that was still hurting from the news of both parents dead in that car accident, leaving a brain-damaged twelve-year-old Eddie in her care. She was only nineteen years old when she was suddenly left with two siblings and a sheep farm to care for. When did Bathilda get to be happy and carefree? When did Bathilda get to have the life she chose?

While she was walking, lost in thought, Shep came tottering towards her, so excited to see her. Bathilda bent down to scratch his neck, and Shep leaned his whole body against her legs. She knew the exact spot that made Shep's eyes close, lost in pure pleasure. Good old Shep. After all these years, he was still her best friend. She didn't know what she'd do without him.

Ivy

IT WAS A BREEZY Monday and warm enough that all the windows on the bus were open. Ivy had had a pleasant ride home, helping Mary with her reading. They were halfway through *Little House on the Prairie*, a book Ivy had loved in middle school, never dreaming that she'd be living on a prairie farm one day. At least it wasn't in a sod house like the real Laura Ingalls Wilder. Still, sometimes it felt like country living was a step backwards in time.

Ivy gathered her things as they got closer to her farm. Bert slowed down for Ivy's driveway. "Hold on, Ivy. Melvin is just putting the mail in your box. Let's give him a minute."

Ivy grabbed the shiny handrail and watched the mailman close the door on the metal mailbox and pull away in his rumbling white Dodge.

"Have a good evening now," Bert said as he yanked on the handle to open the folding door.

"Night, Bert." Ivy climbed down the steps and walked to the mailbox. Usually, Grandma had picked up the mail by now; Melvin was later than usual.

Ivy pulled out the mail along with The *Prairie View Register*. As she walked up the driveway the warm breeze carried the sweet smell of the lavender lilac bushes – a whole row of them planted along the driveway. Grandma said they were her favorite flower – a sure sign that spring had finally arrived. Ivy looked through the mail to see if there are any letters for her. She hadn't heard from Val in a couple of months and wasn't expecting anything from her mother. Their last phone call had not ended well. Ivy was starting to think she might be stuck in Prairie View until she was eighteen and could move back to the city.

She was almost at the house when she glanced at the newspaper. The headline read, "Elmdale man sentenced for manslaughter." She glanced at the man's name in the photo caption: Hank Red Feather. *Hank?* The name jumped out, and she felt a sharp twinge in her gut.

When she reached the back step, she perched at the edge to read the story before she went into the house.

Hank Red Feather, 40, a resident of Prairie View for several years, was sentenced on Friday to seven years in the South Dakota State Penitentiary in Layton, S.D. Red Feather was convicted of manslaughter in the death of Bobby Sears, son of well-known Lincoln County rancher Monte Sears. Red Feather and Sears were involved in an altercation behind a tavern in Elmdale on March 27, and Sears was fatally stabbed.

The jury deliberated for over 22 hours, and Patrick Callahan, attorney for Red Feather, stated that his client was wrongly convicted and called the trial 'a travesty of justice'. Red Feather had been an employee of the Redfield Meat Packing Plant in Elmdale for 17 years after moving from Prairie View in 1947, where he worked as a horse trainer and hired man.

Ivy gazed at the photo of Hank Red Feather. She studied his thick, straight hair and dark eyes, his flat cheekbones and square jawline. He looked handsome, and very sad. She sat there a long time until her grandmother came to the screen door and peered out. "Ivy? When did you get home, sweetheart?"

Ivy didn't answer.

Her grandmother opened the screen door and sat beside her, noticing the newspaper article. She sighed and pulled Ivy into a hug. "I don't know what your mother has told you. She made me promise not to say anything, but she's had her chance, and now it's time to move on, no use trying to keep things hidden. Ask me anything you want."

Ivy blurted out, "Is this my dad?"

"Yes. Your father is Hank Red Feather."

"A murderer?"

Her grandmother closed her eyes and her shoulders dropped with a deep sigh. "Hank Red Feather is a good man. I liked him very much. I don't for a minute believe he did anything besides try to defend that young woman."

Ivy looked at her grandmother, her neck tingling.

"I went over to Elmdale when Hank was first arrested. Spoke to the sheriff on his behalf. I believe Hank was just trying to protect that woman from Bobby Sears. Bobby was the one that had the knife."

Ivy didn't understand. "Then why was Hank sent to prison?"

"Sometimes the law fails people. Especially when it's an Indian man's word against a wealthy white rancher."

"He's Indian?"

"Hank's dad was a Sioux Indian. His mother was white."

Ivy let the truth of all this sink in. A truth that instantly changed how she thought of herself and who she was. The sudden discovery of a missing piece so huge it had left a gaping hole, missing in a way that made it impossible to even imagine a complete puzzle. She was furious with her mother all over again. "How could she not tell me he was Indian?"

"Your mom wanted to protect you. From the same kind of thinking she couldn't protect Hank from. I believe Hank loved her. He would never have left you both if—."

"If what?"

Her grandmother looked away and then said, "Life would have been tough for you and your mother if she had stayed. It seemed best that she go to Omaha to live with your aunt Lil. And have you."

Ivy felt a barrage of different emotions hitting her all at once: disbelief, anger, confusion, and a bit of relief that she finally knew who her father was. She wasn't sure she could take in much more information. But there was one more thing she needed to know. "Did Hank ever try to meet me?"

"For a while, he tried to keep in contact with me to get news of your mother. I sent him pictures of you for a few years. But finally, we both decided it would be best for all if he left it alone."

Ivy's mind spun with so many more questions, but none she felt ready to ask. Her grandmother squeezed her before she stood up. "How about you and I take a walk to the garden and see if there's any lettuce ready to pick?"

"That's okay, I don't feel like it."

Her grandmother laid her hand on top of Ivy's head, and it felt comforting. "Your father is a good man. Don't ever let anyone tell you otherwise."

Ivy nodded. Her grandmother started toward the garden and then turned back. "And now that the secret is out, there's nothing to stop you from contacting him. I can get his prison address if you're interested." She gave a little smile as she walked away.

Ivy sat a little longer, staring at the photo. She reread the story. Horse trainer. Hired man. The man in the picture in the white cowboy hat, the one she'd been carrying around in her diary. The one she had found tucked in her mother's jewelry box.

285

She focused on her heartbeat, wondering if she might feel something between herself and the man in the newspaper picture. She waited, hoping. Any thin thread that would finally, after all these years, connect her to her father.

But she didn't feel anything.

Tilly

TILLY TOOK ONE LAST look around the trailer as she heard the annoying "yoo hoo!" She was feeling confident, sure she had prepared for everything. The house was picked up, and the toys were put away. All the dishes were washed, the table was set, and the casserole dish was in the refrigerator, marked with instructions. There was a large can of green beans on the counter ready for James to heat up, apples ready to slice for the boys, with a can of James' favorite fruit cocktail ready for dessert. The can opener was on the counter beside the cans. Even the boys were cooperating – TJ and Robby were playing nicely in their bedroom, and Milo was napping.

"Come in, Mildred." Tilly pulled out a clean dishtowel to hang on the oven handle.

"Hello, Tilly," Mildred's eyes scanned the living room and kitchen as she stepped through the doorway. "The house is looking nice."

"Thank you. I've been working hard today." It was rare for Mildred to compliment Tilly. Maybe she was in a good mood today.

"James should be here right at six. He's getting a ride from Al. If you wouldn't mind, I have macaroni and cheese you can put in the oven at five-thirty, so it'll be ready for him. Then he won't have to do much to get supper on the table."

Mildred surveyed the counter. "Green beans in a store-bought can? Don't you have any of those nice beans from the garden I canned?"

"Oh, we used them all up a while ago. They were so delicious. The kids loved them."

Mildred smiled. "Now, why is it you have to go into the store today?"

Tilly explained for the second time. "Mr. Cranston and his wife are leaving for Madison in the morning for his nephew's graduation. He wants to go over the advertisement for next week's *Register*. We're having a big spring sale, so he's taking out a full-page ad."

Mildred pursed her lips. "When will you be giving your notice?"

"My notice?"

"Well, now that James is back at the elevator, surely you're going to end this little job."

Instantly, Tilly felt her cheeks get hot and her teeth clench, but she decided she'd better stay calm. "James is only back at the elevator part-time. Only a few hours a week until things get busier next month."

"You'll let Mr. Cranston know you'll be leaving then?"

Tilly kept her voice low and calm. "I'm not planning to leave. James and I have talked about it, and I will keep working for a while. I'll be starting to look for a babysitter. Just someone for the few times James can't be here – like today. I do appreciate you watching the kids for an hour."

Tilly wondered if she'd said 'an hour' with enough emphasis. It was ridiculous how Mildred made it such a big deal to spend time with her grandchildren.

"I can't believe you're that hard up. I know things have been tight, but James could always ask me if he needs to borrow a little." Mildred's tone had a nasty edge that Tilly was all too familiar with.

"It's not only about the money. I like what I'm doing, Mildred."

"You like what you're doing? You like having your husband make dinner for your children?"

"But Mildred, I—"

"Hiring a stranger to watch them? I thought you wanted to be a good wife and mother. That's what you told me when you got married."

"But I am a good wife and mother. With a job!" Tilly raised her voice, her frustration growing.

"You can't have both. It doesn't work that way. I'll be talking to James about this when he gets home," Mildred threatened.

"You go right ahead!" Tilly walked out of the living room and into the boys' bedroom, her heart pounding fast. She kissed TJ and Robby on their cheeks. "Mommy has to go now. You be good boys for your grandmother. Daddy will be home soon."

The boys said goodbye and kept playing with their toy farm animals.

Tilly grabbed her purse as she stomped back to the living room. She mustered every bit of self-control as she said through gritted teeth, "Thank you for watching the boys, Mildred. I appreciate it."

Mildred didn't answer her.

She was a mile down the road when she rolled down the window, stuck her head out, and yelled into the sky, "I can't stand that woman!" Then she let out a long primal scream. Would she ever get away from that horrible, mean Mildred?

Ivy

Dear Hank,

You don't know me, but it seems you're my father. I didn't know about you until a few weeks ago when my mother (Vonda Marie) finally told me. Then I saw the story about you in the paper. My grandma said it would be okay to write, so here goes.

In case you didn't know, I was born exactly 17 years and two months ago in Omaha. I lived there with my Aunt Lillian, but she died when I was ten. Then it was just me and Mom. And Mom was working all the time. In August, Mom dropped me off in Prairie View with my grandparents on her way to California to seek her fame and fortune. She's still seeking it and keeps saying I'll be moving to California to be with her soon. I don't think it will ever happen.

I'm not really cut out for rural living, but I do like riding my horse-on-loan, Bearcat. He's a Quarter Horse, 17 years old, just like me. A beautiful dapple-gray. This will probably make me sound like an idiot, but I didn't know I wasn't supposed to let him into the green *pasture, and he almost foundered. I felt horrible, and my grandpa was furious at me. Luckily, Bearcat seems to be doing fine and we're not seeing any limping. I read that you used to break horses, so I'm wondering if you have any experience with founder?*

I'm not sure what else I should write about. I just wanted you to know I'm alive.

Sincerely,

Ivy

P.S. I'm sorry they sentenced you to prison time. Grandma says she knows you didn't do it. It happened on my birthday. Weird, huh?

June 1964

Hattie

HATTIE SAT IN HER chair, rocking back and forth, with Pup on the small, braided rug in front of her. She'd been listening to the chair's squeak on the wooden floor for so long it had nearly hypnotized her. After the little wooden bird popped out and cuckooed long enough to shake Hattie from her ruminations, she realized it was eleven o'clock. She'd been sitting here almost an hour.

She should get up and get busy; there was so much to be done with only two days until Wednesday Club — and the shower she was hosting for Etola. Hattie wasn't sure why she'd been so tired lately; even a trip to the chicken coop required a major effort. She didn't feel sick; it's just that her zest for life had disappeared.

She was still trying to convince herself to get out of the chair when Pup announced the arrival of a visitor. *Oh dear! Who could this be?* Hattie popped out of the chair and snuck a peek at herself in the hallway mirror. She was a mess, hadn't even taken out her pin curls yet, and the house was a bigger mess. She peeked out the window and recognized Cora's car. She scurried to the kitchen, removed her soiled apron, and piled her breakfast dishes into the sink before going to the kitchen door. She remembered her hair, but it was too late.

"Good morning, Cora," Hattie said, forcing a weak smile.

"Hello, thought I'd drop by the things for the bridal game while I was out," Cora said, holding up a small sack.

"Come in, come in. Let's have a cup of coffee." Hattie motioned for Cora to sit at the kitchen table and pulled out the coffee can. Cora glanced around the kitchen before she sat down. Hattie saw what Cora saw. The table was piled with papers and groceries not put away, the counter was covered with jars and boxes, and the sink was full of dirty dishes.

"Hattie, such good luck! I got the last seven Leister Bridal Shower booklets at Woolworth's. Twenty different shower games. Of course, we'll probably only have time for about six. Do you want to help me choose them?"

"Oh, that's okay. You choose." Hattie waited for the percolator to hiss and bubble. "Sorry about the mess." She cleared a space at the table in front of Cora and started to remove her bobby pins.

Cora smiled. "It's a busy time, that's for sure. May seemed to fly by, and before we knew it, Wednesday Club was rolling around again."

Hattie let out a loud sigh. "I certainly have a lot to do before then."

"Are you okay?" Cora asked.

"Yep, I'm okay. Just haven't had any get up and go lately."

Cora studied her face. "You sleeping?"

Hattie thought about how she must look. Tired. Old. When she had studied herself in the mirror yesterday, she couldn't believe how she seemed to have aged overnight. "It seems like all I do is sleep."

"How long has this been going on?"

Hattie shook her head as she ran her fingers through her curls to smooth them out. "Oh, I don't know, a few weeks. I'm fine;

nothing new is happening, only the usual aches and pains of my arthritis."

"Got the blues?" Cora asked in a gentle voice,

"I guess so." Hattie heaved herself up and headed to the coffee pot. There were no cookies to serve today, an unusual occurrence.

While Hattie poured the coffee, Cora asked, "General blues? Anything bothering you?"

She sat down. She supposed she might as well talk with Cora; she was tired of wearing a groove in her brain, rolling around those same thoughts over and over. "Oh, I don't know. Maybe the news of Etola and Arlo getting married has thrown me for a loop. It's not that I wanted to marry him or anything." A jolt of regret pinged inside her chest.

"It sure did seem like Arlo was smitten with you for a long time. I guess he wasn't your cup of tea?"

"Arlo is a decent man. You probably couldn't ask for a better husband. I'm just not sure any man could be my cup of tea."

Cora took a sip of coffee and spoke slowly. "You've always been very independent. Maybe you prefer to be on your own?"

Hattie almost shouted her response. "What I preferred was never considered. Even after I told Mother, she chose not to believe me." There! She'd blurted it out. She hadn't meant to, but after all these years, she could no longer contain the crack that had opened in her resolve to never speak of it again. There it was. Split wide open.

They both sat quietly for a moment. Hattie wondered if she'd need to explain more or whether the walls of this old house would finally speak the truth of what they'd seen.

"Ray?" Cora finally asked.

Hattie closed her eyes at the sound of his name. "The monster. I guess he turned me against men for good."

"Oh, honey. I often wondered about him. I am so sorry." Cora leaned forward to lay her hand on Hattie's arm. Hattie felt herself tense up as Cora gave her a little squeeze.

"I never was so happy as when he left us early. Then, for a time, I worried that all that hate I felt towards him had caused his heart attack."

Hattie exhaled deeply. It felt like the crushing weight that had lodged for so long on top of her heart had lifted a bit. Just a bit. She continued, determined not to break down. "I never could forgive my mother. She wouldn't believe the man who came to her rescue as a young widow could do anything like that."

"It must have been hard for you to stay here after they both were gone." Cora's voice was tender.

Suddenly, Hattie was right back there; it was the middle of the night, and she'd awakened in a cold sweat in her upstairs bedroom. She lay rigid, not breathing, waiting for his footsteps and the squeaking of the door handle. Then, after a few minutes, reality would set in, and she would remember that Ray was dead. Buried in the church cemetery, right beside her mother. That's when she would begin to relax, a blessed relief washing over her body.

It happened a lot, this nightmare memory.

She answered Cora. "It was more than I could bear to try to sell the farm while I was teaching and managing things on my own. When I figured out I could rent the land and stop working, I felt both free and sort of guilty at the same time. Living off the inheritance of such a brute."

"He owed you," Cora said quietly. "And more."

Hattie's shoulders dropped. "You know, after a while, you just shove things in the attic and close the door. Lock them away for good. At least that's what you tell yourself."

Hattie was pretty sure they both knew it wasn't the physical attic Hattie was talking about. They sat in silence for a minute.

Finally, Hattie relaxed a bit. "It's good to let it out after all these years."

"Of course, it goes without saying that I'll never tell anyone."

Hattie shifted her gaze to the window, to the bright green leaves of the beautiful maple tree. "Maybe the *not telling* has hurt me the most."

Cora nodded. "Why don't I stay on and help you get things cleaned up? Delmar isn't coming in for lunch, and Ivy is babysitting at Tilly's. I've got plenty of time on my hands today."

Hattie knew this wasn't true. Farm women never have plenty of time on their hands. But she appreciated the gesture of friendship. And it would be good to not be alone right now. "Thank you, Cora. I guess talking doesn't get the work done."

It was later, when Hattie was sweeping the floor, and Cora was washing the dishes, that the silent tears came. For both of them.

Wednesday Club Minutes

JUNE 10, 1964

The Wednesday Club met at the home of Miss Hattie Dunlop. The meeting was called to order by President Miss Bathilda Baldridge. The club motto was recited.

The roll call topic was your best idea for fighting garden pests. Everyone liked Cora's suggestion for fighting snails by filling a low container with beer. It seemed the snails can't resist it.

Ivy Hanson read the minutes from the May meeting. Bathilda asked that we include the first name Wanelda when referring to the late Grandma Harrington, to whom we had sent flowers for her funeral. Members voted unanimously to approve the minutes as amended.

Hattie Dunlop read the treasurer's report. The balance was the same as last month's, $50.13, as there were no transactions. Cora asked if the club would like to donate to the county food pantry, as the paper said donations are running low. The club voted unanimously to contribute $6.00.

Cora reported that some members had discussed the idea of a family picnic for the July meeting. Bathilda said she was concerned that too many meetings were turning out to be social gatherings instead of formal meetings with serious programs. After some discussion, the group decided to move the regular meeting date of July 8 to Saturday, July 11, and hold a family picnic. Cora said she would organize the potluck menu items, with each family bringing something to share. Tilly volunteered to reserve the large picnic area in Pioneer Park.

Bathilda asked how the club would like to handle the election of officers since those usually happened in July. Some members thought officers should stay on until they resigned. Ivy said she didn't think she would be around next year. It was decided that elections would happen at the August meeting.

Etola played the organ and led the group in singing "The More We Get Together."

This month's program was Etola's wedding shower. Cora led the club in several games, including a wedding word scramble, a game called Bells, Bells, Bells, and a quiz called "Well, What D'Ya Know?"

Club members donated their prizes to the bride-to-be, including a spatula, a flour sifter, and a piecrust crimper. Etola opened her shower gifts, which included many hand-embroidered items like hankies, dishtowels, and pillowcases. Hattie's crocheted spring hat toilet tissue cover gift was a big hit.

The meeting ended with the reciting of the club creed.

Hattie served a lunch of egg salad sandwiches, homemade pickles, lime Jell-O with mandarin oranges, and strawberry shortcake.

Ivy Hanson, Secretary

Etola

ETOLA HAD BEEN DRESSED and raring to go for twenty minutes by the time Florence pulled into the driveway in her blue Ford Imperial at precisely ten o'clock. She grabbed her handbag off the dining room table and called out, "See you later. I'll be back in time to get that weeding done and the garden watered. Probably about two or so."

Only a "yep" came from the kitchen to acknowledge that Bathilda had heard her. Etola hurried to the car and hopped into the passenger's side. "Morning, Florence!"

Florence was all dressed up, even wearing a hat. Should she have worn one too? Seemed like she'd never get the hang of the right outfit for the right occasion. Good thing Florence had agreed to take her shopping today.

"Good morning. You're looking very happy today." Florence put the car in gear with the lever on the steering column and pulled slowly up the driveway.

Etola grinned. "I swear, if I get any happier, I might burst like an overfilled balloon." She hesitated briefly before adding, "Seems like Bathilda is getting more unhappy as the wedding gets closer."

"I imagine she is really going to miss you."

Etola sighed. "I know that's true. But when I try to talk to her about it, she says I should concentrate on what's ahead, that she'll be just fine."

Florence gave Etola a smile. "I guess Arlo must be getting pretty excited."

"As much as a man can get excited about a wedding, I suppose. Whenever we talk about the details, he keeps saying that whatever I want is fine – he just wants it to be the happiest day of my life — so far!" Etola smiled to herself, remembering how often Arlo used the phrase 'so far.'

"He's a good egg, that Arlo."

Etola nodded, feeling her heart suddenly warm. "The more I get to know him, the more I think I must be the luckiest gal in South Dakota to marry him."

Florence stopped at the four-way stop sign, looked both ways and then turned right. The sign said 'Halsey 5 miles'. "How will it be moving into his little house?"

"Oh, I'm excited about that. I've been going over to get things situated in the kitchen how I like them. For a bachelor, he keeps a neat house. Guess his mama taught him well. Course, after we're married, I plan to do a little sprucing: some new kitchen curtains and maybe some new wallpaper in the living room and dining room. And I've had my eye on a chenille bedspread in the Sears catalog — a nice lavender color. I read that lavender is the color of romance."

"That sounds nice," Florence agreed. "Any ideas what kind of dress you're looking for?"

"Hattie says most women my age would wear a nice suit, but I have my heart set on something fancier. At least something floor length, not too short." Etola was adamant about this. It nearly broke her heart to finally let go of that beautiful wedding dress that had hung in her closet all those years. She wished she'd never let

Bathilda talk her into giving it away. Truth be told, though, she probably couldn't have fit into it anymore.

Etola continued. "Course, I am a bit nervous about finding a dress with only two weeks until the wedding. Don't know what I was thinking agreeing to a June wedding when we only got engaged in May. But both of us are excited to get on with our lives together. When you're our age, time's a-wastin'."

Florence laughed. "Don't worry, we'll find the perfect dress today. I'm so glad you asked me to help you."

"Oh, I can't tell you how much you're helping. Even getting Bathilda to agree to borrow your dress is nothing short of a miracle. She never would've agreed to stand up with me if she'd had to buy a dress. As it is, I'm sure she's gritting her teeth at the thought of it."

Etola and Florence shared a chuckle at the memory of how Bathilda went from scowling at the notion of being a bridesmaid to reluctantly agreeing that she looked nice in Florence's deep blue dress with a matching jacket. But at the suggestion that Florence do her makeup before the wedding, Bathilda had put her foot down.

"Here we are!" Florence said as they pulled up in front of Thelma's Formal Wear, the only place for wedding and fancy dresses within a hundred miles.

Etola gasped. "Why, look at that beauty! And in lavender, no less."

She gazed at the dress in the front window. Made from lavender chiffon, it had row upon row of gathered and ruffled tiers in the big full skirt, a high neck with another row of ruffles, and oversized puffy sleeves with ruffles at the shoulders and wrists. Lots of lavender ruffles.

Florence paused a minute before she replied. "Let's look at every possibility and try them all; you just never know until you see it on. Let's go see what they have."

Etola and Florence entered the store and searched through every rack. Etola picked out seven dresses to try on. With each dress, she stepped out of the dressing room to show Florence, and each time, she could tell by Florence's expression that she felt the same way Etola did. The lavender dress looked plain silly, even though Thelma, the shop owner, tried to tell them how beautiful it was. It turned out it was the most expensive dress in the store, so Etola wondered if Thelma's advice was reliable.

The white lace dress with embossed roses looked like Etola was wrapped in a tablecloth. The floral dress with cap sleeves looked more like a picnic outfit than a wedding dress. The short pink dress with the poufy skirt reminded Etola of a wad of cotton candy. The navy-blue suit dress felt way too somber. And the bright yellow dress with a brown bow made Etola look like a human sunflower.

Etola had an ache in the pit of her stomach as she got down to the last dress, a long A-line in eggshell satin with an empire waist. It wasn't exactly the look she'd had in mind, but Florence said it was an elegant and modern bride's dress, all the rage. Etola pulled it over her head, put her arms through the long sleeves, and started to pull up the long side zipper. My, this dress was very form fitting. So form fitting she couldn't get the zipper even a fourth of the way up.

Thelma said all the dresses could be altered to be a size or two bigger, but still! Etola looked at herself in the mirror. This would never work. Her thighs were bulging the fabric out in a very unflattering way, and when she turned to the side, her butt jutted out like a round-topped muffin. Her ample bust was ready to burst through the top half of the dress, and there was no way she could suck in her stomach enough to pull the zipper up. She looked like a stuffed sausage.

Suddenly, Etola heard a familiar voice.

"What are you doing here, Florence?" Dear Lord, it was that nosey Mildred Halversen. "We thought that was your car outside. Thought we'd stop in to say hello."

"Just helping a friend," Florence answered. Thank goodness Florence knew better than to give Mildred any extra information.

Another familiar voice piped up. "Oh, is it Etola by any chance?" It was the gossipy Nelda Monroe.

Etola's heart sank. She'd better get out of this dress before Florence asked her to model it.

"Why yes, we're looking for a dress for her," Florence said.

"Must be for her upcoming wedding. I suppose I'll be stuck babysitting since I haven't received an invitation." Mildred sniffed.

Etola heard Florence's cheerful response. "Probably not, Mildred, since Tilly's boys are welcome at the wedding." Touché, Florence!

It was probably faster to lift the dress over her head and pull it off that way. She grabbed the hem and turned it inside out, lifting the skirt up to her elbows. But that was as far as she got it before she heard a slight ripping sound. Maybe it wouldn't come off this way after all.

Nelda continued, "Well, you can't deny that she's getting herself a good husband in Arlo."

Etola tried to pull the dress back down, but it started to rip again. Her arms were trapped inside the dress, and she was now completely stuck. The dress was halfway off, inside out, and wouldn't go up or down. Heavens to Murgatroyd. She had to ask for help.

"Florence," Etola whispered. The ladies continued with their chattering, now they'd moved on to the weather.

"Especially after all that rain."

"Florence!" This time, Etola hissed the name louder.

"Is that you, Etola?"

"Yes, please come in here." Etola shuffled over to the far corner so she couldn't be seen when the door opened.

Florence stepped into the dressing room. "What in the world?" She must look like a mummy. "Shh! I'm stuck, that's all."

Florence tried pulling up the dress, but it wouldn't budge. Etola was starting to feel faint, like she might pass out and keel over.

Florence whispered back. "Kneel down so I can get some leverage."

Etola kneeled and Florence tugged. It felt like her arms were being torn out of their sockets as Florence yanked the dress up to her shoulders. "Just rip the damn thing if you have to!" Etola spit out, careful to keep her voice low.

Finally, with more seam tearing, the dress was finally over Etola's head, and she was free. At another time, this might be funny, but Etola was near tears. "That was the last one. None of them work. Now what am I going to do?"

"Wait here. Don't panic." Florence slipped out of the dressing room, and Etola wondered if Mildred and Nelda were still loitering around, like vultures after an accident.

"But there must be something else that would work!" Etola heard Florence pleading with Thelma but couldn't hear her response. She held her breath, bowed her head, and said a silent prayer.

In a couple of minutes, Florence opened the dressing room door a crack and handed through a garment bag. "Thelma says this dress was returned yesterday because the bride got cold feet on the way to the altar. If it works, it's half-price. She says it's probably about your size."

Etola was so wound up with nerves that she didn't even look at the dress as she pulled it out of the bag and stepped into it. She put her arms through, zipped it up partway, and stood to look at it in the full mirror. Floor length, it was a soft ivory with Chantilly lace covering the bodice and filling in the sweetheart neckline and long sleeves. The dress had a taffeta underskirt from the waist down with three soft tiers of Chantilly lace in a waterfall pattern. It was feminine and flattering, and it fit her like a glove.

When Etola stepped out of the dressing room to get Florence's help in zipping it all the way, she didn't even need to hear Florence's approval. She could tell by the awed expressions on Mildred and Nelda's faces that she had found her dress.

Ivy

Ivy was glad that Tilly wasn't watching as she backed out of the driveway. Her grandfather had been teaching her to drive his pickup and Ivy was having trouble getting it in reverse without grinding the gears. Every time that grinding noise happened, her grandfather looked like he was going to burst a vein on the side of his head, and that only made it harder for Ivy to find the right gear. Her Grandma kept telling him to be patient, since Ivy had never learned to drive from her mother. Ivy figured she was probably the last teenager in Prairie View to be driving, but in Omaha they took the bus everywhere.

It had been a fun afternoon babysitting the boys, just for a couple of hours a day when Tilly left for work and before James got home. It was great to have a part-time job and her own spending money.

Two letters were waiting for Ivy when she got home. She should wash up and help her grandmother with dinner, but when she saw one of the return addresses, she ran up to her bedroom with both letters. She opened her mother's letter first.

Dear Ivy,

I'm not sure how much longer I can stand to be in Los Angeles. Everybody here seems so stuck up like they don't want to make room for anybody else to succeed. Even when I let them know at auditions that I've already starred in a Feel Right commercial, they don't seem to think that's enough experience.

And then there's the directors who promise me a role if I do them a favor first. But I won't go into that.

Last week, I had to move out of Richard's pool house because his wife threw a fit after she returned from Europe. I was just sunbathing, and I could hear her yelling about how I was not an 'appropriate' person to be there. I told Richard I'd be happy to pay rent, but he said there was nothing he could do.

For now, I'm sleeping on the couch in Victoria's apartment, she's a girl I work with at the dry cleaners. It's nice of her to let me stay here, but she has three cats, and you can only imagine how the place smells.

I've been getting such friendly letters from Mel Hartmann. Do you remember him, the owner of the deli downstairs from our old apartment? It makes me a little homesick for Omaha.

You must be done with school for the year and enjoying your summer vacation. Pat your pony for me and don't forget to write. The P.O. box is still the same.

Happy Summer! Mom

Ivy hurriedly stuffed the letter back in the envelope, barely remembering what her mother had written. It was the second letter she was most interested to read.

Dear Ivy,

It meant a lot to get a letter from you. You're all grown up now. After all this time, it was probably tough for you to learn about me. I haven't had the chance to meet you, but I have thought about you every day, and if you felt something extra on March 27th, it's because I was wishing you a happy birthday.

I'm sure it's strange to be on the farm after being a city girl for so long, but I'm glad you're getting to know the good things about country life. Your grandparents are decent people, especially Cora. She has a kind heart and was always good to me.

I'm happy to know you have a horse you're taking care of. I know you feel bad about him almost foundering, but you didn't know, and it has happened to horse owners with far more experience than you. I hope he is still doing well with your careful attention. 17 years makes for a steady Quarter Horse and a good way for you to learn about riding. Don't push him too hard, and make sure you spend time cooling him down slowly if you're running him. And don't pull too hard on his bit, I never could stand to see the way some people keep too tight a rein on a horse. If he's always lifting his head up, you need to loosen up on the reins. I guess you didn't ask for all this advice, but there it is.

You said I used to break horses, but I don't like to use that word. I never wanted to break their spirit, just guide them to go along with what I wanted them to do. I call it horse training, not horse breaking. I'm hoping to get work training horses when I get out of here. I've been thinking that life is short, and you might as well go for your dreams.

I hope you believe that I never meant to hurt that man. I was walking by and heard a woman screaming and I just wanted to protect her. There was another guy there who saw what happened and my lawyer is trying to find him so he can be a witness. I have to keep my hopes up to survive this place. Your letter makes me feel like maybe things are starting to turn around.

Your dad, Hank

P.S. If anything should happen to me, get ahold of my attorney Patrick Callahan in Clover City.

Ivy read this letter a second time, letting Hank's words sink in. She realized she'd been breathing shallowly both times she'd read it – almost holding her breath. She exhaled deeply, blowing air slowly from her mouth. She looked at the writing and tried to imagine him writing the words from his prison cell. It was all so strange and shocking. Then she put it back in the envelope and laid it on the bed beside her mother's — letters from her mother and her father on the same day. Did they ever write to one another? Was there was ever a time they considered being together after she was born? Like everyone else she knew who had two parents.

For a minute, Ivy felt like crying. But then she heard her grandmother calling her. It was time to set the table for dinner. Ivy slipped the letters under her socks in her dresser drawer and went downstairs, her heart still pounding.

Bathilda

THE BRIGHT CORAL SUN was starting to peek over the horizon when Bathilda pulled back the curtain and looked out her bedroom window. It was going to be a hot one. For a minute, it felt like an ordinary Saturday, another working day like every other day, and then she remembered: it was Etola's wedding day. Just the thought of all the fuss and bother ahead made her grumpy.

Even Eddie was caught up in the excitement. He had asked Arlo to show him how to tie his necktie about a dozen times, and patient Arlo had continued to teach him over and over. Arlo had taken Eddie to get a new shirt and shoes, and Eddie was already calling him his new brother. No doubt about it, Etola was getting herself a good man.

The wedding would be at two o'clock at Florence and Lloyd's house. Last week, the ceremony had to be moved from the Lake Dorena Lutheran Church when the plumbing sprung a leak. Etola nearly had a nervous breakdown, but Reverend Gerhardt offered to perform the ceremony in the Lane's backyard, where the reception would be held. Florence had reassured Etola that everything would be perfect. Weird things were always happening to Etola, but Bathilda bit her tongue and didn't comment about it.

There were so many chores that needed to be done before she had to get gussied up. Guests would be driving past the farm on their way to the wedding, so she wanted to make sure the front yard was freshly mowed and looked respectable. Eddie said he didn't have time to mow since Arlo was picking him up at ten to take him for a haircut, so Bathilda had resignedly added it to her list.

By the time she finished her regular chores, it was almost eleven-thirty, and Etola and Eddie were long gone to their wedding preparations. It would be a push to get the lawn mowed and still have time to get ready, but Bathilda was determined. Usually, she tied Shep with a rope to the barn stall while she was mowing because he liked to chase the mower, but since he'd be tied up for a long time while they were at the wedding, she decided to let him stay in the yard. She'd have to keep a close eye on him.

Bathilda was almost finished with the lawn, just two more passes with the mower, when she saw Shep rise from the shady spot under the elm tree and go trotting to the road. That darn Shep was chasing something. Bathilda stopped the mower and was about to look for Shep when she felt it — a sharp whack to her chest that almost knocked the wind out of her. It happened at the exact moment she heard the loud thud. An unmistakable sound. Then a slam of brakes and tires crunching on the gravel. *Oh no, dear God, no!*

Bathilda ran up the driveway and looked down the road. A milk tank truck was stopped at a funny angle, and the driver, Kent Buckley — a decent young man — was crouched down and looking at something on the road. The next few minutes were an otherworldly experience, as if she was watching a scene from a movie that she was not a part of. She heard Kent's plaintive cries of "Bathilda, I never saw him; he ran right under the tire. Oh God, I'm so sorry!" She looked first at the reflection in the stainless-steel tank, at the image of Shep, both back legs bent in an unnatural angle. Then she ran over to him, leaned down close, and saw that Shep was bleeding. Kent stood silently watching. Bathilda lifted Shep's limp and heavy body, carried him to the barn in her aching arms, laid him down on the soft straw, and caressed his head as his eyes lost focus and his breathing became labored. All these things she did as if in a fog.

But everything came into sharp focus when she made the trip to the house to get the rifle, said her final words, "Good boy, Shep," and pulled back the trigger to end his misery. All these things were crystal clear.

Afterward, Bathilda couldn't bear to look at Shep's wounds. She found a burlap bag to cover his body from the neck down and knelt in the straw beside him. She looked at his beautiful face, his mouth permanently open and his eyes glassy and vacant, then put her fingers on his neck, where the skin was thick and the fur long and curly, where he loved to be scratched. Bathilda kneaded his neck, waiting for the tears to come, but she only heard half-choking sounds from her throat. She bent over and rested her forehead on Shep's head. His body was still warm. Finally, she began to moan, and then she sobbed, long gasping sobs that she didn't recognize coming from herself. Even as a young woman, when she was told her parents were both dead, she hadn't cried like this. Eddie and Etola had needed her to be strong.

Then she remembered with a jolt that it was Etola's wedding day, and she was supposed to be getting dressed. It must be almost twelve-thirty by now. She couldn't leave Shep like this on such a hot day when she won't be home for hours. The flies. Bathilda considered some of Shep's favorite spots and settled on the area beside the raspberry bushes, a shady spot where he always laid when she worked in the garden. The dirt was soft there, too.

When Bathilda finished burying Shep, she was exhausted, and covered with dirt and blood. She wanted to pray over the grave, thanking Shep for all the good years, but that would have to wait. She had to make the rest of the day perfect for Etola. Of this, she was determined.

Florence

IT WAS DAYS LIKE this when Florence believed she was doing what she was born to do: party planning, hostessing, creating an event that people would remember for years. When she heard the news that the septic tank at the Lake Dorena Lutheran Church had backed up, flooding the bathrooms and the hallway, she felt almost giddy. Of course, they could have the ceremony here! She had always pictured a sweet little archway in the backyard between the gap in the two large birch trees. It was almost as if they had been planted with a wedding in mind.

When word got around about Etola's misfortune, the whole community had rallied. Bob Cranston from the hardware store had donated wood, and yesterday morning James Halversen and Leroy Davis from the elevator had built a wedding arch in no time at all. Cora and Tilly had added two coats of white paint. Delmar and Lloyd had hauled over all the tables and folding chairs from the church basement. Florence brought dozens of Cecile Brunner climbing rose vines from the back of the garage that she and Todd, home on leave for a few days, had wound around the poles and along the top of the archway. Even using heavy leather work gloves, their arms were still covered with scratches from the rose thorns, but it was a small price to pay for the final effect. Just beautiful. Especially with the white willow stands on each side of the arch holding large bouquets of purple delphinium. She could already picture the bride and groom standing there.

Hattie and Cora set up the chairs in neat rows facing the makeshift altar and tied with large pink ribbons on the end of each row. It was a shame the chairs weren't fancy white wooden ones like they had in Texas instead of beige metal folding chairs, but beggars can't be choosers.

With thirty minutes until the guests would arrive, Florence looked around at the buzz of activity and pulled her list from the front pocket of her ruffled hostess apron. The secret to success was in preparing a thorough list. Everything was timed so Etola would walk down the aisle at exactly two-o-five.

Hattie had covered the serving tables with starched white sheets and was stacking the white dishes borrowed from the Methodist Church. Everyone knew the Methodists had the newest, best-looking dishes in town.

"Don't forget to lay out the extra serving utensils, Hattie," Florence reminded. "They're on the kitchen counter, ready to go." Hattie could be trusted to arrange the arriving potluck foods with the appetizers, salads, and hot foods aligned together in categories.

Ivy set up the table for the punch bowl and coffee, and Florence rearranged the cups, so they formed a perfect semi-circle around the front of the bowl. She glanced at the cake table, where they would place the three-tiered cake after the guests finished their luncheon. Don't want it melting in the hot sun. As it was, there had been a little slip in transporting it, and Florence had to do some patching with the extra frosting the baker had sent along. Good thing she'd added an extra ten minutes in her schedule for 'miscellaneous unknowns.'

Florence glanced over at Tilly, who had set up the table for the guest book she'd made. It was a beautiful book, hand-decorated with tiny pearl beads on the cover. It must have taken Tilly hours to create the romantic picture of a little house and tree, with Etola and Arlo's initials on the front door, made entirely with beads. Tilly supervised her oldest, Robby, who carefully carried small bowls of mixed nuts and molded mints to each table. All three of her boys, even the baby, were dressed in matching plaid shirts Hattie had sewn for them.

Cora placed tissue-wrapped quart jars of her garden flowers on each table: Shasta daisies, snapdragons, delphiniums, and roses made for a cheerful and sweet-smelling centerpiece. Perfect for a country wedding.

Florence consulted her list and then ran to the dining room to get the fancy net aprons she had made for the cake, punch, and coffee servers. Pink to match the bows on the chairs.

And now, as the guests began to arrive with their presents and potluck dishes, it was all coming together perfectly. Florence even managed to intercept Mary Ellen Toefte with her infamous tuna noodle salad, known far and wide for its overcooked pasta shells and completely tasteless dressing. Rumor had it that Mary Ellen used only a single can of tuna and a small jar of Miracle Whip for three pounds of pasta, making it dry as toast and inedible. Florence grabbed the large bowl, saying, "Let me put that in the refrigerator so it doesn't go bad in the hot sun." By refrigerator, she meant all the way to the back, where it would be covered up and accidentally forgotten.

Reverend Gerhardt greeted the guests as they arrived, holding his Bible, and looking relaxed and in charge. A few people asked politely about the church's plumbing problems, and he smiled and let them know they should be open for business next Sunday.

With ten minutes to go, Florence decided to make a trip back into the house to reapply her lipstick and check in on Etola, who was upstairs, remaining out of sight from the groom. She might as well grab the bride's bouquet now from the extra refrigerator in the garage and take it up to her. When Florence opened the door and reached for Etola's flowers, she noticed that the smaller bridesmaid's bouquet was still there. Wait a minute — where was Bathilda? She must have gone directly upstairs without Florence noticing.

On her way up, she poked her head into the dining room, where Lloyd was talking with Arlo and Eddie. Florence had given Lloyd strict instructions that his job was to keep them relaxed before the ceremony. And that didn't mean giving them a few nips to calm their nerves. It looked like things were going well, as Arlo and Eddie had rose boutonnières pinned to their lapels and were playing a hand of Old Maid.

Upstairs, Etola sat quietly beside the window, watching the arrival of the guests. She looked relaxed and composed, soaking it all in.

"Here's your bouquet, dear. Didn't it turn out lovely?" Florence held it out to her and marveled at how a wedding day could turn any bride into a glowing beauty. "Is Bathilda in the bathroom?"

"I haven't seen Bathilda yet. I thought she was outside with you," Etola said. "Isn't she here yet?"

"Oh, I'm sure she is. I'll go find her and give her the bouquet. It's almost time!" Florence handed Etola's flowers to her and hurried out.

Where the heck was Bathilda? Florence dashed down the stairs and out the door. Wasn't it just like her to be late to her own sister's wedding? When everything had been going so perfectly.

Florence surveyed the yard and saw that almost all the chairs were filled with guests, everyone settling in and buzzing with excitement. Florence checked her watch. It was two-o-five. She looked around to see if Bathilda was standing in the back talking to anyone, but she didn't see her. There was only Hattie arranging the potluck dishes.

"Hattie, have you seen Bathilda?" Florence asked.

"Why no, I haven't. Isn't she here?" Hattie furrowed her brow.

"I'm not sure."

Florence made a loop around the house and then walked to the driveway and gravel path around the buildings where all the cars were parked. She searched for Bathilda's Ford pickup but didn't see it, so she ran back to the house.

"Eddie, was Bathilda going to drive over in the pickup?" Florence asked, trying not to let her voice register the concern she was starting to feel.

"Yep, she was. Arlo picked me up, and Bathilda was coming on her own."

Florence trotted back to the yard and rechecked the time. Two-fifteen. She could just throttle that Bathilda! It was way past the time they should keep the guests waiting for the ceremony to begin.

Reverend Gerhardt hurried over to Florence and asked, "Are we ready to begin?"

"I can't find Bathilda!" Now, her voice rose, and her stomach clenched.

Just then, she saw Bathilda's pickup tearing up the driveway, spewing gravel. Florence rushed to tell Bathilda she should park anywhere. Could she hold her tongue? How she'd like to give that selfish old biddy a piece of her mind!

She arrived at the pickup just as Bathilda opened the door to get out. The words were forming in Florence's head. *How dare you do anything to mar your sister's wedding day? Just because you...* But one look at Bathilda's shell-shocked face and Florence stopped. Something dreadful had happened.

Florence stepped forward and gave Bathilda's arm a gentle squeeze. "Everything will be okay. You come with me, and we'll get you freshened up and ready to go."

Together, they entered the house. The guests would just have to wait.

Etola

ETOLA SAT ON A small wooden chair in the upstairs guest bedroom, gazing at the scene below. It was picture-perfect: the beautiful rose-covered arch, the rows of chairs filling up with guests all dressed in their finery, and the minister greeting everyone with a welcoming smile.

After Florence brought her bouquet, Etola wondered where the heck Bathilda might be. Had something happened to her? Then she remembered Arlo's words. "If I'm there and you're there, and the minister is there, everything else is just gravy." Since Reverend Gerhardt was in the yard and Arlo was downstairs waiting for her, it was all going to be just fine.

Etola posed in front of the mirror, holding the bridal bouquet. She smiled at her reflection. Florence had certainly dandied her up. For a moment, she thought about her much younger self, how she'd stood in front of the mirror in her wedding dress twenty-seven years ago, even after John was dead and the wedding was not to be. It was time to let that sad memory go. Wasn't it the bee's knees how everything worked out in the end? Maybe it was better being an older bride, coming to a marriage with a more mature outlook. And to be with Arlo! She took a long, slow breath, conjuring the smell of him, that heady mixture of Old Spice and comfort. Her Arlo.

She sat back down. It must be past time for the wedding to begin, but she reckoned they couldn't start the wedding without the bride. Florence had everything under control and would let her know when it was time to walk down the aisle. Etola closed her eyes and basked in her excited anticipation. Her heart was buzzing.

And then, before she knew it, Florence opened the door, a smile on her face. "Are you ready? It's time."

With her hand on the railing to steady herself and Florence holding the back of her dress, Etola slowly descended the stairs to the open back door. There it all was before her: the smiling guests craning their necks to see her, the back of Bathilda as she rather stiffly walked to the front, Eddie all dressed up and smiling at her, and Reverend Gerhardt holding a Bible. And dear, sweet Arlo, beaming at her with a broad smile. Etola saw an unmistakable look of love and admiration in his eyes. *My, he looks handsome, all dressed up in his suit and tie.* Everything else was a blur as she walked toward her soon-to-be husband. *This must be what it's like to float on air.*

Throughout the ceremony and for the rest of the day, Etola had never known such joy. Everywhere she looked, all she saw was perfection. The perfection of love.

Ivy

It seemed to Ivy that it was well past time for the wedding to begin, but nobody else seemed to be giving it another thought. They were all chatting with each other in their fancy clothes and dress shoes, and Ivy could feel a cheerful anticipation in the air.

And then, suddenly, there was Etola standing at the open door. She paused for a second, and, right on cue, an older guy began playing his violin. It was not the typical wedding march Ivy had seen on TV, but it was a pretty song that seemed vaguely familiar. With everyone on their feet now and turning to see the bride, Etola glided down the aisle towards the grinning Arlo.

Etola looked lovely! Her ivory wedding gown was romantic and old-fashioned, just perfect for her. Ivy knew Florence had helped Etola with her makeup, and Ivy thought it looked nice — soft and natural to let Etola's glow come through. Her short gray hair was styled in soft curls, framed by the waist-length ivory lace veil.

Ivy had heard that women were never more beautiful than on their wedding day. Once she had found a dog-eared *Modern Bride* magazine tucked under her mother's pillow when she went to pull the sheets for the laundry, but she knew her mom had never married. Ivy wasn't sure if she would ever want to marry, though she used to practice writing her name attached to Brad's last name: Ivy Donahue. It did have a nice ring to it.

Ivy watched the sweet ceremony and the couple smiling at one another and looked around at all the people who had come together to make this a happy celebration. Could anything like this even happen in Omaha? Most people only knew a few of their neighbors and only enough for a quick 'hello.'

And then, before she knew it, Etola and Arlo had kissed and were walking up the aisle to hoots and claps, and it was time for Ivy to assume her duty behind the punch table. It was hot, and there were going to be a lot of thirsty people. Florence had insisted that all the servers wear ridiculous pink net aprons with matching ribbon ties. Ivy wasn't sure she and her mother had ever owned an apron. Oh well, she wouldn't complain. This was Etola's day.

While Ivy stood behind the punch table, and the guests clustered in little groups of three and four waiting for the food line to form, Reverend Gerhardt said a lengthy prayer — the fourth one today. As soon as the guests were murmuring their amens, Ivy heard a low voice behind her say, "Good bread, good meat, good gosh, let's eat!" She chuckled, then turned to see who had said it. It was Lance. Ivy rolled her eyes at him and whirled back to the punch bowl. She'd been ignoring him ever since their shouting match in February, and she wasn't about to start giving him any attention now.

Etola and Arlo took their place at the head of the line and began making their way down the food tables. A line of guests formed behind them; some came first to the punch table. Ivy served the Kool-Aid punch spiked with 7-Up. She knew a lot of people here. There was Becky and her parents, three teachers from the high school, and the Wednesday Club husbands. Little Mary from the school bus excitedly said hello as her mother stood shyly behind her. Ivy could tell that her mother was an Indian, could she be related to Hank? There was so much she didn't know about her father.

Lance came through the line three times. Finally, Ivy spoke to him. "So, are you really thirsty or you really like strawberry punch?"

Lance smiled. "Okay, you got me. The punch is just an excuse to force you to talk to me."

"We have nothing to talk about," she said a little more loudly than necessary.

Lance looked around to see who else had heard Ivy's outburst. He lowered his chin and leaned in. "That was mean of me. About the dance. I still feel bad about it."

Ivy tilted her head and cupped her hand around her ear. "And?"

"I know this might sound like an excuse, but I pretty much had to take Wanda. Her mom called my mom and said that I had asked Wanda first. And Wanda had talked her mother into buying a very expensive dress. It wasn't a real invitation from me ... I mean ... we were just talking about the dance. But my mom insisted." Lance shrugged and looked around the room, avoiding Ivy's intense stare. She stayed silent. She wasn't going to forgive him that easily.

"Anyway, I'm sorry." This time, Lance looked at her directly.

"Thank you for the apology. That was a long time in coming."

Lance held out his cup for more punch, and Ivy filled it halfway. "I'd like to make it up to you. There's a party at Lake Dorena next Saturday. Picnic and swimming at Tom Connors' cabin. Do you want to go?"

"With you? I don't think so."

Just then, Ivy's grandfather stepped up to the table for punch. "Howdy do, Lance. How's your dad doing?"

Lance spoke to him. "Oh, he's doing great. Good soybean crop so far." He looked back at Ivy. "Think about it, okay?"

Ivy looked away without answering, turning to her grandfather. "Hi, Grandpa! Want some punch?"

Lance did seem to be sincere in his apology. But her mother had always apologized too. And then went right back to doing things she had promised she wouldn't. Like not coming home all night.

July 1964

327

Tilly

TILLY WAS TIRED BUT happy when she left Coast to Coast at four o'clock to head home. It had been a busy day getting all the signs written for the big Fourth of July sale. Almost every aisle had special savings — from the flowers and plants to the barbecue supplies to the paint. Tilly always added a little drawing or embellishment to the signs, so it wasn't just a price, and Mr. Cranston said that's what put her work above anyone else he'd ever hired. Tilly was even approached by Ben Norris from the Red Owl about making signs, but she had her hands full with this part-time job. Now that James was back to work at the elevator, her income wasn't needed as much, so Tilly was squirreling away a little bit with each paycheck. One day, they'd be able to afford a place that was not right behind her mother-in-law's. At this rate, though, it would take a long time.

Thank goodness for Ivy! As Tilly drove home, she thought about how lucky it was that Ivy has been able to babysit. The boys seemed to like her, and Ivy had introduced all kinds of new things to them, like putting on little plays. TJ insisted on wearing the cardboard crown that Ivy made for him all day long; he'd sleep in it if Tilly let him. And Ivy was teaching precocious, not yet five-year-old Robby to read.

Tilly felt her shoulders slowly relax as she left town and drove along, glancing at the fields. She had always loved the look of the dark green rows of knee-high corn, the sharp leaves trembling in the breeze.

When Tilly pulled up in the driveway, Ivy and the three boys were in the yard, nestled under the low-hanging branches of the willow tree. Robby came running out. "Come into our fort, Mommy!"

"Ok. Are you having fun?" Tilly parted the branches and sank down on the grass. Baby Milo reached out for his mother, and she scooped him into her arms and smooched his cheek.

Robby grabbed his mother's arm. "Listen, Mommy!" He sat beside her and opened a library book, slowly saying the words as he moved his finger along the page. "Oh, oh, oh! said Dick. The house and the barn are down. Who did this to my farm? Who did it? Jane said, Oh, Dick. You can make a new farm. I will help you. Soon, we will have a new farm." Robby stopped reading and grinned at his mother.

"Sweetheart, that's great! I'm so proud of you. Ivy must be a good teacher."

Ivy smiled. "He's catching on quick. And TJ had no accidents today. He told me every time he needed to use his potty chair."

TJ gave a big grin, and Tilly bent forward to kiss his cheek. "Let's go in now so Ivy can get home, and I can start supper for your daddy."

As they headed for the trailer, Ivy reminded Tilly of her schedule. "On Monday, I have my First Aid class so I can get my official babysitting certificate, so I can't be here until twelve-thirty."

"That's fine; I told Mr. Cranston I wouldn't be in until one."

"Are you still enjoying your job?" Ivy asked.

"I love that I get to be drawing and painting, even if it is just signs. Have you ever thought about what kind of job you'd like to have someday?"

"Oh, I don't know. I'm not sure yet. I love to read. And write. But I know it's unrealistic to think I could be a writer."

"I think you can be whatever you want to be. Don't sell yourself short. You're still young and have your whole life ahead of you." She smiled at Ivy.

The trailer was hot and stuffy, even with all the fans going. But all the toys were picked up, and the dishes were done and put away, cleaner than when Tilly had left.

"You've cleaned up. Thank you."

"Sure, the boys took long naps, and I had some time. They would have slept even longer, but Mildred came over to check on them and her knocking woke them up."

"That figures. I'm surprised she even knocked." Tilly sometimes forgot to keep her attitude towards her mother-in-law to herself.

"She did compliment me on how clean things were." Tilly and Ivy shared a knowing smile.

Milo started to fuss, and Tilly put him in his highchair and handed him a set of plastic teething keys. "Do you have plans for the Fourth, Ivy?"

"Not really, we'll have a barbecue on Saturday. And Grandma and I plan to spend some time in the garden over the next few days. Round ten of weeding." Ivy grabbed her purse from the counter.

"It's nice that you and your grandmother can spend time together. I admire Cora; she's such a thoughtful person. I've never heard her say a bad word about anyone."

"She is very kind," Ivy agreed. She hesitated at the front door. "Tilly, can I ask your opinion about something?"

"Of course. What's on your mind?"

"Lance invited me to a Sunday picnic at Tom Connors' cabin. I'm not sure if I should go."

"What's your hesitation?"

"I'd like to go. I just don't know if I can trust Lance, you know, after he stood me up for the dance and all."

Tilly studied Ivy's face for a minute before she responded. "I can understand that. Has Lance talked with you about that?"

"A couple of times now, and I think he genuinely feels bad about it. He calls himself a stupid clod. And I haven't disagreed." They both giggled.

"Has Tom invited you?"

"Oh yeah, he's pretty much invited the whole class. Becky will be there with her boyfriend."

Tilly thought for a few seconds. "I have an idea. Why don't you drive yourself, tell Lance you'll meet him there? Then he can't possibly stand you up again or leave you hanging."

"That's a great idea. And then it doesn't seem like I'm on a date with him."

Tilly said, "Because you're not. You're there on your own, and if you want to talk with Lance at the party, that's up to you."

"I like that idea. Thanks. See you on Monday." Ivy was grinning as she headed out the door.

Tilly stood for a minute, remembering how excited she'd been when James first started asking her out. She was in love with him from the start, with his unruly mop of brown curly hair and long, skinny legs. And those big blue eyes. How long ago that all seemed, six years and three kids later. The romance part seemed to go by so quickly. A twinge of sadness and longing washed through Tilly. Then she heard one of the boys calling her from the back bedroom.

"Coming, TJ!"

Cora

CORA CAME IN FROM the garden holding up her apron filled with string beans. Then she heard the phone ring and hurried into the kitchen, rolling the beans onto the counter before picking up the receiver.

"Hello?"

"Cora, it's Hattie. How are you?"

Cora sat down on the stool beneath the wall phone. "I'm fine; I've been meaning to call you. I know I need to figure out the food for the picnic. I've been so busy with the garden I haven't had a spare minute."

"That's what I'm calling about. I haven't been able to get Bathilda on the phone, and Etola says she's terribly sad about her dog."

"I can imagine. It's probably so lonely for her with Etola not being there anymore ... after all those years."

Just then, Delmar entered the kitchen and stood expectantly. Cora motioned for him to wait a minute as she listened.

"Right. Etola says Bathilda's threatening to not even show up for the Wednesday Club picnic."

Cora wiped her hands on her apron. "Oh dear. What should we do?"

"Well, I was thinking you and I should go visit her. Tell her we need help planning the picnic and can't do it without her."

Delmar sat, drumming his fingers on the kitchen table, and Cora turned slightly away to ignore him. "That's a wonderful idea. How about this afternoon? Shall I meet you there?"

"How about two o'clock?"

"Perfect. I'll see you then. Bye now." Cora hung up the phone and turns to Delmar. "What is it, honey?"

"I need a cup of coffee and a snack. Breakfast didn't hold me this morning."

Cora looked at the coffee pot on the stove and the cookie jar on the counter. She shook her head as she got up from the stool. Good grief! How would he survive without her?

Ivy

Dear Diary,
Today was one of the most fun days I can remember in a long
time. The party at Tom's cabin was a blast.
I ended up giving Becky a ride because Matt had to work,
and he was going to be late. Tom's mom had so much delicious
food for us: deviled eggs, fried chicken, watermelon, coleslaw, and
brownies. There were probably thirty people there and they all
know Becky, and for once, everyone talked to me too. Funny how
I didn't even seem to exist for the first six months I was here, and
now everyone is asking me about Bearcat and my plans for senior
year. The only person who acted totally stuck up was Wanda, but
I pretended like I didn't see her. Rumor has it she still has a big
crush on Lance, but he's not having anything to do with her.
The best part of the day was floating on giant tractor inner tubes.
We had so much fun tipping them over and jumping off them. Some
of the kids were water skiing and Lance tried to talk me into trying

it, but I wasn't feeling that brave. Lance is pretty good; he can even stay up on one ski.

Some of the kids were sneaking off to smoke cigarettes and drink Budweisers. I admit they tasted pretty good on a warm day. I probably would have had more than one if I weren't driving. I might be a teenager but I'm not stupid! And cigarette smoke stinks, no matter how cool it looks!!

I wanted to stay longer but I had promised to be home by seven and the mosquitos were starting to get nasty. I ended up giving Lance a ride home — I have a feeling he planned it that way. He kept apologizing about the dance until I finally told him to shut up about it. When we got to his house, I thought he was going to kiss me, but his dad came out the door just then. I might go to a movie sometime with him. He does seem like a pretty good guy after all but I'm still going to play hard to get for a while. He needs to know I'm not that easy — not like Wanda, ha!

Grandma said she was happy to see I had such a good time.

Summer is the best.

Ivy

Hattie

JUST AS HATTIE PARKED near the picnic area at Pioneer Park, a couple of raindrops hit her windshield. "Oh dear, let's hope this doesn't get worse," she said to Tilly. She had given Tilly and the boys a ride to the Wednesday Club picnic, as James was coming later when he got off work. Hattie gazed at the sky as she helped TJ out of the back seat. A band of dark-bottomed clouds loomed in the north, and the breeze was picking up.

"I didn't hear the forecast for today, did you?" Tilly asked.

"Last night on the news, the weatherman said it would be partly cloudy and humid. I didn't hear anything about rain." Hattie opened the trunk of her blue and white '59 Rambler.

"Robby, you look after TJ, okay? No getting on the seesaw until your daddy gets here," Tilly said.

Hattie watched as Robby ran towards the playground, following TJ, and then she lifted the box holding the paper plates, napkins, utensils, jar of Tang, and bowl of potato salad. She hoped the potato salad had turned out okay; it seemed like it was a little bland. She'd run out of mustard and didn't have an extra jar in the pantry, so she'd added a little vinegar, but it just wasn't the same.

And it wasn't only the potato salad; something just seemed off today.

Tilly held Milo and her Tupperware container of sugar cookies, and they walked toward the picnic tables. Several tables had been moved together, and Cora and Bathilda were spreading sheets over them as Hattie and Tilly joined them.

"Hello, ladies!" Hattie called out.

Cora cheerfully greeted them. Bathilda nodded as she straightened the sheet, so it was even on both sides. Cora came around to kiss Milo's head.

Hattie spied Eddie sitting at the far end of the picnic tables. "Hi, Eddie," she called. Eddie gave a slight nod. Some days, it seemed like Eddie didn't feel like talking and the ladies had learned to respect that and leave him alone. Trying to draw him out only made him withdraw more.

"Did you remember the napkins this time?" Bathilda asked.

"Yep, got 'em here in the box. Where's Ivy?" Hattie asked as she set the box down.

"She'll be here any minute. She had her test for her babysitter certificate this morning, and Delmar wanted to finish mowing alfalfa, so they're driving together."

A few large drops of rain hit the table.

"This is not good. Don't think we had rain on the picnic menu." Bathilda looked up at the sky, and then they all did.

The band of clouds was growing darker, and the temperature was dropping fast as the wind picked up.

"Maybe we should hold off on setting the food out. Wait and see how this develops," Cora said.

Hattie agreed, and they all sat on the picnic table benches. Hattie began a conversation to take their minds off the weather. "How's Ivy's summer going?"

"She seems to be having a good time. She spends a lot of time riding horseback with Becky, and I think she's enjoying babysitting." Cora smiled at Tilly.

Tilly replied, "She is doing such a great job with the boys. They love her. And she's teaching Robby to read." Tilly looked over at the boys on the playground, watching as Robby twirled the merry-go-round, TJ crouched down and hanging on. "Not too fast, Robby!" Tilly shouted.

Suddenly, a gust of wind hit them, and it began to rain.

Tilly handed the baby to Cora. "I'm going to get the boys."

"Oh dear, I certainly hope this is a quick shower," Hattie said. "Those clouds don't look very friendly." The clouds had become thicker and blacker, and they were getting closer. The air felt cloying with a heavy humidity.

Just then, Florence and Lloyd pulled into the parking lot, the back of their pickup piled with folding chairs. Etola and Arlo were right behind them.

Now the rain began pelting down, and the wind blew the trees, leaves flying off, and the sound of the creaking branches adding to the sense of unease Hattie felt. Tilly rounded up the boys and they headed back to the tables.

Arlo ran toward the women. "Let's get the boys to the band shell. Pronto! This doesn't look good." He scooped up TJ as Tilly grabbed Robby's hand, and Cora carried the baby, covering his head. Hattie looked up at the greenish sky, then grabbed the potato salad and hurried for the band shell. The rest of the adults scurried after her.

After the loud boom of thunder, lightning cracked nearby, and the rain began to pour. A tablecloth flew off one table. They let it go and left everything behind as they ran for cover. Hattie's cardboard box blew off as a large branch came crashing down.

Right where they had been standing.

Ivy

WHERE THE HECK WAS he? Maybe she had misunderstood, and her grandfather had already left for the picnic. She was only half paying attention this morning, worrying about passing her test. Should she just leave and head to the park without him?

Ivy paced back and forth between the kitchen and the living room, peering out the windows for her grandfather. She thought she would have heard the noisy tractor drive into the driveway, but maybe she missed him, and he was in the machine shed. She ventured out to have a look.

The morning had started sunny and warm, but now the sky was clouding over, and it was a lot cooler than it had been an hour ago. Ivy walked through the wide sliding door, entering the big, tall-raftered building that smelled of oil, iron, and diesel fuel. There was an empty space where the tractor should be.

Ivy walked back to the house, frustrated that her grandfather must have lost track of time. She looked at the kitchen wall clock. It was twelve-fifteen already, a full twenty-five minutes after he was supposed to meet her so they could get to the picnic by noon.

Ivy went upstairs to get a sweater, remembering that it was shady in Pioneer Park with all the big locust trees. The wind was picking up, she could hear the small branches of the hydrangea bush slapping against the living room window as she came down the stairs. Twelve twenty. She paced back and forth, looking out at the driveway. It didn't make sense; her grandfather was a stickler for always being on time.

As the clock ticked in the quiet house, Ivy made up her mind. She grabbed the keys to the pickup and headed to the driveway. A few drops of rain hit the windshield as she drove down the back road behind the barn and past two fields. The cattle were all bunched up in the corner of the pasture, a sign her grandfather had told her meant a storm was on the way. Ivy drove slowly, expecting to see her grandfather coming up the road any minute. She wasn't certain where he was working, but she was pretty sure she heard her grandmother say something about mowing alfalfa. As flat as the fields were, it should be easy to spot his tractor.

Then she saw it. Off to the right and about a third of the way into the field. The green and yellow John Deere 4020 tractor was stopped. Ivy turned off the engine, climbed out of the pickup, and came around to stand by the passenger door, hoping her grandfather would see her and realize it was time to quit. She waved her arms and yelled for him and then noticed her grandfather was not in the tractor seat. But she could hear the rattle and pop pop of the tractor engine.

It was running but not moving.

Ivy stood for a minute, waiting for her grandfather to appear and climb back up onto the tractor. It was starting to rain a little more, and the wind rustled the poplar branches lining the field. There was no sign of him.

Ivy felt an icy coldness moved through her veins — something must be wrong. She waded through the knee-high alfalfa, run-walking as she got closer to the tractor and mower. Then she spotted him, kneeling between the mower and the tractor, his head bowed forward. When she got closer, she saw her grandfather's face was pale and covered with sweat, his black-framed glasses on the ground. His eyes widened as he looked up and saw her, then he shouted, "Turn off the tractor!" It looked like her grandfather had his sleeve caught in a spinning shaft at the back.

Ivy had never sat on the tractor before and wasn't sure how to turn off the engine. She climbed up and peered at the levers and knobs near the large steering wheel. Her heart raced, but then she noticed the small key and turned it. The engine sputtered to a stop. She jumped down and hurried to her grandfather, who yanked his arm back from the shaft.

"Dammit! I knew better, was hurrying to get a hay plug out."

His sleeve was still wound around the circular shaft. She pulled as hard as she could, and the sleeve tore free. Delmar held up his right hand and stared at his index and middle fingers. At first, they looked white and flattened, but they soon swelled and turned bright red.

"What happened?"

"Didn't put the shield on the power take off." Delmar gasped. He looked at his fingers again and said weakly, "I'm fine. Just let me catch my breath." Sweat was rolling down his face, and his complexion had lost all its usual ruddiness; his skin looked ashen.

"Sit down!" Ivy ordered. She ran back to the pickup and grabbed her sweater, frantically trying to recall the first aid steps she had just learned. There was only a small amount of blood on his fingers, so this must be what they called a crush injury. By the time she got back to him, she could tell he was breathing more rapidly. Pale, breathing fast — was he going into shock?

"Are you feeling dizzy, Grandpa?" He didn't say anything, only nodded.

Ivy wrapped her sweater sleeve tightly around his palm and wrist. It wasn't pretty, but it should stop more bleeding. "C'mon, we need to get you to a doctor. Try to keep your hand help up, higher than your shoulder."

She picked up his glasses, helped her grandfather to his feet, and supported him as they walked to the pickup, then opened the door as Delmar climbed in. As she started to drive, she reviewed what she'd learned about crush injuries — the poisons released by the crushed muscles, the potential for serious tissue injury and organ damage. Things might look fine on the outside, but on the inside, there could be serious damage taking place. She was unsure if this would apply to just finger injuries. At any rate, she was pretty sure her grandfather was in shock.

Ivy drove back to the barnyard and out the driveway as fast as she could. It was starting to rain, the clouds were dark, and the temperature was dropping fast. When they stopped at the red light on the edge of town, Ivy looked up at the blackest row of clouds she'd ever seen, a thin line of green along the bottom. The wind was blowing so hard the tops of large trees were bending, and the traffic light was swaying back and forth.

Delmar leaned his pale head against the door window. For the first time ever, he looked weak. Vulnerable. He said in a cracking voice, "You tell your grandmother how much I love her. She's the best wife a man could ever want."

Ivy patted his knee. "Hang on, Grandpa, don't worry. I'll get you to the hospital."

Ivy stepped hard on the accelerator, eyes on the road and hands gripping the steering wheel, intent on only one thing: to get her grandfather some help. He must be really worried to give her this message for her grandmother.

Tilly

TILLY COMFORTED A WHIMPERING TJ as another loud crack of thunder reverberated through the concrete band shell, followed by a flash of lightning that momentarily lit up the hallway ramp leading from the stage to the restrooms at the back of the building. All eleven of them were sitting together in the dark hallway, their faces barely visible to one another. They'd been there for thirty minutes waiting out the storm. Cora still held baby Milo, who was being surprisingly quiet. Occasionally, one or the other stood up to stretch their legs and peer out at the sky. The cement ramp was unforgiving to the older backs, but everyone knew better than to leave this shelter with the wind blowing as hard as it was.

Cora and Hattie chattered about the various band concerts they could remember seeing performed here, and Cora talked about how, for many years, all the 4-H clubs in the county had a talent show every August on this stage. That's when Vonda Marie had gotten the acting bug, the year she had the lead in the Northview Lassies' performance of a scene from "Oklahoma." The talent shows ended a few years back when Bernadette Fish, the organizer, left town. Bernadette was quite theatrical, having grown up in

California, and there didn't seem to be anyone else to pick up the mantle once she was gone.

Tilly appreciated the distracting stories. Lloyd had been outstanding, venturing out of the band shell a few times and giving them updates on the storm. So far, no one's car had been smashed by a falling branch or flying object, but Lloyd told them it was a mess out there, large locust branches down all over the park.

But what about James? Hopefully he was hunkered down someplace safe and was waiting for the storm to pass, but her worst fear kept surfacing: something terrible happening to her husband. What would she do without him? Thank goodness she was here with her neighbors and not by herself with the three boys in that flimsy trailer or even at Mildred's house. She knew Cora must be concerned about Delmar and Ivy too.

Hattie tried a song to take their minds off the storm and keep the boys occupied. "How about let's sing "Row, Row, Row your Boat"?" She began singing and they all joined in, including Eddie, and then Hattie led them in singing in the round, continuing the song's chorus over and over, well past the time they were tired of it. Even Bathilda, who often refused to sing at Wednesday Club meetings, joined in, her off-key singing echoing loudly off the concrete walls. Finally, after multiple rounds, Lloyd said he couldn't take it anymore and he and Arlo ventured out to look around. The wind had slowed, but it was still pouring rain, and the thunder and lightning continued. They were soaking wet when they returned.

"The sky is lightening up to the north," Lloyd reported.

Arlo followed with, "Wind's gonna push the storm through fairly soon. It's still blowing hard, but I think the worst is over."

Tilly asked, "How does it look out there? On the ground ..."

"Lots of big branches down, and a couple of whole trees toppled over. So far it looks like our cars have been spared."

"Were there any tornadoes?" Bathilda asked.

Lloyd glanced at Arlo for a split second before answering, "Not sure."

"James must be worried sick about us. Do you think it's safe to leave soon?" Tilly asked Lloyd.

"Probably best to wait it out here until we know for sure this thing's died down."

They sat silently, everyone weary of coming up with songs and small talk. Suddenly, they heard a faint voice shouting, "Tilly? Tilly!"

"It's James!" Tilly cried, lifting TJ off her lap and rushing to the stage front. "We're in here."

A soaked James ran to the band shell, where he embraced Tilly. "Oh, sweetheart." He held her for a long time and then looked at her face, where tears rolled down her cheeks.

"Daddy! Where were you?" Robby rushed towards his daddy just as a loud and long rumble of thunder crashed through the sky—a few seconds later lightning cracked. Milo began to wail.

"Let's go back and sit down," James hugged Robby and put his arm around Tilly to guide her back into the hallway. "Everyone okay in here?"

Lloyd answered, "We're all fine, just a little stiff from this concrete. What's it like out there?"

"It's bad. Worst storm I can remember. At least three funnel clouds came through; one of 'em was really wide." He looked at Tilly. Even in the dimly lit space, she could tell that James had bad news.

"What is it, James?"

James put his arm around her. "Our place is gone. Tornado blew the trailer apart pretty bad."

Tilly was speechless while James continued, "The important thing is that you and the boys are fine. The rest is all stuff we can replace, sweetheart."

Tilly felt time stop, her surroundings swirling around her. Nothing around her felt grounded. "But where will we live now?" Even her voice felt like it was coming from outside her body.

James squeezed her. "It'll be okay. We can move in with my mom for a while. Her house is fine; the tornado only blew a shutter off. She rode out the storm in the basement."

That was the worst news of the day, the thought of living with Mildred. Tilly tried to mask her reaction to what she felt inside — horrified.

James said, "It'll be a tight squeeze, but we'll get by."

Suddenly, Hattie piped up with authority. "Now, there's no need to inconvenience Mildred. I have a better idea."

And with that, Tilly's life changed completely.

Hattie

HER MAMA ALWAYS SAID the best cure for about everything was staying busy. While there were plenty of things she'd been wrong about, that one she got right. For the first time in a long time, Hattie felt happy and excited. And more bone-tired than she ever thought possible. What a couple of days it had been.

Yesterday, after the storm, and with all of them sitting helpless in that band shell for so long, they needed to get busy. Looking back, it was quite something how they had put a plan together so fast. Arlo and Etola would go with James to help sort through the rubble of the trailer house to see what could be salvaged. Bathilda would gather boxes for them so they could start sorting and packing up belongings before the rain completely ruined things. Tilly and the boys would go with Florence to have lunch and then try to get the boys to nap. Tilly wanted to see the trailer, but everyone convinced her that the sight would be too hard on the little ones. Lloyd would accompany Cora to check on Delmar and Ivy.

And Hattie and Eddie would go back to her house. She had a lot to do to prepare her house for a family of five.

It didn't take much convincing that her big old four-bedroom farmhouse was the perfect place for Tilly, James, and the boys. Everyone agreed they should move in with her until they had time to figure out a permanent situation.

And now, here she was. Nothing like house guests to force someone to do what they'd meant to do for years. There was already bedroom furniture in the two spare bedrooms, but it seemed like over the years, without any regular visitors, Hattie had turned those rooms into storage spaces. The first step was to clear out all the junk and haul it to the attic and Eddie was a big help to her as he climbed up and down the attic steps. Hattie couldn't believe how much stuff she'd accumulated. Most of it needed to find a new home, but that would have to wait for another time.

She still had her baby crib in the attic, almost an antique after nearly forty years. It was solid oak and heavy, and not easy for her and Eddie to get down and into the bedroom for Tilly and James. Once it was in place, Hattie rested for a minute, looking at the crib. Funny how, for so many years, she'd hung on to that crib — how many times she'd looked at it and dreamed of using it for her own baby. But that was not to be. That would have required a husband. And that was not to be either. Hattie sighed, almost letting herself sink into that regret and sadness and wondering what might have been. But there just wasn't time for that now.

The other bedroom already had two twin beds, perfect for Robby and TJ, and with a big, braided rug between the beds, there was plenty of place to play. Hattie thought about turning the fourth bedroom, a bright sunroom on the ground floor with windows on three sides, into a playroom for the boys, but then she had a better idea.

She and Eddie hauled in an old, flat wooden door from the garage that they set on concrete blocks. It wasn't the prettiest, but it would do for now. A big, long working space. They unrolled an extra rug to warm the floor and positioned a white wicker settee against the wall with a little metal table beside it. It would be a nice place to sit with a lemonade and get inspired. She brought in the large Boston fern from the front porch to add some greenery, then cut a bunch of sunflowers and set the vase on the end of the makeshift desk. It turned out lovely.

Wouldn't Tilly be surprised when she found out she had a room of her own? When she was ready, they'd pick out paints, paper, canvas, and whatever else Tilly wanted. Hattie knew that girl has artistic talent beyond painting signs and windows and the Wednesday Club program covers. She couldn't wait to see what Tilly would create.

And wouldn't it be sweet to have baby Milo in that old crib?

Ivy

It was early when the sun burst through Ivy's bedroom window, waking her. The clock said 5:45 and Ivy groaned and buried her head under the summer quilt to try to get back to sleep. But she could hear her grandmother getting breakfast ready downstairs and so she shuffled from her bed and slipped into her shorts and a sleeveless blouse. It already was hot upstairs, even though the windows had been open all night to let the cool air in.

In the kitchen, her grandmother looked up from cracking eggs and greeted her with her customary bright smile.

"Morning, sweet pea."

"Morning, grandma. Want some help?"

"Sure, why don't you peel a couple of those oranges and put some slices in a bowl?"

A few minutes later, Ivy's grandfather skipped down the steps and strode into the kitchen. He came up to Ivy's grandmother and gave her a peck on the cheek.

"Morning!" He sounded cheerful, as he had ever since his tractor accident a week ago, almost like a different man. Though his hand was still in a sling, and he couldn't use it much, the injury had seemed to make him more appreciative of Ivy and her grandmother.

"How's the babysitting going, Ivy?" he asked.

"Good. It's different being at Hattie's house now, but it's still fun."

Sizzling and popping sounds came from the stove, along with the unmistakable smell of bacon. Ivy loved the taste of bacon, and the aroma made her mouth water. Her mother had rarely cooked it because she said it made the apartment stink too much.

Her grandmother joined the conversation. "How does Hattie seem to be doing with a houseful of people?"

"She seems happy to have them there, and it seems like things are working out well for everyone. Tilly even has her own painting room she calls her studio. She painted the prettiest picture of a vase of sunflowers and give it to Hattie."

"Oh, that's wonderful," Ivy's grandmother said.

Ivy began to set the table. "Don't you think it's strange that Tilly's trailer was the only house in the area to get destroyed by the tornado?"

Her grandfather answered. "Trailer houses always get smashed because the wind gets under them. Wind got up to 80 miles an hour, they say."

Ivy nodded. "It's just so weird how the tornado touched down in just a few places."

"That's pretty typical," her grandfather responded. "Lots of places lost their roofs. We're lucky we just had a few branches come down and didn't lose whole trees like a lot of places."

"At Lance's farm they lost the chicken house but somehow all the hens survived."

"How is Lance?" her grandmother asked as she brought the bacon and eggs to the table.

"He's good. I'm planning to go with him, Becky, and Matt tomorrow to see *The Birds*, it's an Alfred Hitchcock movie. It's supposed to be very scary.

"A double date?" her grandmother asked.

Ivy shrugged. "Kind of."

"Your grandfather wants to ask you something." Ivy could tell her grandmother had nudged her grandfather under the table.

"Um, well, I was wondering if you wanted to go meet your dad."

Ivy felt a little dizzy. Had she heard what she thought she heard?

"You mean in prison?" she said. Ivy looked over at her grandmother for a response, but her grandmother's face was still, not giving away anything.

"I called the warden, and he said visiting hours are on Tuesdays. We're on the visitor's list — unless you don't want to go," her grandfather said, as if meeting her father for the first time at the age of seventeen wasn't any big deal.

"So, we'd go tomorrow?" Ivy's skin tingled with discomfort.

"A week from tomorrow," her grandmother responded. "That is, if you'd like to."

"Yes, yes, I'd like to!" Ivy said with force. But inside, she didn't feel so certain.

How many times in one year could her whole life change so completely? She put her head down and began to eat her breakfast, and it turned out the bacon had no flavor at all.

Etola

ARLO WAS ALREADY DRESSED and out by the time Etola dragged herself out of bed at seven-thirty. It had been a rough night, and she'd flipped and flopped like a fish on the shore until well past midnight. Etola grabbed her lightest summer robe and stepped into her worn slippers. She padded down the hallway to the bathroom, then leaned against the sink to remove a cocklebur that was lodged inside the slipper, biting her heel with every step. The long list of things she needed to do knocked loudly inside her head as she shuffled to the kitchen. So much to get done – of all the days to oversleep! First off, she'd better get those two pies baked pronto. It was supposed to be 103 today, the third day of this melt-your-bones heat wave, complete with high humidity and not a bit of a breeze. Etola could kick herself for offering to bake for the Scandinavian Days bake sale; there was always more than enough pies with all those ladies falling all over each other to impress the mayor. And it wouldn't be right to bake one pie without baking another for Arlo. Arlo did have a mighty sweet tooth.

Etola opened the refrigerator and took out the rhubarb she had picked last night. It was the last of the season, and some of the stalks were as woody as could be. Hopefully she'd have enough to eke out the eight cups she needed. She rinsed the rhubarb and began cutting and dicing, her thoughts settling into the well-worn groove that had kept her awake most of the night. Finally, she had cut enough rhubarb and could make the pie filling. She beat the eggs and added butter, flour, nutmeg, and a pinch of salt. The recipe called for a generous one-and-a-half cups of sugar for each pie, but as Bathilda was fond of saying, rhubarb was tart enough to pucker a pickle.

The darn sugar canister was almost empty, so she'd need to get a new bag from the makeshift pantry off the entryway. Arlo's tiny cupboards left a lot to be desired and Etola was always trying to figure out how to turn his small kitchen into a place for some decent cooking and baking. Before she headed to the pantry, she'd see if there was enough lard for the pastry.

Measuring out the lard and then adding the flour and salt, Etola mixed the ingredients and began to roll out the crust with her rolling pin. What a sticky mess! It was going to be a heckuva day for pastry with this humidity. She added more flour to the top of the dough and the rolling pin. It was still too sticky. She added more flour, then a little more flour. Now the dang pastry was tough as nails, and she could barely move her rolling pin, but she finally managed to get the crusts rolled out and laid into the bottom of the glass pie pans. Etola put half of the cut rhubarb into the pans and then poured the custard on the top. At least she could make lattice top crusts — a lattice top can pretty up most problems. By the time she got both pies done, it was already nine-thirty, two whole hours just to get two pies in the oven, and she was still in her robe. She might as well put up her feet and sit a spell. Before she knew it, she'd dozed off, and she woke with a start when her head jerked forward. Only ten minutes before the pies needed to come out of the oven!

While washing the dishes, she picked up the empty sugar canister, and reality hit. Holy cussing cow! Rhubarb pie without the sugar! Instantly she came unhinged, her pent-up feelings like water boiling over in a too-small saucepan.

She yanked open the top of the kitchen's Dutch door and then propped open the screen door. Using potholders so she didn't burn herself, she stood in the doorway and flung the first pie, pan, and all, towards the edge of the yard and the poplar trees. The pie made it about halfway to the trees, crust and filling flying everywhere. Etola marched back to the oven, grabbed the second pie, and flung it. This time, she put extra muscle into her throw and the pie sailed like a discus straight towards the garden shed. It hit against the wooden wall with such force that the glass pan shattered. Then, she noticed Arlo standing nearby, watching the sticky red and yellow filling slide down the side of the shed.

Etola slammed the Dutch door shut. To hell with everything!

By the time Arlo entered the kitchen, Etola was sitting at the table, her head down on folded arms, weeping. Arlo hurried to her side and gently rested his arm on her back. "You ok, Etola? What in the world happened?"

Etola kept her head down for a few seconds, then spoke through shoulder-shaking sobs. "I miss my marble-topped sideboard."

"What did you say?"

"I miss my marble-topped sideboard. Just right for rolling out pastry. I can't do it on a wooden cutting board!"

Arlo pulled up a chair close to Etola. "Sweetheart, don't you fret. I'll get you a marble board. Is that why you threw the pies across the yard?"

"No, it's not that." Etola lifted her head between sobs. "I forgot to put the sugar in. You can't possibly eat a rhubarb pie without the sugar! You'd have a permanent lemon face."

Arlo started to smile but then bit his lips together. "Well, you're right about that. But did you need to send them flying out the door?"

"I don't know why I did that. Everything is wonky today." She started to cry again.

Arlo sat for a minute with his hand on Etola's back, letting her crying wind down, then asked quietly. "Can I ask you something, honey?"

Etola let out a few hiccups, wiped her nose on her apron, and held her breath to stop herself from crying. "What is it?"

"Are you unhappy here? Do you wish you hadn't married me?"

Etola's heart skipped a beat. "For cripes sake, it's nothing like that. I mean, I'm a bit of a fish out of water here, but you are every bit the doting husband I thought you would be. I don't know what bee flew into my bonnet."

Arlo asked in a quiet voice, "And I'm not asking too much of you ... in the bedroom?"

Etola almost shouted, "Course not, Arlo, that's not it!"

"Well, there must be something that's bothering you. I thought I heard you tossing and turning in the night."

Etola chose her words carefully. "Something is nagging at me. But it's not about you. I'm worried sick about Bathilda. She's just not herself, won't hardly talk to me, doesn't want me coming over; even Eddie says she's barely talking to him anymore. I don't know what to do for her."

Arlo patted Etola's back and kissed her on the cheek. "I'm glad to hear that it's not about us, and I'm sorry about Bathilda. I imagine she's lonely without you there. You know, I might have an idea. Why don't you and I head over to the feed store after lunch? I saw something on the bulletin board I'd like to show you."

Etola had no idea what Arlo was talking about, but the longer she was with him, the more she had learned to trust him. That man just seemed to know how to make everything better.

Bathilda

BATHILDA WAS OUT IN the back pasture, checking the fence line, when Eddie ran up to the edge of the road and wildly waved his arms. *What in the blazes? Was something on fire?* Bathilda rushed to the dirt lane to see what was going on. "What's the matter?" she yelled.

"We need you in the barn."

"What for? And who's we?" Bathilda asked. Her mind raced — there were no sheep in the barn. It should be empty.

Eddie didn't answer; he just started to walk off as Bathilda stomped after him. "Who's we?" she asked, putting more force behind her question.

"Etola. And Arlo. They want you in the barn."

"What's going on? Is something wrong?"

Eddie kept walking, his head down. "I'm not supposed to say."

"Why, that's plain ridiculous. I don't see why I'm expected to follow you with no reason given." She kept following, curiosity getting the best of her.

The barn door was open, and Bathilda stepped over the threshold, her eyes taking a minute to adjust to the dim interior.

Etola and Arlo were looking at something in the corner stall, the stall where Shep used to sleep and the one where he took his last breath. Bathilda hadn't gone into that corner ever since and was unsure she wanted to go there now. She trod along the packed dirt floor of the barn, past the horse stalls and their wooden mangers, gnawed down by nervous teeth. When she peered into the stall, she spied a tiny black and white bundle of fur.

Bathilda whipped her head away from the stall towards the open window and stared at the garden beyond. The raspberry bushes. Where her dear Shep lay. Eventually, she turned back and said, "What's that thing doing in Shep's pen?"

"It's a puppy," Eddie said.

"Of course, I know it's a puppy! Did you think I thought it was a pig? What's it doing here?"

"We brought it for you," Etola said.

"Well, you can just take it back then. I never asked you for a puppy."

Arlo spoke in a gentle voice. "We thought maybe you could use another sheepdog around the place."

Bathilda snorked and looked down at the puppy who looked up at her. Such soft brown eyes. Gentle, but shining with the curiosity and intelligence of a border collie. "Doesn't look like much of a sheepdog to me. Not like Shep."

"That's true. There will never be another Shep," Arlo said.

"Right. And I'm not about to start replacing him now."

"We understand. It's too soon," Etola said. She winked at Arlo. "Let's help Eddie get those sheep moved, and then we'll come back and get the pup. She'll be fine here in the meantime." She grabbed Eddie's arm and pulled him out of the barn. Arlo followed.

Bathilda waited until they were gone and then stepped into the stall and squatted beside the puppy. It came to her eagerly, and when she put out her hand, the puppy licked it and then took a playful nibble. She picked up the roly-poly ball of fur and held it out in front of her. "Why, you little rascal! You stop that now!"

Ivy

IT WAS NINE O'CLOCK sharp when Ivy and her grandfather pulled onto the blacktop and headed towards Layton. She'd changed her outfits four times, finally settling on a simple dress she usually only wore to church. Ivy was at the wheel; her grandfather was still under doctor's orders to wait a few more weeks before driving until his fingers healed completely. She hoped her grandfather wouldn't criticize her driving; she was nervous about driving on the interstate, and her palms were sweaty. She was even more worried about how the rest of the morning would unfold. For the last several days, there had been one question that kept buzzing in her head. What would her father think of her? Her grandpa must be anxious, too, because they rode in heavy silence for most of the ninety-minute trip until he switched on the radio to a country western station. Buck Owens belted out the song "My Heart Skips a Beat."

When they finally arrived at the four-story, grey sandstone building, Ivy was pained by how cold and sterile it looked, all the small dark windows covered with ironwork. This place looked even more dismal than she had imagined. When they entered the front door and stepped into the drab grey waiting room with a front desk and no chairs, she thought it smelled like bottled sadness. They stepped up to the middle-aged guard seated behind a tall metal desk that came almost up to his drooping shoulders. His face looked permanently settled into a look of disappointment, his mouth sullen and silent as he waited for them to speak.

"We're here to see Hank Red Feather." Ivy's grandfather said.

"You on the list?" the guard asked, his tone flat.

"Yep. Name's Hanson. Delmar. And Ivy."

The guard opened his notebook, ran a finger down a list, located Hank's name, and read the notes beside the name. "Visiting time is limited to fifteen minutes. One visitor at a time."

Delmar looked at Ivy with his jaw set. "You go, Ivy."

"Do you want to take part of the time?" she asked, hoping he'd agree.

Delmar shook his head. "No. You take the fifteen." He gave her arm a gentle squeeze.

Ivy nodded, feeling a little shaky and almost sick to her stomach.

The guard didn't make eye contact when he said, "Have to frisk you before you go in. And no purses allowed."

Ivy handed her purse to her grandfather. She stood in front of the guard and felt herself tense up as he ran his hands down her body. A hot sense of shame washed over her, though she couldn't understand why, she hadn't done anything wrong. Then the guard peeked through the small window at the top of the heavy metal door and motioned Ivy into the hallway.

On the other side, a tall, skinny guard with bad skin waited, looking not much older than Ivy. They walked down the hallway, their footsteps echoing off the tile floor, highly buffed and reflecting the dim lines of the overhead fluorescent lighting tubes. It looked like a long line of bars covering the floor. All the identical windowless doors on either side of the hallway were closed and at the third door on the right the guard unlocked it and entered. Ivy followed. Inside the small room were two metal stools, one close to a narrow shelf in front of a large metal framed window where a thick black phone squatted on the shelf. The guard sat down on the stool in the corner without explanation, and Ivy sat on the other. It was cold in this room.

"What am I supposed to do?" Ivy asked.

"When he comes in, pick up the phone," the guard said, sounding irritated, like she should have known. Ivy looked through the window and saw an identical room mirrored on the other side. She felt slightly dizzy and squeezed her fingers to bring some feeling into them. In a moment, the door opened, and a guard escorted a man in blue jeans and a light denim shirt into the room. He had a funny shuffling walk, and for a second, Ivy wondered if he was crippled. Then she realized he was shackled around his ankles. And it hit her — he was an inmate, a criminal. Should she be afraid of him? Ivy held her breath as the man sat on the stool across the window. When he put the phone to his ear and gave a slight nod to her, Ivy picked up the heavy black receiver. Why was she even here? This was crazy.

They stared at each other for a moment until Hank spoke. "You must be Ivy?" Ivy wondered if he was serious; who the heck else would she be? Then Hank broke into a grin and continued, "I bet you were wishing I'd be a lot more handsome."

Ivy couldn't help but crack a smile. "I wasn't sure what you'd look like in person. I've only seen a picture of you in the paper." She wished she hadn't said that part about the paper. And it wasn't true. She recognized his square jawline from that photo she'd kept hidden in her diary.

"I've only seen a few pictures of you when you were young, and your grandmother sent them. All this time, I've been wondering how you turned out. Figured you'd be as pretty as your mother, though. She was the prettiest girl I've ever seen."

They both were silent, and Ivy looked away. It was almost hard to breathe in this small room. How were daughters supposed to act around a father they'd never met? She had a distinct feeling they were both in awe and terrified of one another.

"I guess we have a lot to catch up on. Tell me about yourself, Ivy."

When Ivy spoke, her voice sounded different to herself — higher pitched. And shaky. "Well, I've been in Prairie View almost a year, even though Mom said it would only be a month or two." Ivy realized that she sounded kind of bitter. "I mean, there are a lot of nice people there and all, but it's not nearly as exciting as Omaha, where there are a million things to do."

"What kinds of things did you like to do in Omaha?" Hank asked.

Ivy thought about how this must look to the guard — a young woman talking to a prisoner. Who happened to be her father. It was all so strange. "Oh, you know, I was always going to the movies or shopping with my best friend Val. Sometimes, we'd go bowling or just hang out and talk."

Hank looked like he was listening carefully. "Yeah, I guess you can't do those things in Prairie View." His eyes twinkled, and it almost seemed like he was trying to hold back a grin.

Ivy squirmed. "Well, those things you can. But there are other things like The Durham Museum or the Doorly Zoo. Those things you can only do in Omaha."

"I understand. Maybe Prairie View just doesn't feel like home?" He tilted his head. His eyes were deep brown and wide set, his gaze soft and kind looking.

"Right!" Ivy answered quickly, then wondered if she meant that. What made a place feel like home?

"How's Bearcat doing?"

"He's fine now, not lame at all, thank God." Ivy looked at Hank to see if he'd noticed; she tried not to say 'thank God' around her grandparents, as they said it was taking the Lord's name in vain. "My friend Becky and I have been barrel racing at her farm. She says he's a natural."

Hank sat back in his chair. "Those quarter horses were born to barrel race. Quick, good turners. Are you thinking about trying a rodeo some time?"

Ivy shook her head. "Oh, I doubt it. We mostly do it for fun."

Hank nodded slowly. "How's school going?"

"It's okay. It's easy here."

"I bet you're a smart young lady. Do you think you'll want to go to college after you graduate?"

"Yeah, I think so. I'm not sure what I want to be yet, but I'm pretty sure I'll want to go. Maybe back east somewhere."

"Glad to hear it. School is important. I always thought that if I'd finished high school, maybe even gone to college, my life would have turned out much better." Hank ran his hands through his thick dark brown hair, close-cropped.

"What about you? Are you gonna be stuck in the slammer forever?" As soon as the words came out, Ivy covered her mouth. She had told herself not to use that word! It was only that she'd recently heard Rod Serling use it on an episode of *Twilight Zone,* and it had gotten stuck in her head. She looked at Hank as a hot wave of shame ran through her — but he was laughing. A big old belly laugh. He ended with a wide, full-toothed smile.

Then she noticed it. His tooth. He had the same eyetooth overlapping his front tooth that she had. The very tooth that she stared at so often in the mirror. Suddenly, his tooth, and her tooth, broke something open in her. *It's true. I have a father.* Never mind that she was visiting him in prison. He was real. A sudden warmth spilled over her heart.

Her thoughts were interrupted by the guard, who announced loudly, "Three minutes left."

"I hope to get out of the slammer soon, once my lawyer can find that witness and prove my innocence. And then I'm gonna make a change; I'm done with the meat packing business. Gonna go back to what I love, being a horse trainer. Figure I have a few good years left in me while I can still get on a wild, bucking horse."

Ivy smiled widely at him, hoping he would notice her front teeth. "That's neat. I hope you get out soon."

They sat in silence for a minute, just looking at one another. Ivy felt her shoulders drop a little. She looked at her father's short, thick neck and strong-looking shoulders and wondered how tall he was.

"If, for some reason, I don't get out of here, I want you to know something. Just because I wasn't in your life doesn't mean I wasn't always thinking about you. Every month, I put aside money for you. It kept me going all those years, knowing I was working for you. I've got almost five thousand dollars put away. It's set aside for you to use for college, but once you're twenty-one, you're free to do with it what you want."

Five thousand dollars! That was probably enough money for her to go anywhere she wanted for college. "I don't know what to say; I mean, thank you."

"You're welcome. And no strings attached. You don't have to stay in touch with me. My lawyer, Patrick Callahan, has the money; you only need to contact him."

The guard in Hank's room stood. "Time's up."

Ivy leaned forward, closer to the window; the fifteen minutes had gone by so quickly. "Maybe I'll visit you again. If I'm still in South Dakota."

"I'd like that. Thank you for coming to see me." In an instant, Hank's eyes welled up, but he quickly smiled, showing Ivy that precious eyetooth again.

Ivy stayed seated, watching her father stand up. He was taller than the guard. Maybe almost six feet tall. As he shuffled out of the room, she strained to memorize everything about him, hoping this wouldn't be both the first and last time she saw him.

Then, she couldn't hold it in any longer and a half-swallowed sob escaped her lips. The pimply-faced guard pointed to the box of Kleenex and gave her a little time before opening the door to let her out.

Ivy was finishing saddling Bearcat for an evening ride with Becky when she heard her grandmother calling her.

"Ivy!" Her grandmother poked her head in the doorway. "Ivy, honey. Your mother is on the phone. She needs to talk to you."

Ivy checked to make sure Bearcat was securely tied to the post before she followed her grandmother out of the barn. "What does she want?"

She thought it was strange that her grandmother didn't answer, just kept walking back to the house. Her mother was probably calling with the latest excuse for why Ivy wouldn't be leaving South Dakota any time soon. She picked up the phone. "Hello?"

"There you are. I have the best news for you! Remember when I told you that Mel Hartmann had gotten in touch with me? We've been writing and he's been calling me for the last six weeks, and he's asked me — I mean us — to come back to Omaha. The apartment right next to our old apartment has opened, and Mel has put down the first month's rent for us."

Ivy was silent. A whole mix of emotions came flooding in: anger, shock, disbelief, and hope. Her heart pounded inside her chest.

Her mother continued. "Wasn't that so sweet of him? And isn't that the best news?"

Ivy didn't know what to say. She turned to look at her grandmother seated at the kitchen table. *Does she know?*

"I've had enough of Hollywood. If you're not willing to play their games, you don't have a chance. I have to keep some shred of self-respect for myself. Ivy, are you there?"

"Yes, mom. I'm here," Ivy squeaked.

"Get your bags packed because I'm leaving California next Tuesday. I should be there to pick you up on Friday."

Ivy looked at her grandmother, but her grandmother wasn't looking back. She was staring out the window. "Wow, that's so soon. I don't know if I can be ready by ..."

Now, her mother sounded irritated. "You don't seem very excited, Miss Ivy. I would have thought you'd be so happy to get back to your friends. You've told me so many times how much you miss Omaha."

Ivy felt her stomach clench. "It's just that it's kind of shocking how sudden it is."

"I know, but I need to recognize when a good opportunity comes knocking. I'm done with this place. Too many stuck-up people here. I'd better go; a friend let me borrow her telephone. See you soon, sweetheart!"

Ivy's mother hung up the phone, and Ivy stood motionless. Her whole world was turned upside down. Again. And she couldn't decide if she was happy or sad.

Cora

CORA COULDN'T GET BACK to sleep. She'd tried everything, including counting sheep, and still no luck. And those hot flashes combined with the heat of the evening weren't helping anything. Finally, she got up quietly, guiding herself with her hand down the dark hallway and carefully down the steps to the kitchen.

From the window, Cora stared at the bright yard light, the evening fog creating a narrow beam from the top of the light to the gravel driveway below. The white barn glowed in the distance. The barn made her think of Bearcat. That horse had been good for Ivy, helping her make a friend and connecting her to farm life. Even though the near-foundering incident had been painful and challenging, it was also a good lesson in responsibility.

Cora tiptoed into the kitchen and pulled out the Folgers can to make coffee. No sense trying to get back to sleep; even though it was only four-thirty, she'd just start her day. She could probably get a lot done before the sun rose.

It was hard to believe Ivy had been here almost a full year. It had gone by so fast, and yet so much had happened. It was the best year Cora had had in many years. How she would miss that girl!

She let out a big exhale of air from her suddenly tight chest and kept moving. She was just not going to allow herself to dwell on the sadness. Not yet.

Cora grabbed her always-present list of things to do and a pencil from the counter and sat at the kitchen table, preparing to add more items for the day.

That darn Vonda Marie, always putting herself first. Maybe that's what happened when you have a baby when you're only a girl yourself. It would have been so good for Ivy to finish out her last year of high school here. Ivy had grown so much, softer yet stronger at the same time.

Cora poured her first cup of coffee. Maybe two teaspoons of sugar today to get her going. She picked up the list, scanning it. Everything looked hard today. Even the things she normally clicked off without a second thought seemed particularly tiresome. Cora sat a spell, drinking her coffee while she considered what to do first.

Then she pulled out the flashlight, grabbed her willow basket and shears, and left her house shoes at the kitchen door. Better to be barefoot in the morning dew — then she could hose off her feet before she came in. In the early dawn, Cora carefully shuffled to the flowerbed at the front of the house. There were some bright orange tiger lilies ready to be cut and some of those giant yellow dahlias. Oh, and daisies. Lots of happy white daisies. Daisies would always remind Cora of her granddaughter. Thank goodness they would bloom well into September, even after her precious Ivy was gone.

Florence

FLORENCE COULDN'T SEEM TO concentrate on anything. Usually, with the newest issue of *House Beautiful*, she'd sit right down and spend hours poring over the latest home furnishing and hostess tips. Today, none of it seemed to hold her attention. She kept thinking of Cora and Ivy.

Finally, she put down the magazine and headed to the hallway phone. "Davis 4214, please."

It took a long time for Hattie to pick up the phone, and when she did, Florence heard a baby fussing in the background and two boys arguing.

"Hi, Hattie. Sounds like I've called at a bad time."

"Oh, it's alright. The boys were arguing over a toy tractor, and then it set off Milo. Tilly is here, so they'll soon work it out." Hattie sounded unfazed.

"How's it going over there with your newly expanded household?"

"It's certainly much louder than I was used to," Hattie remarked wryly. "But Tilly is a wonderful mother. And ... she has a new client and can work from her studio."

"Etola said *you've* taken a job?"

"That's right. I'm a summer school teacher. I saw how much I liked being around kids again and decided to apply. I have to say I love it; feels like I have a whole new life. Much happier than my previous one," Hattie said.

"That's just wonderful. But speaking of happy, that's why I'm calling. I'm afraid poor Cora is having a difficult time, what with Ivy returning to Omaha."

"I'm broken up about the news myself; I can only imagine how Cora's feeling."

Florence's plan developed as she spoke. "I've been thinking about what we should do, and I have an idea."

"We should do something. What's your idea?"

"There's only one thing to do. Throw a party. How about next Saturday? Right before Ivy leaves? I think Vonda Marie will even be here by then." Florence hadn't met Vonda Marie and wanted to keep an open mind about her. She'd heard a lot of murmuring, but Florence wondered how much of that was just green-eyed jealousy.

"That's a wonderful idea. The Wednesday Club can bring the food. Can you hostess?" Hattie said.

"Of course. The yard is still looking good from Etola's wedding. Let's say 2:00. Can you get the phone tree going?"

"You betcha. Good idea, Florence."

Florence hung up and strode to the kitchen for her favorite notebook — her party planner. She probably should have asked Lloyd first, but surely, he'd understand. These days, he wasn't hiding out like he used to, and he knew how much Florence loved to throw a good party. Even if it was for a sad occasion.

August 1964

Ivy

IT WAS TOO HOT today to race the barrels – ninety-eight degrees – so Ivy and Becky had taken Bearcat and Storm on a slow walk on the dirt lanes that surrounded the neighboring farmyards and fields. At times they rode abreast, the two horses in sync with their steps, the girls' stirrups occasionally rubbing against each other. Ivy was only half-enjoying herself, dreading the news she would need to share as Becky chatted on in her usual enthusiastic style.

They were almost back to Ivy's grandparents' farm when Becky remembered about the movie. "So, was *Goldfinger* good? Should we see it?"

"It's good, lots of action. And Sean Connery is so dreamy."

"How was the time with Lance?"

"He's a pretty neat guy once you get to know him." Ivy looked off into the distance at the white, puffy clouds in the vast expanse of dark blue sky. She hoped she could always remember these South Dakota skies.

Becky continued. "Do you think he'll ask you to the Homecoming Dance? He's probably going to get chosen for the royalty court, you know."

This was the opening Ivy could no longer avoid. "I won't be going to the Homecoming Dance."

"Why ever not? It's the best dance of the year!"

Ivy hesitated for a moment. "I'm leaving. My mom is picking me up in a week, and we're driving back to Omaha."

The two rode in silence, the only sound the squeaking of the saddle leather. Then Becky blurted out, "When were you going to tell me?" Ivy could tell from Becky's face that her feelings were hurt.

"I just found out a couple of days ago. I was kind of waiting for the right time." Ivy was afraid if she said more, she'd start to cry. They were almost at the fork in the lane where they would split off to head for their homes, and they were both quiet.

Finally, Becky spoke in a low voice, "I'm gonna miss you."

"I'm going to miss you too. But I'm sure I'll be coming back to visit my grandparents."

"What's going to happen to Bearcat?"

"Oh, I suppose he'll go back to the Baldridge's." Ivy tried to sound nonchalant, but her heart was breaking at the thought. "I'm babysitting tomorrow, but do you want to ride again on Tuesday?"

"Sure. I'll call you." Becky turned toward her farm. "See you later."

"Bye." Ivy continued to the north, towards her grandparents' farm. She bent forward to pat Bearcat on the neck. She could hardly bear to think about his future. What *would* happen to him? She feared the Baldridge's would put him up for sale again and wondered who would buy him, whether they'd be nice to him.

Ivy hunkered down in the saddle as they made their way back to the farmyard. Bearcat usually wanted to trot as he got closer to the barn, eager for his oats, but today, he plodded along. It was almost as if he sensed something was going on.

Ivy reached the barn, dismounted, and led Bearcat into the barn and the first stall. She eased the bridle over his ears, and he opened his mouth to let the bit fall out. She held out the halter, and Bearcat put his nose through the opening and stood quietly while Ivy slipped it over his ears and buckled it on the side. She poured a scoop of oats into the manger.

Ivy unbuckled the back cinch, then the front cinch, and lifted the saddle off Bearcat's back and onto the saddle peg in the tack room. Then, she removed the saddle blanket and laid it upside down over the saddle to dry. She grabbed a currycomb and started to groom his back, lost in thought, and then realized that Bearcat wasn't eating his oats.

She sidled toward the manger and looked at the untouched oats. "What's the matter, boy? Aren't you hungry today? You always love your oats. I know ... maybe you'll like this."

Ivy walked back to the tack room and unrolled the top of a twenty-pound bag, grabbing a handful of sweet, dark dried molasses, a special treat for Bearcat. She hurried back to the stall and held her open hand for Bearcat. He gently nibbled at the molasses and then used his long tongue to lick the last crumbs from her palm and between her fingers. She stood facing him, and he rested his head on her shoulder for a second and then nuzzled his nose under her arm. Ivy wrapped her other arm around his neck and leaned her head against the top of his head, her breath on him and his breath on her. If only she could memorize his scent.

They stayed that way for a long time until Ivy's tears tickled Bearcat, causing his big, soft ears to twitch against her cheek. This would be the hardest goodbye.

August 2

Dear Val,

You won't believe this — I promise I'm not putting you on. By the time you get this letter, I'll be almost to Omaha.

My mother isn't staying in California, and we'll be on our way back in three days. She's lined up an apartment for us in the same building we lived in before, on 32ⁿᵈ Avenue. So, we can ride the bus together again. One more year and we graduate! Pretty cool, huh?

It's been a while since I've heard from you. How's everything going? Is Brad up to his old tricks? Please let him know I'm coming back. If he even cares by now.

Do you know what day school starts again? We should have at least a couple of weeks to be free before it's back to the grindstone.

It will be so neat to see you and everyone again. I hope people haven't forgotten me.

I've finally made some friends here, and it will be sad to say goodbye. And it's especially hard to leave Bearcat.

Until soon, Ivy

ALTHOUGH HER GRANDMOTHER HAD made Ivy's favorites of meatloaf, fried potatoes, and corn on the cob, Ivy didn't feel like eating. There was a strain in the air. Her grandfather had a half-concealed scowl on his face, her mother was unusually quiet, and her grandmother's face looked pinched and tight as if she was working hard to not show her feelings.

Her grandfather took small, fast nips in a straight line across his buttered and heavily salted corncob and glanced over at his daughter. "So, what're your plans now?"

Her mother half-shrugged and said, "I'll get a job. My friend Mel says they can probably use me at his brother's bakery."

Her grandfather sucked the corn out of his teeth and didn't say anything.

"It'll be a start — until I can find something else."

Her grandmother smiled, "That'll be good, sweetheart."

Ivy's mom glanced away, then suddenly leaned across the kitchen table, and said to Ivy, "I have an idea! Why don't we get a jump start and leave for Omaha in the morning?"

There was a short, stunned silence around the table until Ivy said, "But what about the party tomorrow night?"

Her mother pursed her lips. "I didn't think you cared about it. Wouldn't you rather get back to your friends sooner?"

Her grandmother responded first. "Everyone here has been looking forward to a chance to say goodbye to Ivy. You can't go before the party."

Her mom looked pointedly at her when she said, "Well, I just –"

Delmar interrupted. "You just what? It's always about you, isn't it, Marie?"

"It's *Vonda* Marie. And no. It's never *ever* been about what I wanted."

"You telling me this," her grandfather pointed across the table at Ivy, "is not what you wanted? Dumping off your daughter so you can parade yourself in front of ..."

"Stop, Delmar!" her grandmother interrupted. She glanced over at Ivy. Ivy felt her stomach sour and wished she were anywhere but here. She had always thought it was strange that they lived only a few hours from her grandparents but rarely visited, and not since Ivy was six. Now she understood why. It was like her mother was still sixteen in her grandfather's eyes.

There was silence as they all waited to see who would make the next move. Finally, her mother spoke. "There's something you don't get, Daddy. I guess you're never going to get it. The best thing — about the only thing — I ever had going for me was my looks."

Her grandfather set down his ear of corn and narrowed his eyes. "You didn't even try to— "

Her mom spit out her words, her eyes flashing. "Exactly what did you expect me to try to do? A young mother? No high school diploma. No husband, thanks to you."

Her grandfather leapt up so quickly that he almost knocked his chair over. His face was red as he shouted. "That is so much B.S.! That was your decision — not mine!" He stomped out of the kitchen as Ivy's mother and grandmother exchanged shocked glances.

Finally, Ivy slid her chair back and stood up. "I'm going upstairs to finish packing."

"I'll help you clean up, Mom."

Ivy climbed the steps to her bedroom and looked around at the two cardboard boxes and her open suitcase. There wasn't any more packing to do. She plopped onto the bed, grabbed a letter from under her pillow, and slipped it into her back pocket. She crept down the stairs, avoiding the areas with the loudest creaks, and out the front door. It was a dramatic sunset tonight, a long line of horizontal layers of clouds stretching across the horizon. She sat on the front step and then decided to walk around the house to the back steps, where she could see the pastures to the west. Bearcat, head down, was grazing on the grass, and her grandmother's and mother's voices came through the open kitchen window.

Ivy heard her grandmother say "I wonder if it's the best thing for her. She seems to be enjoying her life here."

"Maybe she's just learned to adjust," Vonda Marie said. Ivy recognized a tinge of doubt in her voice.

"Why don't you let her finish her senior year? She's made some friends now. And she loves Bearcat so much ..."

"She'll get over that horse — maybe we'll get a cat or something. There's nothing long-term for her here ... so much more opportunity in Omaha. She's a smart girl ..."

Ivy heard the water running in the sink below the open window, her mother rinsing the dishes as her grandmother washed them.

"You've said that before. But there are different opportunities for her here. And there could have been for you, too. I mean, if you had stayed and married Hank ..."

Her mother cut in. "Well, I never had that choice, did I? You both seem to be rewriting history. Someone else chose my future for me ..." She hesitated a moment. "For God's sake, don't you remember? He threatened to have Hank thrown in jail if he didn't leave town!"

Ivy sat motionless, straining to hear.

"And look at him now. Locked up after all."

"You know as well as I do, he never meant to hurt that man."

"Of course, I know. Hank could never hurt a flea."

Her grandmother said, "I should have stood up to your father."

"Yes, you should have protected me. You might have been able to make things different for me." Ivy had heard that bitter tone before.

"It's a regret I live with every day." Ivy's grandmother said. "He thought he was doing the right thing."

"Maybe in the long run he did. It probably wouldn't have lasted between us, even if we had married."

"How do you feel about him and Ivy being in touch?"

Ivy held her body as still as possible, not wanting to miss her mother's answer.

"I don't see the point, but it's fine I suppose, if I don't have to be involved. Hank is behind a door I closed a long time ago. Funny, I never felt like I was lying to her when I acted like he wasn't alive anymore. He really was dead to me."

Ivy had heard enough and needed to escape their voices. She walked to the side of the yard where she could get a closer view of Bearcat grazing peacefully, the setting sun creating a glowing red line across the top of his back. She sat down and leaned against the trunk of an elm tree, hidden from view of the house, and pulled the letter from her pocket.

August 4, 1964

Dear Ivy,

I only have a few minutes to write, but I wanted to share some good news. The witness who saw everything that happened on the night of March 27th says he'll talk to the judge. My lawyer thinks the judge might take another look at the case, and it could get dismissed. He says if I'm lucky and the judge gives me another chance, I could be out of here within a couple of weeks, a month at the most.

And I have more good news. My boss Mitch from the slaughterhouse came to see me, and when I told him I wouldn't be coming back to work, he offered to help me get started with my own horse training business. Plenty of people around here need help getting their colts ready to ride. All I need is a little property somewhere nearby with a nice sturdy barn, and I'll build a small arena. Mitch says he'll invest in it with me.

So, I'm thinking that if it's close enough to Prairie View, maybe you could help after school and on the weekends. A part-time job? That is, if you'd want to, once all this is behind me.

I'll write again soon, but I wanted to tell you what's happening.

Love, Dad

Ivy folded up the letter, tucked it back in the envelope, and stared for a moment at the prisoner number in the return address. Then she returned it to her pocket. Now the orange sun was low on the skyline, beginning to set, the purple line of clouds a dramatic contrast. Ivy watched Bearcat contentedly grazing in the pasture, then shifted her gaze to the fence at the pasture's edge. A lone mourning dove sat silhouetted on the barbed wire, singing its plaintive call. Ivy listened and watched, thinking she would remember this moment for a very long time. Her heart hurt.

Florence

A LITTLE OVER A week was not much time to pull together a party, but Florence thought that if anyone in Prairie View could do it, she could. Lloyd and Arlo returned to the church to borrow the tables and chairs again. They wouldn't need as many as for the wedding, even though Florence had told Ivy and Becky to spread the word to invite more young people.

Florence had hoped that Coast to Coast would have a ready-made 'We'll miss you' sign, but they didn't, so last night she and Etola had painted the words on a long roll of butcher paper. Now, watching Lloyd and Lance hang it from the back porch roof, she thought they could have gotten the lettering a little straighter. She wished Tilly had been able to lend her artistic hand, but Tilly was too busy trying to finish up a gift for Ivy. She wouldn't say what it was.

Florence looked around to see what else needed to be done — the guests would be here in just over an hour. The tables were covered in mismatched tablecloths, which Florence thought looked charming, and each table had a glass vase filled with flowers from Cora's garden. Lloyd had run an electric cord out to the yard, and they'd set up a phonograph for playing records; happy music would be important — the last thing Florence wanted was for this event to be too sad.

The Wednesday Club was bringing all the food, and Florence began putting the dishes and silverware on the row of folding tables. She'd mix the fancy punch with 7-Up and orange sherbet right before the guests arrived.

She was in the kitchen when Lance strolled in. "Hi Aunt Florence, I brought some 45s like you asked for. Stuff me and my friends like to listen to."

"Oh, that's wonderful. You don't think it will be too raucous for the older people, do you?"

Lance chortled. "I don't think so. Unless you call the Beatles and Roy Orbison too raucous." Florence arched an eyebrow but reminded herself this was Ivy's party.

"Say, can you give this to Ivy?" He held out a white envelope.

"Why certainly, but don't you want to give it to her yourself?"

Lance set the envelope on the counter. "I can only be at the party for a little while. Coach called a football practice for this afternoon."

"Oh, that's a shame! Can you come by after practice?"

"I don't think so," Lance said, his voice unusually quiet.

Poor Lance, Florence thought. "Thank you so much for helping us get ready. Much appreciated."

"Oh, sure. Don't forget to give that to Ivy."

"I won't forget." Florence smiled at him. She'd like to say something comforting about Ivy's leaving, but she couldn't think of anything that sounded the least bit sincere.

Florence glanced at her list and continued with the final preparations. Just as she was finishing up, the guests began to arrive, starting with Bathilda and Eddie. Florence asked Eddie if he'd like to oversee the record player. She knew Eddie felt better when he had a job since socializing was difficult for him, and Eddie happily agreed.

Soon, the yard filled up with people young and old, and everyone piled their plates with the abundant food: fried chicken, deviled eggs, potato salad, coleslaw, baked beans, watermelon, and sliced tomatoes with cucumbers and onions. A summer feast.

The teens gathered close to the music, and the men migrated to the yard's far corner to talk about farming. At first, Vonda Marie seemed standoffish, lingering on the side of the yard, smoking one cigarette after another, and looking like she couldn't wait to leave. She was wearing a pastel-striped polyester sheath dress with a matching headband and high heels, overdressed compared to everyone else. Finally, Etola asked her to join the women at her table, and soon Florence heard Vonda Marie holding court, entertaining them with stories from California. When Etola asked about her dramatic black eyeliner, Vonda Marie said the Cleopatra look was all the rage.

Florence kept track of the guests eating and conversing and noticed Lance and Ivy talking in a far corner of the yard. After about thirty minutes, Florence decided it was time. Etola helped her bring out the extra-large sheet cake they'd ordered from Lula's Bakery. It was covered with white frosting and decorated with an outline of the state of Nebraska and a star for Omaha. The words spelled out: 'We'll miss you, Ivy.' Florence rapped a spoon on one of the vases to get everyone's attention. It took a while, and someone finally had to shush Vonda Marie before everyone was quiet.

Florence announced, "Thank you all for coming out to help give our Ivy a big send-off. I know it's not her birthday, but we thought it might be fun to light some candles, and while Ivy is blowing them out, we can all make a wish for Ivy's senior year back in Omaha. Come on up here, honey." Florence lit the seventeen candles while Ivy walked to the front. Ivy's eyes glistened with held-back tears as she pulled in a big breath and blew out the candles. Everyone clapped loudly. Ivy blushed, and Florence expertly cut two pieces of cake. "For you and your mom," she said.

Ivy took the two plates and sat beside her mother, who threw her arms out and gave Ivy a dramatic squeeze and a loud smack on the cheek. Soon, everyone lined up for cake, and a few folks brought Ivy their going-away gifts. Florence sat down near Ivy so she could watch the presents being opened.

First, TJ and Robby walked side-by-side to Ivy. TJ was tightly grasping a glass jar covered with a square of calico fabric, tied with a bow of rickrack. Robby grabbed it away from TJ and handed it to Ivy.

"It's stubble berry jam. Hattie made it."

"We helped pick the berries," TJ announced with pride.

Etola presented Ivy with a small photo album of pictures Arlo had taken with his Kodak Instamatic. They were all photographs of the South Dakota countryside — so Ivy wouldn't forget what it looked like.

Becky gave her a high school yearbook with inscriptions by Ivy's classmates. The yearbook wasn't going to be distributed until school started again, but Becky had gotten a special advance copy. Ivy quickly leafed through and smiled at all the messages.

Bathilda stepped up and handed Ivy a folder with the words 'Wednesday Club 1963–1964'. "I thought you might like a record of the minutes. You did a fine job, Ivy." She eked out a small smile.

Mary, Ivy's school bus pal, had made her a necklace from painted macaroni pieces strung together on kitchen string. Ivy slipped it over her head, grinning.

Eddie shyly stepped up and handed Ivy a small paper sack. Ivy opened it and pulled out a homemade key ring. The top was made from thin leather strips braided together around a six-inch tassel of dark gray horsehair. "It's from Bearcat's mane," he said. "Don't worry, it will grow back."

Finally, Tilly walked up with a large, wrapped gift. Everyone stopped their conversation to watch. There was a murmur of appreciation when Ivy removed the paper revealing a beautiful painting of Bearcat standing in front of a white fence, a deep green pasture in the background. Ivy's eyes brimmed with tears, and Tilly swooped in to hug her and block her face while Ivy composed herself.

Someone asked for a speech, and Ivy stood up and looked around. Florence couldn't help but think she was looking for Lance, but Lance was nowhere to be seen. Ivy raised her voice to be heard. "Thank you all so much for coming today. And thanks to Florence and the rest of the Wednesday Club for putting this party together. I will miss all of you and won't forget how kind you've been to me. You were the first real friends I had in Prairie View." It seemed like Ivy might say more for a second, but she stopped there. When she sat back down, Ivy's eyes were not the only ones filled with tears.

The party was suddenly much quieter, and Eddie seemed to know he didn't need to keep playing records anymore. Folks began to leave, stopping to give Ivy their final good wishes on their way out. Cora busied herself, picking up dishes and carrying them to the kitchen. Florence realized she had hardly seen Cora sit down during the party, always finding something to keep herself busy. This was going to be hard on her.

Finally, the last guests headed out, and Delmar, Cora, Vonda Marie, and Ivy were getting into the car when Florence noticed the envelope on the counter. "Lloyd, stop Delmar," she shouted. She grabbed the envelope and trotted out to the car and up to Ivy in the back seat. Ivy rolled down the window. "I forgot to give you this."

Ivy looked at the handwriting and slipped the letter under her leg.

"Who's that from?" Vonda Marie asked.

Florence replied, "Oh, just one of Ivy's classmates." She figured it was up to Ivy if she wanted to tell her mother. Florence was not at all impressed with that Vonda Marie; in fact, she didn't like her one bit. And she was not happy she was taking their dear Ivy back to Omaha.

Ivy

Ivy's grandfather pulled her mother's Chevy up to the back door as Ivy and her mom walked out with suitcases in hand. He opened the trunk and grabbed the suitcases one by one to situate them.

"I topped off the oil and got the tires pumped up. One of them was low," he said. It seemed to Ivy like he was working hard to be pleasant.

"Thanks, Dad. We're all set then." Her mother's smile was tight.

He pointed to the rear fender. "Where'd that dent come from? You didn't have it the last time you were here."

Ivy looked at the crinkled metal, then back to her mother, who avoided their eyes as she responded. "Just one of the California facts of life. All those cars." He grunted and shook his head, then returned to the kitchen for another load.

Ivy's grandmother came out of the house carrying a small cardboard box covered with a dishtowel. "I've packed enough to get you through to Omaha."

Her mother took the box. "Thanks, Mom. You know, it's only a four-hour drive."

Ivy's grandfather heaved the last box and the carefully wrapped painting into the trunk and slammed the lid shut. "You drive safe now, you hear?" He gave his daughter a stiff pat on the shoulder and said, without looking directly at her, "Don't wait too long to bring her back for a visit." He walked over to Ivy. "Study hard; senior year is an important one." Then he leaned in and said in a fake whisper loud enough for his daughter to hear. "You know I couldn't be prouder of how you've turned out." Then louder: "Don't forget to write to your grandmother." He gave Ivy a quick hug.

Her grandmother was holding back tears. "I'm not going to say goodbye because soon enough, we'll be coming to visit at Christmastime."

Ivy gave her grandmother a long hug. "See you then, Grandma," but she was sure they wouldn't be coming to Omaha. By now, she knew how her grandfather hated to leave the farm, especially in the winter when road conditions were unpredictable. Not to mention how he and her mom didn't get along.

Ivy rolled down the window as her mother started the car and slowly pulled away. As she leaned out to wave at her grandparents, she could see the tears streaming down her grandmother's face, and she felt hot pricks behind her own eyes, a big choking lump in her throat.

Her mother looked over at Ivy, and Ivy turned her head away to stare out the window. They drove down the driveway past the lilac bushes and her grandmother's flower garden bursting with color and turned onto the gravel road. Bearcat was in the pasture, close to the ditch, and Ivy called out to him, but they were going too fast, and Bearcat didn't hear her. Ivy had spent an hour with him at dawn, talking to him to let him know how much she'd miss him. Now, she bit her lip hard to keep the tears from streaming.

They kept driving up the road, and passed Bathilda out in her yard, throwing a stick to Rascal. They drove past Becky's farm and the space between the trees where the three barrels were set up in a triangle. Ivy thought about telling her mom how she had learned to barrel race but decided not to. Some things Ivy got to keep as her own.

After a while, they left Prairie View behind and were speeding down the highway, heading south. Her mother looked over at Ivy. "Ivy, sweetie, can you grab my cigarettes? They've slipped down on your side there."

Ivy picked up the menthol Newports near her feet. It looked like her mother had switched brands. She handed the package to her mother and automatically grabbed the wheel to steer while her mom lit the cigarette.

"Cheer up, sweetheart; in a few hours, we'll be back in Omaha, and you can finally see your old friends. Tomorrow, I'll set up an appointment for a haircut for you. All the girls are wearing bangs and flip-ups in California — that style will be so cute on you!" Ivy didn't say anything; she just gazed out the window at the fields they passed by. She was surprised to realize she could now distinguish what was growing in them: corn, alfalfa, soybeans, and sorghum.

Her mother continued. "That Tilly sure could use a new do. But I guess when you have that many kids, you kind of let yourself go."

Ivy kept her head turned, taking in the scenery. She'd never noticed how pretty the little farms were from a distance. So many beautiful big red barns with a smattering of white farm buildings surrounding the two-story farmhouses, each punctuated with a tall silo and a turning windmill. A stand of trees, mostly pine and elm, surrounded each farmyard. Sometimes, a line of cottonwood trees hugged a winding creek.

Her mother kept talking. "I have to say that Etola looks the best I've ever seen her. Married life certainly seems to agree with her. Who would have thought she'd ever find a husband at her age?"

They passed white-faced calves grazing in the green grass, horses alongside them, swishing flies with their tails. Ivy thought about

Bearcat and her father's letter. Then she thought about the letter from Lance — that was sweet of him to say so many nice things. Like how much he was going to miss her. And how Prairie View High wouldn't be the same without her independent spirit and style. He had turned out to be a pretty good guy, after all.

Ivy leaned her head back and closed her eyes. She thought about Becky, how she'd cried and held her in a long hug when they said goodbye. She thought about her grandfather, how he'd said he couldn't be prouder of her. And her grandmother who was so sweet and soft and smelled like vanilla. Like a warm and yummy sugar cookie. She thought about each of the Wednesday Club members. How much she loved babysitting for Tilly's boys, and how Tilly was someone she could talk to about anything. How goofy Etola could be, and how happy she was now. How sweet, and also reserved, Hattie seemed to be. Like there was something she was hiding. How kind Florence was, once you got past how she wanted the world to see her and got to know the real Florence. How even Bathilda had a soft side underneath that prickly shell. And the way that Eddie and Arlo had helped her with Bearcat.

She thought the longest about Hank and that crooked eye tooth. They were related to one another, father and daughter, and bound together in that crookedness.

Her mother's voice interrupted Ivy's thoughts and she opened her eyes. "I'll bet your friends in Omaha can't wait to see you. Won't it be nice to get back to city living? Prairie View seems to be about five years behind the times, doesn't it? It will be nice to get back there, and to see Mel again!"

Ivy still didn't answer. It was depressing how her mom always put her future in the hands of men, and how she was always disappointed by them. It made Ivy feel sorry for her, and maybe forgive her a little. Just a little.

Her mom kept babbling. "After I get a job, we can see about getting you some braces to straighten up your crooked tooth." She stared at Ivy for a second, then said in an exasperated tone, "Come on. Be my big girl, now, Ivy."

The horizon seemed endless. Vast blue sky as far as her eyes could see. Not a cloud in sight.

Limitless. Filled with possibilities.

Ivy's gaze shifted to the land below that sky, large rectangles of land, some planted with long rows of crops, some open pastureland. Stable ground. Secure.

She thought about yesterday's going-away party and how everyone had wished her well. She was surprised by how many people had turned out and how nice they were to her. All their sweet goodbyes. It would be a little bit weird and kind of embarrassing, but Ivy decided she didn't care. It was her life. She turned toward her mother, determined. "Mom! Stop the car."

Her mother looked over at Ivy, her face frozen and downcast. It was as if she already knew. "What's the matter? Did you forget something?"

Ivy shook her head. Her mind was made up. And her heart felt filled up and warm. There were no cold spots.

She looked straight at her mother as she declared, "Turn around. I'm going home."

Wednesday Club Minutes

AUGUST 12, 1964

The Wednesday Club met at the home of Cora and Ivy Hanson. The meeting was called to order by President Bathilda Baldridge. The club motto was recited.

The roll call topic was 'A Beautiful Spot in South Dakota.' All seven members were present, and each listed a different place.

Cora - The Black Hills

Bathilda – Pioneer Park

Etola - Lake Doreen

Tilly - The Badlands

Florence - Mount Rushmore

Hattie - Custer State Park

Ivy - Prairie View

Ivy Hanson read the minutes from the June meeting, and members voted unanimously to approve them. There were no minutes from the July family picnic (interrupted by the storm) at Pioneer Park.

Hattie Dunlop read the treasurer's report. The balance was $44.13, with no transactions since June. Etola reported that Mrs. David Duffy was hospitalized after female surgery and the club agreed to send flowers. The club also voted to give $7.00 to the Crippled Children's Home.

President Bathilda reminded the members that they had decided to vote on next year's officers at this meeting. Cora asked if anyone wanted to step down from their current office, and all officers agreed to continue in their roles.

The program committee of Bathilda, Hattie, and Cora will meet next week to determine the program for next year, and Tilly will design the program covers in time for the September meeting. Bathilda urged each member to thoroughly prepare when called upon to lead the program. She reminded us that roll call is a very important part of the program.

Etola led the group in singing "My South Dakota."

This month's program topic was a current political situation and what it meant to you. Bathilda reported that President Lyndon Johnson was on national television last week to declare that North Vietnamese ships had fired on American ships in the waters off the Gulf of Tonkin on August 2nd and 4th. The US followed with air strikes. As a result, on August 7th, Congress passed the Gulf of Tonkin resolution that gave the president authority to assist any Southeast Asian country threatened by communist aggression.

Members discussed the possibility of the United States getting into a war with North Vietnam and everyone agreed that they hoped things did not progress to that point. Cora reminded the club that the president had assured the American people he had no desire for war. Florence commented that surely, if war did break out, the United States would quickly win. She certainly hoped her son would not be deployed. Ivy said she was worried about war because so many boys her age would soon be 18 and might get drafted. She said most young people she knew didn't support a war. Everyone agreed that surely cooler heads would prevail, and we will find a diplomatic solution before resorting to a worsening conflict.

The meeting closed with the creed 'Count That Day Lost' by George Eliot.

If you sit down at set of sun
And count the acts that you have done,
And, counting, find
One self-denying deed, one word
That eased the heart of him who heard,
One glance most kind
That fell like sunshine where it went —
Then you may count that day well spent.
But if, through all the livelong day,
You've cheered no heart, by yes or nay —
If, through it all
You've nothing done that you can trace
That brought the sunshine to one face —
No act most small
That helped some soul, and nothing cost —
Then count that day as worse than lost.

Cora and Ivy served a lunch of tuna puff casserole, sliced tomatoes, and apricot-coconut pudding with salted peanut cookies.

Ivy Hanson, Secretary

Author's notes

When my grandmother passed away in 1995, we found a box of worn notebooks—some spiral-bound, others with tattered cardboard covers—all filled with handwritten minutes from her Wednesday Club. The entries spanned from 1927 to 1987, chronicling the monthly meetings of rural farm women in South Dakota, each one conducted with the rigor of parliamentary procedure.

I brought the notebooks back to California, imagining I might one day publish them. They offered a vivid portrait of a bygone world—so different from the life I was living. But like many good intentions, the box sat unopened for years, eventually following me to Oregon.

When I finally began to read through them, I discovered that many years were missing. And while the minutes were heartfelt and insightful, they didn't quite hold together as a stand-alone narrative. Still, they sparked an idea: what if I wrote a novel about a Wednesday Club, filled with fictional characters, and shaped by the same spirit that ran through those pages?

What emerged was a story about women's friendship—how six very different women and one reluctant teenager might find common ground. And more than friendship, what struck me was their quiet, unwavering sense of community. These women didn't just support one another; they showed up for their neighbors, brought flowers to the hospital, raised funds for good causes, and baked casseroles when tragedy struck. Their connection extended outward, like ripples from a stone tossed into the water.

In a time when our lives often feel disconnected—and when transitions like moving, divorce, children leaving home, or simply the chaos of daily life can leave us unmoored—I believe we need community more than ever. We need genuine connection, the kind that grounds us and lifts us at the same time.

While writing this novel, I also began to imagine how women today might create their own modern-day Wednesday Clubs—intentional spaces for friendship, belonging, and support. I built a website to share the story of my grandmother's club and began blogging about ways to bring women together again.

I hope you'll visit https://wednesday-club.com to see photos of my grandmother's club, join my mailing list, and connect on social media. As my character Cora says, "Every woman needs a Wednesday Club in her life."

Acknowledgements

First, to my husband, Michael Connelly—thank you for nudging (okay, irresistibly persuading) me to begin a brand-new chapter in Oregon. This joyful life we've built—and your unwavering support, including the thoughtful gift of trips to a quiet writing cottage on the coast—made it possible for me to write this novel.

Love to my son, Joe Pierce—it's been fun to chase our dreams side by side and cheer each other on along the way.

Huge thanks to Jennifer Afton and Kathleen Caprario Ulrich, who read multiple drafts and met with me from the beginning to hash out ideas, give feedback, and listen to my excuses about my lack of progress. At this point, you probably know the story as well as I do.

To the early readers who generously gave their time, notes, and encouragement: Linda Angelotti, Lynn Ash, Nancy Frame Kammerer, Elizabeth King, Mary Jeanne Lewis, Jennifer Newcomb, Shawn Peterson, Julie Ross, Cathie Royer, Lex Talamo, Mary Lou Talamo, Lou Ann Trzynka, Cheri Wallace, David William Wallace, and Lois Wigdahl—I am beyond grateful. Your belief in this story kept me going.

To Jessica Morrell—editor and time-travel companion—thank you for showing me how to sharpen my writing and keep the 1963 details honest.

To my Saturday Sisters writing group (my real-life Wednesday Club)—Lynn Ash, Carol Brownson, Janet Fisher, Elizabeth King, Jennifer Newcomb, and Susan Wyatt—thank you for all the inspiration, motivation, and yummy food. Special thanks to Jennifer for being my website fairy godmother.

To Jim McBride—thank you for your friendship, your generous marketing advice, and the creative camaraderie we shared over years of screenwriting. And to Nicolle Rodriguez for the beautiful cover design—what a gift it is to work with you.

And to every friend and family member who asked, "How's the book going?"—your curiosity and encouragement meant the world, even when my answer was "Still working on it!" Extra credit to Becca Kuiken, who sent me a gold nameplate that said *Published Author*—it sat on my desk like a dare, and I was determined to earn it.

Finally, to you—thank you for taking the time to read this book. If you enjoyed it, I'd be grateful if you left a short review on Amazon or Goodreads—every one makes a difference. Stories of women supporting women matter, and I believe we need them now more than ever.

About the author

Kristine Jensen is a lifelong writer whose work has spanned video scripts, screenplays, and storytelling for brands and organizations. She has spent her career shaping narratives, crafting voices, and distilling complex ideas into language that connects.

Born and raised in South Dakota, Kristine drew inspiration for her first novel from the minutes of her grandmother's real-life women's club, which met for more than sixty years. She now lives in Oregon, where she writes fiction that celebrates women's inner lives, unlikely friendships, and the quiet power of small towns.

You can learn more about the real Wednesday Club that inspired the novel at www.wednesday-club.com